Praise for Sharon Dunn

"Suspense, combined with fast-paced action, starts immediately and does not let the reader go."
—*RT Book Reviews* on *Montana Standoff*, 4.5 stars, Top Pick

"Strong characters and fast-paced action combine in Dunn's latest."
—*RT Book Reviews* on *Fatal Vendetta*

"A fast-moving, suspenseful story with a good mystery that keeps interest high until the end."
—*RT Book Reviews* on *Dead Ringer*

Praise for Valerie Hansen

"Consistently excellent characters. Kudos to Valerie Hansen for writing an exceptional story with a puzzle that's nearly impossible to solve."
—*RT Book Reviews* on *Hidden in the Wall*

"*Wilderness Courtship* is a sweet story, with just the right amount of intrigue and mystery to keep readers turning the pages."
—*RT Book Reviews*

"A quick, evenly pa[ced book that gets even bett]as tension builds…. A
—*RT Boo[k]eart

D1218656

Sharon Dunn
and
Valerie Hansen

Duty and Honor

Previously published as *Guard Duty* and *Explosive Secrets*

HARLEQUIN® LOVE INSPIRED®CLASSICS

Special thanks and acknowledgment are given to Sharon Dunn and Valerie Hansen for their contribution to the Texas K-9 Unit miniseries.

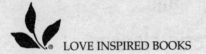

LOVE INSPIRED BOOKS

PLEASE RECYCLE
THIS PRODUCT IS RECYCLABLE

Recycling programs for this product may not exist in your area.

ISBN-13: 978-1-335-14767-7

Duty and Honor

Copyright © 2018 by Harlequin Books S.A.

First published as Guard Duty by Harlequin Books in 2013 and Explosive Secrets by Harlequin Books in 2013.

The publisher acknowledges the copyright holder of the individual works as follows:

Guard Duty
Copyright © 2013 by Harlequin Books S.A.

Explosive Secrets
Copyright © 2013 by Harlequin Books S.A.

www.Harlequin.com

Printed in U.S.A.

CONTENTS

Ever since she found the Nancy Drew books with the pink covers in her country school library, **Sharon Dunn** has loved mystery and suspense. Most of her books take place in Montana, where she lives with three nearly grown children and a spastic border collie. She lost her beloved husband of twenty-seven years to cancer in 2014. When she isn't writing, she loves to hike surrounded by God's beauty.

Books by Sharon Dunn

Love Inspired Suspense

Texas Ranger Holidays

Witness Protection

Texas K-9 Unit

Visit the Author Profile page at Harlequin.com for more titles.

GUARD DUTY

Sharon Dunn

You hear, O Lord, the desire of the afflicted;
you encourage them, and you listen to their cry,
defending the fatherless and the oppressed, in order
that man, who is of the earth, may terrify no more.
—*Psalms* 10:17–18

For Bart, the nervous border collie, who has brought laughter and unconditional devotion into my life.

ONE

"K-9 unit 349. Convenience-store robbery, corner of State and Grand. Suspects are on the run."

As she pushed the talk button to respond to dispatch, rookie officer Valerie Salgado felt that strange mixture of fear and excitement that came every time she responded to a call on patrol.

"Copy. I'm about five blocks from that location. Any idea what direction our perps were going?"

Dispatch responded. "Clerk doesn't know which way they ran. Three males. Two Caucasian, one African American. All dressed in dark clothing."

For the past few months, every call had an extra sense of danger attached to it. A rash of robberies, drugs and murders that had been escalating in Sagebrush for years had recently been linked to a crime syndicate with an unknown leader.

Valerie hit her siren and sped up.

Maybe this was just a run-of-the-mill robbery, but maybe it was another symptom of a city under siege.

In the back of the patrol car, Valerie's K-9 partner, Lexi, paced from one window to the other, emitting an almost ultrasonic whine. The only one more excited to catch a criminal than Valerie was her two-year-old Rottweiler.

Dispatch came across the line. "Clerk says that two of the men were armed."

Valerie took in a deep breath to calm her nerves. "At least we know what we are dealing with, huh, Lex?"

The dog whined as though she understood.

As she neared the convenience store, Valerie scanned the streets and sidewalks for any sign of movement. Now that it was 10 p.m. and dark, it would be easy enough for the robbers to blend into surroundings if they were smart enough to walk instead of run. Traffic was light, and most of the shops were closed. The all-night burger joint up the street had attracted a little bit of a crowd.

Valerie pulled into the convenience store parking lot. The clerk was easy enough to spot, a distraught fifty-something woman pacing by the store entrance. Valerie got out of her patrol car.

The woman came toward her, eyes wide with fear. The unnatural hair color and heavy makeup revealed rather than hid the woman's age.

The clerk wrapped her arms around herself. Her gaze flitted everywhere. The robbery had shaken the poor woman up. Valerie wanted to hug her and tell her it was going to be all right. But that was not what cops did. Instead, she pulled a notebook out of her utility belt.

She hoped her voice conveyed the level of compassion she felt for what the clerk had just been through. "Ma'am, I'm Officer Salgado. Can you tell me what happened here?"

The woman combed her fingers through her hair. "They took over three hundred dollars. My manager is going to fire me." Her agitated state made her south Texas drawl even more exaggerated.

"How long has it been since the robbers fled the store?"

The clerk closed her eyes as though she were struggling to answer the question. "Umm…they made me lay on the floor facedown." She let out a heavy breath. "I waited until I was sure they weren't going to come back. I… I…called as quickly as I could." She put a trembling hand to her chest. "Maybe five minutes."

Valerie felt torn between desiring to comfort the clerk and wanting to catch the thugs who had terrorized her. Picturing her own mother having to go through something like this made her resolve even stronger. The best comfort she could give this woman would be to see that these perps went to jail.

Valerie glanced up the street. Flashing neon signs for budget hotels stood in contrast to the dark Texas sky. In a pursuit, five minutes was a big lead time.

She cupped the woman's shoulder with her hand, hoping to provide some reassurance. "You go back inside and wait. My dog and I will get these guys."

"Thank you, Officer."

Valerie opened the back door of the patrol car, and Lexi jumped out.

"Get 'em," Valerie commanded, leading the Rottweiler toward the entrance of the convenience store. It would take only minutes for Lexi to pick up on the fear odor that people in flight emitted the second they took off running. Though people couldn't smell it, the scent was extremely distinct to a dog trained to detect it.

Lexi placed her nose to the gravel, trotting in wider

and wider circles, returning to the store entrance a couple of times.

Across the street, a dark car with tinted windows came to a stop.

As Lexi worked her way toward the edge of the store parking lot, Valerie glanced at the car. No one got out. The hairs on the back of her neck stood on end as a chill ran over her skin. For weeks now, she had had the sensation of being watched, of eyes pressing on her from dark corners.

The reality of the long arms of the crime syndicate had come home to roost for Valerie. Though she didn't know it at the time, while heading in to the pharmacy a few weeks ago, she'd seen the woman who had most likely murdered Andrew Garry—a local real-estate agent and one of the crime syndicates middle managers. She'd glanced at the woman briefly as she passed her on the dimly lit street outside a vacant building by the corner drugstore. Valerie didn't act on her suspicions that night, but something about the lady in the hooded jacket seemed off. Though she couldn't ID the woman outright, Valerie had the feeling that she would know her when she saw her and that she'd seen her somewhere before. It was just a matter of time before something in her brain clicked.

The initial death threat had come the next day only hours after Kip the cadaver dog and his handler had found Garry's body, confirming her suspicions about the woman she'd seen outside the vacant building. Her police email had been hacked into. The threat flashed on her computer screen… *If you testify, you die…maybe even sooner.*

Living with a death threat had become even more

complicated. Valerie had recently become guardian to her eighteen-month-old niece, Bethany, after her sister Kathleen's death over two months ago.

The department had offered her protection during her off-duty hours. On duty was a little harder, but she noticed that another patrol car always seemed to be close. Sagebrush P.D. looked out for their own. She felt safe while working as long as she had Lexi with her.

Lexi stopped, lifted her head and barked twice. She'd found the trail. "Good girl. Let's go."

Lexi ran hard, leading Valerie up the street. On the opposite side of the street, the dark car with the tinted windows remained. It was probably nothing. She had to let her unfounded fears go. She couldn't do her job if she was suspicious of everything.

Increasing her pace, Lexi pulled through to an alley that led into a residential neighborhood.

Valerie pushed the talk button on her shoulder mic. "I'm on State Street headed south pursuing suspects. I could use some backup."

"Captain McNeal is within a couple of blocks of your location," came the reply from dispatch.

It was unusual for her supervisor to be out on patrol at this hour. As captain of the Special Operations K-9 Unit, Slade McNeal had more than the lion's share of paperwork. Since his beloved K-9 partner, Rio, had been kidnapped by the syndicate, he had limited his time on patrol, utilizing Rio's father, Chief, when needed. A snitch with a long rap sheet had revealed to police that Rio was taken by the head of the local crime syndicate to find something in the Lost Woods, a huge forest on the outskirts of Sagebrush. The snitch was later found dead. The syndicate's structure was such that no one knew the identity of the leader, a man simply known as The Boss.

The loss of Rio over two months ago had been a blow to the whole department. These dogs weren't just useful resources—they were partners and beloved pets. Even though one of McNeal's well-to-do war buddies, Dante Frears, had offered a substantial reward of $25,000 for Rio's return, so far none of the leads had panned out.

Lexi pulled hard on the long canvas leash. Valerie couldn't trouble herself now with what McNeal was up to. After all, she had criminals to catch.

Lexi led Valerie through backyards and over fences, past living rooms with illuminated television sets and houses with dark windows. Though she saw no signs of the suspects, Lexi's persistence told her they were headed in the right direction. The scent trail that a person in flight left was like a glow-in-the-dark line to a dog's keen nose.

Lexi stopped suddenly in a yard that had stacks of roofing shingles piled on the walkway and a ladder propped against the roof. Valerie had noticed another ladder on the opposite side of the house, as well. The dog circled and sniffed the ground again. She'd lost the scent.

"What's going on, girl?"

In the distance, she heard the alto barking of a German shepherd. That had to be McNeal with Chief. The insistence of the barking suggested that Chief was onto something.

Valerie talked to dispatch through her shoulder mic. "Be advised. I am at 620 Kramer. Something is up with Lexi. The trail may have gone cold."

Agitated, Lexi ran back and forth in the yard, stood

by the ladder for a moment and then put her nose to the ground again. What was happening?

She watched Lexi pace the yard, running in all directions. The dog stopped, lifted her head and let out a single "Woof." She still had some kind of scent, but it was confusing her.

Chief's insistent barking reached her. He had definitely alerted to something. But what…? As the realization dawned on her, Valerie pushed her talk button. "I think our suspects split up."

"Copy that. We are sending another patrol unit your way. ETA is about five minutes."

The bushes in the yard across the fence shook. Valerie lifted her head just in time to see a man emerge. The look of fear and guilt on his face told her everything she needed to know.

"Stop! Sagebrush P.D."

The man took off running.

Lexi yanked on the leash, barking and pulling wildly as the man ran around the back of the house. Knowing she couldn't crawl over the fence as fast as Lexi could jump it, Valerie clicked Lexi off the leash. The dog leapt over the fence and bounded after the suspect, her rapid-fire bark a clear sign that she was hot on the trail.

Her heart pumping, Valerie gripped her gun, prepared to run out to the sidewalk and through the gate to meet Lexi. She heard a scraping noise right before something crashed hard against her shoulder, knocking her to the ground.

Dazed by the impact, she stumbled to her feet. Shingles and a busted-open box spread across the walkway. She looked up. Was the second perpetrator on the roof? Had each of the three suspects run in a different direction?

Lexi's barking pressed hard on her ears, but grew farther away. The dog could handle herself. With her shoulder aching and still a little fuzzy headed, she hurried most of the way up the ladder using the roofline for cover.

She lifted her head up a few inches, catching movement by the chimney. "Sagebrush P.D. Drop your weapon." She ducked just as the whiz of a pistol shot shattered the night air. She fired off a round.

Silence.

She lifted her head a couple of inches. The suspect had come out from behind the chimney, aiming his gun at her.

He slipped on the sharply angled roof, falling on his side and dropping the gun. The gun skittered across the shingles and fell to the ground below. This was her chance. She didn't want him escaping down the ladder she'd seen on the other side of the house.

Valerie scrambled up the ladder, attempting to balance close to the top rung and aim her gun at the same time. "Put your hands up."

The man lifted his hands partway and then dropped them, dashing toward her. All the air left her lungs as fear enveloped her and she whispered a quick prayer. He intended to push the ladder away from the roof. She couldn't crawl down fast enough. She grabbed the ladder with her free hand as the man bolted toward her. It had been a stupid mistake to go up the ladder. She'd break her back if she fell that far.

The suspect's feet seemed to be pulled out from under him, and he was slammed facedown on the roof.

Some unseen force pulled him backward away from her. As the suspect scrambled to his feet, she saw the silhouette of a second man, tall and broad through the shoulders.

The second man landed a blow to the suspect's face, knocking him on his back. The perp kicked the man's feet out from under him, and he slid down the steep angle of the roof toward the edge. He caught himself, pulling his body back up toward the suspect who sought refuge close to the chimney.

Valerie climbed onto the roof. Seeking to balance, she lifted her gun. "Put your hands up."

This time, the assailant complied. "I don't want to fall off here."

Neither did she. Valerie looked down and behind her. How on earth was she going to get this guy off here without killing herself and without giving him opportunity to run away?

The man who had helped her apprehend the perp stepped out of the shadows. "Officer Salgado, why don't you crawl down and wait at the bottom?" The man's hand went to a holster on his belt. "I'll stay up here and make sure this guy doesn't get any ideas."

She had no idea who this man was or where he had come from, but everything about him said law enforcement, and he knew her name. Still, this whole thing might have been a setup from the syndicate to get at her. "Who are you?" she shouted across the rooftop.

"FBI Agent Trevor Lewis. I rode in with Captain McNeal and saw that you were in trouble."

He sounded legit. She didn't have a lot of choices and would have to check his I.D. later.

"Okay. I'll go down the ladder first," she said.

Agent Lewis held up his own gun. "I'll make sure this guy doesn't try to get off the roof by way of that other ladder."

She descended the ladder and waited while the suspect followed her. When his feet hit the ground, she pointed her gun at him. "Turn around, on the ground facedown, sir."

A look of hostility compressed his features, his lips curled. "I don't wanna go to jail. I'm innocent." The suspect stepped toward her with his hands out to grab her.

She adjusted her grip on the gun. "I said facedown on the ground, now."

"Do what the lady says," came the strong bass voice from the roof.

The perp tilted his head, grimaced and dropped to the ground.

Valerie pulled the cuffs from her belt. "You're innocent? Like everyone decides to shingle their roof at ten o'clock at night." She was still mad at herself for having climbed up the ladder. She'd broken a cardinal rule of training by putting herself in a vulnerable place.

Agent Lewis climbed to the bottom of the ladder. "At last, we meet." As Valerie stood up from cuffing the suspect, he held out his hand to her.

Why would an FBI agent want to greet her? Along the street, another black and white came to a stop, the additional backup dispatch had sent.

The screams of a man and a distant growl alerted Valerie to Lexi's progress with the other suspect. "Gotta go. Can you watch him until that officer over there can take him into custody?"

No time to wait around for Agent Trevor Lewis to explain why he was with McNeal. She raced out of the yard, pushing through the gate, following the sounds of the shrieking man. She wasn't worried about the suspect's safety; Lexi was trained to hold her suspect without biting. She just didn't want the man to claim police brutality because the dog had her teeth on the man for an excessive time.

She found the man in a grove of trees behind a house facedown with Lexi gripping his forearm in her teeth.

The man screamed in falsetto. "He's killing me. I don't want to die. Don't let that dog bite me."

"For your information, the dog is a she." Valerie clicked the dog into her leash. "Lex, off."

The dog complied but continued to lurch toward the suspect and bark. No one did their job with as much enthusiasm as Lexi. This dog loved to work.

A male officer came up behind Valerie. "That guy over there thought maybe you could use another set of handcuffs."

Valerie looked over at the man who had saved her life on the roof. Guess it was time to find out who Agent Trevor Lewis was and what he was doing showing up to help her on patrol.

Trevor watched the pretty redhead walk toward him. Maybe it was the green eyes bright in the evening lamplight, but there was something open and trusting in her expression as she drew close to him.

For the second time, he held out his hand. "Officer Salgado? Valerie Salgado?"

Still breathless from her pursuit, Valerie nodded and held out a hand. Her fingers were softer than silk, but her grip was strong and confident.

"Two suspects in custody, huh? Quite a night." Her

decision to go up the ladder had seemed a little fool-hardy, but she had handled herself well in every other way.

"I couldn't have done it without my partner." She kneeled, wrapping her arms about the thick-necked Rottweiler. "That's my girl." The dog's bobbed tail vi-brated.

Valerie's shoulder mic made a glitchy noise. She pushed the receive button. "McNeal has the third sus-pect in custody. He's on his way over to talk to you as soon as he puts Chief back in the squad car."

"Copy. I'm standing on the six hundred block of Kramer Avenue. Agent Lewis is with me." Valerie com-manded her dog to sit and turned toward Trevor. "So why did McNeal bring you out to meet me?"

Trevor stared down at the dog, who watched him with a wary eye. The dog was very protective of Val-erie. "I just drove in from the San Antonio FBI office. I'm here to apprehend a fugitive…a Derek Murke."

Valerie shook her head. "The name's not ringing any bells for me."

The hope that this would be an easy capture faded. After two years of Murke popping up on the radar and then disappearing, why had he thought he could just breeze into town and Officer Salgado would know right where Murke was? "Captain McNeal thought you might have heard something. Murke spent his teen years here and has come back several times for extended stays. Since the fugitive used to live in some of the neighbor-hoods you patrol, the captain figured I could get your assistance in finding him."

"I'll help you as much as I can, but I can't neglect my regular patrol duties. What's he wanted for?"

"A few years ago, he robbed a bank in Phoenix." He'd spare her the longer version of the story, fearing he wouldn't be able to keep the emotion out of his voice.

Derek Murke wasn't just any fugitive. He was the fugitive who had shot rookie agent Cory Smith. Trevor had been Cory's training agent for his first field assignment. Cory Smith had been a little too eager to prove himself when he'd been a part of the apprehension team that had cornered Murke in a rental house. The kid hadn't waited for backup to be in place before entering the house. When Cory didn't assess his surroundings from all angles, Derek had seized the opportunity and shot him. Trevor would always wonder if he had given Cory too much responsibility too soon.

The sooner he had Murke in custody, the sooner he would feel like Cory's death hadn't been for nothing.

"I see introductions have already been made." He recognized Slade McNeal's voice behind him.

"Slade and I have done some joint drug task force work together," Trevor explained to Valerie.

McNeal placed his hands on his hips and looked at Valerie. "I thought maybe you could work with Agent Lewis to stir up some leads. He could tag along with you on your patrol, see if you can get any information for him. And in return, you get a little extra protection while you're on duty."

A shadow fell across Valerie's face. "I suppose I could use that."

McNeal excused himself to go talk to the officer hauling away one of the suspects.

Trevor watched him cross the street and then turned back to Valerie. "McNeal explained to me about the death threats against you." News about the crime syndicate Sagebrush was battling had reached other parts of the state. Now as he watched the tall redhead's demeanor change from confident to fearful, all the news stories and police reports seemed a lot more personal. "I'm glad to help out."

The black and white disappeared around the corner. McNeal walked back toward them.

"I'm on the morning shift tomorrow." She still seemed guarded. "I assume you have some sort of file on this guy Murke? Maybe there is something in there that will give me an idea of where to look for him."

She wasn't exactly warming to the idea of an FBI agent tagging along. "I won't waste your on-duty time if I don't have to. I can bring it by before you go on shift. If nothing in the file helps, maybe McNeal has some other ideas."

"That would be fine." Valerie wrote down her home address. As she was handing him the card, her gaze shifted from his face to over his shoulder. Her eyes grew wide as a look of apprehension clouded her features.

Trevor turned, following the line of her gaze. Across the street, a black car with tinted windows slowed to a crawl before speeding up and disappearing around a corner. Alerting on something, Lexi rose from her haunches.

He turned back toward Valerie. Her lips were drawn into a hard, straight line. Something about that black car had upset her.

"Is everything okay?"

She took a step back, shaking her head. "It's…it's nothing." She squared her shoulders and lifted her chin, but her effort at bravado fell short. He could see the fear in her eyes.

Valerie Salgado was living with a death threat hanging over her head. Maybe the car had just slowed down to look for an address, but it had bothered her. Anger flooded through him over the syndicate's stronghold on her life.

If they did end up working together, she wasn't going to die on his watch.

TWO

Valerie peered out the front window of her house. In the early-morning light, she could make out the outline of the police car parked outside. She drew her eighteen-month-old niece, Bethany, closer.

Would she ever get used to that sight? Would there ever be a time when her life wasn't shrouded in danger?

Knowing that the car with the dark windows had been following her last night drove the point home. The syndicate wasn't going to go away. They were just waiting for the right moment to get at her. Sagebrush police knew that one of the middle managers was a woman. That woman, whose street name was Serpent, was most likely the woman Valerie had seen. The Serpent had no way of knowing Valerie couldn't identify her yet. She probably thought it was just a matter of time before she was picked up.

A chill skittered over Valerie's skin when she thought of the woman's eyes meeting hers on the street. Seemingly yellow in the lamplight, they bore right through Valerie. The memory still invaded her thoughts and sent a current of fear through her.

Bethany shifted in Valerie's arms. She jerked her

head back and blinked several times. She was all blue eyes and soft downy hair, just like her mother. Kathleen's funeral had been more than a month ago, but it still felt so raw. While the cancer had slowly drained the vitality out of Valerie's older sister, it had given her time to express that she wanted Valerie to take care of Bethany. The child's father had never been in the picture and had signed away rights even before Bethany was born. Though she felt ill equipped for the job, Valerie intended to keep her promise to her beloved sister.

Valerie held Bethany close, absorbing her softness and that sweet baby smell. Over the months, Valerie had slowly been taking over mothering duties as Kathleen grew weaker. But since Kathleen's death, Bethany had not slept through the night. Though the little girl couldn't articulate it, Valerie knew she was mourning.

Even now, Bethany clung to the stuffed pink rabbit Kathleen had given her. She hardly ever let go of the toy. Valerie swayed back and forth. "I know, you miss your mama." A lump formed in her throat. "I miss her, too."

Bethany melted against Valerie. After a few minutes, the little girl relaxed and her breathing steadied, asleep at last. Valerie padded on stocking feet toward the stairs that led to the bedroom, careful not to jostle the sleeping baby. She glanced at the living room clock.

She stopped so suddenly that Bethany wiggled in her arms. Where had the time gone? She should have been ready for work by now. The sitter would be here any minute. It was easy enough to lose track of time when you got up four or five times in the night to deal with a fussy toddler.

A knock came at her door, loud and intense. Lexi sauntered out of her crate positioned by the sliding glass door. She raised her head and looked toward Valerie, expecting instructions.

Valerie turned toward the door. "Who is it?"

"Trevor Lewis."

And she was still in her bathrobe. What had she been thinking when she had agreed to him swinging by before work? Now that she had Bethany, it took her twice as long to get ready in the morning. Valerie gave the Rottweiler a reassuring look. "Go back to sleep, Lexi. It's okay."

"Just a second." After placing Bethany in her playpen, Valerie took a breath to calm her nerves. She hoped she hadn't seemed too standoffish to Agent Lewis last night. McNeal had been looking out for her when he suggested she work with Trevor, and maybe she'd be able to help him. She probably needed the extra protection, but the partnership was a bitter reminder of how hard the syndicate was making it for her to do her job.

She swung open the door. Trevor looked fresh in a crisp, French blue button-down shirt. His dark curly hair was clipped close to his head and his brown eyes had an intensity she hadn't noticed last night.

His gaze fell to her bathrobe, and heat rushed up her face. "My little one has me running behind schedule." She turned slightly away from the door so Trevor had a view of Bethany shaking the sides of her playpen.

Barely acknowledging the child, Trevor lifted the computer tablet he had in his hand. "I've got Murke's file."

"Come in. I need just a minute to get ready," she said.

Trevor glanced around the room. "Where's the dog?"

"She's resting in her crate." Valerie sighed as she looked at the crate and then at the playpen not too far from it. Lexi had never shown any aggression toward Bethany, but the dog was keeping her distance. Though Lexi was protective of Valerie, it would be a shame if she didn't bond with Bethany. The trainer at the K-9 facility had assured her that dogs were just like people—it took time for them to adjust to new situations.

"Take a seat, Mr. Lewis."

"You can call me Trevor."

Bethany babbled and held her hands up. Valerie gathered her into her arms and grabbed her bottle off the counter. When Valerie offered it to her, Bethany shook her head. She hadn't eaten anything yet this morning. Valerie tried not to give in to worry. She bounced Bethany in her arms. "We don't want you losing weight."

She had fifteen minutes before her neighbor, Stella Witherspoon, came over to watch Bethany. Not enough time to get everything done. This motherhood thing was a juggling act and so far she had dropped all her balls.

She sat Bethany on the opposite side of the couch from Trevor. Valerie smoothed Bethany's silky, soft hair and then handed Trevor the bottle. "If Bethany starts to fuss, see if she will take this."

Trevor's eyes grew wide with fear. "Give her the bottle?" His voice slipped up half an octave.

Valerie shook her head. "It would be a help." You'd think she had asked him to split an atom.

Still flustered by all she had to get done in a short amount of time, Valerie went up the stairs to where her uniform was laid out.

Trevor Lewis shifted uneasily on the couch. The little girl stuck two fingers in her mouth and watched him. With her free hand, she held on to a stuffed pink bunny that had seen better days. One of its ears dangled by a thread. He didn't know that much about kids, but she looked at him like he was a pinned insect.

"Is your name Bethany?"

She continued to stare and suck her fingers. Did kids this little talk?

Valerie seemed distracted. Did she even want to work with him? He stared down at the tablet where he had opened Derek Murke's file. Trying to catch a fugitive without the cooperation of the local police department never went well. She was the most likely candidate to help him. McNeal had mentioned that Salgado was a rookie...just like Cory Smith had been. Icy pain stabbed at Trevor's heart. Could he keep this rookie safe?

Trevor let out a heavy breath and looked at Bethany. And she had a kid.

He held up the bottle to Bethany. "You want this?"

Bethany popped her fingers out of her mouth. She pointed at something across the room and said, "Gaga."

He had no idea what she was talking about. Being around babies made him feel awkward. They seemed so fragile. As if they would shatter like glass if you didn't hold them right. Bethany flipped around to her belly and slid off the couch. She tottered over to him, blue eyes still assessing him.

Her hand rested on his leg with a touch that was barely heavier than air. He held the bottle toward her while she was still standing and fed her as though she were a newborn lamb. She looked up at him with eyes that were filled with trust. He felt a fluttering in his heart. How unexpected that this delicate child was okay with him feeding her.

When he glanced around the room, Valerie stood at

the base of the stairs watching them. Without the utility belt, the uniform accentuated her curves. Her red hair had been pulled up into a ponytail, revealing the soft lines of her face and clear green eyes.

"You can hold her, you know." There was a hint of amusement in her voice.

"We're doing just fine," Trevor muttered.

Bethany pulled away from him and tottered toward Valerie just as the doorbell rang. An older woman with white, fluffy hair that had a tint of blue to it stepped across the threshold when Valerie opened the door. Valerie introduced the babysitter as Stella Witherspoon.

"There's my little Bethie." Mrs. Witherspoon's voice had a charming bell-like quality.

The little girl squealed with delight and kicked her legs while Valerie held her. "Thanks for coming, Stella."

Bethany nestled against Valerie while she gave Stella instructions for the day. Valerie ran a finger down Bethany's cheek and rubbed noses with her when the little girl tilted her head up. She seemed like a natural at being a mom. Where was the baby's father in all this? He hadn't noticed a wedding band on her finger.

After Valerie handed Bethany over, she turned toward Trevor. "Since I'm running late, I can look at the file on the way to the station." She turned back toward the kitchen. "Lexi, come."

The dog trotted out from her crate by the back door.

Valerie grabbed the leash and canine vest by the door and proceeded to put them on Lexi. She rose to her feet. "I hope you don't mind. She goes everywhere with me while I'm on duty."

Trevor nodded. "I understand." He opened the door for her when she had clicked Lexi into her leash.

As they stepped out into the early morning, light shimmered across Valerie's coppery hair. She stopped and stared at where the police car used to be.

"I sent him home since you're with me," Trevor said.

Her voice took on that soft, distant quality. "He usually follows me into the station in the morning."

The inflection in her voice suggested weariness, as though the need for protection had taken its toll on her emotionally.

Trevor glanced around. Other than automated sprinklers turning on, he saw no movement anywhere on the quiet street. He sidled closer to Valerie.

She turned toward him, furling her brow. "You don't need to stand quite so close. I'm a trained officer. I can handle myself."

He had to remind himself that though her irritation was directed toward him, she was probably more upset about the loss of freedom the death threats had created. "I don't doubt you can handle yourself."

She opened the back door of Trevor's sedan to let Lexi in.

On the drive toward the station, Trevor filled Valerie in on the investigation as she flipped through the file. "We knew that Sagebrush was one of the places Murke had ties to. He lived here during his teen years and has come back several times since. He's on the FBI's Most Wanted list, so his picture has been out there. We had an anonymous tip, someone who saw him in a store here in Sagebrush."

Valerie stared at the photo of Murke on the tablet. "Sometimes people are mistaken about identities." She flicked through the pages of the file.

"I know that. It makes sense, though, that Murke

would come back here," he said as doubt tapped at the corners of his awareness. Valerie had to find something that would give them a lead. The urgency to catch Murke was stronger than ever.

Valerie looked up from the tablet. Her eyes lit up as they passed a schoolyard just starting to fill with children. She really seemed to gravitate toward kids. Having kids, being married, none of that had ever been on his radar. His father had been a brute of a man, cruel beyond reason. If it hadn't been for a youth pastor, who had turned his heart toward God, Trevor could have gone down that same road. The way he had it figured, he didn't want to risk having those patterns of violence emerge in his own life. He was a better help to humanity as a lawman.

"So it's just you and Bethany?" The question had spilled out. He had to admit, he was curious.

Valerie laced her fingers together and bent her head. "Bethany is my sister's child. I recently became her guardian when Kathleen died." Her voice trembled.

Trevor retreated, aware that he had stepped on an emotional land mine. "Well, you seem like a natural mom."

Her face glowed, and her voice fused with warmth. "Thanks. It's been an adjustment for both of us."

He hadn't counted on the compliment meaning so much to her. He took a quick sideways glance at her. Shorter hair that had escaped the ponytail framed her soft features, and her full mouth curled into a faint smile. Was she still thinking about what he had said?

Valerie looked back down at the tablet. "Murke robbed a pawn shop with a guy named Leroy Seville?"

Trevor's spirits lifted. "Yeah, do you know him?"

"No, but I know an elderly lady named Linda Seville. I don't think she ever said anything about a son, but they could be related."

"It's worth a shot." This could be the lead he had hoped for.

She lifted her head and peered through the windshield. "We're actually pretty close to where she lives. Let's just go there now. Four blocks up and one over." She paused. "I know the street, and I'll remember the house when I see it."

He caught a whiff of her floral perfume as she leaned closer to him to point through the windshield. He leaned toward her as his stomach tightened.

He pulled to the curb, scanning the area as he got out of the car. "This is the street?" The neighborhood consisted of older homes built close together and several apartment buildings.

She looked at him over the top of the car. "Yep, this is the neighborhood I patrol." She spoke with affection as she lifted her chin and looked around. "If I remember correctly, I met Linda on a stolen television case." She studied the line of houses as though she was trying to jar her memory about where Linda Seville lived.

A girl of about seven road by on a bike. "Hey, Officer Salgado."

A trilling laugh escaped Valerie's throat. "Hey, Jessie Lynn. I see you found a new chain for your bike."

The kid was half a block away when she shouted, "Yes, ma'am, I did."

She turned to face Trevor. "Jessie loves that bike. She always gets a ride in before school."

Valerie cared about the people here. That much was

clear, but sometimes emotions got in the way of the job. He hoped she could keep them in check.

Valerie came around the car and joined Trevor on the sidewalk. She looked up at him, expectation coloring her lovely features. She had a spray of freckles across her nose and cheeks, and her voice had a soft quality that made him think of lullabies. He shook himself free of the warm, fuzzy feeling he got when she stood close to him. Okay, she was attractive and smelled nice. So what? He had a job to do.

Valerie pointed to a bungalow-style house with flower beds that were overgrown with weeds. "That's it, right there. Now I remember. It wasn't a stolen television—it was a missing pet."

It sounded like Valerie didn't know Linda Seville all that well. They made their way up the sidewalk. Worry twisted into a hard knot at the base of his stomach. What if this lead didn't pan out? Would they be back to square one?

As though she had read his mind, Valerie said, "We might be able to get a line on Murke some other way if this turns out to be nothing."

He appreciated her optimism, but in his mind, there were no second shots. Murke had evaded him since Cory's death, leaving whatever town he'd drifted into the second he got wind that the Bureau was onto him. The capture needed to be swift before Murke had a chance to run again.

He knocked on the door. Through the sheer curtain, he could see that all the lights had been turned off, and no one stirred inside. He could feel that tightening in his chest. That awful feeling that they'd missed their chance to get the jump on Murke. "Where would this

Linda be if she wasn't at home?" He couldn't hide the urgency in his voice.

"I don't know that much about her. She's not one of the people in the neighborhood who talks to me. I just helped her find her poodle months ago." She turned and looked at the other houses. "I'm sure we can ask around."

Trevor tensed. Too much asking around meant a greater chance of Murke getting wind that the Bureau had found him. "I just want this lead to work out."

She flinched as though he had hit her with his words. "You really want to get this guy, don't you?"

Trevor softened his tone. She didn't deserve to be the recipient of the frustration over his long history with Murke. "He shot an agent I was training. Cory was a rookie fresh out of the Academy, and I know rookies make rookie mistakes, but he didn't deserve to die."

"I'm sorry about the agent being shot." An emotion flashed across her face that almost looked like hurt, though he couldn't figure out why. "I don't think she's here." Valerie turned away and stared up the street.

He'd heard the quiver in her voice. Something he had said had struck a nerve. Women made him crazy sometimes. He was always saying the wrong thing around them and never quite understanding why it had been the wrong thing. Trying to sort it out with her would just make things worse.

Just let it go and do your job.

Trevor scanned the windows of the apartment buildings. No doubt the neighborhood had eyes everywhere. They'd expect to see Officer Salgado around, but would wonder what he was doing here. And then they would start to talk. If Murke was in this neighborhood, how long before word got back to him?

When he turned toward Valerie, she still had her back to him. She let out a soft gasp as her shoulders stiffened and she reached for her gun. He followed the line of her gaze.

Derek Murke sidled up the street holding two plastic bags and a six-pack of beer.

THREE

"Police, stop."

Valerie sprinted across the grass and drew her weapon.

Shock registered on Murke's face. He dropped his groceries and dashed up the alley.

Murke was headed for the warehouses behind the bungalows. Valerie called out to Trevor. "Stay with him. I'll grab Lexi."

Trevor had already drawn his handgun. He raced past her down the alley. Murke bolted over a dilapidated fence with Trevor on his heels.

Valerie ran to Trevor's car and opened the back door for Lexi. With the dog pulling hard on the leash, Valerie circled around the fence. She entered a two-block area containing a series of metal buildings, some still in use and others abandoned. She saw no sign of Murke or Trevor. She took Lexi over to the other side of the fence where Murke had probably landed. Lexi picked up the trail right away.

They jogged past a tire shop that was still operational, but closed at this hour. There was a risk that Lexi had picked up on Trevor's scent and not Murke's since both men were running. Following a scent was not a perfect science, but she'd trust Lexi's nose over searching blindly.

Heart pounding, she took in her surroundings as she ran. The Rottweiler pulled toward a large warehouse. Metal slapped against metal. The sound of a door slamming against the frame or the wind blowing? Valerie followed Lexi into the warehouse through a place in the exterior wall where the corrugated metal had been bent back from the frame.

Once inside, she waited for her eyes to adjust to the dimness. The warehouse was a big open area with a balcony all around it. This had been a clothing factory at one time. Pieces of abandoned equipment provided numerous places for Murke to hide. Trevor might have lost sight of him and gone off in the wrong direction.

She studied the stairs leading up to the balcony where the offices used to be. Now they were just gaping holes, the office doors having long since been looted.

Lexi kept her nose to the ground, though her pace slowed.

A creak of floorboards caused Valerie to turn. She waited for another sign of life. If Murke was close, Lexi would have been more excited. Valerie licked her dry lips. Blood whooshed in her ears as she adjusted her grip on the gun. Water dripped somewhere in the building. The steady tap, tap, tap of the droplets hitting metal overtook the leaden silence.

Lexi ran back and forth. The scent had become muddled.

Though Valerie's hands remained steady, sweat trickled down her back. Someone was in here. She could feel eyes watching her. Lexi stopped sniffing and lifted her head.

Valerie tuned in to the sounds around her as she breathed in the musty air. Lexi's panting became more pronounced.

Seconds passed. The sense that she was being watched had been with her since the Andrew Garry murder. Was she just imagining it now? She'd give anything to replay the tape of her life and go back to that night—to make different choices. When she'd passed that woman wearing the hooded jacket on the street, something had seemed amiss…but she had ignored her instincts. The next day, Garry's body had been found by another K-9 unit. By then, the woman had disappeared.

Valerie's father, a retired detective, had always said that instinct was a cop's best asset. She had made a stupid rookie mistake and ignored the prickling of the hairs on her neck when that woman had looked at her. Trevor Lewis had no idea that his comment about rookies making mistakes was like a dagger through her chest.

Her life would have been different if she had followed her gut and stopped to engage the woman in conversation. The woman's guilt might have risen to the surface, and Valerie could have detained her for questioning. She certainly would have gotten a better look at the person who later became their prime suspect.

Another noise jerked Valerie away from her regret and back into the warehouse. The balcony creaked. Was the wind blowing through here strong enough to do that? She examined the balcony segment by segment.

Lexi sniffed the ground and then sneezed.

"He got away." A voice boomed in her ear.

Though her training kept her from dropping the gun,

the voice had startled her. "Agent Lewis, do you always creep up on people like that?"

"Sorry, you were so focused on that balcony, there was no way not to surprise you." The arch of his eyebrow and slight upturn of his mouth suggested amusement.

Valerie holstered her gun and squared her shoulders, hoping he hadn't picked up on her loss of composure. She should have heard him coming no matter how closely she was watching the balcony. Tunnel vision while on duty could be deadly. Another stupid rookie mistake. She steadied her voice. "Murke got away?" She pointed to the dog who was working her way to the opposite side of the warehouse. "Lexi picked up on something in here."

"The dog's right. He did run through here, but then he doubled back and went out to the street."

That explained why the scent had become muddled for Lexi.

"I caught up with him on the street." Frustration was evident in Trevor's voice. "He got into a car and took off. No way could I catch him. But I know the make and model, and the first two letters on the plate. We'll post notices out to the locals and the highway patrol. Murke will most likely try to leave town now that he knows we're on to him."

She surveyed the warehouse one more time. She had to let go of the idea that the syndicate could be everywhere and was watching her. "Guess we better get back to the station."

She couldn't read Trevor's expression, but his voice softened. "Maybe next time we need to work on not getting separated like that," he said.

His tone of concern touched her, but she needed to be able to do her job. "Splitting up is standard procedure. Lexi can be a real asset in these situations."

"Sometimes there are things that are more important than procedure," he said.

The smolder in his voice made her heart flutter. Was he that worried about her well-being? He barely knew her.

He stepped closer to her, his hand brushing her forearm. "I said I'd protect you. I don't want to break my promise to McNeal."

Was that all it was about, keeping his word to an old buddy? She struggled to let go of her disappointment. And then wondered why it had even mattered to her that he had expressed concern for her that seemed to go beyond work requirements. "I have paperwork to catch up on back at the station. I still have to do my regular job." She headed toward the door of the warehouse, yanking on Lexi's leash. The dog was reluctant to leave the spot where she'd picked up the scent again. "Come on, Lex."

Once they were in his car, Valerie directed Trevor to the Sagebrush Police Station, a one-story, red-brick building. She led him around to the back where the K-9 officers had a separate entrance. She could feel his body heat and sense his proximity as he walked behind her. There was no chance of them being separated now.

He was one of those men who seemed to live in a state of heightened alert anyway, and he was taking watching her back seriously. Asking him to hang back a little ways wouldn't do any good. She'd just have to get used to it for the time being. "I've got some reports to complete, and I'll pull Leroy Seville's file to see if

I can find out anything more. I'm sure I'll be safe at my desk."

Trevor took a step back. "Great… I'll brief the other officers in the station on Murke. Then maybe we can see if we can track down this Linda Seville lady, find out if Murke was staying at her house or just somewhere on that street." His voice became more intense. "We need to jump on this. Murke is famous for leaving town as soon as he knows we're closing in on him."

As she and Lexi passed the other K-9 officers' desks, a black lab lay by Detective Jackson Worth's chair while he bent over a report. Titan lifted his head when she passed by but didn't move. The lab's job was to stick near Jackson, to watch over him. The devotion of the dogs to their handlers filled her with gratitude. Truth was, she felt safe as long as Lexi stayed close. The dogs remained with the officers most of the time, because having the K-9 as a pet as well as a partner was the best way to ensure unwavering obedience.

Valerie scooted her chair up to her desk and opened up a database that listed Sagebrush felons. Leroy Seville was recently out on parole after five years in jail. Linda Seville was listed as an emergency contact and identified as his great-aunt. They could catch up with Leroy later and see what he knew about Murke. She doubted Murke would go back to Linda's home.

In the small Sagebrush station, Trevor's warm bass voice carried across the room as he showed Murke's picture to the other officers. She tried to focus on her computer screen instead of the joking that seemed to be going on between Trevor and the other officers.

She adjusted her chair for the umpteenth time and leaned closer to the monitor. Trevor hadn't hidden his ire at getting close to Murke, yet not catching him. Did he blame her for that? It was her own insecurity that made her wonder if he was fishing around for a different officer to assist him.

She could only pick up bits and pieces of the conversation, and yet she had assumed that that was what was going on. Why did she even care? Having to help Trevor took away time from her regular work.

Okay, so he didn't like rookies. McNeal had paired them up for a reason. It couldn't just be because it was extra protection for her. Trevor wasn't going to ditch her for a more experienced officer who didn't have any connection to the neighborhoods where Murke was likely to be. Valerie chided herself for worrying. Fine with her if he wanted to work with a different officer.

She picked up a pen, making lines on a legal pad so deep they nearly cut through the paper. That caring tone he had used back at the warehouse had messed with her initial impression of him—that he was one of those lawmen who was good at his job but not so good at connecting with people. Maybe there was some chink in his armor. It wasn't her job to try to find it. The sooner they caught Murke, the sooner Trevor Lewis would be gone.

Pushing all thoughts of the impossibly handsome agent out of her head, she focused on the monitor, opening up a report she needed to complete. The voices around her faded, and all she heard was the tapping of the keys....

She completed the report and opened her email. She smiled as she read the thank-you notes from children at a school where she and Lexi had given a K-9 demonstration. She loved teaching members of the community about what the K-9 units did.

An email from her mother caught her attention as she scrolled down. Her mother usually used her private email. Her skin prickled as apprehension invaded her body.

She opened it up and read.

Bethany is such a pretty baby. It would be a shame to have anything happen to her.

The temperature in the room seemed to drop ten degrees as she stared at the computer screen. It was clear what had happened. Her mother would never send such a horrible email. So now the syndicate was hacking into family members' emails and threatening the life of her niece?

Her hands were shaking as she grabbed the phone to dial her home number.

Stella picked up on the first ring. "Hello."

Valerie took a breath, hoping to hide the anxiety in her voice. "Hey, Mrs. Witherspoon, I was just checking to see how Bethany was doing."

Stella's voice exuded cheerfulness. "She's such a doll. She just finished her cereal and is playing with her blocks."

"So, everything's okay?"

"Couldn't be better." Stella paused as though she were thinking something over. "Are you having a little separation anxiety, dear?"

Valerie gripped the phone a little tighter. "That must be it."

"It happens to every mother. Call here a thousand times a day if you need to."

Though she couldn't let go of the fear over harm coming to Bethany, Valerie relaxed a little. Bethany was in good hands. "Mrs. Witherspoon, you are an answer to prayer."

Valerie said her goodbyes and hung up. She called her mother who said she didn't think her email had been hacked. She barely turned her computer on. These guys were good. She pressed her trembling hands, palms down against the desk. Tuned into Valerie's heightened emotion, Lexi lifted her head and looked at her with dark brown eyes.

The words echoed through her mind. *It would be a shame if anything happened to her.* She felt like she was being shaken from the inside. Would Garry's murderer hurt Bethany to get to her? Now she knew for sure she was being watched. They must have seen her with Bethany.

"Everything okay?" Trevor stood beside her desk.

She straightened her spine and squared her shoulders, forcing her voice to sound professional. "Sure. Why?"

He sat down in the chair beside her, concern etched across his face. "Your complexion's the color of rice."

"It's nothing." She couldn't explain to him. He wouldn't understand why she was so upset. It was just an email, right? It wasn't like a gun had been pointed at her. "My face is always this color. I'm a light-skinned redhead."

He cracked a smile. "That you are, Officer Salgado, but that doesn't explain why your hands are shaking." He reached over and cupped his hand over hers.

She'd laced her fingers together so tightly her knuckles were white. He pulled back and studied her while the warmth of his touch lingered. Would he think she lacked strength as an officer if she revealed how much the threat had shaken her up? Cops were supposed to have titanium spines, right? There probably wasn't anything in the world that made Trevor Lewis afraid…except maybe feeding babies.

The warmth in his eyes, the same that she had seen at the warehouse, told her she could risk sharing.

She drew in a breath and turned the computer monitor toward him. "I just got this." She pulled the photo of Bethany off her cubicle wall and held it to her chest. Images about bad things happening to Bethany rampaged through her head. She shivered.

Trevor's jaw hardened as he looked away from the screen. He shook his head. "Unbelievable. This has got to be the syndicate's doing. Your mother would never send an email like that, right?"

Valerie nodded. "Who else would do this but the syndicate? The first threat came in an email, as well."

His presence had a calming effect on her that she didn't understand. Maybe it was just because he looked like he could smash small buildings with his fist. Being able to share with him had eased her fear. Now that she could get a deep breath, she felt like she was seeing things more clearly. "They wouldn't actually hurt Bethany, would they? It's me the Serpent is after."

"It doesn't matter if they will or won't. They are threatening your kid and upsetting you. It's all part of a game they're playing." His tone suggested deep offense at what had been done to her.

She exhaled. "It might be that it was meant to scare me. You know, the syndicate's reminder that they are still watching and waiting for their chance to kill me." She just didn't want to believe that anyone would harm an innocent child.

Trevor touched his clean-shaven face as his eyes narrowed. "I've seen this before with witnesses we were trying to protect. The intent is to break you psychologically. You don't want something bad to happen to your kid, so you back off from finding this woman."

"I can't even identify the woman yet for sure. We haven't been able to put together a sketch or a police lineup." She turned back to her computer and clicked out of her email program. "I just know that if I saw this woman that we think is the Serpent again, I would recognize her."

Trevor sat back in his chair. "The murderer doesn't know that, though. She probably thinks it's just a matter of time before the Sagebrush police track her down. These people are ruthless. They'll do everything they can to shake your resolve."

"I wish there was protection for Bethany when I'm not with her." Talking with Trevor had eased some of her fear, but every time she looked at Bethany's picture, she felt a jab to her heart. If anything happened to that little girl….

"Maybe the department can provide some protection," Trevor suggested.

"I can ask, and I'll let the captain know about the email, but it's always a funding and resources issue," she said.

At the other end of the administrative area, Captain McNeal stepped out of his office. "Dispatch just got a call from a black and white downtown. The car you saw Murke drive away in has been spotted outside a hardware store on Sagebrush Boulevard."

Valerie jumped up and grabbed Lexi's leash. "We might have Murke in custody before the day is over." Excitement pulsed through her. Chasing down Murke would get her mind off the email.

She clicked Lexi into her leash, glad to be doing something she could deal with.

Trevor quickened his pace as he moved toward the door. "Let's go catch a fugitive."

FOUR

Adrenaline surged through Valerie as Trevor selected a parking space with a view of Derek Murke's older-model Buick parked across the street. Murke was nowhere in sight. He had to be in one of the shops. She loved this part of the job—the prospect of catching a criminal brought the importance of her work back to her.

The sidewalks bustled with afternoon activity. Downtown Sagebrush was a mixture of boutiques and restaurants that provided a medley of rustic charm and trendy affluency. She recognized the patrol car up the block and two other unmarked police cars that had moved into place. Now it was just a matter of sitting and waiting. Murke had to come back to his car sooner or later.

Lexi leaned forward and panted.

Trevor angled his head away so he wouldn't get slobbered on.

"Sorry, she just likes to be a part of the action," Valerie explained, smiling indulgently as she stroked Lexi's ears.

The radio sparked to life. "Car two this is car one.

I've got eyes on Murke. He's standing at the check-out line in Bealman's Hardware."

Trevor lurched in his seat. "All right, let's move in. Keep the uniforms out of sight range. I don't want Murke to know we're on to him."

Valerie sat back in her seat trying to hide her disappointment. "I guess that means me, too." She looked down at her uniform.

"He scares easily." He'd already pushed open the door and slipped out of the car. "Radio the other units of his position if you see him."

Trevor attempted a casual but hurried walk across the street. Two other plainclothes officers were making a beeline for the hardware store. Valerie scanned the surrounding shops and the street. Though she accepted the reason for the decision, she really didn't like being put out of commission like this.

If Murke did come this way, her response time would be faster if she and Lexi were already on the street. If he was on the run already, it wouldn't matter if he saw her uniform.

She slipped out of the car, removed Lexi from the backseat and walked up the boulevard, keeping her eyes on the exterior of the hardware store. She shielded herself behind the other pedestrians to avoid being spotted. She walked past Arianna's Diner and a boutique that sold hats and other accessories.

A voice came across her shoulder mic. "Stand down. False alarm. Bad I.D."

Across the street, Trevor emerged from a cluster of people on the sidewalk. The droop in his shoulders communicated his level of disappointment as he made his way to the end of the block. Valerie's awareness switched into high gear. She turned in a half circle. Murke was still skulking around here. He hadn't come back to his car parked close to the hardware store. Sooner or later, he would show.

Walking to the end of the block, she kept her eye on Murke's car. Parking was at a premium in the downtown area. Just because he had parked by the hardware store didn't mean that was where he went. Trevor was doing the same sort of walking surveillance on the other side of the street. One of them needed to get back to the car in case they ended up tailing Murke in a vehicle. She turned and headed back toward the car.

Lexi came to attention and peered up the street. Valerie shifted her gaze. Murke had just stepped out of Arianna's Diner holding two take-out boxes. Recognition spread across his face as he narrowed his dark soulless eyes at her.

She expected Murke to turn and bolt...to make a beeline for his car. Instead, as she drew within feet of him, he charged toward her. Soda and a take-out box filled with a pasta dish showered down on her and Lexi. The crowd around them scattered like cockroaches in the light.

In the few seconds it took her to recover, Murke pivoted and raced up the street. He disappeared into a cluster of people. Murke's dirty-blond head bobbed up right before he entered a men's clothing store. She dashed inside.

Lexi sneezed repeatedly from the spices that had gone up her nose. The dog couldn't focus on Murke's scent trail. Valerie squinted as her eyes adjusted to the dim lighting. Behind the counter, a clerk pointed toward the back door. Valerie hurried into the alley. The sounds of the busy street gave way to a quiet alley. She heard footsteps and ran in the direction of them.

The alley smelled of garbage and Mexican spices and chemicals from a dry cleaners. A door creaked open, and a man came out tossing a trash bag in an open Dumpster. He offered Valerie only a passing glance before going back inside as if cops with K-9 units chased fugitives up this alley every day.

Trevor's comment about them staying together came back to her, but she swiped the thought from her mind. Doing her job had to be priority one. She needed to catch this guy. He'd already killed one lawman.

She radioed her location. Trevor and the others had to have seen the disruption on the street. They were probably already running this way.

Lexi dutifully placed her nose on the ground and sniffed. Then she sneezed. Would Lexi be able to pick up the scent?

She heard no further noise. Unless he'd slipped into the back door of one of the shops, Murke had to be hiding somewhere. She searched each nook and cranny, opened Dumpsters and checked behind a pile of crates.

Lexi pulled a little harder on her leash. "You got something, girl?"

The dog ran toward a stairway that led to a second-floor door. Valerie remained down below with her gun drawn prepared to shoot if Murke was behind the door.

A voice as cold as ice sounded in her ear as the hard blade of a knife pressed against her throat. "Drop the gun."

Her heart lurched. She let the gun fall to the ground.

Lexi was already headed back down the stairs. Murke hadn't noticed the dog.

Hurry girl, hurry.

Valerie let her hands go limp as though she would comply. When she felt his body relax, she slammed her elbow hard into his stomach. Murke groaned. She turned to face her attacker, preparing to land a second blow.

She saw his face, features compressed into an expression of hate. Onyx eyes tore through her. Behind her, Lexi barked.

Murke's eyes grew wide with fear when he saw Lexi. He took off running again. Lexi bolted past her hot on Murke's heels but was slowed down by her sneezing. It took only a moment for Valerie to retrieve her gun and chase after Murke.

Trevor raced through a store that sold Western wear, past puzzled clerks and out the back entrance. A mixture of fear and anger warred inside him. He had told Valerie to stay in the car. Why hadn't she listened? The uniform thing had been his excuse to keep her safe.

It had taken less than three minutes to figure out it was Valerie and Murke causing the ruckus across the street. Her red hair had flashed bright in the noonday sun, then he had darted across the street to find her.

He stepped out of the Western shop into the empty alley. Where had she gone? His heart squeezed tight. All anger washed away as fear took over. What if Murke had killed her?

Not again. God, please, not again.

He scanned up and down the alley, pushing down the rising panic. She had to be all right.

The distant bark of the dog brought a sense of relief. That had to be Lexi. He followed the sound of the barking, heading away from downtown and toward a residential part of Sagebrush. His feet pounded on the sidewalk as he ran past yards just starting to turn green. He stopped to listen again for the barking. He caught up with Valerie and Lexi by some playground equipment that was part of a housing complex.

She turned to face him as he approached. "We lost sight of him." She looked down at Lexi, who sat at her feet, panting. "Her sniffer is all messed up. Daytime searches are harder anyway—too many people running around, lot of scents to sort through."

"One of the units is still watching the car. If he tries to go back that way, we'll nab him." Disappointment settled in his stomach like a rock. Twice in one day, Murke had been within his grasp…and he had eluded them.

"I already radioed a patrol unit to comb the streets." She tugged on Lexi's leash. "We'll walk the neighborhood, see if we can pick up on anything. Maybe somebody saw him."

Trevor stood close to Valerie, expecting to be enveloped in her floral scent. Instead, he smelled… Italian spices? Her uniform had stains on it. "What happened to you?"

"Murke's escape plan involved throwing his takeout at me. Lexi got spices up her nose, and Murke's lunch is all over my uniform." She shook her head and rolled her eyes. "Let's not make a big deal about it or else the other officers will have a nickname for me before the day is over."

"I don't know…you might have started a trend. Marinara-scented perfume could become very popular," he quipped.

She had an easy laugh that helped quell some of the frustration he'd felt at losing Murke again.

They searched the street for several more hours before giving up. The Buick remained parked by the hardware store. Murke wouldn't be stupid enough to return. Maybe he had slipped into a garage or an unlocked house and maybe he had phoned someone and gotten a ride. The point was they weren't going to find him today.

Valerie completed her usual patrol shift. They rolled through the neighborhood where they had first seen Murke, stopping at Linda Seville's empty house. Maybe the older woman was out of town.

As they stepped around from the house, Valerie suggested, "We might be able to catch up with Leroy Seville through his parole officer."

Trevor nodded, unable to let go of his frustration. "That would be the next step." Squaring his shoulders, he ambled toward his car.

Once he was behind the wheel, Valerie commented, "Both times today Murke was trying to get some food, and we kept him from eating." She rested her head against the back of the seat. "Maybe we'll just starve him out."

Trevor laughed. He appreciated her being able to find humor in the situation, but Murke was still on the run. "I thought Murke would skip town after he saw us this morning. Wonder what's keeping him here, risking being caught?"

Valerie shook her head. "You said he lived here when he was a teenager?"

"Yeah, and he's come back more than once," Trevor said.

"My brother David works undercover. He's in touch

with some of the shadier people around Sagebrush. He might know something."

So her brother was a cop, too. "I'd like to talk to him."

"We're having a family barbecue tonight. You're welcome to come."

Social gatherings really weren't his thing, but he was anxious to heat up the trail that led to Murke. After all, there would be no justice for Cory Smith's death until Murke was caught. "I might do that."

She let out a heavy sigh and stared at the ceiling. "I can't wait to get out of this uniform. I smell like an Italian restaurant."

He drove across town and parked in front of her house. The patrol car that was supposed to be her off-duty protection hadn't shown up yet. He raced around to her side of the car and helped her out. He stayed close to her as they crossed the street. As close as he could get with Lexi between them.

In a lot of ways, she was a good cop, even if she was a rookie. "I appreciate the work you did today. How did you know Murke was on that side of the street?"

They came to her door. "I thought it would be better if I got out of the car and was ready for him." She looked up at him without blinking, her green eyes bright and clear. "I know you told me to stay in the car, but sitting on the sidelines is not what a cop does."

The expression on her face sent a charge through him. "You showed good instincts," he murmured.

"Thank you." When she smiled, her freckles seemed more intense.

The glow of appreciation in her voice made his heart leap.

She leaned toward him. "Guess I'll see you later for the barbecue."

"I'm not going anywhere. Your night watch isn't here yet. I'll be parked right along the curb."

"I appreciate that." She opened the door and slipped inside.

As the door eased shut, he could hear the sound of Mrs. Witherspoon's fussing over Valerie, Bethany's gleeful cry and Valerie exclaiming, "There's my girl."

Trevor returned to his car and settled in. He had some calls he needed to make. He scanned the neighborhood, which was a mixture of apartment buildings and single-family homes. Things looked pretty settled, but that didn't mean he could let his guard down. Twice Lexi came to the window and looked out at him, resting her paws on the windowsill.

That dog just didn't know what to make of him.

As he pulled his laptop out and worked through the late afternoon, he found himself looking forward to the barbecue and being with Valerie. What was it about her that was getting under his skin?

FIVE

As she slipped into a purple sundress and contemplated whether to wear her hair up or down, Valerie realized she was making choices with Trevor's reaction in mind.

"Why should I care what he thinks, huh, Lex?"

The dog, who had positioned herself by the bedroom door, tilted her chunky square head sideways as though she understood what Valerie was saying.

"It's not like I don't have enough going on already." She turned away from the full-length mirror to the bed where Bethany was propped against some pillows. The toddler broke out in a grin and then lifted the blanket to hide her face.

"Oh peek-a-boo to you, too." She swept Bethany in her arms as the little girl let out a giggle. She bounced her up and down, making her laugh even more.

Lexi came to attention. The dog had been around Bethany at family gatherings. As Kathleen neared the end of her life, Bethany had stayed at Valerie's quite a bit, but the dog still didn't quite know what to make of this new little person in the house. She showed neither animosity nor affection for the toddler.

Valerie sat Bethany back on the bed and smoothed her troll-doll hair. She retrieved a plastic barrette from the bathroom and placed it in Bethany's blond hair. Bethany fingered the barrette but didn't pull it out. "Now we both look pretty. And we're ready to have a good time." The ache in her heart returned. She stroked Bethany's soft cheek as thoughts of Kathleen returned.

The barbecue had been her father's idea, a way of bringing the family together under more positive circumstances since Kathleen's funeral over a month ago. She understood her father's way of coping, but the cloud of sorrow would be there no matter what.

Valerie grabbed a light sweater as a cover-up. Spring evenings could still be a little chilly. She juggled Bethany, her purse and the diaper bag as she headed toward the door. Lexi followed dutifully behind.

Once outside, the cool March air greeted her. She contemplated how she was going to get her keys out of her purse to lock the door with everything she was holding.

A car door slammed and Trevor strode toward her. "Let me give you a hand."

She caught the moment of head-to-toe assessment he did of her before he spoke. A warm smile brightened his tanned face.

"Thank you." She handed him the diaper bag and placed Bethany in his arms before opening her purse to dig for her keys. "I thought we should take separate cars. I'm sure you need to get back to the hotel or wherever you're staying. The night shift protection will be in place by the time I…" She looked up at him. Bethany sucked on his shirt collar and then patted his chest three times. Trevor stiffened his shoulders. "Babies aren't quite your thing, are they?"

Color rose up in his face. "I just haven't been around them much."

She placed the key in the lock and twisted it before turning to face him. "You never had any little sisters or brothers?"

"No, it was just me." He broke off eye contact.

She had a feeling there was more to the story than he was willing to tell. She'd seen a flash of sadness or maybe it was pain in his eyes. Trevor Lewis was a hard man to figure out. She took Bethany out of his arms.

He held on to the diaper bag. "That's your car over there?"

"Yes," she said.

"It's been parked out here all day. Why don't I take a good look at it before you get in?"

Valerie's breath caught as apprehension returned. She hadn't even thought of the possibility of a bomb being planted. She wouldn't put it past the syndicate, though.

Trevor opened and closed doors, ran his hands underneath seats, searched the trunk and checked the underside of the car. He rose to his feet and dusted off his pants. "Take it slow. I'll follow behind you."

Valerie placed Bethany in her car seat in the back, and Lexi took her position in the passenger seat. As they drove, Lexi alerted to the movement of people and cars on the street. Like any good cop, there wasn't much that the dog didn't notice.

Valerie checked her rearview mirror. Trevor's sedan remained close. They passed the Lost Woods before arriving at a suburb on the outskirts of Sagebrush.

Valerie had pulled Bethany out of her car seat by the time Trevor rolled in behind her in the driveway. He got out of his car and flashed her a quick smile. "We made it."

Her stomach fluttered when he looked at her with those dark, intense eyes. What was it about this guy that stirred up these feelings of attraction? "Come on, let's go meet my family."

Trevor followed Valerie around the side of the house as he took in his surroundings. He hadn't wanted to tell Valerie, to ruin her evening out with her family, but he was pretty sure they'd been followed.

The chatter of voices and water splashing in a pool greeted him even before he saw the huge crowd gathered on the patio. An older man in a Hawaiian shirt flipped burgers while he spoke to a woman in a wheelchair. Young children jumped in the pool and came out shivering. Adults milled in and out of the house or sat at a patio table. He estimated that there were at least ten adults and just as many children.

Valerie leaned close to him. "Don't be intimidated. Not all of them are family—some are friends and neighbors."

A woman with long, blond hair came up to Valerie and held out her arms for Bethany. "There's my sweet baby."

"Trevor, this is Lucy Cullen. We met when I was assigned protective duty for her."

Lucy gathered Bethany into her arms. "And we've been friends ever since."

"She's engaged to a fellow K-9 officer." Valerie

pointed across the pool at a tall, muscular man with light brown hair. "Lee Calloway."

Lucy's gaze fell on Trevor. "I'll watch Bethany for a while. Why don't you relax and enjoy yourself." She sauntered away holding Bethany.

Valerie set the diaper bag down. "My brother David should be around here somewhere." She scanned the crowd. "I'll have you meet my dad first."

She took his hand as though it were the most natural thing in the world and led him toward the man by the barbecue. The softness of her grip sent a surge of heat through him.

She let go of his hand and touched his shoulder. "Dad, this is Agent Trevor Lewis from the San Antonio FBI. We're working together to catch a fugitive."

The older man put his spatula down and offered Trevor a hardy handshake. "Detective Ben Salgado, retired, twenty-five years on the force."

Trevor nodded. "Appreciate your service, sir."

Ben offered him a wide grin. "Trying to talk Valerie into taking the detective's exam. Once she gets done with this dog thing."

Valerie turned slightly and bent her head, staring at her feet. "I enjoy the K-9 unit."

The moment passed quickly, but he had caught a tremor in her voice that suggested hurt.

Oblivious to how his comment had affected his daughter, Ben flipped a burger and then turned to face them again. "This is my wife, Helen." Ben pointed toward the woman in the wheelchair, who nodded.

"I worked dispatch until this muscular disease got the better of me. Ben and I met when we were both employed by the police department." Salt and pepper hair framed Helen Salgado's slender face. Kind eyes looked at him from behind wire-rimmed glasses.

"Daddy, we're looking for David. Where is he?"

"Mary and the girls came separately. David is still on duty. He should be here any minute," Helen said.

Ben slapped Trevor's back. "In the meantime, have a burger. Drinks and sides are over by the table."

While Trevor ate, Valerie retrieved Bethany from Lucy only to have her taken away again by a gray-haired grandmotherly woman. Trevor took a bite of his burger and watched the action around him.

Lexi sat where Valerie had commanded her to stay. Though children would come by to pet her, she remained stoic and vigilant, always watching. When one of the kids had pointed a plastic water pistol at Valerie, Lexi had stirred to her feet, waiting for the command from Valerie to attack. Valerie had given her a hand signal that told her it was okay to lie down.

That was something he had in common with the dog. He'd never been much of a mixer at social gatherings, preferring to remain on the perimeter as an observer.

Valerie walked around the other picnic tables, grabbing the empty plates. The setting sun gave her skin a luminescent quality and her long, red hair had shaken loose from the ponytail. He jumped up when she headed back toward the house with a stack of dirty plates. Maybe that car hadn't been following them on the way in, but he didn't want to take any chance of her being alone or vulnerable. He could stay close without her having to think about the death threat.

He caught up with Valerie just as she placed the dishes in the sink. Her back was turned toward him. The big windows provided too much of an opportunity for Valerie to be seen. It would be nothing for a sniper to fire a shot through them.

They were alone in the kitchen, the noise from the party outside muffled by the patio door. "Why don't we go back to the yard?"

Startled, Valerie turned and placed her palm on her chest. "I didn't realize you'd followed me in." Evening light streaming through kitchen windows washed over her. "I just needed to get away from all the noise for a moment and catch my breath. I kind of like the quiet."

After seeing how shaken up she was from the email threat at the station, he felt the need to protect her not just physically, but emotionally, too. She needed to have a nice night with her family and not have to think about the ever-watchful eyes of the syndicate. "I just think we should get back. I'm sure Bethany is missing you."

She laughed, a soft trilling sound. "I don't think I am going to get that baby back until the night is over."

Headlights created shadows across the living room carpet. Someone was pulling up the street by the Salgado's long driveway.

"Oh, I bet that's David." She rushed through the kitchen toward the entryway and flung open the door.

Trevor followed on her heels, as the evening air chilled his skin.

She ran halfway down the long driveway. He could just make out the outline of the car he had seen earlier.

A man covered in shadows got out of the car.

"David!" she waved.

Trevor caught up with Valerie and wrapped his arm around her shoulder. "Let's go back inside."

She resisted when he tried to guide her back to the house. "What are you talking about?"

The man stopped, then pivoted and returned to the car.

She tensed. "That wasn't my brother."

"No," he said, pulling her close.

"They followed us here. They...they know where my parents live." Her voice faltered and she began to tremble.

He drew her close. "I don't know for sure. Maybe that guy was just lost." She rested her face against his chest. He covered her with his arms and held her until the shaking stopped. Her back expanded and contracted with the steady intake and exhale of her breath.

She pulled back and tilted her head toward him. "I forgot. For just one moment, I forgot that my life was in danger."

"We can't take any chances." He'd do anything to give her back a normal life, but that wasn't within his power. All he could do was protect her and watch over her. "Come on, let's go back to the party."

"What do you suppose that man's plan was?" Fear still permeated her words.

He stayed close to her as they turned to go back inside. "If it was the syndicate, he was probably going to scope out...an opportunity." They walked across the living room floor.

"There's lots of trees around the backyard to hide in. I'm sure he would have found—" she cleared her throat "—a place to hide and get a clean shot."

For now, Trevor's presence had deterred the would-be assassin.

She opened the patio door and the happy noises of the party spilled into the living room. She hesitated at the door, her mouth drawn into a pensive line.

He placed a supportive hand on the middle of her back, leaned close and whispered in her ear. "I know it feels like you can't ever relax because of this. Just know that I'm here."

Mr. Salgado waved at them from a close picnic table. "David's here." He pointed across the pool at a man with long hair sitting in a lawn chair.

"He must have pulled around back because the driveway was full of cars," Valerie said as she stepped outside.

David Salgado pulled his sunglasses off and stood up as Valerie and Trevor approached. He was at least ten years older than Valerie. The long hair was probably part of his undercover work.

"David, this is Agent Trevor Lewis from San Antonio. He's trying to track down a man named Derek Murke." Valerie had a faraway look in her eyes. She was probably still rattled by what had happened in the driveway.

David rubbed his forehead. "Derek Murke. Yeah, I remember him. He was robbing convenience stores when I was still on patrol."

"He's back in town. You have any idea where he might be?" Trevor asked. "He's probably worn out his welcome with his old partner in crime, Leroy Seville, and the aunt he was staying with."

David made a clicking sound with his tongue. "Murke did a lot of petty thievery."

"He graduated up to armed robbery about two years ago," Trevor said.

David rubbed his chin. "Seems like he had a half sister. She had a different last name than him, much more law abiding, too. I'm sure I could track down the name for you."

"Thanks, I'd appreciate that." Trevor slapped David's back and shook his hand before handing him a business card. "Give me a call when you know."

"Will do."

Valerie came up beside him and touched his forearm lightly. "Trevor, I think I'm ready to go home. I don't like the idea of putting my family in danger." Her voice had a pleading quality.

Trevor nodded. "I don't blame you."

As they walked away, David said, "I'll let you know as soon as I remember. Take care of my sister."

He helped Valerie gather up Bethany and the baby's things. David's words echoed in his brain. More than anything, he wanted to keep her safe.

Valerie gave him a backward glance before commanding Lexi to come.

"I'll follow you home," he said. "We need to make sure your night protection is in place."

She nodded, but didn't say anything. He waited for her on the quiet suburban street while she backed out of the driveway. He remained close as they made their way back to town through the city streets to her home. The red glare of her taillights overshadowed the outline of her head and of Lexi's head in the passenger seat.

She slowed when she got close to her house. The police car was already parked outside. Trevor pulled in behind her. He waved at the police officer and followed Valerie up to her door. She had removed the car seat with the sleeping Bethany in it. Valerie fumbled in her purse for her keys. She pushed open the door.

"Why don't you let me have a look around inside first?"

Again, she nodded. He checked both her first and second floor as well as the backyard. Satisfied, he returned to where she waited in the foyer. "All clear." He squeezed her shoulder. "Have a good night."

He waited outside until he heard the lock click into place. He recognized the police officer from the station this morning. The man rolled down his window as Trevor approached. He leaned on the window. "Keep her safe."

"You got it," said the officer.

He got in his car and drove away. He circled the block twice before finally feeling like he could let go. He wanted to stay there all night, to watch over her. But he would be no good to anyone if he didn't get some sleep.

As he hopped on the freeway to head to the hotel, the lights of the city stretched before him. He had always thought there was something comforting about a city at night viewed from a distance. The twinkling lights and the silence masked all of the turmoil taking place on the streets and in some homes at night.

Valerie had a family that loved her and Bethany. She had siblings who cared about her. The whole experience had been surreal to him. He had grown up in a home where all the happy families who cared about each other were on television. Valerie wouldn't want anything to do with him if she knew what kind of family he came from…what his father had done to his mother.

He spotted a sign for the hotel and hit the blinker. Why did she matter so much to him if he couldn't see himself fitting into her life? He went to the hotel room he'd checked into the previous night. The room was clean, but the silence stood in sharp contrast to the chatter of the barbecue earlier. As he tossed his suitcase on the bed and pulled off his jacket, he was struck by a profound loneliness.

Valerie woke in the night to the sensation of Lexi licking her fingers. The room was dark except for a night-light close to Bethany's bed.

"What is it?" Valerie whispered.

Lexi whined.

Bethany stirred in her crib, but luckily she didn't wake up.

Valerie threw back the covers and followed Lexi to the main floor. She checked Lexi's food and water dish, though the dog was not in the habit of waking her for something so trivial. Maybe she was just restless.

Valerie flicked on the faucet and grabbed a cup. When she had finished her water, the dog hadn't settled down. Valerie checked that the police car was still parked outside and all the doors were locked. She returned to the kitchen. Lexi stood at attention by the patio door.

Valerie's hands were clammy as she reached to open the blinds on the glass of the patio door. She hesitated, gripping the string for the blinds. The truth was she didn't want to see what was outside. She didn't want to see a stranger with a gun pointed at her. Or the Serpent's yellow eyes burning through her. Or Derek Murke's face compressed into an expression of hate.

As a cop, she had faced danger before. She'd had guns pointed at her. But this wasn't about a criminal wanting to avoid jail time. This was personal. The syndicate wanted her dead. That took her fear to a whole new level.

As blood thrummed in her ears and she struggled for a deep breath, she found the courage to open the blinds all the way. Dark shadows and movement caused her to take a step back. Lexi came up beside her and leaned against her. She stroked the dog's head, an action that calmed both of them.

"What do you think is out there?" She could not clearly discern anything outside. Maybe someone had been in the yard and maybe it was just her heightened state of awareness. Valerie closed the blinds, and Lexi finally relaxed.

She trudged upstairs. She hovered over Bethany's crib until she heard the soft sound of Bethany's breathing. Assured that the baby was okay, she crawled beneath her covers and pulled her legs up to her stomach.

Seeing the police car outside did ease some of her fear, but she couldn't help but think that she would feel even safer if it was Trevor who was parked outside.

SIX

Captain Slade McNeal strode toward Valerie's desk looking like a man on a mission. Judging from the tightness of his expression, either her paperwork was messed up or he had something very serious for her to do.

She checked the entrance to the K-9 administrative area. Still no sign of Trevor. She'd called him early in the morning, and they'd agreed to meet at the station. Her night duty protection had followed her into the station. She'd looked at Derek Murke's criminal file again but didn't find a mention of a half sister. Hopefully, David would remember the woman's name.

McNeal stopped a few feet from her desk. "Salgado, I just got a call. A group of school children found a dog matching Rio's description collapsed underneath a bush in Palo Verde Park." Though McNeal never gave much away in terms of emotion, there was intensity in his piercing blue eyes that Valerie had not seen before.

Valerie jumped to her feet. "I'll go with you." Rio had been missing since January. If this was McNeal's dog, the whole department would breathe a collective sigh of relief.

Lexi stood up and looked to Valerie, waiting for a

command. Her bobbed tail vibrated in anticipation. "Lex, come."

Trevor was just pulling into the back parking lot as they headed toward the patrol car. He was clean shaven and the light blue windbreaker he wore set off his dark hair and eyes. His smile drew her in.

Trevor glanced from McNeal to Valerie. "Something going on?"

"I've got to take this call at Palo Verde Park." She looked over her shoulder at McNeal. "It's important."

McNeal put a hand on her shoulder. "She'll be all right. She'll be with me."

"I got in touch with Leroy Seville's parole officer. He's got an appointment this morning. It's a chance for me to find out what Murke said to him...if anything," Trevor said. "I can meet you at the park after the interview."

As Trevor returned to his car and pulled out of the lot, Valerie and McNeal rushed to the patrol car, putting Lexi in the back. Captain McNeal radioed the animal warden to meet them at the park. If this was Rio, there was no telling what condition the dog would be in. The syndicate could have beaten him and left him for dead. Or the dog might have become vicious due to mistreatment.

As she drove, Valerie glanced over at her captain. Deep furrows through his forehead indicated his level of anxiety. He touched his dark hair where it was graying at the temple, a gesture that gave away how nervous he was. The burden he had carried since Rio's disappearance had been a heavy one. Not only had he lost his dog, but Slade's dad had also been badly beaten during the abduction. Valerie had heard that he was on the mend, though. On top of everything, Rio had been a best friend and protector to Slade's five-year-old son, Caleb, since the boy's mom had died.

Her heart went out to Slade. He needed some morsel of hope. "Maybe this will be it. Maybe we found him, huh?"

"If it is him, collapsed on a playground is not a good sign." His voice faltered, betraying the level of worry he must be going through. McNeal shifted slightly in his seat. "How are things working out with Agent Lewis?"

McNeal didn't want to talk about Rio, so he'd changed the subject. Though he was a man who kept his emotions in check, Valerie had seen the sorrow over the loss rise to the surface in subtle ways. The loss of a K-9 partner stung as much as if Rio had been human. The dogs were officers and partners in every way. She never doubted that Lexi had her back and would take a bullet for her. She understood about him not wanting to talk about it. "How well did you say you knew Agent Lewis?"

"We've done joint training exercises together." McNeal stared out the window.

Valerie hit the blinker and made the turn into the park. "He's a competent agent. He's a little bit closed down when it comes to sharing much about himself, though."

McNeal nodded but didn't offer any further information. Knowing something about where a person had come from was probably not important to a man. Connection to people, getting to know them, was everything to her. She'd worked at building the trust of the people in the neighborhoods she patrolled and with all the people in her life.

As they pulled into the parking lot, fatigue mixed with the anticipation she felt about finding Rio. She'd only had half a cup of coffee. Not only had Lexi awakened her in the night, but Bethany had stood up in her crib only a few hours after Valerie had gone back to sleep, clinging tightly to the worn pink bunny. It just seemed like Bethany should have fallen into a less restless pattern of sleep by now. Valerie worried that she wasn't comforting and holding Bethany enough. And then she worried that she was holding her too much. She really didn't know what she was doing when it came to being Bethany's mom. Kathleen had been such a natural. Sometimes she wondered why her sister had had so much confidence in her.

When they arrived at the park, Valerie commanded Lexi to follow her. As they got out of the patrol car and headed across the long stretch of grass to the playground, the ache over Kathleen's loss returned. Grief rose to the surface at the strangest times.

I just don't know if I can be a good mom.

A group of children along with a woman who must be their teacher stood by the playground equipment. Valerie could make out the prone body of a German shepherd beneath the bushes.

"Let's approach with caution. We don't know what he's been through." McNeal was already thinking that the dog was Rio.

The teacher came toward them with the children trailing behind her. "I'm Mrs. Scott—we're the ones who phoned in."

One of the children, a girl of about six dressed in a pink polka-dot coat, peeked around Mrs. Scott. "The dog growled at us and then cried out like he wasn't feeling good."

"If you could just stay back," McNeal advised and then looked around. "Where's the animal warden?"

"I'm sure Robert's on his way," Valerie said, turning her attention toward the dog.

"We can't wait for him. Let's just move in slowly and see if we can figure out what is going on with the dog." McNeal's voice was thick with emotion.

Valerie dropped to the ground and approached the dog. Captain McNeal took the lead, and Valerie inched behind him. From this angle, she couldn't see any obvious injuries on the dog. The dog lifted its head with a wary eye toward McNeal.

Valerie made soothing sounds as she eased closer. The dog was laying on what looked like a child's coat and a picnic blanket.

"There, boy," said McNeal.

The dog raised its head and growled. McNeal stopped, unable to hide his anguish. His eyebrows pinched together.

"She doesn't like men. Some dogs are like that." Mrs. Scott had come up behind them.

"Ma'am, please, I'm going to have to ask you to stand back." Valerie knew McNeal well enough to know that the harshness of his tone was not meant for Mrs. Scott. That the dog had growled at the sound of McNeal's voice was not a good sign. Either Rio had been so traumatized that the bond between handler and dog had been broken, or this dog was not Rio.

McNeal patted Valerie's shoulder. "Go ahead and move in."

Valerie scooted closer. The dog lifted her head and

whimpered. It took Valerie only a minute to see blood on the tail and the canine's bulb-like stomach. Valerie closed her eyes in disappointment. "Captain, this isn't Rio. This dog is about to have pups."

Repeated gleeful cries of, "Puppies! Puppies! She's going to have puppies," came from the children.

Mrs. Scott shushed the children and scooted them farther back.

"She's nesting. That's why she dragged that coat and that blanket over here." Valerie turned to look at her boss.

His features were distorted from despair for only a moment before he recovered. "The right thing to do here is to help that dog have her pups and make sure we get her transported to a safe place."

"Yes, sir." Valerie turned her attention back toward the dog. She reached a tentative hand toward the dog's head. The dog whined and stiffened in pain from a contraction. Empathy surged through Valerie's body. "It's all right." She soothed the dog's head.

There were no tags or collar. The dog looked thin but not malnourished. She heard footsteps behind her and turned to see Robert Cane.

Though she addressed the animal warden, she kept her tone soothing so as not to agitate the dog. "She's not crazy about men."

"I'll just hang back here, Valerie. It looks like you're doing fine," said Robert.

The dog closed her eyes and panted. "But I'm not trained for this," Valerie said.

"She'll do most of the work." She could hear Robert repositioning himself behind her. "I can watch from here and let you know if you need to intervene."

Valerie took in a deep breath, hoping to ease the tension in her neck and back. "So I guess it's up to me."

"You got a new job title, Valerie—canine midwife." Slade's voice came from a few feet behind her.

His joking didn't quite hide the undertone of sorrow she picked up in his voice. The man missed his dog, not just for him but for his kid, also.

The first four pups came quickly. The mother licked off the protective air sack of each. With their eyes still closed, they grunted and pushed until they found a nipple to nurse on. A fifth puppy emerged, but did not move. The mother was still occupied cleaning the fourth puppy.

Valerie's hands became clammy. "He's not moving, Robert. This little guy isn't moving."

"He needs to get air into his lungs. Hold him upside down and swing him like a golf club," the animal warden said.

"What?"

"I know it sounds crazy, Valerie, but it works."

Valerie picked up the motionless slimy black body and did as Robert instructed. The puppy still showed no signs of life.

Please, God, don't let this little guy die.

Robert's soft voice didn't conceal his concern. Tension strung through his words. "Try again."

She swung the pup one more time…and waited. The pup let out a noise that sounded like a sneeze and wiggled to life.

Valerie let out the breath she'd been holding. Behind her, she heard the collective sigh of the school children. The puppy moved more vigorously in her hands.

"You're a natural." Robert edged toward her. "Now put her close to the mother so they can bond."

Valerie placed the squirming pup close to the mother's nose. The dog lifted her head and licked the black fur. The instinct to nurture seemed to come easily to the female shepherd. A deeper understanding stirred inside Valerie. Maybe she needed to trust her own maternal instincts where Bethany was concerned. As hard as it was, Valerie couldn't imagine her life without that little girl. She wasn't going to be a perfect mom, but she'd be the best mom she could be for Bethany.

Once the mother dog was done cleaning the pup, Valerie placed him close to the mother's belly so he could nurse. The little pup was smaller than the others, but fought his way to the top of the pile.

Robert came up behind her. The female dog lifted her head but didn't growl. "That little guy has some strong survival instincts."

Valerie nodded. "I suppose we should leave mother and babies alone." She rose to her feet and stood beside Robert. "We'll have to transport her and the pups when she's ready."

"We'll find homes for them when they are old enough," Robert said.

McNeal came and stood beside them. "Maybe the mother would be a good candidate for the K-9 training program."

A blond girl broke away from the group of children watching at a distance. She looped her fingers through the straps of her purple backpack and looked up at Valerie. "Can we see them now?"

"I suppose that would be okay." Valerie looked toward Robert for guidance.

"Just a couple of kids at a time, and you can't touch them," he advised.

The little girl nodded.

Valerie stepped back toward the bushes. The school girl kneeled beside her. Her eyes grew wide when Valerie lifted the branches for a view of the nursing pups. "Wow."

Mama dog licked one of the wayward pups and scooted it back toward the warmth of her tummy and the litter with her nose.

"She takes good care of them," the little girl said. "How does she know what to do?"

"It's just the way God made her. She's wired to be a mom," Valerie said.

They kneeled for a moment watching the pups, some sleeping and others still probing for an opportunity to nurse more. The little girl's hand slipped into Valerie's. She held the warm little hand in her own as though it were as fragile as a snowflake. Bethany would do this in time, and she relished the opportunity to share the wonder of birth with her daughter. Yes, that was it. Bethany was *her daughter* now.

They backed away from the bushes. "Now," said Valerie, "go get three more of your friends and tell them to come over here."

Valerie ushered over groups of two and three children until McNeal tapped her on the shoulder.

"Your partner is here," he said.

Trevor stood by the edge of the swing set some distance from the children.

"I'll finish up here and take Agent Lewis's car back to the station. I know you need to do your regular patrol—Robert can make sure the dog is safe," McNeal assured her.

The school children chimed as she walked by them, "Goodbye, Officer Salgado."

Valerie waved at them before turning to face Trevor. She couldn't read his expression but something about him seemed…softer. She wasn't quite sure what had caused the change. Had he been watching the drama of the puppies being born for some time?

"So McNeal tells me the dog wasn't Rio and now the department has five puppies to deal with," Trevor said as he walked beside Valerie.

Valerie commanded Lexi to come and the dog fell in beside her. "We'll try to find the owner. If not, we'll see that they are placed in homes." They strolled across the stretch of lawn to the parking lot. "So did Leroy make his meeting?"

"Yeah, I'm pretty sure Murke won't be welcomed back. Leroy is working hard at going straight, and Murke wore out his welcome when he took Leroy's Buick." He gazed down at her. "The aunt is out of town for a month or more. When Leroy got out of prison, she said he could house sit. If Murke does show up, I'm sure Leroy will give us a call."

Valerie let Lexi into the backseat of the patrol car. "That's good news. So do you think Murke has left town?"

"I don't know." Trevor got into the passenger seat. "Your brother called me with the name of Murke's half sister. I thought we'd go over there and try to talk to her."

Valerie settled in, started the car and turned around. While she waited for a car to pass by before pulling out into the street, she studied the hard lines and angles of Trevor's face.

He offered her a glance with a smile that was more of a spasm. Something was going on with him.

"So everything was pretty routine this morning?"

He tapped his fingers on the dashboard. "Yeah, sure, why?"

"I don't know. You just seemed different when you were standing in the park…like you were thinking about something," Valerie said.

He picked up a small notebook from the cup holder. "That's the address where Murke's half sister lives. Her name is Crystal."

He was good at changing the subject. She took the piece of paper and read the address while stopped at an intersection. "I know where this is." She sped through the intersection. "So what were you thinking about in the park?" If they were going to work together, she wanted to know more about him. He certainly hadn't revealed anything personal to McNeal.

His eye twitched. "Who says I was thinking about anything?"

She caught the defensiveness in his tone. She focused her attention on the view through the windshield. The car clicked past a mall and some big-box stores. Why did it even matter to her that she wanted to know more about him…to see more of the man underneath that thick exterior?

The silence in the car became oppressive. Valerie rolled down the window, letting the spring breeze caress her face. Lexi leaned over her shoulder to take in the outdoor smells.

"Not every family is like your family, you know," Trevor blurted.

She picked up on just a slight waver in his voice. If she hadn't had interview and interrogation training, she'd never have noticed it. His comment had come out of left field. She wasn't sure where this was leading.

"I think the street is just up here a ways." She took in a breath and glanced over at him. "What do you mean not every family is like mine?"

"You got people that love you and care about you," Trevor said. "They want your career to turn out right, and they help you with Bethany."

"Yes, that's true." She still wasn't sure what he was implying.

His gaze shifted more than was necessary. This wasn't easy for him, whatever he was trying to say. Slowing down as they entered a residential neighborhood, she parked the car outside the house where Murke's half sister lived. Then she looked over at him, waiting for an explanation.

Valerie's gaze was like a heavy weight on him. Sweat trickled down his neck. Now he regretted even breaching the subject of his family. Talking about them was harder than sniper duty in below-zero weather.

She'd run to the hills when she knew what kind of family he'd come from. He'd grown up in a home that half the time didn't have electricity because his father didn't pay the bill. His mom had tried to make the house a home. She had tried until…that night.

"So you're saying your family isn't like mine." She leaned closer. Her green eyes intense as the scent of her perfume enveloped him.

He liked the way she tried to make it easier for him. It loosened some of the tension that was like a cord twisting around his chest. When he had watched her at a distance with the children and the puppies, he'd felt a longing to be a part of the tender moment she had created. That was what had started this whole thing. He didn't want to be the outsider anymore.

"How bad could it be? My family isn't perfect, either." Her eyes seemed to probe beneath his skin straight to his heart. "I wish my dad would get off my case about the detective exam."

She had no idea. He braced his hands on the dashboard and delivered his words in rapid fire intensity. "Your father never murdered your mother."

Valerie's eyes widened and her mouth dropped open as a look of shock and then horror spread across her face.

The comment had come out all wrong. He said it like he was trying to push her away with his words. And maybe that was what he had intended. Her openness and her sweetness enticed and frightened him at the same time. His stomach felt like it was in knots. Why did he push her away when what he wanted more than anything was to draw her close?

He couldn't look at her. For sure now, she wouldn't want anything to do with him. He opened the door. He should just do what he was good at—work. They had an interview to conduct. He could hear her footsteps behind him as he strode up the sidewalk and pounded on the door.

He couldn't bring himself to look her in the eye when they stood on the porch waiting for someone to come to the door.

A boy of about five wearing a T-shirt that hung down below his knees answered the door. The kid had the telltale signs of having eaten a peanut butter sandwich, a smear of grape jelly at the corners of his mouth.

"Is your mom home?"

The little boy led them through the house to the backyard where a woman was placing plants in a flower bed. Crystal Stern was a plump woman with brassy blond hair held back by a scarf. She looked to be in her late thirties. She assessed Valerie's uniform and asked, "Is this about Derek?"

"So you've been in contact with him?" Trevor said.

The little boy lingered by the door until Crystal commanded, "Taylor go on inside and finish your lunch."

Taylor made a noise of protest but turned and marched inside.

"My boy doesn't need to hear any more about his wayward uncle." Crystal looked up at them, shading her eyes from the sun. "I don't want anything to do with that man. Any nice thing he does is just a setup to take advantage of me."

Trevor cleared his throat. "Ma'am, he's wanted for armed robbery and killing an agent in Arizona. If we can catch him, we can put him away for a long time."

Crystal picked up another plant and turned it upside down. She dug a hole with her trowel. She was probably mulling over what he had said, debating her options.

Trevor glanced over at Valerie who seemed to understand that it was better to remain silent. Give the woman time to think.

Crystal let out a heavy sigh and placed her hand on her hip. "He was here yesterday. Came by with a new toy for Taylor and a bunch of promises I know he won't keep."

"I take it he didn't stay here last night?"

"No. He wanted to. Said he was going to come into 'a big score.'" Crystal made quotation marks with her fingers. "He said he could get it in the next few days and that it was easy money no one could touch."

Valerie shifted her weight. "Those were his exact words—'easy money no one can touch?'"

"Pretty much. And he wanted his father's old gun, which I wasn't about to give him." Crystal wiped the sweat from her brow with the back of her hand.

So Murke was looking for a gun. Could the score he talked about be another robbery? "Did he say anything else?"

"He said he could pay me rent once he got this score." She blew out a puff of air that made her lips vibrate. "Trust me, I heard it all before where Derek is concerned. He's the king of the broken promises. I've waited my whole life for him to act like a real big brother."

Trevor tried to keep his conversation casual, though he felt a sense of excitement. The trail to Murke was heating up. "Any idea where he might have gone?"

She shook her head. "Derek is a master manipulator. I'm sure he'll find somebody to take him in. I don't think he has much money."

Valerie glanced around the yard. "So do you think this big score he talked about is why he came back into town?"

Crystal exhaled slowly. "Actually, he said something about getting even with an old girlfriend who double-crossed him years ago."

Valerie shifted her weight. "Do you know the name of this woman?"

Crystal shrugged. "Derek left Sagebrush when he was eighteen. He's been back a couple of times, but I'm not able to keep track of all the girlfriends he's had over the years. Quite frankly, I try to associate with him as little as possible."

She pulled off her garden gloves and assessed her fingernails. "I can tell you one thing. Whoever she is, he's plenty mad at her. He all but spit venom when he talked about getting back at her."

"You sure he didn't say a first or last name?" Valerie asked, stepping toward Crystal.

"The name he called her is not fit to be spoken, if you know what I mean." Crystal turned and wandered toward a small shed at the back of the yard. "That's all I got to tell you. You can let yourself out through the side gate."

As they strolled toward the side of the yard, Trevor could see Taylor with his face pressed against the sliding glass door. Something about the kid reminded him of himself at that age. A lonely boy making peanut butter sandwiches and watching cartoons.

Once inside the patrol car, the uncomfortable silence settled between them like an oppressive fog. Lexi whined in the backseat as though she had picked up on the mood. Trevor clenched his teeth. All he had to do was apprehend Murke and leave town. Why did he feel this need for Valerie to know the ugliness of his childhood?

Valerie offered him a faint smile. "So what do you suppose the big score is that Derek told Crystal about?"

He had tensed for a moment when she had looked

at him, fearing she would want to resume the conversation where they'd left off. He had probably shocked her so badly, she wouldn't want to know anything more about his private life. "Hard to say. Since his specialty is robbery, it sounds like he's looking for a gun. It's interesting that he said it was money no one could touch."

Valerie nodded. "That caught me, too, like he was talking about money that was obtained illegally in the first place or laundered."

Valerie rolled through a middle-class neighborhood. She glanced over at Trevor and then focused her attention straight ahead. She pulled the car over to the curb and turned to face him. "I don't know exactly what happened between your mom and dad, but it wasn't right to put a kid through that." She shook her head as tears formed at the corners of her eyes. "That sort of thing is never right. Never."

Warmth pooled around Trevor's heart. She wasn't crying for him. She was crying for the twelve-year-old kid who had come home and found his mother dead. He swallowed the lump in his throat. "It's over now. It's the past."

She held his gaze even as a tear flowed down her cheek. "No one would ever know that about you by meeting you today."

"I had some help along the way. Good foster homes. A pastor who loved me like a son." He reached over and brushed the tear off her cheek with his thumb. All the shame of the past fell away with her acceptance of him, of where he had come from.

She placed her hand over his. With her hand warming his, he felt closer to her than he had ever felt with anyone. Her green eyes held such depth of compassion.

The female voice of the dispatcher came through the radio, causing both of them to jump. "K-9 Unit 349, we have a domestic in progress at the end of Wilshire. House number 787."

Valerie picked up the radio. "Copy. We are about five blocks from that location."

Dispatch continued to relay information as they drove. A neighbor had phoned in when the squabble had escalated.

Valerie sped up as she merged into traffic. Sensing the excitement, Lexi twirled in circles in the backseat and let out yipping sounds. The car motor revved in time to the pounding of Trevor's heart.

The moment between them had been broken by the reality of her job, but he would not be the same after this. She had not run when he had revealed the harsh truth of his childhood.

Valerie slowed the car, nearing the address dispatch had given her. She sat up a little straighter as the worry lines on her forehead intensified.

Something was making the red flags go up for her. Trevor leaned forward in the seat. "What is it?"

SEVEN

Valerie came to a stop by the house. The hair on the back of her neck stood up. Lexi, who had ceased turning circles in the backseat, let out a single yip.

"Something wrong?" Trevor asked.

The house was one of five homes that occupied a city block. They had just passed two empty lots where houses had been torn down. On the other side of the block was an apartment building still under construction. Construction trailers, heavy equipment and materials surrounded a multi-story building that was mostly framing and scaffolding. This was a neighborhood in the midst of renewal. It looked like these were the last five old houses left.

"I'm not so sure anybody even lives here." Valerie clicked out of her seat belt and keyed the radio. "Be advised, this may be a false alarm."

There were still some signs of life in the house next door. A child's tricycle, some wilting plants in the flower bed and a car that looked like it still ran parked at the curb. The house at the end of the block had a sprinkler turned on. Signs of habitation, but still something didn't feel right.

"We still have to check it out," Trevor said.

Valerie nodded. "I'm leaving Lexi in the car. Sometimes adding a dog trained to protect to the mix of a domestic makes things worse. I can deploy her if I need to."

Trevor got out of the car and continued to survey the scene. Two blocks away, the noise of people driving up and down the street, children playing and dogs barking was muffled by distance.

Valerie approached the house with her hand on her gun. As a patrol officer, she had to assume worst-case scenario even if things looked benign. "Sometimes the most critical moment in a domestic is when things get quiet. The man could be holding a knife or gun to his wife's throat right now."

Trevor nodded before walking across the brown lawn to assess the side of the house. He returned to her side and grabbed her elbow. "There. I saw movement by that window."

She'd seen it, too. A glimpse of a man in a sleeveless white shirt and then he'd disappeared into the darkness of the back of the house. "I'll circle around the back." She didn't give him time to protest. "You take the front."

Once at the back door, she eased it open. From the front of the house, Trevor knocked and identified himself. "Sir, we know you are in there. Please come to the door."

She waited a few minutes for the man to respond. Nothing. A musty smell hit her as she stepped into a long hallway. When she passed a child's bedroom, only a mattress and few broken toys were left on the floor. The place looked abandoned. Yet she had clearly seen someone in here.

The front door creaked open, and Trevor stepped inside.

She moved through the hallway, clearing another room and checking a closet as she moved toward the other side of the house. She heard footsteps, probably Trevor's, as he cleared the living room and the kitchen. She came to a final closed door at the side of the house. She took in a quick, sharp breath. All the other doors had been open. If the man was hiding anywhere, it had to be in here. The floorboard creaked as she eased forward and reached out for the doorknob.

She feared the worst. A woman tied up or restrained...or dead already. She twisted the knob, gripping her gun with the other hand.

The hall closet slid open and a man caught her from behind. "Drop your gun right now."

She felt the cold hard steel of a gun barrel pressed into her temple.

Trevor had cleared the kitchen and living room, and was headed up the stairs when he heard what sounded like a scuffle at the far end of the house. He scrambled down the stairs, leaping over the railing when he was five steps from the bottom.

He checked rooms as he dashed down the hall toward a closed door and an open closet. He kicked open the door, fearing he would find Valerie on the floor in a puddle of blood. The room was empty. As he stepped outside the room, he saw her police-issue Glock dropped on the floor by the closet.

"Valerie." He took off in a dead run. The back door was flung open. He dashed outside, training his eyes on the construction site. He saw them for only a split second. The man had his arm around Valerie's neck as they disappeared behind a backhoe.

He ran the short distance to the construction site. He saw no sign of them and heard only the metal beams creaking in the wind. They could be anywhere in this labyrinth of construction materials, equipment and trailers. Clearly, this wasn't a domestic. Why had the man taken her? An icy chill filled his veins. *The syndicate.* They'd been set up.

He turned a half circle, scanning the trailers and piles of wood planks as alarm spread through him. If this man was intent on killing Valerie, Trevor had only minutes to find her. He had to be precise in his search.

He ran back around to the car, called for backup and then peered over the seat at Lexi.

"Can you help me find Valerie?"

The dog licked her chops and stepped side to side. He opened the back door of the patrol vehicle and Lexi leaped out. She looked at him as if waiting for a command. He grabbed Valerie's police hat and allowed Lexi to sniff.

"Find Valerie, find her."

He didn't know what the proper commands were. Would the dog even understand? Did she know how to track?

He pulled on her long canvas leash. "Come on, this way, Lexi." He pulled her to the back of the house by the open door where the man had exited with Valerie.

The dog kept looking at him as though waiting for clearer direction. This had to work. He couldn't wait any longer.

He waved the hat beneath her nose one more time. Lexi wagged her bobbed tail and whimpered. She was waiting for him to give her a command. "I need to find her." Desperation colored his words.

Lexi lifted her head, sniffed the air and then put her nose to the ground. She ran in circles that grew wider and wider and then bounded in the direction of the construction site. The dog had picked up on something.

He raced after her, praying that Lexi was following the scent that would lead them to Valerie before it was too late.

Overpowered by her assailant, Valerie struggled to find an opportunity for escape. With one arm, he pressed the gun into her side. The other arm locked her neck in place. When she twisted side to side, he applied pressure to her neck, cutting off her breathing.

Images of piles of wood and steel and some kind of large moving equipment with a bucket on it flashed by her as he dragged her deeper into the construction site. She dug her heels in, hoping to slow him down.

If Trevor's stomping had not scared the assailant, she probably would have been shot on the spot. But why? Who was this man?

Valerie stopped struggling for a moment. If she couldn't use force to get away, maybe reason would work. "Please, I'm an officer of the law. You'll go to jail for a long time."

The man spoke forcefully into her ear, his voice like a pounding drum. "With what I'm getting paid, lady, I can get away and never be found."

Panic coursed through her. Only the syndicate had that kind of money to hire someone to kill her. He kicked a door and dragged her through some kind of structure. It looked like they were on the ground floor of the apartment building under construction.

He grabbed the collar of her uniform at the back and pushed her forward. She fell on the concrete floor. He pulled the slide of his gun back and released a sinister chuckle. She rolled sideways and caught a glimpse of him, a colossus of a man with black wavy hair. His bulbous lips furled back from his mouth. He aimed the gun at her.

She took in a breath that felt like it was filled with jagged glass. Her stomach tightened into a hard ball as he lifted the gun. She couldn't outrun the bullet.

Then she heard it—the faint barking of a dog. Her heart nearly burst with relief. Lexi was coming for her.

Panic filled the man's features as he lifted his head and turned, comprehending what the sound of the approaching dog meant.

Valerie used his moment of inattention to pull herself to her knees. Before she could get on her feet, he had run toward her, yanking her by the collar and pulling her up. The fabric choked her. She gasped for breath.

"Up those stairs," he commanded. He pushed her toward stairs that led to the second floor. She climbed, and he followed close on her heels.

The one thing she had in her favor was that this man did not want to be caught in the act of killing her. It had stopped him once. When she glanced behind her, he had the gun aimed at her. There was nowhere to go but up.

As she climbed, she could still hear Lexi's barking, but it had grown more distant. Had the dog been thrown off by some other smell? Trevor would only be able to guess at the right commands.

Oh, please, God, bring her to me.

When they stopped climbing, they came out on what must be the fourth or fifth floor, which consisted of a plywood floor and the metal framing of the outside walls. As he pushed her toward the edge of the structure, she could hear only the faint sounds of Lexi's searching.

"Back up more," the assailant ordered.

She stood on the edge of the floor. He'd shoot her, and she'd fall off the edge. If the bullet didn't kill her, the fall would. He lifted his gun and took aim. The trigger clicked. She closed her eyes and said goodbye to the life she had loved.

Lexi had taken the stairs to the second floor and then bolted up the ladder that led to the third without hesitation. Her ears were drawn back on her head as she focused only on moving ahead. As they reached the third floor, a popping sound slammed against Trevor's eardrum. Fear sliced through him. He tilted his head. A gunshot.

Dear God, don't let us be too late.

Lexi stopped and raised her head, letting out two quick barks. And then she ran for the ladder that led to the fourth floor. Helpless to do anything else, he followed the dog.

As they climbed, the sound of creaking metal surrounded them. Something crashed into something else on the outside of the building. Lexi came out on the fourth floor, which was empty except for some power tools and stacks of wood.

He heard another crashing noise and ran to the edge of the open floor. A large man with dark hair skirted around a work trailer and disappeared. Trevor's heart seized. Had that man shot Valerie and then run off?

Lexi ran the length of the floor with her nose to the ground.

Trevor edged toward the perimeter of the open floor, fearing the worst. He braced himself for a vision of Valerie's prone body on the ground, crumpled and deformed by the fall and bleeding from the bullet. When he peered over the edge, he saw only the construction materials and a work truck.

Lexi came to the edge of the floor opposite him, her bark insistent. She twirled in circles and barked again.

Trevor ran to where the dog kept returning. Lexi sat back on her haunches, barked and then got up, pacing. He peered over the edge. At first, he saw nothing. Lexi kept going to the edge of the floor, whining and looking up at Trevor. When he peered over the edge again, some of the scaffolding looked like it had given way and hung at a slant.

Lexi leaned over the edge and barked. Wild horses weren't going to drag her away from that spot. The dog knew something.

He looked again. "Valerie?"

Dare he hope?

No response came.

And then he saw it. Beneath the scaffolding that was at a slant, a hand. Trevor leapt over the side of the building and climbed down the scaffolding. When he looked up, Lexi was watching him. Her big ears flopped forward.

He reached out for the metal frame that held the plywood floor of the scaffold. The whole structure creaked and swayed. It wasn't as sturdy as it should be. He jumped to the scaffold that stood at a slant. Gripping the edge, he peered underneath it.

Valerie's hand was twisted in a piece of broken cable. Her head hung to one side.

He said her name again, but she didn't respond.

Aware that the scaffolding could give way, he inched toward her and reached out to grab her feet. He still saw no indication that she was alive. He shimmied to the edge of the plywood platform. The whole structure creaked. By leaning out and risking falling himself, he was able to wrap his hand around her waist and reach up to untwist the cable that had kept her from falling to the ground.

He gathered her into his arms. Her body was still warm. Blood stained the sleeve of her uniform. He brushed his hand over her face. She had hit her head on something, but she hadn't been shot there. He touched her stomach and her shoulders, no sign of a bullet hole or bleeding. His hand moved to her neck. Her pulse pushed back against his fingers.

Joy flooded through him, and he drew her close. She was alive. She was breathing.

He pressed his face against her cheek. "I thought I'd lost you." His throat tightened with emotion. He'd saved lives before because it was his job, but this was different. He had felt his heart open up to her in a way it never had before. He buried his face against her neck. "I didn't want to lose you."

In the distance, he heard the sound of sirens as backup pulled onto the street where they had received the false call for a domestic disturbance. It would be a matter of minutes before the cops figured out they were at the construction site.

Overcome with emotion he didn't understand, he held Valerie close and waited for her to regain consciousness. She had to be all right. She just had to be.

EIGHT

Valerie felt as though she were being pulled out of a deep pit, upward toward light and sound. Voices around her became more distinct.

She heard her mother. "You gave us quite a scare there, Junebug. Thank goodness there were no broken bones."

No matter how old she got, the sound of her mother's voice would always be a comfort.

Then she heard her father's gravelly voice, "She's a Salgado. She's made of indestructible iron, just like the rest of us."

Her eyes opened. She blinked. The images in front of her were blurry. Three indistinct faces surrounded her.

"There you are," her mother said again. A tender sound to her ears.

"Give her some space, people." That was her dad.

"Her pupils look normal." A third voice she didn't recognize.

She could feel people fussing around her, tucking blankets underneath her. The smell of bleach filled her nose. She was in a hospital bed. That third voice was probably a doctor.

Her mind struggled to put the memory back together about what had happened at the construction site. Knowing she was out of options, she had leapt off the building seconds before the large man had pulled the trigger, hoping he would think he had hit his target.

Her father stood by the bed. Her mother had pushed the wheelchair close. Her brother David and his wife, Mary, sat on chairs not too far away. Standing away from the others toward the back wall was Trevor. Her vision cleared. Trevor lifted his chin to indicate he saw her. There was a brightness in his eyes she hadn't seen before.

Then she remembered being held so tightly and someone crying over her. His voice had been a mixture of joy and anguish. She glanced again at Trevor, whose gaze was downcast. Was that really a memory or was her mind filling in blank spaces?

"Boy that dog was something else, wasn't she?" Her father turned slightly to address Trevor.

While she had been absorbing her surroundings, a conversation that she hadn't totally been aware of had been going on. The doctor had left the room.

Her mother leaned close to her and patted her hand. "We thought that dog wasn't going to let the doctor have a look at you."

"They had to call one of the trainers from the center to come over and get her," said her father. "Trevor said Lexi insisted on riding in the ambulance. Nothing anyone did or said would change her mind."

She'd come to in the ambulance only for a few moments. Lexi had licked her hand, and Trevor had hovered over her. He had brushed her forehead with a touch so gentle for someone who was so strong. The concern for her etched in his features burned into her memory.

From the back wall where he stood, Trevor cleared his throat. "Lexi really proved herself out there today. She is completely devoted to Valerie. I don't think there is anything that dog wouldn't do for her."

Valerie settled back on her pillow. All the weeks of training she and Lexi had gone through had paid off. But it was more than the training that bonded them. She loved that dog and Lexi loved her.

Her mother rolled back from the bed. "I suppose we better let you get some rest. The doctor wanted to keep you overnight."

"Overnight." Valerie sat up. "Who is going to take care of Bethany?"

"Relax, honey, your friend Lucy said she could take her for the night. She'll bring her by first thing in the morning when you check out. It's all been taken care of."

Pain sliced through her arm. She must have scraped it in the fall, and her head hurt. Uneasiness stirred inside her. She wanted to be home with Lexi and Bethany. They were a family. They needed to be together.

Her family filed out with Trevor being the last to leave.

Tears warmed the corners of her eyes. The day had been too long and too hard. She missed Bethany. Her arms felt empty.

Trevor returned a few minutes later. "I just called the station. There'll be a night duty officer coming by in a few hours for protection. I can stay with you until he gets here."

She turned her head away and nodded. Reality hit her like a semi truck. The syndicate's desire to kill her had not gone away. If anything, what had happened today revealed how far they would go to kill her.

Trevor leaned over the bed. "You okay?"

She swiped at her eyes. "I'm missing Bethany. I know Lucy will take good care of her, but I'd feel better if I could be with her."

He studied her for a moment. "Do you want me to see if I can get you something to eat?"

She wiped another tear off her cheek. Her distress was probably too much for him to deal with, so he was focusing on doing things for her. "Just a drink of water would be nice."

He poured the water and held the cup, tilting the straw toward her mouth. She wasn't that injured, she could hold the cup herself, but he seemed to like helping her in that way. Absently, she draped her fingers over his beefy hand.

He sucked in a breath of air, and his eyes widened. She searched the depth of his dark brown eyes as heat spread over her skin. He looked away. Did he really not want her to see what was in those eyes? It had taken courage for him to share the darkness of his childhood. Maybe he was still afraid she would reject him over it.

She could not imagine what kind of a home he had known if it had ended with his father killing his mother.

The sound of her swallowing augmented in the silence between them. She finished drinking, and squeezed his fingers, hoping to communicate her acceptance of him.

Your secrets are safe with me, Trevor.

He pulled away and placed the plastic cup on the tray at the end of her bed. Then he sat down in a chair. "So that had to have been the Serpent who sent that guy to kill you. The whole thing was a setup."

Valerie pulled the covers up to her neck and shuddered. She didn't want to revisit the attack and could only manage a nod. How far did the syndicate's arms reach in this town, anyway?

Even as the fear returned over her own life being in jeopardy, resolve as hard as steel formed inside her. Her part in ending the control the syndicate had over Sagebrush was with identifying the Serpent and seeing that she was put in jail. Once she was back out on patrol, she could garner information that would lead to the downfall of the syndicate.

Trevor shifted in his chair. "I was thinking if Murke couldn't get a gun from his sister, he'll try to get one some other way."

Valerie nodded, grateful the subject had changed. "People I've arrested have dropped names about where they got the guns they used in crimes. We might be able to track some of these people down. With his record, Murke's not going to be able to get a gun legally."

He patted her shoulder. "We'll get started on it tomorrow." His voice filled with tenderness. "You've been through a lot. Why don't you get some sleep?"

She liked the way he used the word *we*. They were a team. Desire to catch Murke almost overshadowed her need for recovery. "You're probably right." She turned her head and closed her eyes. At first, her awareness of Trevor in the room made it hard to fall asleep, despite how exhausted she was. Gradually, the heaviness of unconsciousness invaded her mind like a fog. She drifted off.

She awoke once in the night. Trevor had propped a laptop up on a heater and was typing. He glanced in her direction when she stirred. His vigilance made her feel safe, but when was he going to sleep? He had been through almost as much as she had. She fell back asleep.

When she opened her eyes a second time, Trevor was gone. She stared at the empty chair for a moment as her heart filled with longing. The night officer must be stationed outside her door.

She stayed awake, listening to the sound of footsteps, the wheels of gurneys turning and faint conversations. She lay with her eyes open in the dark room. A chill crept beneath her skin. Though she told herself it was only the nighttime and the quiet of the room that was scaring her, she couldn't let go of her fear that one of the Serpent's henchmen would burst through the door or break the window at any moment. Her sleep was fitful until morning sun streamed through the crack between the curtains.

Trevor met Slade McNeal at the end of the long hallway that led to Valerie's hospital room. The look on Slade's face was grim. A sudden dread gripped Trevor that something had happened to Valerie in the night.

Even though he knew Valerie didn't go on shift until later in the afternoon, he'd been anxious to check on her. He'd slept only a few hours at his hotel before worry over her safety had gotten him out of bed.

Though concern pressed on him, he kept his voice level and managed a smile. "McNeal, you coming to check on Valerie?"

"I was hoping to talk to her, but maybe she'd take the news a little better if it came from you." The captain placed his hands on his hips.

Trevor shook his head, not understanding where McNeal was leading.

"In light of what happened yesterday, I'm going to ask Valerie to take a couple of sick days until I can think things through. Both you and Lexi were with her, and the syndicate still found a way to get at her." The worry lines in McNeal's forehead became more pronounced. "I just don't know if she can do her job safely."

Though he didn't disagree with the decision, he doubted Valerie would be happy about it. "She wants to catch the members of the syndicate as much as you do. She's been a big help in chasing down Murke, but I understand your reasoning."

They walked together down the hall toward Valerie's room. "I hate doing it to her, but I can't put a good officer at risk. I'll see that she has protection while she's at home."

"I can stay with her this morning. We're trying to track down some of the guys that might sell Murke a gun under the table. We know from his half sister that he is trying to acquire one."

McNeal nodded. "Making some phone calls would be fine. It gives me some time to speak to the chief and move the duty roster around so we can provide her with more protection at her home."

As they made their way toward Valerie's hospital room, he saw Lucy enter, carrying Bethany in one hand and a car seat in the other.

Trevor had that sinking feeling that no matter how McNeal's decision was presented, Valerie wasn't going to take it well.

"There she is. There's my girl." Valerie thought her heart would burst into a thousand pieces when Lucy carried Bethany into the hospital room.

Bethany kicked her legs and reached out for Valerie,

who was dressed and past ready to leave the hospital. The light blue floral dress with a ruffle offset Bethany's eyes. Lucy had placed a sunhat on Bethany's blond head. Valerie pulled her close and Bethany snuggled against her.

"She's a busy little thing." Lucy set the diaper bag down. "She kept me on my toes."

"Thanks, Lucy, for watching her," Valerie said.

"It was no trouble. I wish we could do more. You know that." Lucy pulled a teething ring out of the diaper bag. "She was fussy last night. I'm not sure what is up with that. She might have some teeth coming in."

Valerie looked into Bethany's blue eyes while she sucked on her teething ring and clutched her pink bunny. "She's still adjusting…to things. It's hard for her to sleep at night."

Lucy said her goodbyes, hugged Bethany and Valerie and left. Bethany wandered around the room while Valerie gathered her things. The shiny black buckle shoes made her little feet look so small.

Bethany pointed at the bed and said, "Ahh?" Her word for what is it?

"Bed. That's a bed, sweetie." Valerie held her hand out to her. "Come on, let's go." Bethany's hand slipped into hers. Valerie took smaller steps so Bethany could keep up with her. In the hallway, she was surprised to see Trevor and McNeal.

As she looked over at Trevor, the seriousness in his eyes gave her pause. Was he bringing bad news?

She swept Bethany into her arms. "I didn't expect to see you both here. I'm not on shift until later."

Trevor offered her a quick smile. "I thought I would keep you company."

She glanced from McNeal to Trevor. "What's going on?"

McNeal rubbed his temple. "I want you to take a few days off."

Valerie held Bethany a little tighter. "Why? I'm ready to go back to work. I feel fine… I just got a few bruises and scrapes." She couldn't do her part in taking down the syndicate if she was sitting at home.

"In light of what happened yesterday…" Trevor's gaze darted from McNeal to Valerie. "He seems to think you might be in too much danger on the streets."

"Are you thinking I need to be on desk duty for a while?" She loved doing patrol with Lexi. Sitting at a desk would drive her insane, but at least she would still in some way be helping take down the syndicate.

McNeal shook his head. "I don't know. I just know it's not safe for you to be out on patrol."

Valerie gazed at Trevor for a moment. It annoyed her that he wasn't protesting McNeal's decision—especially since he of all people knew she could handle herself.

Valerie clenched her teeth. So she wasn't even going to get desk duty. What if McNeal decided she couldn't do her job at all? A couple of days could turn into weeks. She knew they only wanted to keep her safe, but being on patrol was like breathing to her. "I could have died out there yesterday, and I didn't."

"You made incredibly smart choices." Trevor's voice tinged with admiration. "I just don't think the police department fathomed the power and the resources the syndicate would utilize to get at you."

Frustration rose to the surface. "If only I could re-member who this woman was…where I've seen her before."

McNeal gripped her forearm. "I know this is not

what you wanted to hear, but I have to keep my officers safe." He turned and headed down the long hallway.

Valerie's throat went tight as she watched her captain disappear around a corner. Couldn't he see that she only wanted to do her job?

"McNeal said take the day off, so do as he says and enjoy yourself. I'll keep you company." Trevor's voice held a tone of false cheerfulness. He was trying to make her feel better, but why hadn't he stood up for her more?

"I guess I have no choice." Bethany rested her head against Valerie's neck as if to comfort her. "I'm going to call Slade later so he can clarify whether this is a few days or until the Serpent is in custody." The prospect of being a prisoner in her home or having to restrict her movements for months frustrated her.

They stepped out into the sunlight of early morning, and Trevor directed her to his car. She placed the car seat Lucy had brought in the backseat.

Once they were settled in, Trevor turned to her. "So what's the plan?"

"We need to go get Lexi. I was planning on taking her and Bethany to the park this morning, anyway…so we might as well do that."

"All right then, let's go." Trevor's effort at trying to sound positive was commendable, but none of it made McNeal's decision sting any less.

How long would this go on? If only she could remember the woman's face more clearly. She had sat down with a police artist twice and attempted to recall the details in the face she'd seen for a split second, but always the image was blurry. They looked through police photographs of women who had a record. Nothing clicked.

Trevor started his car. "Where am I going?"

"Same park as where the dog had her pups yesterday." Valerie laced her hands together and tried to let go of the bad news that had started her day. She looked out the window. It was a beautiful sunny day. The sound of Bethany babbling in the backseat lifted her spirits. She needed to focus on what was right in her life.

After getting Lexi from the training facility, Trevor pulled into a lot of the park that faced a duck pond. "This all right?"

She rolled the window down, enjoying the warmth of the morning sun. Maybe by the end of the day McNeal would change his mind. "Let's go have some fun."

Trevor carried the diaper bag while Valerie lifted Bethany out of her car seat. She rubbed noses with the little girl, which caused a squeal of delight. Bethany offered her a smile, revealing a front row of pearl-white teeth. "How could anyone be sad around you, huh?"

Lexi followed dutifully behind as they found a park bench. Valerie pulled a flat beach ball out of Bethany's bag and blew it up. She rolled it toward Bethany who sat in the grass a few feet from the bench.

Valerie sat down on the grass beside Bethany, and the dog situated herself close by.

Trevor paced the length of the bench and then walked a half circle around them. Valerie rolled the ball to Bethany. Trevor stopped and stared at a grove of trees. His posture stiffened.

Valerie followed the line of his gaze. Her heartbeat kicked up a notch when she saw the man partly shielded by the trees looking in their direction.

NINE

Trevor zeroed in on the man in the wooded area. The stranger slipped deeper into the trees and disappeared. Why was he trying to conceal himself?

Still not willing to let his guard down, Trevor surveyed the park, making a note of every person within a hundred yards of them and watching the comings and goings in the parking lot. Behind the bench, a jogging trail ran along the upward slope of the hill. Though he could keep an eye on the people in front of them, someone could come up over the hill and close in on them without much warning.

An open park like this was precarious in terms of safety for Valerie. However, she'd had a traumatic day and a disappointing morning. He didn't want to add to her frustration by telling her she couldn't take her niece to the park.

Bethany lifted the beach ball and carried it toward Lexi. The dog nudged the ball with her nose, and Bethany clapped her hands in delight. The Rottweiler wagged her tail. Valerie remained close to Bethany, talking into her ear and pointing. She twisted her long red hair and held it in place before looking over at Trevor.

That open and honest gaze that she had was enough to make him weak in the knees. She was a beautiful woman. And once the Serpent was caught and this was all over, she would have a beautiful life, a little girl to care for and job she loved. He had seen the worst of humanity in his life and his work. Even as he felt his heart opening to her, he knew they were two very different people.

A car pulled into the lot, and a large man with black hair got out. Trevor moved a little closer to Valerie. Tension eased when the man opened the back door and two young boys tumbled out.

As he drew closer, the man only vaguely resembled the assailant from yesterday. The boys both placed sailboats in the pond. The man took a bench on the opposite side of the pond.

Valerie studied the woods where he had seen the man. Her mouth twitched, and a look of sadness clouded her features for only a moment before she managed a smile. Her efforts at not giving in to despair were deliberate.

Bethany had just rolled the ball down the hill toward the pond when Trevor noticed the man sitting on a bench on their side of the pond. The same man he had seen hiding in the trees. Valerie and Bethany walked toward the pond with Lexi trailing behind. The ball slipped into the water.

Trevor hurried down the hill toward Valerie, training his glance toward the man without turning his head. The man wore a jacket that was too heavy for the warm weather and could easily conceal a gun.

Bethany and Valerie made an utterance of disappointment as the ball rolled into the pond. Valerie commanded Lexi to get the ball. Without hesitation, the dog jumped in the water, but only managed to push the ball toward the center of the pond.

The man in the coat sat on the bench above them. Trevor glanced up at him. The man's gaze followed Valerie as she moved closer to the water.

Lexi got out of the water on the side of the pond, some distance from Valerie and Bethany. The two boys with sailboats cheered and clapped, encouraging the ball to float completely across the water.

Trevor swooped down the hill. "Why don't we go for a walk?" He pulled Valerie up by the elbow.

"But we need to get the ball." She opened her mouth to protest more and then noticed the man on the bench rising to his feet. "Oh." Her voice filled with fear.

She gathered up Bethany. Trevor fell in step behind her, and Lexi took up the rear. When he looked at the bench again, the man was gone. He wouldn't try to take a shot at them as long as they were in the open and around people, unless he could shield himself from view.

Trevor placed a protective hand on the middle of Valerie's back, a move that made Lexi grunt in protest.

Trevor looked at Lexi and shook his head.

We're both trying to do the same job, girl.

"She doesn't like it when you touch me." Valerie kept her voice upbeat, but her gaze darted around at her surroundings.

There were a dozen trees the stranger could hide behind.

Trevor pointed to a gazebo by an ice-cream stand.

"Let's go over there." The gazebo was in a flat, open area. He would have a full three-sixty view of the park.

As she sat down in the gazebo, Valerie said, "Maybe we should just go home." She kept her voice sing-songy for Bethany's sake, but he picked up on the undercurrent of tension.

Trevor took a seat opposite them. He wanted her to have at least a few hours where the threat wasn't foremost in her mind. Couldn't he at least give her that? "We'll be fine here. That man could have just been out for a walk."

Valerie let out a heavy sigh. Bethany wiggled out of her arms and sat on the wooden floor of the gazebo. She continued to talk to the child in a positive tone, but Trevor saw the pensiveness in her eyes.

"Come on, I'll buy you two some ice cream. Isn't that what people do in parks?"

"It's kind of early in the day, but sure," Valerie shrugged. "Since Bethany can't eat a whole cone, just ask for a spoon and I'll give her bites of mine."

Trevor stepped out of the gazebo and walked a few feet to the ice-cream stand. "Can I get two vanilla cones?"

"Coming right up." The ice cream vendor's white apron covered his rotund belly. His bald spot glistened in the morning sun.

Trevor turned to check on Valerie, who had gotten down on her knees to point things out to Bethany as she took in her surroundings. Lexi stood guard outside the gazebo.

The man handed Trevor an ice-cream cone with a generous scoop. "That's a nice family you got there."

Was that how they looked to the outside world? Just

a family enjoying a morning in the park. No one else could see the level of fear Valerie lived with every moment. "Thank you," Trevor said as he took the second cone from him.

Trevor resumed his spot on the bench in the gazebo and watched Valerie give Bethany spoons full of ice cream while the little girl held on to Valerie's leg and bounced. Her mouth opened bird-like every time Valerie tried to get a bite of ice cream for herself.

"She's getting more of that than you are."

"That's usually how it works." Valerie wiped Bethany's ice-cream-stained face with a paper napkin.

A chuckle escaped his throat. He couldn't help it—watching Bethany made him smile. Valerie relaxed, too. She laughed as Bethany tried to grab the spoon to feed herself.

Trevor's cell phone rang. "Agent Lewis."

The voice that came across the line had a slow Texas drawl. "This is Detective Jackson Worth. I think I may have a sighting on your fugitive."

Trevor sat up a little straighter. "Really?"

"A man matching Derek Murke's description just checked in to the Rainbow Motel—it's a fleabag not too far from the industrial district."

Trevor's voice betrayed his excitement. "How did you find out?"

"I kind of put a bug in the ear of a couple of people in that area I know I can trust. One of them saw a man matching his description going into the hotel."

"How long ago did he check in?"

"I got the call less than an hour ago," Jackson said.

"Thanks, I'll look into it." Trevor slammed his phone

shut. The elation he felt over a new lead faded when he saw the drawn look on Valerie's face.

"So sounds like you may have found Murke." She offered him a faint smile, but her eyes never brightened. "That's good news."

"I'll take you and Bethany home." As anxious as he was to see if the lead checked out, he understood her frustration at being put out of commission. He'd never been very good at sitting still and doing nothing if he knew he could put a criminal in jail. She was probably the same way.

She nodded and bit her lower lip. "I guess I'll just have to enjoy my day off." She sounded like she was trying to convince herself.

They walked back across the park to his car. He drove her back to her place, calling to make sure a police officer would be posted outside her house as soon as possible.

The officer had just pulled into place when he brought his car to the curb.

Trevor escorted Valerie and Bethany to her house, then searched both floors and walked around to the fenced backyard before he was satisfied that no one was lying in wait for her.

As he drove away, Valerie stood at the window.

Unable to reach McNeal by phone, Valerie spent the afternoon cleaning her already clean kitchen. McNeal owed her an answer as to how long her exile would go on. What she feared most was that he would ask her to take a permanent leave of absence until the Serpent was behind bars.

By late afternoon, she had worked off some of her

frustration. Fatigue set in as she lay Bethany down for a nap. The physical trauma of yesterday's confrontation was catching up with her.

Before lying down to rest, she checked to see the officer parked outside. The afternoon sky had darkened with the promise of rain. Always a welcome event in southwest Texas.

Bethany lay in her bed on her tummy. Her cheeks rosy and her downy hair sticking out at all angles. She had seemed fussier than usual before her nap. Valerie stroked the toddler's back and then lay down herself to sleep.

She awoke hours later to the sound of Bethany's crying. Wind rattled the glass panes, and the sky had grown dark.

Bethany's cry sounded different than her usual I'm-awake-please-hold-me cry. Valerie sat up and threw back the covers. Bethany wasn't standing up in her crib. Instead, she continued to lie on her tummy rubbing her face against the blankets.

Lexi whined from the door where she'd been standing watch.

When she gathered the toddler into her arms, the heat of the little body stunned her. Her cheeks were even redder and her forehead was hot. Valerie tried to soothe the little girl.

"You got some teeth coming in? Is that what's going on?" When she opened Bethany's mouth, the gums didn't look swollen. Maybe it was something more serious.

Valerie stared at the ceiling as she fought against the onslaught of anxious thoughts. Bethany had seemed fine this afternoon. But Lucy had said she was fussy the night before. Maybe it hadn't just been about being away from familiar surroundings.

Bethany rested her chin on Valerie's shoulder and continued to fuss and cry, wiggling and writhing in Valerie's arms. Her little body stiffening in pain. "You poor thing."

Worry spread through her as she made her way downstairs to the kitchen to find the children's fever reducer. Bethany cried louder when Valerie put her in the playpen, so she could root through the drawer where she kept baby medicine, ointments and bandages.

When she opened the bottle of fever reducer, it was empty. How could she have been so forgetful to not pick up more? What kind of mom was she to let her baby be in pain like this?

Bethany's crying became more intense. She touched Bethany's hot cheek and then put the thermometer in her ear. She read the digital numbers. 101. Not good.

She needed to get Bethany's fever down so she would sleep. She paced the floor and then picked up the phone and dialed Mrs. Witherspoon's number. The phone rang five times before the answering machine came on. Lucy wasn't answering her phone, either.

She grabbed the empty medicine bottle, slipped into her coat and raced outside, tapping on the window of the officer on duty.

"I need you to do something for me. My little girl is sick. I need to get her some more of this." She showed him the bottle.

"Ma'am, I'm not supposed to leave my post."

"Please, it will take you twenty minutes at the most. There's an all-night drugstore ten blocks away. It would be more dangerous if I went out myself, and I don't want to take my little girl out in this rain."

The officer stared at the bottle of medicine.

"Please, for my little girl. She'll have a miserable night if I don't break her fever."

He nodded. "Okay, but don't tell my supervisor I did this."

She watched his two red taillights distorted by the rain as he drove away, and then ran back inside where Bethany continued to cry. Lexi paced and whined by Bethany's playpen. The dog licked Bethany's fingers, something she had never done before. Lexi's concern for Bethany indicated that she was bonding to the little girl.

Valerie stroked the Rottweiler's head and ears. "I know you want to make it better, don't you?"

She swept Bethany up and walked back and forth the length of the kitchen floor while bouncing Bethany and singing to her. The little girl stiffened in her arms and tugged at her ear. Her cheeks flushed a deep red from the fever.

Valerie felt like her heart had tied itself into knots. The worst thing in the world was seeing your child in pain. Bethany stopped wailing for a moment and stared up at Valerie with her wide blue eyes.

She pressed her face against Bethany's hot cheek and could almost feel the child's pain.

My baby. My sweet baby.

Bethany took in a shaky breath and resumed her crying. Her little body was rigid from pain. The doctor wouldn't be open at this hour, but if she could get the fever down, she could have a restful night. In the morning, if the fever came back, she'd have to see the pediatrician.

Valerie walked a circle through the living room and kitchen with Lexi following her. When twenty minutes passed and the officer hadn't returned, she peeked out the window. A car she didn't recognize was parked across the street. An icy chill crept over her skin. Was her fear real or imagined? Someone in the neighborhood could just have a visitor.

She picked her cell phone up off the kitchen counter where she had left it. Calling the department would get the officer in trouble. It wouldn't look good to McNeal, either, for her being put back on duty. Maybe she hadn't made the best choice in sending the officer to the pharmacy, but concern for Bethany took priority over everything else.

She ran her fingers over the control panel of the phone. Maybe she could call Trevor. She dismissed the thought. He was working surveillance trying to track down Murke. It would be selfish to call him away from his job.

Maybe he had even caught Murke by now. Sadness and frustration over not being able to be a part of such a coup was like a knife to her heart.

Bethany screamed in her ear and then rubbed her face against Valerie's shoulders.

Valerie prayed for her fever to go away.

Where was the police officer? Her mind grasped for an explanation. Maybe he hadn't been able to find the fever reducer and had gone to look at a different store. Valerie moved one more time to the window where the strange car was still parked.

She picked up the phone again. Maybe she should call Trevor now?

Trevor had watched the entrance of the Rainbow Motel all day and into the evening with no sign of Murke. Showing Murke's picture to the desk clerk meant that the fugitive might be tipped off. He didn't want to risk it.

The motel was situated in a less than desirable part of town that featured a lot of bars and greasy-spoon restaurants and secondhand stores. Sitting here watching the door of the motel was starting to feel like a waste of time. Maybe the guy who had checked in only looked like Murke. However, he wasn't ready to let go just yet. Maybe Murke had spent time in some of the businesses around here. Someone might recognize his picture.

After alerting the other surveillance unit of what he was doing, Trevor pushed open his car door, turned up the collar of his coat against the rain and walked up the sidewalk. He peered into a window of one of the restaurants. Most of the customers ate alone at the counter. One table had a mother and father sitting with their two children. He watched for a moment as the mother scooped up applesauce and fed it to a baby who wasn't much younger than Bethany. Funny how his thoughts went back to the little girl.

He'd lingered at the window long enough for people to start to look at him. Best to go inside and see if he could spot Murke. As he opened the door to the restaurant, a cacophony of noises assaulted him, people talking, dishes clattering, waitresses yelling at cooks.

Several people craned their necks in his direction as he stepped inside. The place was dimly lit, making it hard to see the faces of the people in the booths. He found a chair at the counter and ordered a soda. He walked the length of the room, studying each face without staring. He stepped into the men's room where the walls muffled the noises, waited a moment and then stepped back outside. He performed the same discreet survey of faces on his way back.

The waitress had left his soda by his place at the counter. He drank slowly, swung around on his stool and did one more survey of the restaurant.

"Can I get you anything else, honey?" With her steel-gray hair and heavily lidded eyes, the waitress was probably someone's grandmother.

"No, thank you." Trevor put his empty glass back on the counter. He pulled the photo of Murke out of his chest pocket. "Can you do one thing for me? Can you tell me if this man has ever come in here to eat?"

The waitress put his bill on the counter, glanced at the photograph and shook her head. "He sure looks like a mean one, but I ain't seen him around here."

Understatement of the century. He gathered up the photograph. Maybe the Rainbow Motel was a dead end, after all.

Trevor put payment for the soda and a tip on the counter, then walked toward the door.

When he stepped outside, light rain sprinkled down on him. Across the street, teenagers had set up a make-shift game of soccer in an empty lot. He watched them kick the ball through the mud, slapping each other on the back and offering verbal jabs as they raced across their small field.

The rain distorted the lights from the streetlamps and the whole scene had a surreal quality to it. He couldn't help but think that if Valerie were with him, she would strike up a conversation with the teens if she didn't know them already. Yes, his thoughts always seemed to circle back to her, too.

He turned and headed back toward the hotel. He'd

give surveillance one more hour. He had just opened his car door when his phone rang.

Valerie's phone number came up on the screen. "Hello?"

"Trevor." The single word carried a note of desperation.

"Valerie, what is it?" He could hear Bethany crying in the background. His heart lurched. "What's going on?"

"I sent the officer away to get some fever reducer for Bethany. It's been forty minutes. He hasn't come back. There's this car outside that concerns me. I know you are working, but I didn't know who else to call."

"I'll be right over." He hung up and ran the half block to his car. After informing the other surveillance team that he was leaving, he shifted into gear and sped toward Valerie's house, praying that nothing bad happened to her before he got there.

TEN

Lexi's scratching at the sliding glass door was insistent.

"You have to go, don't you?" Valerie had been so preoccupied with Bethany, she'd forgotten about Lexi. Bethany had settled into a fitful sleep in her playpen, waking and crying every ten minutes.

Valerie slid open the door. The steady fall of rain greeted her ears. Lexi slipped past her. The dog's dark fur disappeared against the blackness of the night as she ran to the edge of the yard. Only the tinkling of dog tags indicated where she was. "Come on, Lex. Hurry it up."

Valerie took in a breath of rain-freshened air. Though worry still plagued her over Bethany and over the officer's delay in returning, she had breathed a sigh of relief when she heard Trevor's voice over the phone. He was on his way.

Inside the house, Bethany wailed. Valerie slid the glass door shut and ran to get her. Lexi let out two quick barks. She gathered Bethany in her arms, walking and swaying with her to quiet her. She worked her way back to the sliding glass door, opened it and called for Lexi. All she could hear was the pattering of the rain.

"Lexi?" Panic coursed through her. "Lexi!" she shouted.

Lexi had never run away before. Bethany wiggled in her arms. She couldn't stand out in the rain with the baby, and she couldn't leave Bethany alone to look for Lexi.

She tried one more time calling for Lexi as a sense of foreboding overtook her. Aware suddenly of how vulnerable she was, she closed the door and latched it. The police officer was gone. Lexi was gone. Valerie could feel the walls closing in on her as Bethany's cries echoed in her ears. She raced upstairs and placed Bethany in her crib.

She opened the window that faced the backyard to see if she could see anything. The porch light illuminated only a small area close to the house. The rest of the yard was still dark. No sign of Lexi anywhere. Her breath caught as she shook her head in disbelief. This couldn't be happening. Someone had taken her dog… or worse.

This had gone too far. It was time to alert the police. She needed to go downstairs, get her cell phone and call the station.

Bethany stood up in her crib, shaking the railing and crying.

"I know, baby. I know you're hurting." She gathered Bethany into her arms.

Bethany wailed, jerking her head back. Valerie patted and rubbed her back. Bethany pressed close to her shoulder, her cry reduced to a whimper.

Silence enveloped them, as Valerie's mind filled with anxiety over what had happened to Lexi.

Downstairs, a window shattered.

Trevor struggled to stay under the speed limit as he got closer to Valerie's house. He understood her desper-

ation, but it was foolhardy to send the protective officer
away. Why hadn't she just called him in the first place?

As he neared a stretch of road that led to her subdi-
vision, flashing police lights caused a knot of tension
to form at the base of his neck. He pulled his car over.
A police car had been run off the road, and an ambulance had been called to the scene. He recognized one
of the policemen talking to a woman, who had probably witnessed the accident. Trevor approached him.

"What happened here?"

"As you can see…someone ran one of our own off
the road." The officer pointed to the police car angled
into the ditch with a crushed front end and bent back
bumper. "Knocked him up pretty good, too. He lost
consciousness."

Trevor didn't know the name of the policeman assigned to watch Valerie, but he suspected it was the
officer being loaded into the ambulance. Somebody
didn't want that cop to make it back to Valerie's house.
"Do they know what the cause of the accident was?"

"It looked to me like a black car hit the patrol car
on purpose," said the witness. The woman fanned herself with her hand and shook her head. "And then he
just drove off."

Trevor didn't wait around for further explanation.
He jumped in his car and sped up the street to Valerie's
house. He wrestled with his fear as he gripped the steering wheel. If anything happened to her, he didn't know
if he could forgive himself. He should have stayed with
her and let someone else run the surveillance on Murke.

He braked forcefully and jumped out of the car.
When he knocked on the door, there was no answer.
Anxiety coiled around his chest, making it hard to

breathe. He knocked again, this time harder. When he tried the door, it was locked.

He ran around to the side of the house, but paused when he noticed a main-floor window that had been shattered. Had the storm done that? He reached inside, undid the latch and crawled through the window. He thought to call out Valerie's name, but caught himself. Something about the room felt off.

The main-floor area was eerily quiet. Valerie's phone rested on the countertop in the kitchen. A bottle was on the kitchen table. Lexi hadn't come out to bark at him. Then he saw the rock on the carpet not far from the broken window.

With his heart pounding against his rib cage, he drew his gun and moved slowly up the stairs. The bedroom was empty. One of Bethany's blankets lay on the floor in a haphazard way in sharp contrast to the otherwise tidy room. His anxiety grew when he pushed open the closet door, but found nothing.

When he stepped back into the hallway, Valerie was pointing her gun at him. She let out a breath as her hand went limp.

"Why didn't you call out for me? I thought you were the intruder." Her voice was shaking from the adrenaline rush.

Even though his heart was still racing from having had a gun pointed at him, a sense of joy spread through him. Valerie was okay. "I saw signs of a break-in. I wanted to have the element of surprise on my side if the intruder was still around."

Bethany's cry came from what must be an upstairs bathroom.

Valerie set her gun on the hallway table and went

into the bathroom. She returned a moment later, holding Bethany. The little girl's cheeks were red, and she sucked on her fingers. The distraught look on Valerie's face intensified as she tried to comfort the fussing baby.

Valerie talked at a rapid pace, growing more and more distraught. "I heard a window break when I was upstairs with Bethany."

"Someone did break a window, but it was still latched. Something scared them away."

Valerie didn't seem to be able to process that the intruder had been foiled. The panic-stricken look on her face never wavered. "I couldn't get to my phone. I left it downstairs. I grabbed my gun and hid in the bathroom." Her voice faltered. "I didn't know what else to do. Oh, Trevor, Lexi is gone."

Bethany stopped crying and rubbed her face against Valerie.

Trevor wanted to alleviate Valerie's distress—not add to it—but it looked like some careful planning had gone into the attack. It had probably involved several people if they had been able to take Lexi and run the police officer off the road. "How long ago did you hear the window break?"

"Maybe five minutes before I heard you in the hall."

So it had been his arrival that had scared the would-be intruders away. "I'll help you look for Lexi. We'll get some more protection here for you."

Bethany took her fingers out of her mouth and cried.

"Please, the first thing we need to do is get Bethany some fever reducer from the drugstore up the street."

Such a small thing in the gamut of everything that had happened in the last hour. "Sure, I can take you."

"I'll call the station. Maybe they can bring a K-9

tracking unit out here to look for Lexi. I have a feeling someone has hurt her or taken her." Valerie's agitation showed in her wavering voice and the deep crevice between her eyebrows.

He'd do anything to ease her worry, but he didn't know what to say. "We'll find her." He tried to sound reassuring, but what if the Serpent had done something horrible to Lexi and tossed her out on the road somewhere? Just the thought of it chilled him to the bone.

Valerie looked up at him, her eyes filled with pain. "I hope so."

Bethany quieted for a moment, resting her head against Valerie's neck. Trevor reached up and touched the toddler's tear-stained cheek. "We'll do all we can to find her," he said.

Valerie's lips parted slightly, and she managed a nod. He found himself leaning toward her, wanting to kiss her, to comfort her and hold her. Would his love be enough to calm her? In an instant, she blinked and looked away.

"I can grab my coat and phone downstairs." She swept past him. Her arm brushed over his. "I'll call the station before we go."

He followed behind her. Bethany looked over Valerie's shoulder, studying him.

As they drove to the drugstore, Bethany continued to cry. Valerie turned toward him. "Can you just go inside and get it? Bethany is so fussy. I'll wait out here with her."

Trevor glanced around at the parking lot. The syndicate was pulling out all the stops to get at Valerie tonight. He wasn't about to leave her alone for even a few minutes. "You better come with me. I have no idea what I'm supposed to get. What if I get the wrong thing?"

Valerie scanned the area around her as well and let out a heavy breath. "I suppose you're right."

He didn't need to mention the syndicate by name for her to know that was what he was thinking about.

Valerie pushed open the door and got Bethany out of the backseat. The little girl quieted again when Valerie lifted her out of the car seat and placed a blanket over her.

The neon sign of the all-night drugstore had a warm, welcoming glow as did the lights inside the store, which seemed to cast a golden hue over everything. There were only a few other patrons in the store at this hour. An elderly couple waited by the pharmacy counter and a teenaged girl dressed all in black browsed through cosmetics. Neither seemed like a threat. All the same, he watched the door and the parking lot.

Valerie swayed and bounced with Bethany as they stood in front of the shelves of children's medicine.

"Which one do you want?" Trevor asked.

"I need to read the labels." She handed Bethany over to Trevor before he could protest.

Still obviously in pain, Bethany slammed her head against Trevor's chest, but didn't cry. Her little hand reached up and held on to his shirt collar. He could hear the sucking noises she made as she placed her fingers in her mouth. Her head was clammy from the fever, but her body was warm against his. Her chest moved in and out, pressing against his own.

Valerie picked up several bottles and read them front and back. "I don't remember which one Kathleen used to get..." When she looked at Trevor, her expression suddenly changed. The worry seemed to fall from her face and was replaced by a warmth that softened her features and made her even prettier. "You don't need to look so scared. You're doing just fine with her."

"I just..." He didn't want Bethany to break into a million pieces, but he couldn't tell Valerie that. It sounded ridiculous when he thought about it. "She seems so fragile."

"She's stays pretty calm when *you* hold her." Valerie stepped a little closer to him. "I think she likes you."

"She's just sick, is all," he said, dismissing the idea that anything he could do would comfort a child.

Valerie reached up and soothed Bethany's hair. "This is the quietest she's been all night."

Valerie's hand brushed the bottom of his chin. Heat rose up his face when he looked into the deep green of her eyes. Once again, he wondered what it would be like to kiss her. Right there in the aisle of the all-night drugstore, he was thinking about how soft and full her lips were. What would it be like to pull her close and hold her? To breathe in the sweet smell she exuded.

The moment of reverie was broken by the sound of sirens on the street.

"That must be the units coming to help look for Lexi," Valerie said, her face contorted with worry.

"We should probably get back to the house so you can brief them on what you know." After picking out two different fever reducers, they raced out to the car and headed up the street.

Valerie took a deep breath to try to dispel some of the fear that was making her chest tight. Her house, with two police units parked outside, came into view.

A new wave of tension caused her muscles to contract. What if Lexi was dead?

Bethany's low-level fussing in the backseat only added to her anxiety. She felt pulled in two directions and helpless. She couldn't leave Bethany to go look for Lexi.

"I suppose you will want to lend a hand with finding Lexi," Valerie said.

Of course he would. Trevor was the type who had to be part of the action, not doing something as mundane as taking care of a sick baby.

He studied her for a moment. "Looks like they have enough men on this. I'll stay with you until Bethany quiets down." His gaze flicked around the car and he added, "If you want me to."

"I'd like that," she murmured. Trevor was full of surprises. She hadn't realized how wearing it was to deal with a sick baby alone. His presence did seem to make the worry and anxiety more bearable. "I'll go tell them what I know, if you want to get Bethany out of her car seat."

She saw that flash of fear in his face again and couldn't help smiling. "It's easy to take her out. Just unclick the latch and lift her. Be careful not to hit her head on the door frame." How ironic to see this man, who could probably take down half a dozen criminals, single-handedly turn to a puddle of mush around a toddler.

The bloodhound Justice and his handler, Austin Black, from the K-9 Unit waited for her on her lawn. Justice's tracking skills were second to none. She approached Detective Black.

"I'm glad you could make it out here to help. The backyard was the last place I saw her." Her throat had gone tight from the surge of emotion over the loss of Lexi.

Compassion etched across Detective Black's face as he squeezed her elbow. "We'll find her."

"She wouldn't run away. Someone took her. I just know they did." She couldn't hide her desperation. Life without Lexi was unimaginable.

Austin looked toward the door of her house where Trevor had just stepped inside. "Looks like you got your hands full. We'll take care of this."

As she retreated toward the house with the sound of the baying bloodhound pressing on her ears, the feeling of being pulled in two directions intensified. She longed to be a part of the search. It would ease the angst if she could be doing something to find Lexi. But the thought of leaving Bethany tore her insides up.

When she stepped into her house, Bethany was crying. Trevor held on to her while she arched her back.

"What should I do?" The helplessness on his face was endearing.

"Sit down with her in the rocking chair. I'll get her medicine measured out." Every cry from Bethany was like a stab to Valerie's heart. She'd do anything for her not to be in pain. She'd take the pain on herself if she could. She measured the medicine out into a syringe and hurried into the living room.

"She doesn't like having the medicine. You're going to have to hold her so she can't turn her head away," Valerie said.

Trevor's eyes grew wide.

"She'll be all right. Just hold her chin with her mouth open. Then I can shoot this far enough down her throat so she won't spit it out."

Trevor's forehead wrinkled. "Are you sure about that?"

"Trevor, I've done this before. She needs this medicine."

Gingerly, he cupped his fingers around Bethany's chin.

Valerie soothed Bethany's hot cheek. "All right baby, open your mouth for me."

Bethany jerked her head to the side. Trevor pressed his hand flat against Bethany's cheek and pulled her mouth open with his thumb. Valerie shot the medicine toward the back of Bethany's throat before she had time to react.

Bethany's features pinched together in a look of utter betrayal.

"I'm so sorry, pumpkin." Valerie stroked her blond head.

Trevor sat back in the rocking chair. "Whew. Glad that's over." He continued to rock Bethany as her crying subsided.

Valerie returned the medicine to the kitchen cabinet. When she looked across the island into the living room, Bethany was gripping Trevor's finger while he pretended to try to pull away. Then he bent his head toward Bethany's and a look of pure delight filled Trevor's face as he elicited a smile from the sick little girl.

The moment passed quickly when he glanced up and saw Valerie. He frowned and bent his head self-consciously. He seemed almost embarrassed that she had caught him showing affection for Bethany.

After getting Bethany a bottle, Valerie collapsed on the love seat opposite the rocking chair. She was beyond exhausted.

"Do you want to take her?"

"You're fine. Let me catch my breath." She tilted her head and closed her eyes as the heaviness of fatigue settled in.

She rested for maybe fifteen minutes. When she opened her eyes, Bethany was taking the bottle while Trevor held her. Her eyelids flicked up and down and then closed altogether as she sucked on the bottle.

Trevor's stiff posture had softened a bit. He stared down at Bethany. What was he thinking right now? Did he care about Bethany or was she just an encumbrance to getting his job done? Why, then, had he offered to stay with them when he could have been part of the action combing the countryside for Lexi?

She wondered, too, what he had been thinking when he looked at her so intensely at the drugstore. He had leaned toward her as though to kiss her. She'd seen the smolder in his eyes and been pulled in by the magnetic force of his gaze. As the hours passed and they took turns rocking Bethany, the glow from the sunlight spread across the living room, giving everything a warm, golden quality. She wondered if maybe there could be something more between her and Trevor than a working relationship.

Trevor lifted his gaze toward her. That same look, filled with longing, colored his features and brought light to his eyes. Something had changed between them after their long night together with Bethany.

"Looks like you got her to sleep," Valerie murmured.

"I didn't think I would ever experience something like that." He looked down at the sleeping toddler. "Have a baby fall asleep in my arms."

She detected just a tiny hitch of emotion in his voice.

She heard baying and voices at her back door and got up to see what the noise was about. Her heart fluttered as she neared the sliding glass door. She opened it, half-expecting to see Lexi with her heavy jowls and dark eyes and her little bobbed tail vibrating in joy at seeing Valerie.

Detective Black stood outside, holding the leash while Justice sniffed the grass in vacuum-like fashion.

Valerie's hand went to her heart. "Did you find her?"

Austin Black shook his head, unable to hide his disappointment. "We lost the trail. I brought Justice back to see if we could pick it up again. I'm concerned that maybe at the point we lost the trail, Lexi was stashed in a car and taken somewhere."

Valerie took in a painful breath. What was the syndicate doing to poor Lexi?

Austin's voice filled with compassion. "I want to find her as bad as you do, Valerie. I know how much she means to you."

Valerie thanked Austin and returned to the living room with a heavy heart. Trevor, still holding Bethany, had drifted off to sleep. They looked so cute together. Both Trevor's and Bethany's head were angled to one side, their mouths slightly open…almost like they were father and daughter.

Valerie gathered the sleeping baby in her arms and trod upstairs to her room. She lay Bethany on her tummy, rubbed her back a few times and placed a blanket over her. Bethany stirred, rubbing her face against the sheet. Valerie braced for another bout of crying, but the baby quieted and grew still.

She tiptoed toward the door.

Trevor was standing in the hallway waiting. With

his broad shoulders and firm jawline, he was still an imposing figure. But she felt as though she had seen a softer, more vulnerable side to him.

"She still sleeping?"

Nodding, Valerie turned and eased the door shut.

When she pivoted, Trevor was standing even closer to her. He gathered her in his arms, drawing her close and pressing his lips on top of hers.

She responded to his kiss. A tingly sensation, like warm honey moving through her veins, overtook her. Her hand rested on the hard muscle of his chest. He backed her up to a wall and deepened his kiss.

With his face still close to hers, he pulled her away from the wall and encircled her with his strong arms. He held her close. His kiss had left her breathless and wobbly in the knees. Trevor didn't seem to want to let go of her. She sensed his longing and was overcome by the tenderness of his embrace.

He pulled away for a moment and looked at her. His lips parted as though he wanted to say something to her. He cast his gaze downward and pulled her back into a hug that completely enveloped her.

It didn't matter to her if he couldn't express what he was feeling. The power of the kiss and the tenderness of his embrace spoke volumes to her.

I could stay in his arms forever.

The sweetness of the moment was broken by the sound of the doorbell ringing.

ELEVEN

Trevor was still reeling from the sweetness of Valerie's kiss when he opened the door and saw one of the officers who had been involved in the search.

"We found Lexi in the brush by the river. She's alive, but highly unresponsive. They are taking her over to Dr. Mills."

Valerie, who stood behind him, gasped.

"Thanks...we'll get over there as fast as we can," Trevor said.

He closed the door and turned to face Valerie. All the color had drained from her face, and the look in her eyes was frantic.

"I can go check on her if you need to stay with Bethany," he offered.

The enchantment of the kiss faded as harsh reality barged into his awareness. Valerie's life was still under threat. She wasn't safe. The syndicate may have killed her dog.

Valerie turned one way and then the other. "I can ummm..." She held a trembling hand to her lips, then let out a breath and straightened her shoulders. "I can call Mrs. Witherspoon in a little bit. She's supposed to come over today, anyway. I forgot to cancel her after McNeal told me to take sick leave."

As he watched her struggle with the decision, he was filled with compassion. "Hey." He grabbed her delicate hand and pressed it between his. He wanted to tell her that Lexi was going to be okay, but that might be a lie. He moved toward her, brushed a strand of hair out of her eyes and kissed her forehead. "I'll wait with you, and we'll go together to see Lexi."

Once Mrs. Witherspoon showed up, they sped across town toward the vet clinic.

"Which way?" Trevor glanced over at her.

Her fingers were laced tightly together and resting in her lap. Her lips were pressed into a hard, straight line. Nothing he could say to her would take away the worry. All he could do was walk through it with her.

"Take a left at this next street," she said, releasing a heavy sigh.

As he drove, he saw signs that indicated an area called the Lost Woods was close by. The vet clinic was set off by itself on a large piece of land. Two horses, one with a bandage on its leg, ate grass in a fenced field next to the stark white building. Valerie jumped out of the car almost before Trevor had come to a stop. He followed behind her.

Valerie rushed over to the woman behind the counter. "There was a police K-9 brought in just a little bit ago?"

"Oh, sure, Dr. Mills is just back there with her now." The receptionist pointed to a door behind her.

Trevor followed as Valerie pushed through the door. Dr. Mills was a slender fiftyish woman with pronounced eyebrows and candy-apple-red hair pulled back in a bun.

Valerie stopped short when she saw Lexi lying on

the sterile, metal exam table. She shuddered. Trevor came up from behind, wrapping his arms around her.

Valerie glanced from the prone dog to the vet. "How is she?"

Lexi managed a tail wag at the sound of Valerie's voice.

"She's becoming more responsive. The wagging tail is a good sign." The doctor put the half glasses she had on a string on her face.

Valerie stepped toward the exam table and rubbed Lexi's ears.

"What happened to her?" Trevor asked.

Valerie bent her head close to Lexi's ear and made soothing noises while she petted her. Her eyes glazed as she stroked the dog's belly.

"The department ordered a tox screen on her, but my guess is she was given some kind of drug that paralyzed her. She's just now starting to show movement in her extremities."

Valerie didn't look up from the dog. "The drug wears off after a while?" She held her hand close to the dog's mouth. Lexi licked her fingers.

"If that's what it is, she should have a full recovery." The vet leaned toward the dog, touching her front flank. "There's some barbs in her fur consistent with the use of a taser."

Valerie shook her head. "That would be the only way they would have been able to drug her in the first place." Her voice tinged with anger as she stroked Lexi's head. "I can't believe they did this to her."

"Can Valerie take her home?"

Dr. Mills stuck her hand in the pocket of her white

lab coat. "I'd like to watch her for a couple more hours until the drug wears off completely."

Valerie straightened her back. She bit her lower lip and turned her head away. Trevor's ire rose over what had been done to Lexi. How dare the syndicate put Valerie through this emotional turmoil.

"You're welcome to stay with her for a little bit, but she needs to rest." The doctor pulled a chart off a wall. "I've got a sick parakeet to look after." She left the room.

Valerie looked at Trevor. "If it's all right with you, I'd like to be alone with Lexi."

"Sure," Trevor said, trying to hide his disappointment. He wanted to be with them, but he needed to honor her wishes. He left the exam room and found a seat in the waiting room. Valerie and Lexi were a tight team, partners, and he wasn't a part of that. Despite the kiss, he was still the outsider.

Valerie emerged from the exam room about twenty minutes later. Her eyes were red from crying.

Trevor struggled to find words to comfort her. What could he say to make her feel better? As they stepped out into the parking lot, his rage over what the Serpent had done returned. The syndicate represented the worst kind of evil, and now they were trying to get at Valerie while she was in her home.

Once they were in the car, Trevor put the key in the ignition. "You want me to take you back home?"

"I'm going to call McNeal and see if he has changed his mind. I don't like being on the sidelines like this. If I can work the streets, maybe I can take this syndicate apart piece by piece." The ire he heard in her voice was the same that he had felt. But her drive to make a difference was overshadowing her sense of self-preservation.

"Valerie, I've been thinking… After what happened last night, maybe it's not good for you to stay at your house." Trevor pulled out of the parking lot.

"I can't go to my parents'. That would put their lives in danger, too. My dad has his hands full taking care of my mother. Maybe I could stay with Lucy or one of my brothers."

He shook his head. "You need something with a higher level of security. Maybe the department can set up a safe house for you."

Her voice rose half an octave. "So then I become the prisoner. I can't work, and I can't be in my own home. It could be months before we bring the Serpent in."

"The Serpent's ability to get at you seems to be escalating." He only wanted to keep her safe. His protection and what the department could manage didn't seem to be enough.

She rubbed her temple as her voice gave way to frustration. "Bethany is just starting to adjust to all the changes. She'd be in a new strange place again and have to adjust all over." She ran her hands through her hair. "I understand what you are saying, I do, but I just…" Valerie turned away and stared out the window.

Trevor took a moment to gather his thoughts before speaking. He checked his rearview mirror. Only one dark-colored car was behind him on the long stretch of country road.

He understood her point of view, but his desperation to protect her pressed in on him from all sides. "Maybe it would be best if McNeal extended your sick leave for a while."

"I want to do my job. I want to get these guys out of Sagebrush. If you two want to lock me up in some stuffy safe house all day, it's like the syndicate has already won. Do you think I can't do my job?"

"Valerie, that's not what I meant." Trevor felt like he was slipping down an icy wall. Valerie thought he was insulting her ability to do her job. Frustration over not being able to shield her from harm gnawed at him.

He'd been so intent on their conversation he hadn't noticed that the dark-colored car behind him had pulled up beside them without passing. When he looked over, he saw Derek Murke's leering face as he raised a pistol and aimed at Trevor's window.

Trevor swerved, and the shot went wild.

Valerie screamed and ducked beneath the dashboard.

Trevor accelerated and checked his rearview mirror. The car was behind them but closing in fast.

Trevor turned onto a dirt road just as Murke's bumper hit his. Another shot shattered the back window. Then he heard an odd popping sound. The dirt road was surrounded by trees on both sides. He sped up, creating a dust cloud that made it hard to gauge where Murke was.

His car fishtailed and then vibrated. Now he knew what that popping sound had been. Murke had shot out a back tire. He braked with force, causing the car to spin in a half circle. They weren't going to get anywhere on a bald tire.

"Get out." He pushed his door open.

As the dust cloud settled, he could see Murke's car careening toward them. He ran around to Valerie's side of the car where she crouched low. He grabbed her hand. Murke got out of his car and ran toward them. Trevor pulled his gun and fired a shot. They'd find cover in the trees thirty yards away if they could make it without being hit. Pulling Valerie with him, he ran. Murke stalked toward them. He'd have to get pretty close to have any accuracy with a pistol.

They were ten yards from the trees. Trevor stole a glance toward Murke as he lifted his gun. He dove to the ground and scrambled toward the trees. Valerie stayed low, as well. The pistol shot he'd braced for never happened.

A panicked look spread across Murke's face as he stared down at his gun. He was out of bullets. He raced back to his car.

This was his chance to take Murke into custody before he drove away. He turned to Valerie. "Hide in the trees. Wait for me."

"No way! I'm coming with you."

"You're unarmed," he growled. "You need to lay low. And besides, you have Bethany to consider…"

Valerie's eyes clouded over, but she obeyed without protest. He could see the yellow of her jacket as she stepped behind a cluster of trees.

Murke crawled back in his car and disappeared beneath the dash. Trevor ran toward the car, ready to shoot. This was his chance. He could get Murke.

Murke popped his head up behind the steering wheel and lifted a rifle, aiming it in Trevor's direction.

Trevor hit the ground and then soldier-crawled toward the cover of the trees. His pistol was no match for a rifle. A shot zinged over his back. Murke's footsteps pounded hard ground.

When he entered the trees, Valerie found him and pulled him to his feet. They ran deeper into the Lost Woods as shot after shot reverberated around them, breaking branches and stirring up dust.

With no clearly defined trail in front of them, they pushed through the thick underbrush and trees. He held on tight to Valerie's hand. Another shot rang out, and a branch above them broke. Murke was gaining on them.

They zigzagged through more trees, their feet pounding the dusty earth, both of them growing breathless from exertion. When twenty minutes passed without any indication that Murke was still close by, Trevor stopped, taking in a raspy breath. Valerie pressed close to his back.

"It looks like Murke is playing offense and has decided to take me out of the equation," Trevor said.

Valerie nodded. "This score he told his half sister about must be pretty big for him to take this kind of a risk." She leaned over, placing her hands on her knees and drawing in deep breaths.

All the trees around him looked exactly alike. "How do we get back to the main road?"

Valerie shook her head, turning in one direction and then the other. "I have no idea."

Going back to the car wasn't a viable option. He didn't have a spare, and trying to drive with a bad tire would just make them an easy target for Murke. He pulled his cell phone off his belt. No reception. He had to find a way to turn this thing around and take Murke down, but how?

"Let's just keep moving in the general direction of the main road. We got to come to it sooner or later." She placed her hand in his.

Despite their earlier fight…despite snapping at him for suggesting the safe house and forgoing her job… Valerie trusted him enough to lead her out of the Lost Woods.

As they started running again, he prayed that trust wasn't misplaced.

TWELVE

Valerie's leg muscles burned from running, and her lungs felt like they had been scraped with a steak knife. Her throat was parched.

Trevor continued to lead them through the woods, but every bunch of trees looked like the one before. They might even be going in circles. They risked running around a cluster of trees and ending up face-to-face with Murke.

She had to get her bearings, had to obtain some sense of direction. There was a reason these were called the Lost Woods. She'd heard the stories of people who went in and never came out. The thick undergrowth and trees were like a maze.

Trevor stopped. "I've got one bullet left," he said, clicking the magazine out of his gun. "Murke has outmatched us firepower-wise, but maybe we can still catch him."

Valerie swallowed, trying to produce some moisture in her mouth. It felt like she had swallowed dust. How much longer could they keep this up? "Maybe we should just try to get back to the main road."

Trevor glanced at his phone panel again. "If I could

get some cell reception, we could get backup out here. Murke wouldn't be able to leave these woods."

Murke could be lying in wait for them around any corner. How on earth would they catch him? Valerie studied her surroundings. They'd been running for at least half an hour. She wasn't so sure they could even find their way back to the car if they had to.

They heard voices, two men exchanging verbal jabs and raucous laughter.

"Maybe we'll get some help." Trevor's voice tinged with hope.

As the conversation carried over the trees, something about the way the men talked seemed menacing. "I'm not so sure about that. Let's hide." She pulled on his shirt and then slipped behind some thick undergrowth.

He hit the ground and scooted toward her. "What are we doing?"

"Lot of drug deals go down here and lots of transients hang out here, too," she whispered. "Let's see if we can get a read on these guys before we go asking for help."

She lay close enough to Trevor to feel his body heat. His soapy-clean scent mixed with sweat. Despite the fear coursing through her, his closeness calmed her.

The voices of the two men grew distant and then loud again. As their conversation became more distinct, it was obvious that they had been drinking. They could have been on a bender and been out here for days. There was no guarantee they even had a car. They might have hitchhiked and been dropped off, or come from one of the low-rent housing districts that were close to the woods.

As the men passed within twenty feet of them, Trevor

turned to look at her, rolling his eyes. He was probably thinking the same thing. Not the rescue party they were hoping for.

When the voices faded, they crawled out from under the bush. Valerie dusted off her pants. It had been a while since they had seen or heard any sign that Murke was close. Maybe he had given up or gotten lost himself. She reached out for Trevor's hand, but he didn't notice.

Now that the threat from Murke had died down, she could feel the wedge between them again, probably over their fight. Trevor had been so great in helping with Bethany, and the kiss had been wonderful, but he seemed to be closing down again. His feelings for her were even more unclear.

He walked with his back to her, talking over his shoulder. "What kind of drug deals take place out here?"

If he only felt comfortable talking about work, she would talk about work. "It's one of the syndicate's favorite places to do business. It's a hard place to patrol. We usually know something has gone wrong when we find a body."

She stared at his back as the emotional chasm between them seemed to grow. Was he just preoccupied with dealing with Murke?

She scurried to catch up. "Captain McNeal thinks that Rio was taken because the syndicate needs him to find something that is hidden out here."

"Really?" Only half his attention was on the conversation as he turned in one direction and then another.

All around her, the trees and boulders looked the same. She struggled to shake off that sinking feeling. They were lost. "Maybe we should try to get back to the car. We can navigate our way out from the road."

He stopped and looked directly at her. "Good idea. Which way would that be?"

She turned a half circle until her gaze traveled toward a high rock formation. She caught movement on top of the rock. An instant after it registered that what she was seeing was a man holding a gun, she heard the zing of a rifle being fired.

Trevor pulled her to the ground, shielding her with his arm. They crawled behind a boulder.

Trevor spoke into her ear. "We know where he is at now. I'm going to see if I can sneak up on him."

She grabbed his sleeve. "Trevor, I don't know if that is a good idea." He was down to only one bullet. He'd be walking into a death trap.

"He's got to come down off that rock sooner or later…and I'll be ready for him." He pulled his cell phone off his belt. "Keep trying to get some reception. Backup would be nice, but if I have to do this myself, I will."

Staying low and moving quickly, he disappeared into the brush. Valerie beat down the approaching sense of doom. Maybe Trevor could succeed. She hadn't had time to notice if there was brush around the boulder Murke had climbed onto. There might be a place for him to hide.

After slipping out of her yellow coat, which made her too easy to see, she angled around the thick brush where they had found shelter. She spread the coat over a bush, so it would serve as a decoy.

Valerie soldier-crawled on the ground until a rock outcropping came into view. The rock formation was at least twenty feet high. Cell reception might be better up there, and it would allow her a view of the landscape.

Pushing aside the worries about Trevor that plagued her, she found a foothold and climbed up to a flat spot. A finger-shaped rock that was higher than the flat spot shielded her from view on one side.

She craned her neck around the rock. She could see the boulder where Murke was perched. Though the sniper's movements were small, she caught the glint of his rifle barrel in the noonday sun. When she scanned the surrounding area, she saw no sign of Trevor.

Dear God, keep him safe.

She checked the phone and breathed a sigh of relief. She had a signal. Dispatch promised to send three patrol cars, but she could only give them a rough idea of where they were at in the Lost Woods.

The dispatcher's voice came across the line strong and clear. "Then we'll probably have to send a chopper, too."

Valerie hung up. It would take at least twenty minutes for the units to mobilize and get out here. She peered out at the landscape again. Murke was crawling down from the boulder. Where was Trevor?

Murke stopped and looked in her direction. She swung around and pressed hard against the finger-shaped rock. Had he seen her?

With her heart racing, she rolled over on her stomach and peered out. She still saw no sign of Trevor. Had he even made it over to the boulder? The view from high up made the layout clear, but it would be easy enough to get turned around if you were on the ground.

Valerie heard branches breaking some distance from her. Several deer jumped out of the brush and bounded toward a clearing. She caught a flash of movement not too far from where the deer had been. That had to be Trevor.

A rifle shot shattered the stillness. Murke had spotted the yellow coat and taken aim. The shot reverberated off the cliffs and rocks. The deer scattered, their hooves pounding hard earth. Valerie had a clear view of the action below. She gasped.

Trevor had mistaken the echo of the rifle for the rifle shot and was headed in the wrong direction, but that was not what had sent a charge of fear through her. Murke was stalking toward where Trevor had been. It was only a matter of time before Murke saw Trevor.

As Murke closed in on Trevor, Valerie's heart seized up. She couldn't cry out. That would put both of them in jeopardy. Murke drew closer to the rock where she hid. Murke kept looking through the sight of his rifle. He must have spotted Trevor moving through the brush and was trying to line up a shot.

Murke was almost even with the rock where Valerie hid. She had only one option to stop him and a split second in which to do it. She peered out behind the outcropping and waited until Murke was directly below her.

Valerie leapt from the rock, landing on top of Murke and taking him to the ground. The rifle fell from his hand. Valerie struggled to get Murke into a hold by immobilizing his neck. Murke swung free of her grasp and reached out to hit her. She angled away, grabbed his foot and pulled him to the ground.

Murke let out a groan, showing his teeth. The sneer on his face communicated pure hatred. He meant to kill her. He leapt toward her, hands curled like claws.

Trevor came up behind him and wrestled Murke to the ground.

Sirens sounded in the distance, and the mechanical hum of a helicopter grew louder.

Murke twisted and writhed and cursed, but Trevor held him down face-first.

Valerie tore the heavy-duty laces from her boots. "Tie him up with these. They'll hold until backup gets here."

Within minutes, the helicopter was low to the ground and directly overhead. The sirens grew closer. The helicopter must have alerted the police cars to their position.

Trevor placed a knee on the small of Murke's back to keep him from moving. He looked up at Valerie. Gratitude colored his voice as his mouth turned up in a smile. "Thanks…you saved my life."

"It's what partners do for each other." However, what she had done was more than just one lawman looking out for another. She cared about Trevor.

"You could have died. You didn't have to do that for me." The tenderness in his eyes made her heart flutter.

"Your life was worth saving." She looked at him for a long moment, expecting him to say more. His gaze rested on her, but he remained silent. What words had gone unspoken between them? What was he thinking?

"You're hurting me." Murke cursed and struggled beneath the weight of Trevor's knee. Trevor focused his attention on making sure the fugitive stayed put. Valerie picked up the rifle and kept it trained on Murke until help arrived.

About twenty minutes passed before the first of several officers emerged through the trees. One of the officers pulled his handcuffs from his tool belt. Trevor stood up, his hand on his gun while the officer cuffed Murke and pulled him to his feet.

Trevor spoke to the officer who had cuffed Murke. "I want to interview him as soon as he is processed. He's got a lot of questions to answer."

Murke looked at Trevor with his dark soulless eyes and then spat on the ground before being led away.

As she watched Murke being escorted through the trees, a sense of satisfaction swept over her. Trevor had his fugitive.

Detective Jackson Worth emerged through the trees with Titan taking up the lead. The lab's black fur shone in the sun. Seeing Titan was a sad reminder that her own K-9 partner was not with her.

Jackson held out a hand to Trevor. "Job well done. They are going to take him in the chopper to get him to the station faster." He shook Valerie's hand, as well. "I saw what he did to your car. I bet you two could use a ride back into town."

Trevor nodded. "I suppose I will have to make arrangements for my car to be towed." With Jackson and Titan in the lead, Trevor and Valerie followed, pushing brush out of the way until the dirt road came into view.

"I'd like to swing by Doc Mills's place and see if Lexi is ready to come home," Valerie said as she walked beside Trevor.

"Consider it done," Jackson replied.

"I need to be dropped off at the station," Trevor said. "So I can find out what this big score is that was Murke's undoing."

Trevor's words brought her frustration to the surface. She couldn't be a part of that questioning, not as long as McNeal had her on forced sick leave.

Trevor must have sensed her disappointment. He reached over and touched her hand, squeezing her fingers. With Murke in custody, it would only be a matter of days or even hours before Trevor returned to San Antonio. She might never see him again.

They drove along the road that bordered the Lost Woods back to the vet clinic. Jackson had barely stopped the patrol car when Valerie pushed open the door and rushed into the clinic.

Doctor Mills's assistant stood behind the tall counter. Recognition spread across her face when she saw Valerie. "She's in the kennels out back. You are free to take her home."

Valerie rushed down the long hallway and pushed through the door. The first kennel had a collie with a cone around its neck and the second was empty. She found Lexi lying down in the third kennel. The dog leapt to her feet and trotted over to Valerie. She stood up on her hind paws, resting her front paws on the chain-link fence.

Bursting with joy, Valerie leaned down so Lexi could kiss her face. "I missed you." The dog's face with the light brown markings above her eyes and the head tilted sideways communicated love. She wrapped her hands around Lexi's thick neck.

Dr. Mills came and stood by the back entrance. "You might want to walk her around a little bit, let her get her land legs back. We just put her out in the kennel a few minutes ago."

Valerie took the leash from Dr. Mills and opened the gate. "Lex, come."

The dog looked up at her, but didn't move. Then she bowed her head. Valerie thought her heart would break. Lexi had been traumatized by what she had been through.

Trevor came and stood at the edge of the building. "We should get going. I've got to make arrangements for Murke to be transported back to San Antonio."

Valerie stepped into the kennel. "Can you just give me a few minutes? Lexi is still not herself." Her voice faltered. Seeing her strong, brave dog cower because of the abuse she had endured tore Valerie to pieces. "I can get a ride into town some other way if you're in a hurry."

Trevor put his hands in his pockets. "No, we can wait." His voice filled with compassion. "Take all the time you need."

She clicked Lexi into the leash and pulled. Lexi obeyed, but the confidence she had always seen with Lexi seemed to be deflated. The dog hung her head as Valerie led her around the field by the clinic.

Valerie dropped to her knees and wrapped her arms around the dog's neck. Lexi's coarse fur was warm against her skin. "What did they do to you?"

The dog licked her cheek as though to reassure her that everything would be okay. Valerie pulled back and rubbed Lexi's velvety ears. Dark brown eyes looked back at her. "We'll get through this together."

She took in a breath and rose to her feet. Valerie worked with her a little longer, hoping to see some of Lexi's tenacious spirit return. Though she obeyed the commands, the drive that had made Lexi such a great K-9 wasn't there.

Valerie glanced over her shoulder where Trevor had been watching at a distance.

She moved toward him. "I know…we need to get going."

Trevor seemed to be all business now that Murke was caught. Had the kiss meant anything to him? She longed for an opportunity to be alone with him to talk before he left, but she didn't see how that would happen.

Valerie rode in the back of the patrol car with Titan beside her and Lexi on her lap. She didn't mind. It felt good to have Lexi close. Holding the dog might even help with her emotional recovery.

Jackson turned onto the street where she lived. Her heart sank. She might be saying good-bye to Trevor for the last time. He turned his head sideways but didn't look at her from the front seat. He hadn't said much of anything since catching Murke.

As they pulled up, she was surprised to see Captain McNeal standing on the sidewalk by her house. The expression on his face was grim, and his shoulders bent forward.

What was going on here?

THIRTEEN

Anxiety stabbed at Trevor's nerves as Jackson pulled up to the curb. McNeal had come over to Valerie's house instead of meeting him at the station. Something pretty serious must be going down.

Trevor got out of the passenger seat and hurried to open the back door for Valerie. She looked up at him, her round, green eyes filled with trust. Heartache over having to say goodbye to her had made it hard for him to say anything at all to her. It didn't make sense that their lives should go on in separate directions and yet, he was afraid to tell her how he felt about her. What if the feelings weren't mutual?

Lexi jumped out of the backseat first. The dog seemed to be perking up a little, though he had yet to see that bobbed tail wag with enthusiasm. He took Valerie's hand and helped her up to the sidewalk.

Jackson got out of the driver's seat and rested his forearm on the top of the police car. "I've got to get back to work. Take care of Lexi, Valerie."

She nodded as Jackson got back into the white SUV and drove off.

McNeal strode toward them. "I'll spare you the small

talk. Murke escaped. Once the chopper landed, he over-powered the two officers who were escorting him to processing."

The news was like a boulder slamming against Trevor's chest. "Did he have help?"

"I don't think he had inside help. But someone picked him up on the street once he got away." McNeal shifted his weight and rested his hands on his hips. "When you didn't show up at the police station, I figured you were here with Valerie. I wanted you to get the news in person."

"We stopped to get Lexi," Valerie explained.

A mixture of frustration and despair wrestled within Trevor as he struggled to find solutions to getting Murke back into custody. How could this have happened? "I assume you have units out looking for him?"

McNeal nodded.

Valerie stepped forward. "It's going to take more than patrol units to find Murke. We have to be strategic about where we look."

McNeal turned toward Valerie. "You two have been working this case together, and I'll take any input you have, Valerie. But I still don't feel comfortable putting you back out on the street."

Valerie's jaw went slack as a veil of disappointment shrouded her eyes, but she lifted her head and squared her shoulders as a show of acceptance like the true professional she was.

"With all due respect, sir, the syndicate is going to get at Valerie no matter where she is," Trevor said. "They almost got into her home last night. Valerie is the reason we even got Murke into custody in the first place. She risked her life to save mine." He scrubbed a hand across his face. "Now that Murke has decided taking me out of the equation is the solution to his problems, there is no one I would rather have my back than Officer Salgado."

Valerie's face glowed with gratitude.

Raising his eyebrows, McNeal glanced over at Valerie and then rested his gaze back on Trevor.

Trevor feared he had overstepped the boundaries of McNeal's authority, but he had meant every word he said. Locking Valerie away wasn't going to make her any safer and being overly protective of her wouldn't bring back Agent Cory Smith. The syndicate had ways of getting to her no matter what. Valerie was ten times the professional Cory had been. She'd shown herself for the fearless and quick-thinking cop she was out in the Lost Woods.

McNeal cleared his throat. "Well…your point is valid. She's vulnerable staying at home, too, and she's an asset in catching Murke. I'd feel better about putting Valerie back out on the street if you were with her. Once you go back to San Antonio, I'll reassess."

Valerie grabbed McNeal's hand and shook it vigorously. "Thank you, sir."

"For now, the two of you need to focus on finding Murke," McNeal said. "We'll figure out the extent to which you can resume your patrol duties later."

"Yes, sir," said Trevor.

"I got to get back to the station." McNeal ambled toward his car where Chief perched faithfully in the backseat.

Valerie turned toward Trevor and mouthed the words "Thank you" as McNeal drove away. The look on her face and the warmth in her eyes were captivating. There was so much more he wanted to say to her, but now was not the time. "So what is your theory about where we'll find Murke?"

"We backtrack to where we know he has been. We know he has had contact with Leroy Seville, as well as his half sister, and someone had to have sold him those guns."

The half sister and Leroy seemed like dead ends. Murke had burned his bridges with them. It could take days to track down whoever had sold Murke the guns. His mind went through the catalog of Murke's known movements. If only they knew what this big score was that Murke was after.

"What about Arianna's Diner? Maybe he said something to the waitstaff or was meeting someone there," Valerie said.

Trevor lifted his head. "It's worth a try."

"Let me just go inside and give Bethany a hug and then we can get going." Valerie turned and headed up the sidewalk.

"I'll come with you…if you want." He wanted to make sure Bethany had made a full recovery as much as she did.

"That would be nice," she said softly.

He stepped into line a few paces behind her. "Valerie?"

"Yes." She looked over her shoulder, offering him a smile that melted his heart.

"It's good to be working with you again."

"You, too."

Valerie pushed open the door. Mrs. Witherspoon and Bethany were sitting on the couch reading a storybook. Bethany burst out in a smile when she saw

Trevor. The surge of joy he felt at such a small gesture surprised him.

With Mrs. Witherspoon's assurances that Bethany's fever had not returned, Valerie felt comfortable going. At Stella's request, Bethany opened her mouth and showed everyone where a tooth had poked through her gum.

After getting back into uniform, Valerie drove with Trevor and Lexi to the station to get the patrol car.

Arianna's Diner was on the main floor of a large brick building in downtown Sagebrush. The decor featured distressed wood floors, soft lighting and a tin ceiling. Though the restaurant was known for its coffee and pastries, it also served sandwiches and light Italian dishes.

At this time of day between the lunch and dinner hours, the diner was virtually abandoned. A waiter stood at the corner of a counter folding silverware into napkins. A fan whirred on the tin ceiling.

Only two customers sat at separate tables, a college-age girl with a cup of coffee and an open journal and an older man enjoying a plate of pasta.

Trevor walked in behind Valerie. "Do you eat here ever?"

"Lots of the officers stop here because it's on the way to the station, but I think I've only been in here once or twice," Valerie said.

They were really grasping at straws to come back here, but Trevor had vowed not to leave Sagebrush without Murke in custody. Thin leads were enough to keep him hoping. He could sense the clock ticking though. Would the big score Murke had told his half sister about be enough to keep him here now that the law had managed to catch him once? However clever Murke was at escape, he had to be shaking in his shoes over being taken into custody.

When they walked across the diner floor, the waiter at the counter lifted his head. "Yes, may I help you?"

Trevor waited for Valerie to take the lead.

"We have some questions to ask you about a man who was in here a few days ago." She pulled Murke's picture out of her pocket and laid it on the counter.

The man stared down at the picture. Trevor tensed when the waiter shook his head.

"What day would he have been in here?" the waiter asked, looking back at them.

"Tuesday afternoon."

"I wasn't on shift that day. Maryanne might have been. Just a minute. I don't think she has left yet." He disappeared behind a swinging door.

Trevor studied the restaurant walls, which were decorated with photographs and fifties memorabilia.

A moment later, the waiter returned with a plump, forty-something woman with bouffant blond hair. Dark eyeliner rimmed her eyes. "So y'all are wonderin' about a feller who came in on Tuesday." She raised an eyebrow at them. "Honey, do you have any idea how many customers stomp through here in a day?"

Her comment was a bleak reminder of how thin the lead was.

Valerie pushed the photograph across the counter. The woman glanced at it, shook her head and then looked away.

Disappointment fell on Trevor like a lead blanket. The woman stopped as she was turning to go back to the kitchen. She angled back toward the counter and picked up the photo again, nodding slowly.

"Actually... I *do* remember him. We were really busy that day, but this guy wanted to talk to the boss."

"The boss?" Valerie stepped closer to the counter.

Maryanne put her hand on her hip. "Arianna Munson—she owns the place."

"Is Arianna here now?" Trevor shifted his weight, excitement colored his voice.

"She only comes in once in a while to make sure everything is running smoothly." Maryanne made a face. "Arianna's good at the business end of things but not so good with the customers."

"Can we get an address for her?" Valerie asked.

"Sure." Maryanne pulled a pen from behind her ear and grabbed a paper napkin. She talked as she wrote. "I don't know what they talked about in her office, but Arianna was white as a ghost when she came out."

Was it possible that Arianna was the girlfriend that Murke had wanted to get even with?

Trevor stepped toward the counter. "Did she say anything to you about the meeting?"

"Hard to say. She's not exactly a woman who's in touch with her feelings." The waitress shrugged her shoulders. "She was just crabbier than usual with the chef and waitstaff for the rest of the day." She pushed the napkin with the address on it toward Valerie.

"Thank you for all your help." Trevor felt a lightness in his step as they headed out the door toward Valerie's patrol car. If Arianna was the old girlfriend, she might be able to answer a lot of questions for them. She might even know where Murke was.

Valerie checked the address before handing the napkin to Trevor. "It won't take us but ten minutes to get there."

Valerie adhered to the speed limit through downtown and turned off on a wide street that featured luxury high-rises and lots of greenery. The Mercedes and BMWs parked on the street indicated that the neighborhood was high income.

Valerie pulled over to the curb and pointed. "She's in the Merill building. It used to be a fancy hotel, but it's been converted to high-end apartments."

"Restaurant business must be doing her pretty good," Trevor mused.

They entered the lobby, which featured a marble floor and wide, sweeping staircase. Valerie pointed toward the elevators. "Fifth floor."

They stepped inside, waited for the doors to close and pushed the button for the fifth floor. Trevor could feel his anticipation growing as the number three and then four lit up on the panel. "Maybe we'll get some answers from this woman."

Valerie nodded.

The doors swung open. At the end of the hall, a woman in a white coat with her back to them stood holding a suitcase and sticking a key into a doorknob.

When she turned around, Valerie gasped, her eyes going wide with recognition.

"The Serpent," she whispered.

FOURTEEN

The shock of seeing the Serpent was like being plunged into ice water. Valerie struggled for a deep breath as her hand went for her gun. Arianna and the Serpent were one and the same.

"Stop. FBI." Trevor ran down the hall with his gun drawn.

The woman dropped her suitcase, dashed inside the apartment and slammed the door. As Valerie ran behind Trevor, she could hear a locking bolt sliding into place.

Trevor pounded on the door. "Ma'am, we need to talk to you." He waited only a second before lifting his leg to kick the door in. The first kick only shook the door.

"I don't hear anything. She might have a back exit from the apartment." Adrenaline coursed through her. "I'll go down to the ground floor and see if I can catch her."

Trevor grabbed her arm. "No, I can't let you. This woman wants you dead. We don't know if she's armed or not."

"But Trevor…"

He kicked the door a second time, splintering it off its hinges. He grabbed her hand. "You're staying with me."

They entered a huge living room done mostly in white. While Trevor searched the room, Valerie ran to the window. A large parking garage was across the street.

Trevor shouted from a second room. "This way!"

She ran to a back entryway where Trevor stood by an open door with steps that led down.

When they were halfway down the exterior stairs, Valerie scanned the area below them. Arianna was weaving her way through the cars in the lot toward the parking garage, her white coat easy to spot among the darker cars.

They reached the bottom of the stairs just as Arianna disappeared into the parking garage.

"I'll grab Lexi." While Trevor headed toward the parking garage, Valerie ran the short distance to the patrol vehicle and opened the back door. "Lexi, come."

The dog leapt out of the car and bolted toward Valerie. Valerie grabbed the long canvas leash and commanded, "Get her. Get her."

The light diminished by half when they entered the dark cave of the parking garage. The dog pulled hard, making her way past the parked cars, her ears back and her nose low to the ground. People who were being chased put out an unusual amount of adrenaline. Lexi's nose was sensitive to pick up on the scent.

Valerie glanced up ahead, hoping to see Trevor. Toward the entrance of the garage, a car started up and pulled out of its space. Lexi moved in the opposite direction. She'd trust the dog's nose over any theory she might have. She was confident the car leaving the garage was not Arianna's.

Approaching footsteps seemed to echo. A moment

later, Trevor came around a curve. He held his gun in his hand and spoke between ragged breaths. "No sign of her yet."

"I'll call and see if I can get another unit to watch the exit. I don't think she has left here. She's got to be hiding in her car or somewhere in this garage. Lexi will find her."

The dog pulled hard, stopped for a moment, retracing her steps. When she finally picked up the scent, she made yipping sounds that suggested extreme excitement.

Using her shoulder mic, Valerie radioed in for backup to block the exit. Lexi stopped, lifting her head and sniffing the air. She ran ten yards in one direction and then ten in the opposite.

"What's going on?"

The leash went slack. "She's lost the scent. She'll find it again."

Lexi continued to sniff the ground, but not as frantically. Both of them slowed their pace. Valerie listened for footsteps but didn't hear any.

"What do we got here?" Trevor turned side to side. "Three stories of cars."

Valerie ran over to the elevator that lead to the higher floors. The elevator wasn't in operation, and Lexi didn't alert to anything outside the doors. "She's still on this floor. She has to be."

They walked, catching their breath and listening for the sound of a car engine starting up or lights turning on. With Valerie at her heels, Lexi wove through the cars. Arianna must have crouched and used the cars as cover on the way to her own car. She probably ditched the white coat, too.

Trevor lifted his gun and edged toward Valerie. "Stay close to me—she might see this as an opportunity to take you out."

Valerie tensed. Trevor was right; she could be walking into an ambush. The woman had clearly recognized her. After all her efforts at sending henchmen to do her dirty work, the Serpent probably would have no qualms about finishing the job herself.

Lexi's yipping and sniffing vocalizations grew more intense. She pulled hard on the leash again. "She's got it. She's close." Valerie let go of the leash. "Get her, get her."

They ran past several compact cars then turned at a circular angle leading upward. Lexi had separated from them and was running hard. Tires screeched on concrete as a car backed out of its space. Lexi yelped. Valerie couldn't see her dog behind the car. Had she been hit?

In an instant, the roar of an engine surrounded Valerie. Terror invaded every muscle as headlights blinded her. She froze. Trevor's arms surrounded her, lifting her off her feet. Her body impacted with the hood of a car, and they rolled over the top and onto the concrete. Arianna's car screeched, taking a hard turn as it roared through the parking garage.

Arianna had used her one chance to kill Valerie and now she was focused on getting away.

Trevor helped her to her feet. "You all right?"

Lexi. She had to get to Lexi. Half stumbling and half running, she made her way up the ramp. Was her partner lying run over in a pool of blood? She couldn't see anything. Couldn't hear anything.

Yelping and barking some distance away reached her ears. Relief spread through her. Lexi was okay. The sound was coming from the exit to the parking garage. That dog never gave up the chase. Valerie and Trevor ran toward the sound of the barking. They found her at the exit to the parking garage, barking and pacing up and down the sidewalk.

Valerie scanned the street. Arianna's silver Mercedes was long gone, and Lexi was inconsolable. Valerie picked up the leash. "It's all right, girl. You did good."

Trevor touched her elbow. "You're sure you're okay?"

She nodded, barely comprehending what she'd just been through. "We lost her." She couldn't stop shaking. "I can't believe she got away." Her voice faltered.

"Hey." Trevor placed a comforting hand on her cheek. "We'll catch her. We know what the car looks like. We'll put an APB out."

The delayed reaction of what had happened finally kicked in. She'd almost died. Arianna would have crushed her under her tires like she was an insect.

Thank you, God, that I'm still alive.

She must have given her fear away in her body language. Lexi whined and looked up at her, growing agitated.

Trevor gathered her into his arms. "It's okay to be scared."

"She could have killed me just that fast if you hadn't reacted so quickly." The warmth of his arms surrounded her. Lexi pressed against her leg but didn't object to Trevor's hug.

He held her for a long moment. She rested against his chest. His breathing, the rise and fall of his chest, surrounded her. She closed her eyes until her own heart stopped racing and her resolve returned. Now she was mad about Arianna's getting away. "Where's that backup I called for, anyway?"

Valerie radioed in the details about Arianna's car as she looked back at the entrance of the parking garage. Her gaze traveled up and down the long street and to the surrounding side streets hoping to see some sign of the silver Mercedes. Several cars passed by, but there was no sign of Arianna's car. She was long gone.

Trevor looked back toward the apartment complex. "She had a suitcase with her. She must have been planning on leaving town."

"I wonder why?" Valerie wanted to believe that the Serpent leaving meant her life could return to normal. But it was too much to hope for. Arianna would probably just give her death orders from afar. Her fear fueled her desire to catch the Serpent. She could clearly identify her now. She wanted that woman behind bars.

Trevor placed his hand on Valerie's lower back. "Let's go find out what the neighbors know."

They walked back to the apartment complex. Valerie opened the back of the patrol car for Lexi. The dog moved slower than usual. The chase had worn her out. "Lexi is still recovering. I don't want to overwork her. I think I want to take her back home and let her rest up for the day."

Trevor nodded. "Sure, we can do that." He touched her arm lightly.

Valerie was still shaken from having nearly lost her life. The warmth of Trevor's touch smoothed over much of her anxiety. He seemed to instinctually know that she needed that sense of security his nearness evoked.

They entered the back parking lot. "If Arianna is the

girlfriend Murke told his half sister about, that links him to the syndicate," Valerie said.

Trevor nodded. "I can't help but think that big score he talked about is the same thing the syndicate is looking for in the Lost Woods, the reason they took Rio."

A man in the parking lot stood by his SUV, pulling out golf clubs.

Valerie walked over to him. "Excuse me, sir, do you live in this building?"

He was an older man with a deep tan and white hair. "That's right, third floor suite." He patted his clubs. "Love being so close to the golf course."

"Do you know the lady who lives on the fifth floor… Arianna Munson."

"I know her in passing, not a very friendly lady, though." The older man picked up one of his golf clubs and twirled it in his hand. "Kind of hard to start a conversation with her. Guess she owns a swanky diner downtown?"

"When was the last time you saw her?"

"Matter of fact—" the man put the golf club back in the bag "—I just saw her today right before I left to play a few holes."

Valerie's heart skipped a beat as she straightened her spine. "Really?"

"Sure, out here in the parking lot she was talking to a gentleman, and I tell you what, neither one of them looked none too happy."

Trevor cut a glance toward Valerie, lifting his eyebrows. He pulled the photo of Murke out of his chest pocket. "Is this the man you saw?"

The older man took the photo and stared at it for a

long moment, rubbing his chin. "Yeah, that was the feller."

Valerie's anticipation grew. They'd been that close to Murke. Their trail was hot again. "Could you tell what the conversation was about?"

"I was too far away to pick up any words, even though their voices were raised. If I had to venture a guess, I would say that Arianna lady seemed afraid. This guy—" he shook the photograph "—pointed his finger at her like he was demanding something from her. I'm tellin' ya, the lady looked really scared. Then he grabbed her arm. She got real quiet and said something that made him let go of her arm."

"How long ago would you say that was?"

The man wiped sweat from his forehead with the back of his hand and thought a moment. "I'd say an hour or two ago, I only played nine holes and there was hardly anybody else on the course."

"Thank you, sir, you've been a great help." Trevor patted the older man's shoulder.

"Always happy to lend a hand." He tilted his golf club bag, which was on wheels, and rolled it toward Merill Towers.

Valerie pieced together the information the man had given them. "Sounds like Arianna was leaving town to get away from Murke."

Trevor nodded. "I guess it's pretty clear that Murke is demanding something from Arianna, threatening her, even. He must have found the Serpent as soon as he escaped. His desperation is growing since we are getting so close to him."

"From the way our witness describes the interaction, Arianna said something to placate him," Valerie said. "Do you suppose she knows where this big score is that the syndicate has been after, or knows how to get it for him?"

Trevor scanned the parking lot. "I'd say it's a high probability."

Valerie was surprised that news about Arianna's car hadn't come across her radio yet. A fancy car like that would be easy enough to spot. "We're only a step or two behind Murke. We ought to be able to stir up something." She walked back to the patrol car where Lexi waited just as another police car pulled up. Jackson Worth got out. The black lab Titan sat nobly in the back-seat, his chin jutting up.

"Are you the backup I called for?" It wasn't like any of the Sagebrush police to ignore a call for back up, especially Jackson.

"There was a huge drug bust on the north side. All available units were called out. Otherwise, I would have gotten here faster," Jackson said. "You said you were trying to track down guys who deal guns to people with a record. One of the perps they brought in on this drug bust is Dwayne Wilson, aka Babyface. He's known for selling guns to criminals."

Valerie perked up. Hours of work in finding someone like Dwayne Wilson had just been shortened. "You think he might have sold those guns to Murke?"

"You can question him while he's in custody," Jackson said.

"Let's get down to the station." Trevor was halfway to the patrol car.

Valerie thanked Jackson. A sense of urgency sped up her steps to the patrol car. They were two hours behind

Murke in tracking him, and they knew the identity of Garry's murderer.

Once they were both inside, she started the patrol car and shifted into Reverse.

After dropping Lexi back off at the house, Valerie drove toward the station. As she pulled into the back parking lot, she couldn't help but feel that they were closing in.

FIFTEEN

Trevor stared at the door marked *Interview Room 2*. A mixture of excitement and anxiety twisted his stomach into a tight knot. They were so close to wrapping this case up. Murke had a link to the syndicate. Arianna and Serpent were one and the same.

Valerie returned from the vending machine holding the soda they would offer to Babyface, aka Dwayne Wilson, as a way of building trust. She had a file tucked under her arm.

"Why don't you take the lead on the questioning," Trevor suggested.

"Thanks!" Valerie said, appreciation evident in her tone.

She deserved it. Inside the interview room, Dwayne Wilson sat in a hardback chair, arms crossed and chin resting on his chest. He looked up when Valerie and Trevor entered.

His street name fit. He was a chubby-cheeked man with small beady eyes and a tuft of brown hair that stuck straight up.

Valerie sat the soda on the table and slid it toward

Dwayne. "Thought you might be thirsty." She took a seat while Trevor remained standing.

"I don't know why I'm even in here." Babyface tilted his chin toward the ceiling.

Valerie rested her elbows on the table and laced her fingers together. "Weren't you part of a drug bust, Dwayne?"

Babyface drew his thick eyebrows together. "I don't sell drugs. I don't do drugs."

"But you do sell guns, right?"

Trevor liked the way Valerie kept her tone neutral, even though she was making a strong accusation.

Dwayne touched his fingers to his chest. "I'm the victim here. I was in the wrong place at the wrong time, but I wasn't doing anything bad."

Valerie flipped through the file she had brought with her. "So are you saying you weren't in the middle of some kind of gun transaction when you were picked up?"

Babyface jerked in his seat. "I was just there for a social visit."

"Really?" Trevor rested his palms on the table and leaned toward Dwayne. "We're not the guys who can put you in prison, but we are the guys who might be able to get you a lighter sentence. You being a victim of circumstance and all."

Dwayne looked squarely at Trevor. "What do you need?"

"Derek Murke," Trevor said, his heart hammering at the mention of the name.

"Who?" Dwayne looked to one side as his shoulder twitched. Body language that indicated he was lying.

Valerie slid the photo of Murke across the table.

"Selling guns to a felon is pretty serious business, Dwayne."

Babyface pursed his rosebud lips and narrowed his eyes, but did not look at the photograph. He wasn't going to give in easily.

"I got to tell you, Dwayne. It doesn't look good that you were at that house with all those bad people," Trevor said.

Babyface swallowed, his Adam's apple moving up and down.

Valerie allowed for a long moment of silence, time for the man across the table to think about the charges he was facing. She flipped through the file she'd brought with her, which contained a litany of Dwayne's previous crimes. Sweat beaded on Dwayne's forehead as he looked Valerie in the eyes. The man was scared, that much was clear.

"I told you I'm not into drugs. The people at that house were in the market for some handguns. That's why I was there."

Valerie still didn't respond. She deliberately kept her face void of expression. Sometimes silence was a powerful tool.

Dwayne looked at the ceiling and let out a heavy breath. "Yeah, I know Murke."

She shifted in her chair. "Where is he staying?"

Though her voice remained even, Trevor detected a hurried quality that suggested she was as excited as he was about closing in on Murke.

Dwayne shook his head. "He's moving around a lot. I don't know." His gaze didn't waver.

Dwayne was telling the truth. Trevor's spirits deflated. Babyface wasn't going to lead them directly to Murke.

"What can you tell me about his connection to Arianna Munson?"

Valerie's questioning was tenacious and smart. He would have given up thinking Babyface could be of any use to them.

Dwayne leaned back in his chair. "She dumped him years ago and took a bunch of jewelry he had procured through illegal means. Every time I saw him he talked about getting back at her. He thinks she used the money from the jewelry to start that restaurant and make herself all respectable."

Dwayne seemed to relax a little. He was more comfortable talking about what Murke was up to than focusing on his own pending legal troubles.

"So how was he going to get back at Arianna? Is that what the gun was for?"

Dwayne shook his head. "He said the gun was to get some Fed off his back, so he'd have the freedom to tap into this big score that Arianna knew about. The way he had it figured, Arianna owed him money."

Trevor felt a tightening through his chest as his hand curled into a fist. He wasn't afraid of Murke, but it made him irate to think about how low the fugitive would stoop to get what he wanted.

Trevor pushed himself off the wall where he was leaning and moved back toward the table.

Dwayne took a sip from his soda can and licked his lips.

"When was the last time you saw Murke?" Trevor continued to watch Dwayne's body language.

Dwayne shook his head. "I haven't seen him for a

couple of days…not since I sold him the guns." He sat up straighter in his chair. "So am I free to go?"

"Not quite, but we will put in a good word for you." Valerie pushed her chair back and grabbed the file.

After they left the interrogation room, Valerie turned toward Trevor. "That narrows it down. The guns were probably to get rid of you. He's not planning some kind of robbery spree. This score he's talking about has to be the same one the syndicate is looking for, whatever it is that is hidden out in the Lost Woods."

"I just wonder what kind of information Arianna gave him. Where's he going to go next?"

Valerie shook her head. "Something Arianna would have access to or something he thinks she has access to."

"Do you suppose Murke knew Arianna was the Serpent?"

"I think he must have figured it out. Maybe that's why she was scared. She was afraid he'd blow the whistle on her," Trevor said.

Jackson came up to them outside the interrogation room. "Valerie, we just got a call that Arianna's Mercedes was found abandoned on the edge of town."

"No sign of Arianna?" Valerie's voice trembled slightly.

Jackson shook his head. "Woman like that probably has lots of resources. Somebody could have picked her up."

Valerie pulled a strand of red hair behind her ear. "The question is…did she get out of town or is she still hiding somewhere in the city?" Valerie looked up at Trevor.

She didn't need to say anything more. The fear in

her eyes said it all. Whether Arianna was still in town or halfway around the world, she could still direct her thugs to take out Valerie. Now that Arianna knew that she'd been named as the Serpent, things were only going to get worse. Valerie had probably hoped for news that Arianna had been picked up and put in jail. Short of death, nothing else would make the Serpent back off.

"Also, Trevor, they towed your car in and replaced the tire." Jackson excused himself and headed back toward the desk.

Trevor checked his watch. "You're off duty in twenty minutes. I'll follow you home." His heart ached for her. He would do anything for her to feel like she was safe again.

Valerie nodded. "I just got some paperwork I need to finish up."

Half an hour later, Trevor kept an eye on the taillights of Valerie's compact car as they headed toward her place. Their lives seemed to have fallen into a routine of him escorting her home after her shift and waiting for her protection to show up. Despite the apparent safety of routine, their encounter with Arianna was a bleak reminder that Valerie was far from safe.

A black van edged between Valerie and Trevor's car. He couldn't see around it. Traffic was too heavy to move out into the passing lane. Not having a view of her car made him nervous.

As they passed a side street, the van turned off. He breathed a sigh of relief until he looked ahead. Valerie was no longer in front of him. He checked the rearview mirror and caught a flash of red. Valerie had turned off on a street that wouldn't take her home, and the van was following her. Valerie must have suspected the van was tailing her and was trying to lose him.

Trying not to panic, he hit his blinker and turned as soon as he could. He'd have to circle back and search for them on a side street. His phone rang.

Valerie didn't wait for pleasantries. "He's following me." The strain in her voice was evident even over the phone.

Trevor's pulse raced as he gripped the phone. "I know. I'll get there as fast as I can."

"I'm parking on Sagebrush Boulevard," she said. "I'm going to get out."

"Val, wait." He wasn't so sure getting out of the vehicle was the best option.

He heard a door slam. Her words came in breathless gasps. She must be running up the street. "He has a gun. I saw him lift and aim it through the windshield when we were in traffic. That's why I turned off. There's lots of people here. I don't want to risk harming them by shooting this guy. I can hide in the crowd."

He scanned the street name as he passed it. Sagebrush Boulevard had to be close.

"I'm at this outdoor café." Her words came in a harsh whisper. "He just pulled up across the street. I'm at a back table. I don't think he can see me."

Trevor saw the sign that indicated Sagebrush Boulevard and turned off. He pressed the phone against his ear. He passed her little red car, but couldn't spot her. There were no parking spaces left. He was going to have to park on the next street. He pressed the phone hard against his ear. "Valerie?" He pulled into a space and climbed out of his sedan.

"He got out of the van. Trevor, he's walking this way."

Her voice quivered with fear. Desperate to get to her before it was too late, Trevor raced around the block and pushed through the crowds on the street. He saw two outdoor cafés on opposite sides of the street. He passed the first café. No sign of Valerie. He spotted the black van but not the would-be assailant. He must be concealing his gun in a coat or something.

Loud mariachi music poured from a Mexican restaurant as he approached the second café. Valerie was seated close to the entrance, hiding behind a menu. He recognized her shoes.

When he scanned the crowd on the street, he located the large man with dark hair. The same man who had tried to shoot Valerie at the construction site. Trevor slipped into a store entrance as the man passed by. The man walked up the street past the café.

Trevor crouched low and edged toward where Valerie was seated. The assailant was headed up the street toward her car.

"Valerie, come on," Trevor rasped out.

He grabbed her hand and pulled her behind a crowd of people. He whispered in her ear. "He's headed up the street. We can't get to your car, but we might be able to get to mine."

It was only a matter of time before the thug turned around and started looking closer at the people on the street. The crowd cleared, and Trevor directed her toward the door of an open shop.

When he glanced over his shoulder, the assailant had turned back and was headed toward them. Recognition spread across the man's face before Trevor could duck. Hatred filled his eyes as he pushed people through the crowd, making a beeline for them.

The doors of the Mexican restaurant burst open, and revelers, complete with a mariachi band, spilled out into the street, blocking the assailant's direct path to them.

Trevor shielded Valerie as they worked their way up the street. With this many people, the sniper could shoot Valerie at point-blank range and become a face in the crowd before she hit the pavement.

Valerie pressed close to him, her arm wrapped around his waist. The thug's head towered above the others.

"This way." He held her close, directing her into an art gallery.

A college-age woman with blond spiky hair approached them in the brightly lit space. "May I help you?"

"I'm a federal agent and this woman is in danger." Trevor flashed his I.D.

"Oh, my." The woman's hand fluttered to her chest.

"Is there a back entrance we can use?" In his head, he could hear the clock ticking. How long before the assailant figured out where they had gone?

The woman shook her head.

"A window we can crawl out of?"

She pointed toward the back of the gallery. "In the storage room."

"If a big brutish man comes in here, pretend you never saw us, please," Trevor said.

He was pretty sure the clerk would be unharmed. The sniper wouldn't risk getting caught unless it meant getting his target. The woman nodded. The bell that indicated someone entering the store dinged just as Trevor closed the door to the storage room. He pushed the knob in on the door, locking it.

He could hear the shop clerk talking in that polite tone, her voice elevated slightly with fear. The thug was in the shop.

The storage room contained canvases and frames, an antique desk piled with papers and a laptop. The window was small and situated high up.

Outside the door, the woman spoke more rapidly. Trevor heard a low guttural male grunt. The man's words were indiscernible but demanding in tone.

Valerie pushed a wooden chair toward the window and flipped it open. She'd slip through fine, but it would be a tight fit for him. He boosted her up.

The doorknob shook.

"Sir, you can't go back there. That's private." Though there was an attempt at calm, the shopkeeper's voice had become more agitated.

Valerie's feet disappeared. Trevor stepped onto the chair and pulled himself up to the windowsill.

The thug pounded on the door and shook the knob again. "Get the key," he demanded.

Trevor pushed through the window, stretching out his hands so his head wouldn't hit the sidewalk. Inside, the door opened on squeaky hinges.

"See, sir, there is nobody in here," the clerk said.

On the street, Valerie helped him to his feet. He had expected to end up in an alley, but instead the street featured more shops with smaller crowds. Several people stopped to stare at him as he brushed the dust from his pants.

Trevor grabbed Valerie at the elbow. "We owe that lady a big thank you."

"At least." Valerie let out a heavy sigh, agitation evident in her expression as she pressed her lips together. "What now?"

She was shaken by what had just happened. He grabbed her hand and held it, hoping to calm her.

"We can get to my car without being spotted." Trevor stepped forward, still holding on to her hand. "We'll have to make arrangements for your car to be picked up later."

Valerie looked up and down the street. "I have a couple of friends I can call. They'll come by for the key and bring the car back."

"We better hurry. This guy is dedicated. I'm sure he's still combing the streets." Trevor glanced down at her. "Walk fast, but don't draw attention to yourself by running."

Trevor was grateful he had had to park on a side street, otherwise they'd still be evading the Serpent's thug. He opened the passenger-side door for Valerie, scanning the surrounding street as he walked over to the driver's side.

He phoned in to the police station with a description of the man who had chased him and Valerie. Maybe the Sagebrush P.D. could catch him.

Valerie was silent on the drive home. She stared out the window without focusing on anything. He knew that look, an emotional exhaustion was setting in for her. He'd seen it on witnesses he'd been assigned to protect. The constant barrage from every angle by the Serpent's henchmen was wearing on her.

When they got to her home, her nighttime protection had already pulled into place by the curb.

Maybe the policeman outside could protect her physically, but she was being worn down emotionally, as well. Trevor scrambled to make an excuse to be with her until she was on stronger footing. "I'll stay with you until your car gets here."

Her expression softened as gratitude filled her voice. "That would be nice. I can fix you some dinner."

Trevor waved at the cop on duty as they walked past him and entered Valerie's house. The heaviness that pressed down her shoulders seemed to lift when Valerie saw Bethany. The little girl toddled toward her mother, arms lifted up.

Mrs. Witherspoon rose from the couch where she had been stacking blocks on the coffee table with Bethany. "She's always so glad to see you."

Valerie nestled close to Bethany as her tiny hands wrapped around her neck. As always, Lexi greeted Valerie by wagging her bobbed tail and licking her owner's hand.

"Poor dog slept most of the day," said Mrs. Witherspoon. "You were smart to bring her home."

Lexi resumed her post in the corner keeping watch, lifting her head slightly to each movement the people around her made. The dog had never greeted him when he had come into Valerie's place. Though Lexi was not openly hostile toward him, she seemed to be reserving judgment on him for now.

Valerie thanked Mrs. Witherspoon. The older woman left after giving Valerie a hug.

She turned to face him. "I hope you like grilled chicken and a big salad because that's what is on the menu."

"Sounds great," said Trevor.

"Can you keep an eye on Bethany while I work in the kitchen?"

Trevor settled down on the couch. Lexi moved to her bed in the living room, which provided her a better angle to watch Trevor.

Valerie handed Bethany a cup with a lid before moving to the kitchen.

Trevor held up one of the blocks toward Bethany. "You want to play?" He stacked one block on top of the other. Bethany watched him for a moment before retreating to the dog bed where Lexi had settled. She used the dog as a back rest while she drank from her sippie cup.

A moment later, Valerie came into the living room and swept Bethany into her arms. As she made her way back to the kitchen, bouncing Bethany and singing to her, Lexi rose to her feet and followed them.

Trevor sat in the living room alone. He heard the back door slide open. Valerie must have stepped out to grill the chicken. He walked to the open door where Valerie had started the barbecue. Lexi and Bethany lingered on the patio. Bethany balanced against a lawn chair while Lexi sniffed the perimeter of the yard, her bobbed tail swinging like a metronome.

The Serpent had managed once to get into Valerie's yard; she might try again. He peered over her fence at the surrounding backyards.

After placing the chicken on the barbecue, she looked up at him. Weariness marked her features; her eyes lacked that sparkle that he loved. What he wouldn't give for the light to return to her eyes, to see her smile and hear her laughter.

As Valerie sat in the lawn chair and gathered Bethany into her arms, Lexi stopped her patrol and settled down on the patio beside them. Bethany crawled out of her lap, wrapped her arms around Lexi's thick neck and kissed her. Valerie leaned forward to stroke the dog's head. They had become a tight cohesive unit— Valerie, Bethany and Lexi. Each of them looking out for the other.

Neither one of them had said anything about the attempt on her life less than an hour ago. Yet that reality hung in the air like a thick fog.

If they could make it through this, there would come a time when Valerie's life was no longer in danger. Things would return to normal for her. She could take Bethany to the park without fear.

As he watched Valerie slip down to the patio to talk to Bethany and stroke Lexi's ears, he wondered if there was room in their world for him after she no longer needed his protection.

Even as Valerie rose to her feet to turn the chicken, he sensed the chasm in his own heart. She deserved better than him. Someone who understood the meaning of happy family.

She touched his hand lightly on her way back to where Bethany was nestled against Lexi. He felt a stirring deep inside, an overwhelming longing stabbed at his gut. These three females had been what he had been searching for all his life, but was there room in their world for him?

SIXTEEN

Valerie awoke to the sound of her phone ringing beside her bed. Struggling to get past the fog of sleep, she flipped open her phone. "Hello." Her voice sounded like she'd been eating gravel. She cleared her throat.

"Valerie, it's Trevor. Looks like Babyface is willing to squeal on Murke if he thinks it will reduce his own charges. He heard through the grapevine that Murke was eating at a truck stop outside of town last night. Maybe he'll come back." He paused. "Officer Worth and I are heading down there now to ask some questions and watch the place a while. I'll catch up with you at the station when you get on duty."

She looked at the clock. She had over two hours before she needed to be at the station. "Okay, sure."

"Have your nighttime protection follow you to the station. Let's not take any chances."

Valerie took in a deep breath. "Yes, I will." She pressed the phone against her ear. "Did any of the officers have any word on Arianna's whereabouts?"

"You know I would tell you the second I heard anything."

Her throat tightened as she fought back frustration.

"I know." What if Arianna had left town and would never be caught? "Guess I was just looking for a little hope to hang on to that all of this will soon be over."

She said goodbye and hung up, rolling over on her side and pulling the covers up to her neck as she prayed for a sense of peace even though the Serpent was still not in custody.

Bethany slept on her belly in the crib. Her sweet face turned toward Valerie. She'd gotten through the entire night without waking or fussing, a victory and a sign that she was adjusting to her new life. Lexi slept protectively beside Bethany's crib, a sure sign that Lexi had bonded with Bethany.

Valerie rose from bed, showered and dressed and was ready to go by the time Mrs. Witherspoon knocked on the door. Bethany was up and sitting on the couch with her sippie cup. She clutched her pink rabbit in the crook of her elbow.

Valerie kissed her soft head. "See you in a little while, my sweet princess."

The drive to the station was uneventful. She finished up paperwork from the day before and checked the clock. She couldn't wait any longer to go out on patrol. Her neighborhood needed her. Trevor would just have to catch up with her on the street.

Captain McNeal caught her on the way out the door. "Where's Agent Lewis this morning?"

"He had a lead on Murke he had to take," Valerie said. "I think I'm ready to go back out on patrol."

Concern etched across McNeal's face.

"I'll be all right," she assured. "Lexi is coming with me. Trevor should be done shortly."

"There is a patrol car three blocks away from your

regular beat following up some house burglaries. They're canvassing the neighborhood so they should be there for a couple of hours."

McNeal never stopped thinking about the safety of his officers. He was one of the reasons she was so proud to be on the Sagebrush force.

She knew McNeal had been torn up about not being able to protect his own father when Rio had been kidnapped. "How's your dad doing by the way?"

McNeal offered her a quick smile. "He's coming around since he woke up from his coma."

"That's good to hear." She headed out to her patrol car.

Not wanting to interrupt him if he was on surveillance, Valerie texted Trevor, advising him of the neighborhood she'd be patrolling for the next few hours.

The day was sunny and clear as she parked her car and prepared to patrol on foot. She opened the back door for Lexi. The number of children playing on lawns suggested that it must be a school holiday.

Several children came up to greet her and pet Lexi. The dog relished the attention, her little bobbed tail vibrating at a furious rate. She'd taken Lexi for talks at the local schools and all the kids knew her. Lexi seemed more energetic, more like herself.

Jessie Lynn rode up on her bike, her light brown hair catching glints of sunlight. She'd attached metallic streamers to her handlebars. Several children rode behind her.

"Officer Salgado." She braked, her eyes wide with excitement.

"You got your bike looking pretty spiffy there, Jessie Lynn," Valerie said.

A second child, a boy of about six, came up on a

bike and stopped behind Jessie Lynn. Two more children stopped, as well. All of them looking up at Valerie.

"What's going on here, kids?"

Jessie Lynn, the official spokesperson for the group, gripped her handlebars. "Are you still looking for that police dog that was stolen?"

"You mean Rio?"

"We saw a dog just like him over by the old auto shop." The boy pointed over his shoulder.

"Yeah, it was a German shepherd," said another child.

All the children nodded in unison before a third one added, "It was all mean and scary-looking."

"It wasn't mean." Jessie Lynn put her hand on her hip. "We saw him from far away."

"Yeah, we saw him running," a chubby-cheeked little boy said.

"He was running toward the old auto repair place?"

"Like sniffing around it," another child piped in.

Valerie listened intently. Could this be Rio? "Was there a person with him?"

All the children shook their heads in unison.

"All by himself," added the chubby-cheeked boy.

"I'll check it out. Thanks, kids." Valerie jogged down the street with Lexi taking up the lead. The old auto shop building was one of the abandoned warehouses in the area where she and Trevor had first spotted Derek Murke.

So much had changed since that first morning. Trevor's aloofness because of her rookie status was no longer an issue. He seemed to respect the work Lexi did. Yet, there was still some part of Trevor that held back. She'd noticed it last night at dinner.

The bike convoy of children followed her to the end of the block.

As excited as the band of junior detectives were, she couldn't put them in any danger. "Why don't you kids wait here?" As if on cue, four sets of shoulders drooped and heads bent in disappointment. "I'll let you know if I find anything." She turned a corner and headed up the street.

Strange that Trevor hadn't called her yet in response to her text, or showed up. If Murke was going to show at that truck stop, he should have been there by now. Maybe Trevor and Jackson had caught up with him and he'd run again. She felt a twinge of regret at not being able to be there when Murke was finally apprehended.

She approached the warehouse with caution. The kids had said the dog was roaming free, but that didn't mean that some member of the syndicate wasn't close by. She radioed dispatch to let them know she might need assistance. If this dog was Rio, it was possible that he had served his purpose for the syndicate and had been turned loose.

She pulled her flashlight off her utility belt and entered the warehouse. The shell of an old truck—tires missing and doors torn off—rested in the middle of the concrete floor.

Lexi hadn't alerted to anything. If there was another dog in the proximity, she would have smelled it. Lexi licked her chops and whined when Valerie looked down at her.

"Nothing, huh?"

She walked the interior perimeter of the shop. There were plenty of busted-out windows and a back door where the dog the children had seen could have gotten out.

She stepped out into the sunlight. Her cell phone rang. She clicked it on, expecting it to be Trevor.

"Hello."

Silence on the other end of the line and then the line went dead. Valerie clicked through to see what number had dialed her. A sense of apprehension crept in when she saw that it was Mrs. Witherspoon's cell number.

She dialed the number, pressing the phone hard against her ear. It went immediately to message. Had something happened to Mrs. Witherspoon? She wasn't a young woman. What if she was having a heart attack and Bethany was alone in the house? Valerie quelled the rising panic with a deep breath.

She didn't know anything yet for sure. Even as she tried to convince herself that her fear was unwarranted, thoughts of the threat that had been made against Bethany only days ago overwhelmed her.

Lexi stirred at her feet and looked up at her.

The phone rang so suddenly, she nearly dropped it. She pressed the receive button expecting to hear Mrs. Witherspoon's chirpy voice.

"Valerie?"

Normally, Trevor's voice would have brought a sense of relief, but not this time.

"Oh, Trevor." She still couldn't let go of her fear.

"Listen, I don't think Murke is going to show. I got your text. Where is your patrol car at right now?"

"I'm not too far from the warehouse district where we first saw Murke."

"Is everything okay? You sound upset."

Invisible weight pressed on her heart. "Trevor, I... think I'm going to drive back home real quick." She wouldn't be able to let go of this distress until she saw that Bethany and Mrs. Witherspoon were safe and sound.

"What's going on?"

"It's just… I'm worried about Bethany. I need to check on her. It's probably nothing, but Mrs. Witherspoon called and hung up…and now she's not answering her phone at all."

"I'll meet you over there," Trevor said, concern saturating his voice.

"It might be nothing…" said Valerie.

"We can't take that kind of a chance with Bethany, can we?" Trevor said.

"No, we can't." She liked the way he used the word *we* and how willing he was to drop everything just to check on Bethany.

Valerie left the abandoned auto shop and stepped out onto the street. Lexi's ears perked up as her attention was drawn up the block. A black dog crawled out from underneath a pile of old tires and rubble.

To the trained eye, the dog was clearly not a German shepherd. But children eager to help her find Rio could have easily made such a mistake. The dog offered them a passing glance as it slinked away.

Valerie jogged back to the patrol car, stashed Lexi in the back and slid into the driver's seat. As she pulled away from the curb, she glanced in the rearview mirror at a woman pushing a baby carriage up the sidewalk. Anxiety twisted her stomach into knots.

The car gained speed and she prayed that Mrs. Witherspoon and her precious Bethany were okay.

Rising tension bunched the muscles at the back of Trevor's neck. Traffic moved at a snail's pace as the streets filled up with commuters. He never should have separated from Valerie. If he had just stayed with her, they could have gone back to her house together.

He and Jackson had staked out the truck stop for over three hours. The only good thing that had made the morning not a total waste of time was that one of the waitresses had remembered serving Murke the night before. If this was Murke's new favorite hangout, they'd catch up with him soon enough.

His thoughts drifted back to Valerie. While Lexi provided some protection, he didn't like the idea of her being in the patrol car alone after what had happened last night. The dog would be no help at all if someone decided to run Valerie off the road.

Three cars behind him, Jackson Worth sat in his patrol car with his dog Titan. He had offered to go with Trevor to check on Valerie and Bethany.

The cars came to a complete halt behind a red light. The traffic was so backed up in this part of town, it would be several light changes before he even got through the intersection.

Valerie had sounded so afraid over the phone. His longing to be with her and comfort her made him want to jump out of the car and run the rest of the way to her house.

He gripped the steering wheel. Of course that wasn't rational. Even with the cars moving as slowly as they were, he couldn't run the mile or so to her house faster than driving.

Trevor shook his head. He'd had lots of irrational thoughts like that in the days since he'd met Valerie.

He had always thought of himself as a guy with two feet planted solidly on the ground, a reasoned and dependable problem solver. Not so, when it came to Valerie.

He gripped the steering wheel with clammy palms. If anything had happened to Bethany…

Valerie hadn't said anything on the phone, but when she had suggested that Mrs. Witherspoon might not be okay, the first thought he had was of the Serpent.

His stomach clenched.

He looked out the window at the clear blue sky. The concern could be over nothing, too. Maybe Mrs. Witherspoon had just dropped her phone and couldn't get to it.

He glared at the red light, willing it to change.

Valerie pulled up to the curb of her house and jumped out of the patrol car, opening the back door so Lexi could get out, as well. No strange cars were parked on the street. The neighborhood was quiet. Unlike the neighborhood she patrolled, this area of town had mostly working couples without children, and senior citizens.

Only the sound of sprinklers and a car pulling into Mrs. Witherspoon's apartment building parking lot disturbed the silence.

On her drive over, she had tried Mrs. Witherspoon's phone number several more times. Each time the call went to message, the weight on her chest increased until she felt like she couldn't breathe at all.

Lexi's feet tapped on the sidewalk as they made their way toward her front door. Valerie twisted the doorknob and stepped inside.

"Hello, Mrs. Witherspoon? It's me, Valerie."

The ceiling fan twisted above her, making a slight whirring sound.

Valerie's throat constricted as her heartbeat drummed in her ears. "Mrs. Witherspoon?" Her voice cracked. "Beth—any?"

From this angle, it didn't look like anyone was in the kitchen. Still, the hair on the back of her neck stood up. Bethany's stroller was by the door. Mrs. Witherspoon hadn't stepped out with her.

She walked toward the sliding glass doors with Lexi trailing behind her. The dog stopped suddenly and made a noise that was somewhere between a whine and a growl.

Bethany's bottle was on the counter, and there was a pot on the stove with steam rising out of it. Valerie ran around the island. Mrs. Witherspoon lay crumbled on the floor, not moving. Had she had a heart attack?

As she kneeled to check for a pulse, Valerie's mind raced at lightning speed. Where was Bethany? Mrs. Witherspoon was alive but unresponsive.

Valerie rose to her feet, intending to look for Bethany. Her finger touched her shoulder mic as she prepared to call for an ambulance for Mrs. Witherspoon when she noticed the sliding glass door to the patio was open. Valerie commanded Lexi to search the yard. A woman stepped out from behind her patio curtains and slid it shut, trapping Lexi outside. The woman ran toward Valerie.

Valerie had only a second to register that it was Arianna holding a canister of something. The Serpent lifted her hand and sprayed Valerie's face. The sting was instantaneous. Her nose and eyes felt like they were on fire.

She heard Lexi scratching frantically at the patio door. Her bark was muffled by the glass.

Unable to breathe and with limited vision, Valerie reached for her gun even as she reeled backward toward the island.

"Oh, no, you don't." Arianna grabbed her hand and twisted it, trying to pull the gun free.

Her eyelids felt like they had hot acid poured on them. She closed her eyes against the pain. She held on to the gun while Arianna clawed at her arm.

Arianna grabbed Valerie's shoulder mic, ripped it off and threw it against a wall.

Behind her, she could hear the pot boiling. She reached back for it and flung it toward where she thought Arianna was.

She was rewarded with a blood-curdling screech. Hot water sprayed across her arm, as well, and she let go of the gun involuntarily. She heard it hit the floor, but couldn't see where it landed.

As she struggled to orient herself with limited vision, Arianna grabbed her by the hair and dragged her across the room. Valerie tried to twist free. The swelling inside her mouth and nose made it hard to breathe. Arianna pushed Valerie to the floor and bound her hands and feet with what felt like a scarf. She could barely keep her eyes open from the pain.

As she listened to Lexi's frantic barks outside, Valerie's anger intensified. She could not give up. All she had to do was stay alive until Trevor got here.

"What have you done with Bethany?" Her voice didn't even sound like her, filled with agony and terror.

"The same thing I am going to do to you," Arianna retorted.

Terror collided with her resolve at every turn. She

would not let herself think about what might have happened to Bethany. "They will catch you."

"Fires are accidents, my dear, and that is what this is going to look like." Arianna spat out her words.

The Serpent's voice chilled Valerie to the bone. An image flashed through Valerie's head. Arianna had been wearing gloves when she stepped from behind the curtain. Even if anything from the fire survived, there would be no evidence that Arianna had ever been here. Valerie had been lured here. It was probably Arianna who had made the phone call after knocking out Mrs. Witherspoon.

Arianna patted Valerie's bound hands. "Don't worry. Those will come off once the fire gets going. We don't want any signs of foul play, and I have a way of making sure you don't escape the fire." When Arianna stood close, Valerie could see where the hot water had burned the Serpent's arm. Her shoulder was soaked with water, as well.

The Serpent's voice grew a bit more distant as her heels tapped back into the kitchen and Valerie could hear her moving around in that room. "Your foolish old housekeeper left the stove on and it caught on fire. You came home and tried to stop the fire, but were overcome by smoke inhalation."

In the living room, Valerie struggled to break free of her bindings. Her instinct was to close her eyes against the pain from the pepper spray, but she forced them open. Every time the Serpent turned her back or looked away she wiggled her feet, loosening the bindings.

Arianna poured oil on a dishrag, turned the flame up on the gas stove and set the rag beside it. Flames shot up from the stove.

"I have fellow officers coming."

"Sure you do." As the flames spread across the countertop, Arianna poured more oil and added newspapers and magazines to the growing fire.

"They will be here any minute," Valerie said.

Arianna cackled.

What was keeping Trevor and Jackson, anyway? They should have been here by now. She had to hold on.

Though she held her feet together to make it look like she was still bound, all she had to do was slip out of the loose restraints. Her hands were tied more tightly behind her back. She pulled the fabric and twisted her hands to loosen the restraints.

Arianna retrieved her purse and pulled out a hypodermic needle.

Valerie had a feeling it contained the same drug that had been used on Lexi a few nights ago. If she was not able to move, it would indeed look like she had come through the door and been overcome by smoke inhalation. The flames on the countertop grew higher as the room filled with smoke.

Arianna moved toward her with the needle pointing straight up. Valerie could see her gun sitting on a chair by the island. The flames had engulfed most of the island as bits of burning debris fell to the floor.

On the other side of the island, Mrs. Witherspoon coughed. Would she wake up in time?

Valerie's vision was still fuzzy as though petroleum jelly was smeared across her eyes. Arianna drew closer.

She had to wait for the exact moment to pounce on Arianna. Too soon, and the Serpent would have time to move away. Too late and the needle would be embedded in her flesh, poison sinking in and paralyzing her.

Still standing, Arianna lifted the needle. Valerie had expected her to kneel on the floor beside her. Valerie worked free of her loose bindings and scooted away as Arianna brought the needle down toward her shoulder.

She grabbed Arianna's foot, pulling her off balance. Arianna crashed to the floor, but didn't drop the needle. Arianna lunged toward Valerie, but she angled out of the way and scrambled across the floor toward the gun.

Though her eyes still stung, her vision started to clear.

Arianna grabbed her foot. The grip was like an iron claw around her ankle. Valerie flipped back over and kicked Arianna, landing a blow to her burned shoulder. Arianna let go of her. Valerie coughed from the accumulating smoke as she ran to grab the gun by the island. Mrs. Witherspoon groaned and coughed. She must be coming to.

Lexi howled at the sliding glass door.

Valerie wrapped her fingers around the gun. Arianna pounced on her. The gun flew out of her hand. The two women scrambled across the floor toward the gun.

A stack of magazines by the kitchen island caught fire. The smoke thickened.

Arianna retrieved the gun and jumped to her feet. She pointed the gun at Valerie, who was still on her knees.

"Fine. I'll shoot you if that's the way you want it." She lifted the gun and took aim.

Valerie's breath caught as she stared down the barrel of the gun. What would happen to Bethany if she wasn't around to take care of her? Where was she now?

Lord, keep her safe. Whatever happens to me, keep that little girl safe.

Arianna's lips curled into a sneer. She put her finger on the trigger.

Trevor burst through the door with Jackson on his heels. He fired two shots. Arianna slumped to the floor.

Jackson kneeled on the floor beside the dying woman. He leaned close to the Serpent while she whispered something to him. Her body went limp and motionless. He called for an ambulance and then grabbed a wool throw from the living room and began to swat at the fire.

Trevor gathered Valerie into his arms.

Valerie was shaking uncontrollably. She clung to Trevor while her heart pounded against her rib cage and her thoughts raced at lightning speed. "I need to find Bethany. I need to find my daughter."

Trevor let her go and rushed over to put the fire out. "Get out of the house."

Valerie stumbled toward the stairs. "I have to find Bethany." She still couldn't see clearly. She reached out for the banister which guided her to the top of the stairs. She held a hand out and pushed open the door of her bedroom.

Bethany lay in her bed. As Valerie drew close, Bethany did not stir or cry out.

Valerie fell to her knees, weeping and shaking. She heard the shrill scream of ambulances and fire trucks growing louder.

SEVENTEEN

Though his first instinct was to follow Valerie up the stairs, Trevor helped Jackson subdue the flames that were spreading across the kitchen counter. His gut twisted from thinking about what might have happened to Bethany.

Arianna lay prone and lifeless on the floor. When Trevor came around the island, he saw Mrs. Witherspoon on the kitchen floor. He kneeled. The older woman still had a pulse. He lifted her up and carried her outside.

Lexi howled and barked, clawing at the door.

Trevor found himself longing to be with Valerie. Was Bethany upstairs? Was she safe or had the syndicate made good on their threat and harmed her? His heart ached over the possibility.

"We need to get everybody out of here." Jackson opened doors and windows as the ambulance and fire truck sirens wailed through the city, growing louder and closer.

Trevor raced up the stairs. He found Valerie on the floor of her bedroom clinging to Bethany. The little girl was motionless in her arms.

His chest squeezed tight. "Is she...?" He couldn't say the words, his throat tightened with pent-up anguish.

Valerie looked up at him. Her green eyes glazed with tears.

Bethany lifted her head off Valerie's shoulder and turned to look at Trevor.

"She's all right." Valerie's voice faltered. "She slept through the whole thing."

A flood of love and joy that he had never known before brought tears to Trevor's eyes. He wrapped Valerie and Bethany in his arms. They were safe.

He couldn't imagine life without the two of them. He didn't know what he was to Valerie. His feelings for her were stronger than ever, but what did she think of him?

Valerie's eyes were swollen. He could see the effects of pepper spray.

"We need to get you ladies downstairs and outside until the smoke clears." He led the two of them downstairs.

When they got downstairs, Arianna's body was being loaded onto a stretcher.

Trevor helped Valerie over to the ambulance where Mrs. Witherspoon had come to. The older woman held an oxygen mask to her face and had a blanket around her shoulders. She greeted Bethany and Valerie with a fierce hug.

Valerie repeated over and over, "I'm so glad you're okay."

Trevor spoke to one of the EMTs. "Valerie was sprayed with pepper spray."

"The effects will wear off in about forty-five minutes." The EMT rose to his feet and opened a drawer in the back of the ambulance. "I have some drops to help cleanse your eyes."

He took the drops from the EMT. "Valerie, I got something for your eyes."

Valerie handed Bethany over to Mrs. Witherspoon and turned toward him. "Thank you. They're still stinging."

She tilted her head back. Standing close to her, he touched her cheek and put the drops in. She bent her head and blinked.

"Better?"

She nodded.

Lexi came bounding around the house. Someone must have let her out of the backyard. She ran past Trevor, not even seeing him.

As Valerie kneeled beside him and spoke soothingly to the dog, he realized that was the bottom line. Even if Bethany and Valerie would welcome him into their lives, the dog didn't totally trust him. Lexi would do the job she was trained to do, but she had not given any indication that she had bonded to Trevor. She tolerated his presence because she was such a well-behaved dog, but he was still an outsider to her.

Valerie stroked the dog's face and ears. "Poor girl, I know you wanted to help me." The dog licked Valerie's face.

Gradually, the crowd dispersed and the ambulance took Arianna's body away. The fire department allowed Valerie to return to her house to get a few things. They advised her to find somewhere else to live until the smoke damage could be taken care of.

"Why don't you stay with me tonight, dear?" Mrs. Witherspoon said.

"I think we will do that." She turned and looked at Trevor. "After that I can probably stay with my folks or one of my brothers since Arianna is no longer a threat." Her soft, sweet voice radiated gratitude. "Thanks for coming to my rescue."

"I just did what any officer would have done," Trevor said.

She linked her arm through his. "You saved my life."

"Trevor, why don't you come in and have something to eat with us?" Mrs. Witherspoon ushered him toward her apartment. "You all could probably use a little break."

Valerie pleaded with her eyes. "Stay a while."

Trevor shrugged. As much as he loved his work, he'd rather be with Valerie and Bethany any day.

As they walked back to Mrs. Witherspoon's apartment, there was something different in Valerie's demeanor. She seemed to hold her head a little higher as though a burden had been lifted off her shoulders. Her life was no longer in danger.

Though the need to catch Murke still loomed large, he felt a sense of relief, too. They spent the afternoon baking cookies with Stella and Bethany.

Trevor could have almost fooled himself into believing that they were an ordinary family spending the day together until his phone rang.

Trevor recognized McNeal's number.

The captain spoke in rapid-fire manner. "We just got a call. A man matching Murke's description has broken into a woman's house and is holding her hostage. The SWAT team is always deployed in a hostage situation, but you and Valerie should take the lead on this."

"We can do that," Trevor said. He got the address

from McNeal and hung up. He summarized what McNeal had told him and then added, "You can go if you feel up to it. You've been through a lot today."

Valerie looked over at Mrs. Witherspoon who said, "You go. Do your job. I can watch Bethany."

Valerie's gaze was intense and unwavering. "You helped me take down the Serpent. I want to be the one who helps you get Murke."

In the short time they'd been working together, she'd changed a great deal from a rookie to a confident police officer. There was no one else he would rather take this call with than her.

Lexi rose to her feet. "I think she's ready to go, too," Valerie said.

Trevor touched Valerie's arm. "Let's go get him."

Once they were in the patrol car and speeding across town, Valerie radioed in to dispatch for more details while Trevor drove.

"The woman has locked herself in the closet…and she told us she's three months pregnant." The female voice from dispatch offered the last little bit of information in a neutral tone.

Valerie's gaze flitted toward Trevor. A hostage situation was dangerous enough. Now there were two lives at risk.

Valerie swallowed to push down some of her anxiety and keyed the radio. "Does this hostage have a name?"

"Her name is Nicki. Nicki Johnson."

"Thanks. Keep us advised." Valerie put the radio back in its slot.

Trevor turned onto the street that led out of town to the Lost Woods where Nicki's apartment building was.

"We'll just have to make sure Nicki and her baby get out unharmed."

Lexi paced in the backseat ready to go to work. Valerie felt a fluttering in her stomach, a mixture of excitement and fear. Beneath the surface emotion, there was a deeper resolve. They would get Murke this time and he wouldn't get away.

She clicked off the radio and looked over at Trevor, whose jaw had formed a hard line. "This is it. I can feel it."

"Me, too," Valerie said.

The address dispatch had given them was on the edge of the Lost Woods. A series of run-down two-and three-story apartments and box-like houses in need of paint jobs. "Lot of drug arrests in this part of town. I wonder why Murke is here?"

Trevor shook his head. "It's not too far from that truck stop we had staked out."

Up ahead, the SWAT team had moved into place, taking cover behind cars and crouching by the building.

Trevor got out while Valerie opened the back door of the patrol car for Lexi. A man in a bulletproof vest walked toward them. "Second-floor apartment. We've evacuated the building. The woman is hiding in a closet and has turned off her phone. She doesn't want to risk Murke hearing her talk."

"Why is Murke up there?"

The sergeant shook his head. "All she was able to tell us was that she's pretty sure he is armed, and he's been screaming something about a code."

"A code?" Trevor shook his head. "Let's see if we can talk him out. He doesn't know we are here yet, right?"

The SWAT team leader nodded. "It's been about ten

minutes since the woman made the call. It's only a matter of time before he figures out she's in the closet and breaks it down."

Valerie stepped forward. "How many points of entry do we have?"

"A back door with a fire escape and patio, a front door inside at the end of a hallway." The SWAT leader turned toward the apartment building. "And she was able to tell us that the closet is at the back of the house."

From what she had seen with Murke so far, he wasn't going to give up without a fight, and he'd run the first chance he got. What would he do if he was backed in a corner and couldn't escape? If he got to the hostage, he'd use her as a shield. "We've got to keep that hostage safe. I say we don't let him know the whole SWAT team is here. He'll panic and start shooting or worse. We got to get him separated from the hostage." Valerie squared her shoulders. "I'll go to the front door and see if I can keep him distracted. Agent Lewis can go in the back and be in position to take him down if needed."

Trevor's face shone with admiration for Valerie. "I think Officer Salgado has a good idea."

"We need some kind of wire so Trevor and I can communicate. If it looks like Murke is going to harm Nicki, all bets are off. You guys can storm the place."

It took only a few minutes for the team to equip Valerie and Trevor with earpieces and bulletproof vests. As they walked toward the building with Lexi heeling beside her, Valerie's stomach knotted with anticipation.

When they reached the entrance, Trevor clasped her arm and turned her toward him. He drew her into a hug, stroking her hair and kissing the top of her head. "Stay safe."

"You, too," her voice welled with emotion. This might be the last time he held her. They could both die. She closed her eyes and pressed her ear close to his beating heart while his arms surrounded her.

After a long moment, Trevor pulled away and rested his hand on her cheek. "Let's do this." He stepped away and disappeared around the back of the apartment building.

Valerie pushed open the front entrance where there was a series of mailboxes and doors for the main-floor apartments. Taking in a deep breath, she traversed the stairs with Lexi beside her to the second floor. She walked down a silent hallway, her footsteps barely audible on the worn carpet. When she came to apartment 210, she stared at the chipped and peeling green paint of the door.

Inside, she could hear Murke calling Arianna names and ranting about how she owed him big time.

She touched her earpiece. "Trevor, I'm at the door."

"I'm headed up the fire escape to the back door. Looks like there is a curtain across it, so Murke won't be able to see me even if it opens up directly into the living room." Trevor's breathing indicated that he was moving quickly.

Valerie closed her eyes and prayed as she raised her hand to knock on the door.

Oh, God, help me.

She knocked three times and then pressed her back against the wall, raising her gun in case Murke decided to start shooting.

In her earpiece, she heard Trevor whisper, "I'm in place by the back door."

From inside, there was more banging and pounding and Murke screaming, "You better let me in or I'm going to shoot this door down! Tell me the code, Nicki."

Time was running out. Murke had figured out where Nicki was hiding. With her heart racing, Valerie knocked again, this time louder.

The silence that followed was disconcerting.

"Derek Murke?" She spoke in a loud, clear voice even though her legs were wobbly. "This is Officer Salgado from the Sagebrush PD."

"Officer Salgado." Murke's voice dripped with sarcasm.

Down the hallway, the rest of the SWAT team had moved into place. Murke's voice had sounded like he was still halfway across the room. She needed him right by the door, away from Nicki before she gave Trevor the okay to enter.

"Why don't you come with me now, and we can all walk out of here in one piece." Valerie gripped Lexi's leash a little tighter. The dog tilted her head as though to give her a vote of confidence.

There was a long silence and then Murke's voice seemed to be right against her ear, even though there was a door between them. "How did you know I was even here?"

Valerie cringed. Saying that Nicki had called them would put the hostage's life at risk. "A neighbor saw you walk into the building holding a gun."

She stepped away from the door, not wanting to risk Murke hearing her and spoke to Trevor. "He's by the door."

"I'm going in." Trevor's voice was steady and filled with determination. "Looks like there is a hallway before the living room but no closet door. It must be at the other end. Can't get to it without Murke seeing me."

Valerie wiped the perspiration off her forehead. Now all she had to do was keep Murke talking.

"So what do you say, Derek? Open the door and everyone here gets out alive."

She held her breath during the long silence. Had Murke gone back to the closet or heard Trevor entering?

"And I go to jail, right?" Murke's voice blasted through the thin wood of the door.

"I could put a good word in for you," Valerie said.

Several moments passed but all she could hear was the sound of Murke's heavy breathing.

She stepped away from the door and whispered. "Trevor, where are you?"

He spoke in such a soft whisper she could barely hear him. "In the hallway. I can hear Murke. I'm about to turn the corner. Keep him talking. Going dark. Don't want to be heard."

She turned back toward the door. "So what do you say, Derek? How about you unlock this door?"

Seconds ticked by. What was he doing in there?

"Derek?"

Nothing. No noise. No indication of a fight. Had Murke gone back to the closet where Nicki was? Had he figured out that Trevor was in the house? Certainly she would have heard the sound of a struggle.

Lexi looked up at Valerie, licking her chops.

She made a split-second decision, stepped away from the door and charged it, lifting her leg to break it down. The thin door crumpled like balsa wood. She took in the scene. Murke hiding behind a china hutch, Trevor turning the corner and looking at the door, where Murke should have been. Murke raising his gun. Lexi bounding across the carpet as a pistol shot shattered the silence.

Lexi yelped and fell to the floor, blood spreading across the carpet. Murke had shot the dog. Lexi had taken the bullet intended for Trevor.

"Drop the gun!" Trevor yelled. "Down on the ground."

Valerie moved in, her own gun drawn. "You heard him, hit the floor."

Lexi's anguished yelp pierced her heart, but she couldn't help her. Not yet. Not until Derek was no longer a threat.

Murke lifted his hand and let the gun fall. Valerie kicked it away so he couldn't pick it up again. The SWAT team swarmed in.

Trevor turned toward one of the SWAT team members. "Hostage is down that hall in the closet."

Valerie fell to the floor and wrapped her arms around Lexi. The dog licked her hand twice and then lost consciousness.

One of the SWAT team members escorted a slender woman with brown coppery hair into the living room.

Nicki swiped at her eyes that were red from crying. "He kept shouting about a code. He said Arianna told him I had the code."

"You know Arianna?" Trevor was already kneeling on the floor beside Valerie.

"Yes, she's my cousin." Nicki let out a cry when she saw the injured dog on the floor. She looked down at the dog, her voice filled with sympathy. "What happened?"

Valerie could feel herself shutting down, going numb. All she could think about was Lexi. Trevor's voice pulled her out of shock. "We need to get her to a vet."

More SWAT team members came into the house. Two of them had already gotten Murke to his feet and were leading him out.

Murke thrashed like an animal caught in a trap when he was led out. "That score should be mine. By rights that score should be mine."

Nicki had retreated to the kitchen and returned holding three clean white towels. "Here, for your dog." She kneeled beside Valerie and gazed at her with kind blue eyes.

Valerie placed the towels over the hole where the bullet had gone in on Lexi's back flank. So much blood.

Trevor placed a hand on Valerie's shoulder. "We can get her to the vet's faster than they can get here."

Trevor gathered the Rottweiler into his arms. She looked so lifeless…like a rag doll. As he raced out of the apartment and down the hall, Valerie slipped past him. "I'll bring the car around."

Her feet pounded down the hallway. Inches felt like miles as she ran outside to the patrol car, praying that Lexi wouldn't die.

The lump in Trevor's throat made it hard to swallow. Lexi was warm against his chest as he ran down the stairs. This dog had saved his life. She wasn't going to die on his watch—not today, not any day.

Outside, the bright sun stunned him. He hadn't noticed what a beautiful day it was, not the kind of day you expect to lose a dog you've come to love. And she had proven that she loved him, enough to give her own life to protect him.

Valerie pulled up to the curb.

Still cradling Lexi, he got into the passenger side of

the SUV. His shirt was covered in blood. The dog's rib cage still moved up and down, but her body was limp and lifeless.

Valerie sped away from the curb. "I've already called the vet. She's prepping the surgery room." She glanced from the dog to Trevor.

He wanted to offer her reassurances, but as he held Lexi, he wasn't so sure he could do that. She was barely hanging on. She'd lost a lot of blood. "It shouldn't take us long to get there." His voice was solemn.

Once she was away from the residential areas, Valerie accelerated. Plowed fields and then the trees of the Lost Woods clipped by.

Please, God, don't let this dog die, Trevor prayed.

Dr. Constance Mills was waiting for them outside when they pulled up. "Let's get her inside. We're all ready for her."

Trevor carried Lexi into the operating room and laid her on the metal table. Two assistants went to work putting an IV in her leg while Dr. Mills assessed the wound. She spoke to one of the assistants. "We'll need a 7 mm trach tube and some lactated ringers."

Valerie shuddered and let out a gasp.

Dr. Mills looked up at her. "You should wait outside. Use my office, it's more private. You might be able to find a clean shirt."

Trevor glanced down at his own shirt. It was covered in blood. He felt as though he were walking under water as he pulled Valerie out of the operating room. He stood in the hallway for a long moment, not able to process what he needed to do next.

Valerie rubbed her temple. "Umm… I think her office must be this way." She stopped, bursting into tears.

"What am I going to do without her? What if she doesn't make it?"

Trevor gathered her into his arms. Anguish twisted inside him, made his throat tight. He couldn't speak. He held her until her crying subsided. He opened the door to the office where they found a T-shirt for Trevor with the name of the vet clinic on it and an operating smock for Valerie.

When Valerie looked down at her own bloody shirt, the tears started all over again. He held her again.

As he drew her close, he prayed.

"God, I don't know what your will is for Lexi, but we sure like having her around." His eyes grew moist. Life without Lexi... He didn't even want to think about it.

After several minutes, Valerie pulled away. She looked up at him with glazed eyes, still unable to say anything. He held her for a moment longer.

After they both had changed out of their bloody shirts, they stood in the hallway.

"I don't want to go back into the regular waiting room. Someone is bound to ask me what my pet is here for, and I just can't bear that kind of small talk." Valerie's voice was paper thin.

He led her out to the back exit of the clinic where horses trotted around a small corral. The sun warmed his skin.

Valerie looked up and stared at the sky, placing her hands over her face. "I need to see how Bethany is doing."

She pulled her phone off her belt and stepped away from him. He caught bits and pieces of the conversation. A desperation colored her words as she suggested that Stella bring Bethany to the vet clinic. Her eyes met

Trevor's as she finished her sentence, "...so we can all be together."

Is that how she saw them now, as family that needed to be together during this uncertain time? She hung up the phone and offered him a faint smile. Her wide green eyes were filled with affection that drew him in.

He stepped toward her, ready to take her in his arms again. The moment was shattered by his phone ringing. He stepped away, a sheepish grin on his face. He looked at the number on the phone. "Sorry, it's Officer Worth. You might want to listen in, too."

He rested an arm on the corral as Valerie came and stood beside him, resting her hand on his shoulder and leaning close to him.

"Hello, Jackson. Valerie is here with me."

"Yeah, I heard about the dog. I hope she makes it," Jackson said.

Trevor swallowed hard. "Me, too."

"McNeal asked me to fill you guys in. They've got Murke down at the station." Murke hadn't escaped custody this time. And Trevor knew he would be put away for good. Finally, he had some justice for the death of Agent Cory Smith.

Jackson continued. "Since he's not talking, McNeal thinks we might have to bring the woman at the apartment in for questioning. This Nicki Johnson. She was related to the Serpent. She might know something."

"Yeah, we don't know what her level of involvement is. Derek seemed to think she had some sort of code that would help him with his big score, which has to be whatever it is the syndicate has been looking for in the Lost Woods. Arianna must have known something about it, and Murke must have coerced her into telling him that this Nicki person had it."

"That's what I wanted to talk to you about. When Arianna was dying, she whispered three words to me that make sense now," Jackson said.

"What did she say?"

"Cousin. Code. Danger."

"Sounds like the Serpent was having some last minute guilt pangs over sending Murke to terrorize her cousin," Trevor said.

"Maybe. Hard to say." Jackson seemed to be mulling all the information over and had fallen into a silence.

Trevor's own thoughts wandered again to the fate of the loyal dog lying on the operating table. "Listen, I got to go."

"A lot of people in the department are praying for Lexi," Jackson said. "I know I am."

Trevor hung up the phone and turned toward Valerie. "Did you get all that?"

She nodded. "I don't want to think about any of that right now." Anxiety showed itself in the deep furrows between her eyebrows. No doubt, her mind was on Lexi, too.

He brushed a strand of hair from her face. "Let's just walk." He took her hand and walked around the corral and into a field of bluebonnets. They walked without saying a word. There was nothing he could say to ease the fear. He felt it, too. That voice resonated deep inside of him.

What if Lexi didn't make it?

Twenty minutes later, Mrs. Witherspoon pulled up with Bethany. They ran to meet her in the parking lot of the vet clinic. Bethany's bright smile cheered him as

Stella handed her over to Valerie. She offered Valerie a hug and kiss and a promise to keep praying for Lexi before driving away.

Bethany reached over and patted Trevor's cheek. As he leaned close to Valerie, their shoulders touching, he was overwhelmed with the love he felt for her and for Bethany.

He did love them both…and he loved that dog, whose life hung in the balance.

One of the assistants who had been with Dr. Mills opened the door to the vet clinic. "There you two are. You can come in and see Lexi now."

Valerie looked up. "Is she…?"

The assistant offered a quick smile that didn't quite reach her eyes. "I'll let the doctor explain."

Valerie tensed and looked up at Trevor. "Do you think we should take Bethany in the operating room?"

"I think we should all be together, whatever the news." He rubbed her back.

They stepped through the waiting room where a woman sat holding her cat and another woman sat beside a little girl who had a birdcage on her lap. A little yellow bird tweeted inside the birdcage. The cheerful tweeting of the bird stood in sharp contrast to the sense of dread he felt. What if they were being ushered into the operating room to say goodbye to Lexi?

They slipped inside the operating room where Lexi lay motionless on the table with a blanket over her. She had a breathing tube in her mouth. An IV stand was close to the operating table. The steady beep of the monitor indicated that Lexi had vital signs.

Dr. Mills looked like she had aged ten years. She leaned back against a cabinet filled with medicine.

"How does it look?" Valerie's voice wavered, fear evident in every syllable.

Dr. Mills pulled off the surgical cap and rubbed her eyes. "It was really touch and go. She lost a lot of blood at the outset. The muscle in her back leg is just torn to pieces. She's going to have a long recovery ahead of her."

Valerie let out a heavy breath. "But she'll make it." She handed Bethany over to Trevor and rushed to stroke Lexi's ears.

The doctor nodded. "She'll make it."

Bethany wrapped her arms around Trevor's neck as though it were the most natural thing in the world for him to hold her.

"I'll leave this little family alone with her for a minute." Dr Mills left, closing the door softly behind her.

Valerie spoke without taking her eyes off Lexi. "She thought we were a family."

Then she looked over at him, green eyes shining. He took in the wonder of holding Bethany, of having the little girl feel comforted in his arms. Trevor's heart pounded and in that moment, he knew what he needed to say. "That sounds like a pretty good idea to me."

She blinked, color rising up in her cheeks. "What are you talking about?"

Trevor moved around the operating table so he stood face to face with Valerie. "I would like for us to be a family."

Valerie rubbed Bethany's back. "Do you mean that?"

He nodded as joy welled up inside him.

Bethany patted his chest and made "Ba ba ba" sounds.

"All three of us?"

"All three of my girls." This is what he had been looking for most of his life…a family.

Her eyes were radiant with love. "Yes, I think we would like that."

Trevor brought Valerie into a hug with him and Bethany.

Lexi let out a faint whine and licked Valerie's hand. "I think she approves."

They laughed. Valerie tilted her head. He kissed the woman he wanted to spend the rest of his life with.

* * * * *

Valerie Hansen was thirty when she awoke to the presence of the Lord in her life and turned to Jesus. She now lives in a renovated farmhouse in the breathtakingly beautiful Ozark Mountains of Arkansas and is privileged to share her personal faith by telling the stories of her heart for Love Inspired. Life doesn't get much better than that!

Books by Valerie Hansen

Love Inspired Suspense

Military K-9 Unit
Bound by Duty

Classified K-9 Unit
Special Agent

Rookie K-9 Unit
Search and Rescue
Rookie K-9 Unit Christmas
"Surviving Christmas"

The Defenders
Nightwatch
Threat of Darkness
Standing Guard
A Trace of Memory
Small Town Justice
Dangerous Legacy

Visit the Author Profile page
at Harlequin.com for more titles.

EXPLOSIVE SECRETS

Valerie Hansen

I will give you a new heart
and put a new spirit within you.
—*Ezekiel* 36:26

To my "partners in crime,"
Shirlee McCoy, Margaret Daley, Sharon Dunn,
Terri Reed and Lenora Worth, who were a joy
to work with on this series. To Joe and Karen,
beloved proofreaders who catch my boo-boos. And
to my personal K-9 corps, Charlie Brown and Lucy,
two rescued Labs who see to it that I don't spend
every waking hour sitting at my computer.

ONE

Nicolette Johnson was about to leave for her night-shift job at The Truck Stop Diner when her cell phone rang.

She slipped it out of her jeans pocket and hesitated while she listened to the ringtone playing "The Yellow Rose of Texas." Most of her recent callers had been nosy reporters or curious neighbors wanting to ask what she knew about her cousin Arianna Munson's recent murder.

"That would be *nothing,* just like I told the police," she muttered. But since her curiosity was aroused, she gave in and answered. "Hello?"

"Hello, Nicki, darlin'."

The slow, deep drawl was dripping with menace, sending chills up her spine. "Who is this?"

"Never mind who I am. You need to stop holding out on us," the man warned. "Remember, we know where you live."

Nicki swallowed past the lump in her throat. "I don't know what you're talking about. Leave me alone."

"That's not going to happen, lady. That idiot Murke blew it the other night, but we can still get to you, just like we got to the Serpent."

"Who?" She rued the telltale tremor in her tone.

"Arianna Munson." He gave an evil-sounding chuckle. "That was our pet name for your dearly departed cousin."

There was a pause while the caller laughed as if he'd just told a great joke. "We eliminated her, and we can do the same to you. If you think you can run or hide, just ask the Sagebrush cops what happened to one of their wives a few years back." He chortled again then shouted, *"Boom!"*

Stifling a tiny shriek, Nicki immediately ended the call. Many of the specifics of the man's threats had already become a confusing muddle, but one fact stood out. The way he had barked *boom* left no doubt that she was dealing with a deadly enemy, one she should not try to defeat on her own.

Shaking, Nicki managed to punch in the phone number from the business card the police officers had left with her a few days before. She held her breath and counted the number of rings while she waited for someone to answer.

"Sagebrush Police Department. How may I help you?" a friendly sounding woman asked.

Nicki had intended to report the sinister warning calmly and with little emotion. When she heard the dispatcher's voice, however, she blurted, "I need help. Somebody just threatened to blow me up!"

"K-9 unit 463, your position?" the patrol radio broadcast.

Jackson Worth keyed the mic. "Sagebrush Boulevard and Main, headed north."

"We have a possible bomb threat at 3274 Lost Woods Road, apartment 210. See the woman."

"Affirmative. On my way. ETA approximately ten."

"Copy. Advise if you need backup."

Jackson flipped on his light bar and spun the wheel of the SUV. In the backseat, his black Labrador retriever, Titan, was panting rapidly, knowing they were about to go to work.

The big dog's enthusiasm made Jackson smile. They were so much a team it was as if Titan could read his mind. He could certainly tell what that dog was thinking. When they were on duty his canine partner was all business, even when he acted as though he was still battling the negative effects of their previous assignments in war zones.

"We both came through the fire okay then, didn't we, old boy?" Jackson said affectionately. "And we're still doing it."

Titan wiggled, but remained disciplined enough to stay seated and not fight the restraints that kept him safe when he wasn't riding in his portable kennel. Jackson hated to cage the tractable dog so he used every excuse not to.

They pulled to the curb in front of the apartment building on Lost Woods Road, and stopped. Jackson barely had a chance to climb out when a slim, young woman in jeans and a pink T-shirt raced over and grasped his sleeve. Her wide eyes were as blue as a summer sky, and her coppery-brown hair fell softly around her face, its silky length brushing her shoulders.

"Are you the party who placed the call for police assistance?" Jackson asked.

"Y-yes. I thought they'd send the same officers who were here before."

He politely touched the brim of his cap, then opened

the rear door to leash Titan as he explained, "I'm Detective Worth, ma'am. You must have mentioned a bomb threat when you contacted the station or they wouldn't have sent us."

"I did. That's really the only thing I can remember clearly. The man who called me said I should ask about a policeman's wife getting blown up and then he hollered, *'Boom!'* Just like that." She tried to catch her breath. "I didn't know what else to do so I called the number on the card those other officers left when they were here a few days ago."

"You did the right thing by waiting outside, Ms..."

"Nicolette Johnson." She pointed to the upper story of the poorly maintained apartment building. "That's where I live. I was about to leave for work. After I got the threatening phone call, I didn't know what to do."

Jackson straightened with Titan at his side. "Okay. Let's start from the beginning. Tell me your version of the trouble you had here recently."

"Okay. A man broke into my apartment. I hid in the closet and called 911. When the other officers got here there was a fight and some shooting. That's when a police dog was wounded. It was awful."

Jackson nodded soberly. "I understand how upsetting that must have been. A fugitive named Derek Murke was arrested."

"Right. He was an ex-boyfriend of my late cousin, Arianna Munson. That's another reason I got scared. The man who called me today mentioned her. Only he called her a snake or something."

"You mean *Serpent?*"

Nicolette nodded, her eyes wide. "That was it. Serpent. He said that he had killed her."

"In those exact words?" Jackson knew that the Munson woman had died during a shoot-out with the police, so why would anyone claim murder as a threat? He had to make an effort to control his excitement. Any clues, no matter how obscure, that brought the department closer to finding the gang of killers and drug runners causing mayhem in and around Sagebrush were definitely top priority.

"I—I don't know. I'm sorry. I can't remember his exact words. I guess I was too scared."

Or up to your eyeballs in the whole criminal mess, he thought, keeping that notion to himself for the time being. "Suppose we get off the street and go check your apartment before we do anything else?"

"Okay." She was wringing her hands. "I feel silly causing such a fuss, but he sounded really serious about hurting me."

"Did he say why?"

"Yes. He seemed to think I was withholding some kind of information. Murke said the same thing when he held me hostage the other night."

"Are you?"

"Of *course* not. If I did know something, I'd have told the officers who arrested him." She shivered. "He's still in jail, isn't he?"

"Yes, ma'am. And he will be for a long time if I'm any judge. You don't need to worry about him coming back to bother you."

"Oh, good! What about the wounded police dog? Is she going to make it?"

"Yes. The muscle in her hind leg was torn up pretty bad, but the vet says Lexi will be back on duty in due time."

"That's a relief."

Nicolette was reaching for the outer door to the complex when Jackson stopped her. "You'd better wait while we check the premises. I'll signal you to come and unlock your apartment when we're sure the halls are clean."

She seemed reluctant. "Okay, but…"

"Just stand where we can still see each other," Jackson told her. "If Titan finds anything suspicious, he'll sit down by it, and then I'll call for backup and evacuate the building. If he doesn't react, you'll know everything is fine."

"What a beautiful, intelligent animal," she said softly as man and canine started to walk away.

Jackson watched Titan methodically check every corner and sniff at every door on the ground floor. Then they returned to Nicolette.

"Coast is clear down here. Where's your apartment?"

"Second floor, far end of the hall." She held up a key. "Do you need this?"

"Not yet. Let us take the lead. You can follow at a safe distance. When Titan is satisfied, you can come and unlock the door for us."

It would have given Jackson a better feeling if he'd had at least one more officer with him to guard the young woman, although in this case it seemed unnecessary. Whoever had tried to frighten her had succeeded, yes, but that wasn't proof of real danger. As long as Titan didn't alert, he'd be satisfied that the place was free of explosives. That was the main thing.

Finished with the second phase of the sweep, he paused at apartment number 210 and motioned to Nicolette.

Watching her hurry to join them he was taken by her grace, her natural loveliness. So many women he'd known in the past seemed to think that painting themselves up was the key to beauty. As far as Jackson was concerned, a naturally pretty woman like Nicolette Johnson was far easier on the eyes.

You're on the job. You're not supposed to notice things like that, his conscience reminded him.

That made Jackson smile slightly. He might be working. And he was certainly not in the market for romance of any kind. But that did not mean he was unable to appreciate this kind of loveliness, any more than he could overlook a gorgeous Texas sunset or the shining, coppery coat on a special chestnut-colored mare out at his ranch.

His smile threatened to widen and he had to stifle it. He could just imagine what Ms. Nicolette Johnson would think of having her beauty compared to that of a fine horse, even if it was one of the nicest compliments he could have bestowed.

Nicki's hands were trembling so badly she had trouble fitting the key into the lock. When she was finally successful, she stepped back and let the dog and his handler enter while she waited by the door.

It was interesting seeing how they worked as a team with the dog leading the way and the man indicating when he wanted him to proceed to another room.

If the apartment hadn't been so small and sparsely furnished, she would have worried more when they both disappeared into the bedroom. Thankfully, there wasn't much to see and their inspection was complete in a matter of minutes.

"You can come in and relax now," Jackson called. "The place is clean. There's no danger."

Frowning, she poked her head in first. "You're sure?"

"Titan is," Jackson said with a smile. "You can trust him. I do."

"Okay." She took a few steps closer and eyed her tiny living room. "I suppose I'd notice if there was anything out of place. It's just that the last few days have been so awful. The landlord repaired my front door after the female police officer forced it, but I thought I'd never get the stains out of my rug from where that poor dog was wounded."

"I understand your concern." He waited for her to sit in the only easy chair before taking a place across from her on the slipcovered sofa. Titan lay at his feet. "Now that we can take it easy, how about starting from the beginning and telling me what's been going on?"

Sighing, she began. "I feel like I've just run a marathon instead of sleeping 'til noon. I work nights at The Truck Stop Diner out on Highway 20 so I don't get up very early." Her stomach fluttered, then settled, much to her relief. She didn't think it was this officer's business that she was expecting a baby so she kept that information to herself.

His eyes never left her face as he asked, "I take it that's your normal schedule. Are you a waitress?"

"No. I'm one of the short-order cooks. I've worked that shift for the past year."

"How about neighbors? Any trouble with them lately?"

"No."

"Boyfriends? Anybody you may have argued with?"

Hadn't he heard a word she'd said? "I told you what

the caller wanted. He knows—knew—my cousin, Arianna. That's what this is all about. Everybody thinks she told me some secret, but she didn't."

Nodding, he seemed to be trying to stare right into her mind because his gaze was unwavering. "I'd like to believe you, but there's a problem with that," Jackson said.

"A problem? What?"

"I heard your cousin's dying declaration with my own ears. She said, 'Cousin. Code. Danger.'"

"Now you sound like Murke!" Nicki jumped to her feet and began to pace the small room. "Arianna and I were related, yes, but we weren't close. Not anymore. There's no reason for her to even mention me."

"Does she have other cousins?"

Nicolette's shoulders slumped and she shook her head slowly. "Only one that I know of. I have a half sister somewhere back East. Since even *I* don't know where she is, I'm sure Arianna couldn't have meant her."

"So, that leaves you," he said calmly.

"I know, I know." She blinked back unshed tears, unwilling to let a stranger see how close she was to losing control of her emotions. That was another of the side effects of pregnancy, or so she had read, and she couldn't believe how often she'd fought mood swings lately.

"We'll need your half sister's name." He poised to write in a small notebook.

"Her maiden name was Mae Johnson. I heard she got married. I don't know what her last name is now."

"We'll track her down, just in case." He stood and pocketed the notebook and pen. "Are you sure there's nothing else you'd like to tell me?"

"No! Nothing. I don't know why nobody will believe I'm innocent."

"It doesn't matter what I do or don't believe, Ms. Johnson. I'm just doing my job."

"I know you are. Sorry."

He nodded stiffly. "No problem. I'll be glad to escort you to work if you want."

Nicki almost told him to go away, to leave her alone and stop treating her as though she was lying. If she hadn't still been so afraid she might have done so.

"Okay. I guess there's no sense sitting home brooding," she finally said with a muted sigh. "Besides, I can't afford to make my boss mad. When I had to call in sick the other night after Murke came gunning for me, Lou told me it had better not happen again or I'd be fired."

"In that case, we should get going. If you receive more strange calls or notice anything unusual, feel free to call us again. That's what we're here for."

"Thanks." She hesitated. "Would you mind walking me to my car and having the dog check it, too? Just in case."

"Sure. Be glad to."

Nicki grabbed her wallet off the end table and fisted her keys. They jingled, attracting the dog's attention and making him pant and wag his tail.

"Looks like your partner is ready to go for a ride."

"Titan is always ready for adventure." Jackson stepped to the side while Nicki opened the apartment door.

She halted abruptly, staring at the floor. Someone had tucked a small, fresh flower arrangement in the doorway so that she couldn't miss seeing it.

"Oh, how pretty. I love daisies."

Jackson frowned. "I thought you said you didn't have a boyfriend."

"I don't. Not since Bobby Lee got so mad and took off. Maybe he changed his mind." She bent and reached for the flowers.

To her left, she saw Titan plop down into a sitting position so fast the movement was a blur.

Jackson shouted, "No!" and lunged for her.

Half bent over, Nicki was almost toppled. She recovered, managing to rescue the bouquet by clutching it to her chest.

Titan began to bark.

In what felt like one fluid movement, Jackson grabbed the flower arrangement from her, threw it inside the apartment, shoved her and the dog into the hall and slammed the door. Then he covered and shielded them both as best he could with his own body.

Moments later, a loud explosion shook the building and made Nicki's ears sting as if they were being stabbed by needles. Stunned, she could hardly breathe.

The flowers! She could have been killed. So could her innocent baby. But they were safe! *Thank you, Jesus.*

As the officer slowly straightened and allowed her to move, she felt so light-headed she was afraid she might faint. If she hadn't already been sitting on the floor she knew she would have been reeling.

Tears gathered and spilled down her cheeks. So utterly thankful she could not speak, she threw her arms around the dog's neck, pressed her face into his fur and silently wept as the reality of her situation dawned. There would not always be a police officer at hand to rescue her at the last second, so what could she do? What *should* she do?

Nicki was at a loss to know. Death had stalked her, and she had once again triumphed. The question was, how many more narrow escapes could she hope to endure before some lurking, unnamed evil slipped through her meager defenses and succeeded in ending her life?

TWO

"It doesn't make any sense for them to want to hurt her when they think she's keeping secrets," Jackson told Captain Slade McNeal as they stood apart from the other officers at the scene of the chaos. "If the gang wants the information Arianna gave her, they need to keep her alive and well."

"Unless they knew you were with her and figured your dog would identify the device before it was touched."

"Possibly."

"How's the woman doing?" Slade asked.

"She's scared silly. Who wouldn't be?" Jackson paused and raked his fingers through his short, dark hair. "I can't believe how close we all came to buying the farm."

"Yeah. It wasn't a big explosion, but it sure made hash out of her apartment. I'm having the paramedics hold her in the ambulance until the ATF boys get here. They may have a few questions for Ms. Johnson, too."

"Makes me wish we had our own bomb squad right here in Sagebrush."

"Can't afford it."

"Yeah, I know. I'm just glad you hired me and Titan." He sobered even more as he regarded his superior. "We're all sorry about what motivated you."

"Thanks. I still blame myself. If you'd been here then, my wife might have been warned in time, and Caleb would still have a mother."

Chagrined, Jackson shook his head and thrust his hands into his pockets. "Don't be so sure about that. I messed up on this one."

"You saved the woman's life. I'd hardly call that a failure."

Jackson snorted derisively. "Tell that to Ms. Johnson when she gets a look at what's left of her place. It's a shambles. Every window is blown out, and the furniture looks like a wildcat on meth shredded it."

"Yeah…but she's still alive. If I were you, I'd remind her of that before I let her go up and look. The bedroom seems to have escaped damage, except for lots of plaster dust and smoke, so she will still have clothes and personal items to salvage."

"I hope that helps. She has every right to be furious with me."

"You're too hard on yourself," McNeal told him. "Why don't you go see to your dog and check on Ms. Johnson while I wait for Boomer."

"Right." Hearing the familiar ATF agent's nickname almost always made Jackson smile. Any guy with the initials TNT was a shoo-in for a bomb-investigating job. Timothy Nelson Taft was not only good at his job, he seemed to enjoy the good-natured teasing he usually received when people realized why he was called *Boomer*.

Several other members of the Sagebrush P.D. and fire department were milling around the rescue and police vehicles parked in the street. Some regular officers had cordoned off the apartment grounds and were detouring traffic. That was probably unnecessary, yet Jackson didn't complain. He had mistakenly underestimated their foes and an innocent bystander had almost paid for his laxity.

He went first to Titan and the fellow K-9 officer who was tending to him. Valerie Salgado's Rottweiler had been the one wounded on these premises a few days ago and since Valerie was on her own for the present, she had volunteered to look after Titan while Jackson spoke to their captain.

A tall woman with green eyes, freckles and long, reddish hair, Salgado was seated in one of the SUVs, petting Titan to soothe his jangled nerves.

"How's he doing now?" Jackson asked, approaching.

"Better. He's not shaking nearly as much as he was when I got here. What happened, anyway? Didn't he alert properly?"

"The dog did fine." He reached toward his canine partner to affectionately ruffle his velvety ears. "I was the one who messed up. I let a civilian get ahead of me and she picked up the bomb before I could stop her."

"That's when it went off?"

"No, thank God. Literally. I had a few seconds to grab it and throw it. Unfortunately, the only place I could pitch it was into her apartment."

"Better a few dented walls than dented heads." She gently stroked Titan's broad back, wiggling her fingers, much to the dog's delight. "What a good boy."

"Do you have time to mind him for me a little while longer? I want to check with the EMTs and see how the vic is doing." Jackson inclined his head toward a parked ambulance.

"Sure. No sweat. I'll take him back to the station with me and you can pick him up there later, if you want. Lexi won't be able to work for a while yet, and I miss relaxing like this." She sighed. "Petting a dog lowers your blood pressure and does all kinds of good things for your state of mind."

"I know. Just save me a little Titan chilling time. I'll need it after I get through showing the lady over there what happened to her apartment."

He could hear Valerie's light laughter behind him as he started for the ambulance.

One of the paramedics headed him off before he got all the way to where Nicolette was being treated.

"Worth. Hold up," the medic said. "I need to talk to you for a sec."

"Sure." He peered past the shorter, younger man's shoulder. "Is there a problem?"

"Not yet. At least not that I know of, but you should know that this victim is pregnant before you continuing questioning her."

That brought Jackson up short. "She's okay, though? I hit her pretty hard when I was shoving her out of the way."

"Seems to be. It's early in the pregnancy so she's not showing. There's no way you'd have known unless she chose to tell you."

He huffed quietly. "I figured she was holding something back, but I had no idea that was it. No wonder she seemed so overwrought."

"Yeah, well, I wanted you to know."

Jackson clapped him on the shoulder and stepped past. "Thanks, man. I owe you one."

The ambulance was positioned at an angle to the curb so it could go into action without delay. Jackson made sure he was smiling as he circled it and came face-to-face with Nicolette.

The woman's eyes were misty as she looked up at him and asked, "Are you okay?"

"I'm supposed to be the one asking you that."

"I'm fine." She returned his smile. "Well, relatively fine."

When he said, "I'm really sorry about your apartment," he saw her face grow ashen.

"How bad is it?"

"Truthfully? It's a mess. But the good news is we're all safe and sound." Noticing that her arms were crossed to hug her torso he added, "*All* of us."

Rosy patches replaced the lack of color in her cheeks. "The medics told you?"

"About the baby? Yes. I hope I didn't hurt you when I knocked you down. I had no idea…"

"I'd lots rather be knocked over than blown to bits, so thank you for saving me—us. When I saw your dog react that way, I didn't put two and two together fast enough. If you hadn't been there…"

She raised her eyes to the apartment building. "I can't see any damage to the outside."

"It wasn't a large explosion," Jackson explained. "I don't think they actually intended to kill you. Not if they really do think you're withholding information they need."

Nicki rolled her eyes. "I am *not*. What do I have to do to convince everybody of that?"

"I don't know that you can. Or if you should," he replied soberly. "You might be better off if the criminals keep on believing you do have info they need."

Shoulders slumped, she exhaled noisily. "Okay. What's next? How long before I can go back inside?"

"Hours, at least. The bomb crew and our local techs need to comb the wreckage. If the captain okays it and you're up to it, I suggest you go on to work for the present."

"Will that be safe?"

"You're safer in a crowd than you would be alone in that apartment." He smiled. "Besides, I plan to accompany you."

"My boss won't like it if you just hang around and watch me work. He never approved of my... Never mind."

Jackson assumed, judging by the face she was making, that she was remembering her now-absent boyfriend. How any man could abandon a woman like that, after what he'd done to her, made Jackson furious. "You're sure there's no way your ex could be the one harassing you?"

"No way. After I told Bobby Lee about the baby, he said some really awful things and insisted he never wanted to see me again." She grimaced. "I know it's not him."

"You're positive?"

"Absolutely. He packed up and left the day we argued while I was at work. Friends tell me he was headed for Dallas. Personally, I don't care where he is. As far as I'm concerned, good riddance."

"He's a fool" was all Jackson dared say. If he had

opened up and told her everything he was thinking, she would have been even more embarrassed.

He'd always had a strong sense of honor, of right and wrong. Maybe that was why his job seemed to fit him so well. And why he felt such an undeniable obligation to step up and take care of Nicolette when her need was so great. She would never know how deeply, how personally, her plight affected him, of course, because he would never tell her.

But he would be there for her, helping and guarding her to the best of his ability, for as long as she needed him to be. It wasn't only because she might help the department solve a difficult case, either.

Looking after her was simply the right thing to do.

Whether she liked it or not.

Whether she was helping the investigation or not.

During the drive to work, Nicki had visualized her poor apartment, imagining the worst. The place hadn't been much to start with, but it was hers. The landlord had just repaired the door the police had damaged when they'd burst in to arrest Murke. No telling how upset the apartment manager was going to be when he saw what had happened today. She hoped there was insurance to cover this new damage because it was bound to cost a lot more than the broken door had, and she was pretty sure the authorities were not going to pick up the tab this time.

She parked her trusty old sedan in the usual spot behind The Truck Stop Diner and paused to try to compose herself. She'd been just getting over the jitters left after Murke's attack only to have her life thrown off-kilter once again.

If the familiar police car hadn't been following close behind her all the way, she wasn't sure she'd have been able to convince herself to go ahead and report for work. But there he was, on duty as promised.

His dog was absolutely precious—so sweet-natured and friendly. Nicki smiled to herself, noting that both man and canine had the same dark, silky hair and puppy-dog brown eyes.

She looked in the car's mirror and fastened her long hair out of the way as her job required. Two quick twists of an elastic band and she was good to go. "I can do this," she told herself. "I've worked here so long I could fill the orders in my sleep."

A smile lifted one corner of her mouth as she climbed out of her car, locked it and pocketed the key ring. Considering her lack of adequate sleep since Murke's break-in, and the adrenaline she had expended today, she just might doze off at the grill. The books she'd read about pregnancy had said to expect changes in her metabolism, but they hadn't told her how tired she'd be. Of course, those writers hadn't allowed for repeated attacks and terrifying threats, either.

Nicki glanced over to the visitor section of the lot where Jackson was parking the police car, then started for the back door leading to the kitchen. Wafting odors of burnt grease and accumulated garbage overflowing the trash receptacle instantly set her stomach churning.

Seeking to escape the cloying stench, she held her breath and chose a roundabout route instead of heading straight for the door.

A shadowy figure, hardly more than a blur, appeared for an instant in her peripheral vision. If she had continued along her usual path without diversion they could have collided!

Startled, Nicki shrieked. Whirled around. Started to run without waiting to see who or what had scared her.

A dark shape loomed directly in front of her. She crashed into a hard chest and would have fallen if the man had not quickly grabbed and steadied her.

Clenching her fists, she began to beat on him.

"Whoa. Take it easy. It's me. It's me."

As the voice penetrated her fog of fear, she realized it was familiar. Gasping, she looked up at Jackson Worth and managed to croak out, "Somebody tried to grab me!"

"Are you sure? Where? I didn't see a thing."

"Back by the trash bin." She struggled to catch her breath.

Bright lights twinkled at the corners of her eyes. Her head spun. Her legs refused to support her.

She could sense that she was being lifted and cradled protectively just as the parking lot vanished and blackness wrapped her like a warm blanket.

Fighting was useless. Surrender felt too good.

Bearing his lightweight burden, Jackson shouldered through the front door of the main service station complex and carried Nicki past racks of cellophane-wrapped snack food and into the dining area. Their passage generated a few raised eyebrows but apparently his uniform, badge and gun were enough to keep any of the truckers or other customers from interfering.

As she began to stir, she slipped an arm around his neck, laid her cheek on his chest and clung to him as if she knew what she was doing. That was troubling. So was his reaction. Having her show such reliance felt far too good. It was also something he could not permit. He'd learned the hard way that romance and being a cop did not mix.

He lowered her to sit on the edge of one of the green plastic booth benches, unwrapped her arm from his neck and steadied her as she regained full consciousness. Her color was wan, her eyes blinking rapidly.

When she pushed him away, he realized that her earlier actions must have been instinctive rather than an effort to sway his opinion of her. That was definitely a good sign—a point in her favor.

A chubby, uniformed waitress appeared at Jackson's elbow with a glass of ice water. He nodded as he took it from her. "Thanks."

"Is Nicki okay?" the older woman asked.

"I think so. Just got too much excitement."

"I sure hope that's all it is. Big Lou is already complaining because she's late again. He's gonna have a cow if she can't work tonight."

Jackson turned his attention back to Nicolette as the waitress left. He bent and held out the glass of water. "Here. Drink this."

"I'm not thirsty." She tried to rise, getting only partway to her feet before she plopped back down on the spongy green seat. "Uh-oh. Still dizzy."

"Let me take you to the E.R. for a checkup. You may be feeling the effects of the blast."

"No way. If I don't work, I don't eat. I'll be fine in a few minutes." She grimaced. "Sure wish I didn't have to deal with all the strong odors in that kitchen, though. Seems like everything makes me queasy these days."

"That's normal, isn't it?"

"So they say. It's just a bummer to work around food when even the thought of it makes you sick."

Jackson had to smile at her wry expression and the way she accepted her new limitations. "I can see where that might be a drawback."

A hard tap on his shoulder diverted his attention. He straightened, instinctively resting his palm on the butt of his holstered gun as he faced the burly, stubble-chinned man who had joined them. "Yes?"

The man cocked his head toward Nicolette. "She gonna work or not?"

Nicki was quick to reply, "Of course I am, Lou."

"Then get into the kitchen. I don't pay you to sit around entertaining cops."

Jackson wanted to defend the young woman by explaining what had happened to her earlier, but figured she didn't want or need his help. It was clear from her demeanor that she was used to facing down her taciturn boss. If she wanted this Lou character to know about the threats and the explosion, she'd tell him.

"I'm going to go have a look around the parking lot," Jackson explained, "and see if I notice anything out of the ordinary. You couldn't tell what startled you?"

"No. I thought there was a funny shadow back by the trash bins. I assumed it was a man. Since you didn't see anybody, maybe there was nothing there. I have been awfully jumpy lately."

"That's understandable." He took a slow step backward. "Will you be okay or do you want me to hang around for a while longer?"

"I'm fine." Pushing away from the worn, Formica-topped table, she swiveled and stood next to the booth.

A relieved smile spread across her face and she held out her arms. "See? Perfect. Not dizzy at all."

"Good. I'll be in the neighborhood. Just call if you need help again and be sure to let us know when you're ready to go home. We'll have an officer stop by to escort you." Jackson eyed the portly man in the stained apron, bid him a terse "Good day" and turned to go.

He was halfway to the exit before he glanced back. The man called Lou was in the lead.

Head held high, back straight, Nicolette followed him through a swinging, half door into the busy, steamy kitchen.

Jackson paused. Found himself wishing he could help her more. But how? As things stood, it was highly likely that she was embroiled in her cousin's confusing transgressions whether she knew it or not. Therefore, unless she could prove that she and Arianna had had no contact at all, she was going to continue to be of interest to many folks.

On both sides of the law.

If she'd thought her life was complicated before, she was probably going to discover that her ordeal was just beginning.

THREE

Nicolette tried to breathe shallowly as she entered the crowded, overheated kitchen. Steam rose from stainless-steel pots simmering on the stove, and filled the air with pungent odors.

A tall, thin guy she didn't recognize was standing at the grill, flipping burgers. Judging by how stained his apron was, he'd been there for some time.

Grabbing a clean, white apron from a waiting stack, she slipped the top loop over her head, crossed the strings in the back and tied them in front at her waist.

Her eyes met Lou's. She nodded toward the man at the grill. "Who's that?"

"My sister's boy." His graying eyebrows arched as he gave her the once-over through rheumy eyes. "Had to get him to fill in for you a couple of nights ago and he worked out real good. What's wrong with you, anyways? You look kinda peaked."

"I'm fine," Nicki insisted. "Just had a really rough morning." She swallowed hard, fighting the stomach upset that kept sneaking up on her. Pregnancy wasn't predictable the way she'd assumed it would be. There seemed to be no way to avoid occasional waves of nausea, yet at other times her mood might soar for no apparent reason.

"Life ain't easy for any of us, missy. You man the grill while my nephew takes his break," Lou ordered.

"Okay. No problem." Nicki said it automatically. Only she was not okay. Not even close. Her stomach was roiling, and she wondered how long she was going to be able to control herself.

The new cook started to pass her the spatula.

Nicki reached for it, noticed it was dripping with yellowed, half-congealed grease. *Uh-oh.*

Spinning, she raced for the ladies' room.

Lou was waiting in the hallway when she finally emerged. His hairy, tattooed forearms were folded across his chest and he was glaring at her. "Well?"

"I just needed a quick break, myself, that's all."

"Tell you what," he drawled. "You can have a long break. A permanent one, starting now. You're fired."

"But…"

The man already had his back to her.

"Wait, please, Lou. I need this job."

He turned and gave her a once-over. "Yeah? So why were you late again today?"

"There was trouble in my neighborhood this morning. I had to stay until the cops said I could leave."

"Okay…suppose I buy that. How come you keep complaining you're sick all the time?"

"Not all the time. Honest. I just can't help it." Hoping the truth about her pregnancy would soften his heart she blurted out, "I'm going to have a baby."

"Uh-huh. That's what I figured. Like I said, you're done here. Pick up your final check on Friday."

"No, please. How am I going to survive?"

"Should of thought of that before you messed around and got caught."

Left alone in the dingy hallway, Nicki leaned against the wall. She felt as drained as if she'd just run a marathon. What was she going to do now? Her bills were already steep, thanks to her conniving former fiancé, Bobby Lee Crawford, and his liberal use of her credit cards without her knowledge. She was behind in the rent, too. Not to mention how expensive it was going to be to repair the damage she imagined had been done to her apartment and her furniture. Those repairs were likely to cost a lot more than she had in the bank, which was pretty much nothing.

Untying the apron, she wadded it into a ball and threw it onto a chair as she stomped out of the truck stop. What a day this had already been. She could hardly wait to see what other disheartening surprises awaited her.

This was *not* how life was supposed to be when a person became a Christian, was it? She had no idea but she was certainly going to ask Pastor Eaton the next time she saw him. Instead of life getting easier, it seemed as if her problems had become a lot more complicated since she'd turned to Jesus for help, asked for forgiveness and surrendered to the Lord a month ago.

So, now what? Nicki wondered. What, indeed? She was without a job, had no savings and was still two months in arrears on her rent because she'd believed Bobby Lee when he'd taken the cash from her and lied about paying the landlord. What a blind fool she'd been where that smooth-talking Romeo was concerned.

Her hand rested at her waist and she sighed. "Poor

little baby. You sure picked a mama with her share of problems, didn't you?"

Now that she was outside in the fresh south Texas air and sunshine, she took a few deeper breaths and began to feel better. Yes, she was in a pickle because she'd trusted the wrong man with her heart, but she was strong and smart and resilient. She'd had to be to have survived thus far. There were other jobs, other cafés.

She'd never consider applying at Arianna's place, even if her cousin were still alive to give her a job, but there was the Sagebrush Diner and even the Youth Center. They might need a good cook or kitchen assistant. As long as she could ventilate the work area, she should be fine. She wasn't trained for any other decent-paying jobs, and as soon as her pregnancy started to show, she knew she'd have an even harder time finding steady work.

Determined to start looking immediately, Nicolette rounded the corner and stopped dead in her tracks. Shading her eyes, she squinted in disbelief.

There sat her car, her only means of transportation, with all four tires totally flattened!

Jackson's pager went off just as he got back to the station and reclaimed Titan.

With the dog trotting happily at his side, he headed for Slade McNeal's office to find out what was up.

"You wanted to see me, Captain?"

"Yeah. What kind of shape was the Johnson woman in when you left her?"

"Pretty good, considering." Jackson's hand rested on Titan's silky black head and he absently ruffled the dog's ears as he continued. "She thought she'd seen somebody coming after her behind the truck stop, but I didn't find anything odd when I checked that area. Why?"

"Because she just called to report that her tires had been flattened. I asked her if they'd been slashed but she didn't know. She apparently took one look and high-tailed it down the road before she used her phone." He cleared his throat. "Says most of her personal belongings are still locked in the car, and she's not going back there for any reason until you show up to keep her company."

"Me?" Jackson could tell he was coloring but chose to pretend otherwise. "Why me? Was there another bomb threat?"

"No. Apparently you impressed her, Detective. She said she'd promised you she'd call."

Jackson scowled. "Hold on. She works nights. She shouldn't have even looked at her car 'til almost dawn. What was she doing out there now?"

"Guess you can ask her that when you see her." He checked a note on his desk, then handed it over. "You'll find her at the Jiffy-Suds car wash on Highway 20, down the block from where she works."

Jackson turned to leave, Titan at his side, when the captain added, "Give your dog a break and let him sniff around there if he wants. I know he's not a tracking dog like my Rio or Austin Black's bloodhound, Justice, but he has a good nose. A little cross-training might prove useful."

"Yes, sir."

"I suspect the Johnson woman is more scared than anything. Since she's apparently taken with you, I'll expect you to continue to cultivate her confidence and get us some answers."

"You still believe it's all connected? The murders, the drugs, the bomb, everything that's been happening in Sagebrush these past few months?"

The captain's jaw clenched. "It's entirely possible. Remember, one of our primary objectives is still to find my Rio and bring him home. Soon. Before the syndicate that kidnapped him decides to put a bullet in him—if they haven't already." He sighed heavily. "Caleb would never understand losing his best buddy for good. You can't explain things like that to a five-year-old. The poor kid's been a nervous wreck ever since Rio was dognapped."

"I'll do my best, sir," Jackson said. "How's your father doing? Any lasting effects from the beating he took back then?"

"Some. Dad's not himself, that's for sure. He still has to have nursing care at home. I wish I knew if the dognappers beat him because he tried to do the right thing and stop them from stealing Rio, or if they acted from plain meanness. Guess it really doesn't matter." He paused, pensive, before ordering, "Get going, Worth. Find out what the Johnson woman knows."

"Yes, sir," Jackson said, saluting as he took his leave.

The whole K-9 team had been searching for Rio— McNeal's multipurpose, elite German shepherd—since January, with little result. Whoever had taken the dog had obviously known exactly when to strike, assaulting the captain's elderly father, as well, and putting him in the hospital in a coma. Their K-9 unit had managed to rescue a neighborhood child who had been snatched after seeing Rio abducted, but as far as finding the dog went, they'd drawn a series of blanks.

Jackson gave his black Lab an additional pat as he loaded him into one of the unit's special SUVs. Losing a beloved partner like Titan the way McNeal had lost Rio would be devastating.

The search for Rio had had one unexpected benefit, however. It had given the police more leads to a crime syndicate operating in and around Sagebrush. Unfortunately, that discovery had also resulted in a string of violent deaths, the last being that of Arianna Munson—aka "the Serpent."

"So, what do you know about all this, Ms. Johnson?" Jackson muttered to himself. "And why won't you tell us?"

Maybe a better question would be, *How can I convince you to trust me?* If Nicolette didn't realize she held the key to the puzzle that had gotten her cousin into so much trouble, perhaps he could still succeed. All he'd have to do is get her talking, and listen very carefully to everything she revealed.

If the answer was there, he prayed he'd recognize it quickly. Before it was too late to save Rio and before something else happened to the Johnson woman.

There was no doubt in his mind. Someone was out to get her. And they had nearly succeeded at least twice, maybe more.

Nicki paced, perspiring more from anxiety than from the warm Texas evening temperature. She scanned passing traffic. She could see the truck stop far in the distance, but figured as long as she stayed near the activity at the car wash she'd be safe enough, at least for the time being.

The approach of the distinctively lettered K-9 unit elated her so much, she couldn't help grinning. In seconds, she was standing beside the driver's-side window.

Jackson rolled it down and leaned a bent arm on the sill. "I hear you have another problem."

"You could say that. Somebody flattened all my tires."

"Good thing you discovered it before dark," he said. "Why did you?"

"Why did I *what?*"

"Go outside. I didn't expect you to venture into the parking lot until you were off work. I don't suppose whoever messed with your car did, either. So, why were you out there now?"

"I was trying to go home," she replied with a grimace. "Right after you left, I started to feel sick. I told Lou why and he fired me."

"That's against the law. You can't be fired for being pregnant."

"No, but I can if I'm no longer able to work around food, and that's the only job I know. Besides, he's got his nephew working there now, and I have a feeling he was looking for a good excuse to let me go." She shrugged. "If it hadn't been that it would have been something else, like my being late for work again."

"Do you want me to have a talk with him? Explain the other problems you've been having and what held you up today?"

"Don't bother. I told him enough. Besides, it's none of Lou's business." She started to circle the black-and-white. "You can give me a lift back to my car, though, so I can show you what happened to it."

Jackson unlocked the passenger door with the flick of a switch. "Okay. Climb in."

Titan stuck his head over the back of the seat and panted in her ear while she fastened her seat belt.

"I'm glad you brought your buddy," Nicki said, tickling the dog under the chin. "I know he's not a protection dog, but I still feel safer when he's around."

"So do I. We've been partners since we were deployed in Afghanistan. Actually, Titan outranks me. It's customary for all the working dogs to hold a higher rank than their handlers."

"Really? How did you manage to bring him home with you when he was trained for the battlefield?"

"It's a long story." In her peripheral vision she saw the man glance lovingly at the dog before he added, "Have you ever heard of PTSD?"

"Freaking out from stress? Sure."

"Well, dogs can get it, too. Titan and I were traveling in a convoy when the vehicle directly ahead of us was blown up by an improvised explosive device. After that, he was never the same. He still works okay, but he's just too jumpy for military service. That's how I was able to keep him after my discharge."

Suddenly, a lot of things made sense to her. "I get it. And you came here to Sagebrush because of that old explosion the lowlife on the phone was bragging about."

"That's part of the reason. My boss, Captain McNeal, lost his wife in that attack. When Titan and I applied for a job with the K-9 unit, he had a strong personal reason to convince the commissioners to hire us."

"That is so sad." She pointed toward her car as they drove closer. "There. See it? All four tires are flat."

"You stay here with Titan, and I'll go have a look.

Since there's no hurry getting you back on the road, I want to examine the scene carefully."

"It could be just vandalism."

She watched him hesitate long enough to report his location to dispatch, then open the door and put one foot outside before saying, "I don't think this is any more random than the attacks at your apartment, Ms. Johnson. If you're smart, you won't get complacent."

Nicki knew he was right. Like it or not, she had become the target of some shady characters who apparently had ties to Arianna.

The biggest question was how in the world could she hope to convince them—and the police—that she was innocent. Clueless. Not worth bothering with.

Except for this particular officer, she added silently. Given a choice, she would just as soon have him hanging around a little while longer, at least until the threats stopped.

It wasn't sensible.

It wasn't logical.

But it was true. She felt a lot safer when he and his big, black dog were close by.

Like right now.

As far as Jackson was concerned, the pretty cook had dodged a theoretical bullet once again. If she hadn't been fired and, therefore, left work before nightfall, she could easily have become a crime statistic.

He swept the general area, checked inside her car and retrieved her personal belongings, then returned to Nicolette and Titan. They both seemed very glad to see him.

"Looks like somebody let the air out of the tires instead of slashing them, so you should be good to go as soon as we get them inflated."

"But…why would someone do this?"

"You really don't see the possibilities?"

"No."

He turned sideways in the seat to partially face her. "Okay. Here's what I think… I think somebody still believes your cousin told you something important, and they're determined to get the secret from you."

"By letting the air out of my tires? That's crazy."

"Not if it meant you'd be stranded at night, all alone, behind a building that provides plenty of cover from passing witnesses."

He could see that his frankness was making an impression with her. Judging by the paleness of her cheeks, he wondered if he'd gone too far.

Instinct told him to reach out to her, to squeeze her hand, to offer comfort. Training and experience warned against getting too friendly. Before Jackson could decide which concept to employ, his dog settled the question for him.

Titan stretched his big head over the seat and gave the frightened young woman a kiss on the cheek. The slurp was audible.

If she'd looked the least bit upset, Jackson wouldn't have laughed. However, when she squealed, "Eww," and swiped at her damp cheek with her palm, he had to chuckle. "Sorry. I think he wants you to know you're safe with us."

"Safe, maybe. Wet, too. Is he always this slobbery when he wants to show affection?"

"As a matter of fact, no," Jackson told her. "I guess he remembers you hugging him after the blast."

"It's a good thing I didn't give him any treats, too, or he'd have *drowned* me!"

Pointing at the dog Jackson ordered, "Down. Stay." And Titan plopped onto the backseat as if he'd had that pose in mind all along.

"He really is amazing," Nicki said. "I've never seen such a well-trained animal. Do you get to take him home with you at night?"

"Yes. I have a little ranch east of here where he can run around and unwind." He smiled. "Me, too."

"That's nice." Nicki paused and sighed. "So, what shall I do about my car? I'll need it if I'm going to go job hunting."

"I'll radio Arnie's Garage for a service truck. If the driver can't take care of your tires on the spot, I'll have the car delivered to you later. In the meantime, suppose you let me buy you a cup of coffee and maybe a bite to eat?"

"Not here," Nicki said quickly, eyeing The Truck Stop Diner. "Any place but here."

"Fine." He used his radio to order the roadside assistance, then started the SUV. "All set. How does the Sagebrush Diner sound?"

She smiled. "Wonderful."

"Good." *And while we're there,* Jackson mused, *we'll relax and talk about a lot of things, including what your crooked cousin may have told you.*

It didn't matter how much he happened to like this woman or how smitten his dog was with her, there was no way he could believe she didn't know more than she was willing to admit. Nobody her age could still be this naive, this innocent. Nobody.

This woman was hiding something. Something that was liable to get her killed if she didn't confess soon.

FOUR

Nicki rolled down the SUV window and let the balmy April air caress her face as the K-9 cop drove her into town. Many businesses were located on or near Sagebrush Boulevard, as was the large, redbrick church where she had so recently become a Christian.

They pulled up to the familiar storefront diner. "While I'm here, I can ask if they need a cook," Nicki said. "I need to find something that I can keep doing while I'm waiting for the baby."

Jackson rolled down the windows partway to give Titan fresh, cool air before he circled to open her door. "Isn't it going to be hard to be on your feet a lot?"

"I haven't had any problems yet. The biggest drawback at the truck stop was that tiny, stuffy kitchen."

She accompanied him to the diner and felt a rush of cool air as he opened the glass door in the brick facade. This place, too, smelled of cooking, but not in the way her former job had.

The booths along one wood-paneled wall beckoned, and she headed straight for the most distant one.

"I can't let you pay for my order," she insisted, scooting in. "This is not a date."

"Of course not."

"Good, because I don't want you to think I'm trying to take advantage of your kindness."

The astonished look on his handsome face almost made her giggle. It was ludicrous to suggest that anyone could take advantage of a man like this unless he permitted it. Still, she had to wonder why he was being so solicitous. Perhaps his motives were not as pure as hers.

As soon as Nicki had ordered a slab of apple pie à la mode and coffee she leaned back, folded her arms across her chest and spoke her mind. "Okay. Here we are. Now why did you *really* invite me?" The odd arch of one of his brows caused the beginnings of a cynical smile at the corners of her mouth. "Well?"

"I don't suppose you'll believe it was out of the goodness of my heart?"

"Nope. I've had my fill of manipulative men, particularly lately. Try telling me the truth."

"Fair enough." Leaning forward, his hands clasped atop the faux-wood table, Jackson spoke quietly. "My boss wants me to talk to you about what Arianna said with her last breath."

"You mean that ridiculous *code* thing that Murke was screaming about before the shooting started? Forget it. I don't know anything about any codes. I told you— my cousin and I hardly ever spoke. I am the *last* person she'd have shared an important confidence with."

"Okay. Suppose I buy that."

"What do you mean, *suppose?* It's the truth. I don't know a thing about her business or her criminal activities. She and I were at odds from the time we were teenagers. Arianna used to laugh at me for being too goody-goody. She made no bones about it."

"Then why would she waste her last breath warning you?"

"How should I know?" Nicki could tell from the warmth of her cheeks that she was getting upset. "Maybe she was trying to get me into trouble for the fun of it. She did that lots of times when we were kids."

"Okay." Jackson unfolded his napkin and eased back in the booth to make room for their orders. "Eat your pie and then we'll talk to the manager in case there's a chance for a job here."

"What about my poor apartment and my tires?"

"If the car isn't ready soon enough, I'll drive you home and the garage can deliver it later."

"Assuming I have a home. You haven't really told me what to expect."

"It's probably not as bad as you're envisioning." He paused to add cream to his coffee. "I didn't get a detailed look at it, but they tell me your bedroom is still in pretty good shape so you can salvage your clothes and things like that."

"Oh, spiffy. And I can sit in the middle of an exploded sofa to watch TV?"

To his credit, he winced. "No TV, I'm afraid. No windows, either."

"What? I can't even lock myself in?"

"Probably not, now that you mention it. I'll have a talk with your landlord and see about getting you moved into another unit."

"I don't want another unit. I want my home back. I want my job back. I want my *life* back."

"One step at a time. One day at a time," he said so calmly she wanted to scream.

Who did this cop think he was, lecturing her? He

probably had a family and a real home. That was all she'd wanted. To belong again, the way she had once, when her parents were alive and life had been so peaceful. It wasn't fair that they had both been taken from her when she was in her teens and made her grow up overnight.

In retrospect, she could see that that desire for normalcy was what had gotten her into trouble with Bobby Lee, yet it had also ultimately led her back to church and had resulted in her recently renewed faith, so she could hardly complain. Now she understood how desperately she had needed God's forgiveness, His unconditional love. She still did. And so did her unborn baby.

They would make a family of their own someday, just the two of them. Nicki knew she could handle being a single mother. Her fondest hope was that raising her child alone wouldn't be too hard on the little boy or girl.

It was becoming clear that the Lord had been protecting her when He'd allowed her to glimpse Bobby Lee's true character. Being deserted by a selfish liar like that had to be better than having him co-parenting their child.

The only thing she would have done differently, given another chance, was avoid listening to her biological clock and believing the sweet lies and so-called marriage proposal of that handsome cowboy-type in the first place. Anybody could look good in a Stetson. It took a special man to deserve to become a father.

The trip back to Nicki's apartment was short and uneventful. Jackson pulled up to the curb and stopped. "I truly am sorry you lost your job."

"Yeah, me, too." She sighed wearily. "I'm beginning

to realize how hard it's going to be to find another cooking position. Sagebrush is too small."

"You'll find something. I know you will. My earlier offer stands. If you want me to speak to Lou for you, I'll be glad to."

Nicki shook her head. "No. I can't go back to work there. Just the thought of that steamy, stinky little kitchen turns my stomach."

"Okay." Jackson circled the SUV to open her door. "First things first. I'll walk you up to your apartment so you can get some of your things."

"Then what? I have no place to go."

"There must be an empty suite close by, hopefully in this same building." He saw she was standing strong, unwavering. Nevertheless, he felt it would do her good to have Titan along so he also leashed the dog and let him jump down. "Let's stop at the manager's unit on the way up and ask."

"Whatever you say. I'm beyond logical thought right now. It seems like my whole world has been turned upside down."

Jackson smiled to reassure her as they made their way along the front walk. The old concrete was so cracked and uneven, he almost cupped her elbow to steady her without thinking of the possible negative consequences.

Reaching past her, he opened the worn exterior door and held it while she passed through. He'd seen plenty of dumps before, but this building was close to the worst. Moving out might be the best thing for her. Getting into a safer neighborhood wouldn't hurt, either, particularly since she had her baby's welfare to consider as well as her own.

Jackson paused to knock on the manager's door, then turned to Nicki when no one responded. "Guess they're not home."

"The TV is blasting so maybe they can't hear us over that noise. Let's go on up to my place and see what's left. We can stop by again on our way out."

Jackson's smile spread. "See? There's nothing wrong with your thinking. That's a very sensible suggestion."

"Yup. That's me. All brains."

"Don't put yourself down," he said with a scowl. "I don't know very many people who could cope with the stresses you've faced, and do as well as you are."

Her expression was one of astonishment when she glanced up and murmured, "Thanks."

"No thanks necessary. It's the truth."

"Well, thanks, anyway. It's nice to get a compliment that has nothing to do with my looks—or my cooking."

He was pleased to see her blush slightly, and hear her soft chuckle in spite of the trying situation. The woman was a survivor. That inner strength would stand her in good stead in the coming months, particularly if she failed to find a new job.

Climbing the stairs, Jackson noted that Titan seemed reluctant. That figured. The halls still smelled of smoke and undoubtedly of the chemicals used to formulate the explosive. Plus, the dog would remember this place as being the one that had originally frightened him.

"Let me go to your door first," Jackson said.

Wide-eyed, she stared at him. "You don't think…?"

"No. I don't think there's another bomb. It never hurts to be careful, though. Let Titan and me do what we're trained for. It'll only take a second."

"Okay," Nicki replied, smiling slightly. "But if I see

anybody trying to deliver more flowers, I may shove him back down the stairs first and ask questions later."

Jackson could tell she was trying to find humor in spite of her fear so he played along. "You probably won't have to. The department has been grilling every florist in town as if they're hiding Public Enemy Number One behind the bouquets in their coolers. After that, I doubt any of them would accept an order for delivery to this address."

"Good to hear." She rolled her eyes. "Did you figure out where those exploding flowers came from?"

"Not yet. There wasn't much left to go on and no record of a cash-and-carry sale." He held up his hand like a traffic cop. "Wait there. We'll only be a minute."

He approached the ruined apartment. There was a plain, white envelope bordered in duct tape stuck to the outside of the door.

On the front was printed *#210*. That was all.

Donning latex gloves, he carefully pried the tape loose and opened the envelope, fully expecting another threat.

Instead, he found an eviction notice.

Nicki watched the K-9 officer from afar. She could see that he'd discovered something on her door, but until he motioned her to come closer, she had no idea what it might be.

He handed the paper to her. Immediate incredulity was followed closely by a teary blurring of her vision. She was being thrown out. She'd been a good tenant until recently. Didn't the past count for anything?

"I'm sorry," Jackson said.

What could she say? The notice spelled out several

plausible reasons for her eviction, besides the bombing. She sighed and shook her head. "It's okay."

"You were behind in your rent?"

"It's a long story," Nicki told him. "I guess I can understand why this mess might be the last straw. I just wish I still had a job and references so I'd have a better chance of getting another place to live."

"First things first," he said matter-of-factly. "I have permission for you to pick up your clothes and some personal items as long as you confine yourself to the bedroom and bath, in case the crime scene techs want to go over the living room again. Then we'll find you temporary quarters somewhere. Maybe at one of the motels downtown."

"I can't afford to do that," Nicki said, feeling utterly defeated.

"Let me handle the details. The department has an agreement with several businesses to temporarily house crime or disaster victims. Your situation qualifies. Don't worry about the cost."

"Temporarily?"

"One day at a time," he said solemnly.

She had to smile. "How about an hour at a time? I don't think I can handle another day like this one has been. Not all at once."

"She didn't even own a suitcase, so she threw her clothes and stuff into pillowcases. I placed her in the motel closest to downtown, that way she can walk to the store or to church if she wants," Jackson reported to Captain McNeal. "Arnie's delivering her car to her there."

Slade stared into space for a few moments, his blue

eyes narrowing, before he replied, "It's stretching the rules to include her in that relief program."

"Yeah… I know. But I couldn't figure what else to do with her. She really seems clueless about her cousin's criminal activities, but she may be in danger just the same. I had her program my private number into her cell phone, too, in case she needs it."

Opening a file folder on his desk, Slade scanned the loose pages. "The Johnson woman is thirty-four. She's hardly naive. She *has* to know more than she's admitting."

"What do you want me to do next? As long as she's out of a job, all we can do is keep an eye on the motel, in case she has visitors, and monitor her calls."

"How's your uncle Harold these days?"

Jackson's eyebrow arched. "He's fine. Why?"

"Just wondering. Last time you mentioned him, he was carping about having to do all the cooking while you were on duty, wasn't he?"

"Oh, hey. Hold your horses, Captain. Harold and I make out fine by ourselves. We don't need a cook. If I was in the market for help I'd hire a cowpuncher to manage my livestock—not that I run many head."

Slade's gaze narrowed. "I've been giving this situation a lot of thought. I definitely think you need kitchen help. Matter of fact, I know just the person. She's a pro and she needs a job. Plus, if she was at the ranch with Harold all day, he could help us keep an eye on her when you're working. What could be better?"

"Anything but that," Jackson grumbled. "My uncle thinks he missed his calling when he became a sheriff's deputy instead of a stand-up comic. Now that he's retired, he drives me crazy with his stale jokes. Ms.

Johnson would never put up with him on a daily basis. I barely manage."

"I'll talk to Harold myself, tell him to cool it and give him the idea that it's an unofficial assignment. He'll love it. Once a cop, always a cop. You know that."

Jackson wasn't convinced that the captain's conclusions were right. He had one last hope. "What if she turns me down?"

"She won't. I've already warned off every restaurant and greasy spoon in and around Sagebrush," Slade said flatly. "Ms. Johnson can't leave this area because she's a person of interest in her cousin's murder case, and she won't find a job in town. She's out of options. She'll agree to work for you."

"You've really thought of everything, haven't you?"

"That's my job," Slade drawled, obviously pleased with himself.

Jackson was anything but happy. "There must be another way."

"Not as perfect as my plan. I think it would be best if you approached Ms. Johnson ASAP. No use taking the chance she might decide to apply for a different kind of position. The sooner she moves out to your ranch and starts cooking for you two starving bachelors, the better."

"And if I refuse to hire her?"

"I can't order you to comply, but you're a good man and a smart cop. If you're truly concerned about her being innocent and in somebody's crosshairs, you'll move her to where she's a lot safer." He paused and closed the file folder. "And if she's as guilty as I think she is, we all need to do everything we can to prove it."

He reached for the phone on his desk and lifted the

receiver, holding it while he added, "I'll take care of briefing your uncle. You go hire yourself a cook."

Jackson was muttering to himself all the way to his patrol vehicle. He loaded and secured Titan, then slid behind the wheel. The captain's idea had merit—he simply didn't want to bring Nicolette into his personal life.

And why is that? he asked himself. The honest answer was not only a surprise, it was an unwelcome one. He didn't want to take the chance of getting closer to her. If he had to interact with her all the time, he'd have to really guard his heart because he already liked her far too much for his own good. Or for hers.

FIVE

Nicki had freshened up at the motel and then began using her cell to phone every place she could think of that might need a good cook. After her problematical parting with Lou, she suspected he must have been bad-mouthing her because all her polite inquiries about work were summarily dismissed.

Discouraged, she was planning to make the rounds in person, first thing in the morning, when there was an unexpected knock at her door. Was it safe to answer?

One look through the peephole showed she had nothing to be afraid of this time. The exterior walkway lights illuminated a familiar, most welcome figure.

Grinning broadly, she jerked open the door and greeted the K-9 officer. "Hello! What a surprise." She scanned the sidewalk. "Where's your furry buddy?"

"In the car. Can we talk?"

"Sure. Come on in," she replied.

"You aren't afraid of harming your reputation?"

Nicki had to laugh. "Me? I'm pregnant and alone, just got fired…and my apartment was bombed right before I was evicted. How much worse can my reputation get?"

"You have a point there."

He removed his cap and stepped through the door. The way he was worrying the brim of the hat telegraphed unusual apprehension, particularly since his demeanor was normally so calm and unruffled.

"So, what brings you here, Detective Worth? Am I in trouble again for something I didn't do? Because if that's what you came to tell me, I'd just as soon skip it."

"Actually, no," he said slowly.

"Then what's wrong? You look as if some lowlife just tried to kick your dog."

"You're mistaken," Jackson insisted with a smile that seemed forced to her. "Actually, I came to tell you I've arranged for your undamaged furniture to be stored, and found you a new job."

"Really?" Nicki was so elated, she almost forgot herself and hugged him the way Southerners commonly did when celebrating good news. "Where? Did the Sagebrush Diner reconsider?"

"No. Nothing like that. This is a private residence that needs a cook. I figured, since you were so short of cash, you wouldn't care where you worked."

"I guess I don't. What's the catch?"

"No catch. You'll have room and board plus a negotiable salary. You'll be expected to serve three meals a day and keep the kitchen clean. Anything you need will be provided to you, within reason of course, and you'll have your own private room with a bath."

"Go on. Who's my boss? Some lecherous old guy who'll chase me around the kitchen for fun?"

"I hope not." He blushed. "The only older man in the house will be my uncle Harold, and I'll make sure he's on his best behavior."

Nicki could feel the beginnings of a headache thrumming at her temples. "Hold on. You're asking me to work for your uncle?"

"And for me. Harold and I live together on the ranch I told you about. He's been managing the place when I'm gone but he hates to cook and when he tries, it's barely edible." A smile quirked the corners of Jackson's mouth. "Just don't tell him I said so, okay?"

"Slow down. I haven't agreed to take the job. I don't want charity."

The K-9 officer seemed to be warming to his subject because his smile widened more naturally. "Believe me, you'll earn every penny. Harold is a nice guy but his sense of humor can be a bit much sometimes. Your only problem with him will be trying not to groan when he tells the same lame joke for the tenth time."

She met his eyes. "Where will you be all this time?"

"At home, whenever I'm not on duty. I don't have to stay in town as long as I can be paged and respond quickly. The ranch is only about a twenty-minute drive from the station."

"What about housekeeping? I'm a cook, not a window washer."

"No windows." Jackson raised his hand as if taking an oath. "I promise. We have an older woman who comes in to clean once a week. Other than that, it's just Harold and me and Titan. I was hoping that wouldn't be a problem for you."

"I guess it isn't," Nicki said after a short pause. "When do I start?"

"Um, well, I suppose you should spend at least one night here to give us a chance to get a room ready for you."

"Very sensible. One thing, though."

"Yes?" he asked.

"I won't stay at the ranch if I get an offer for a regular restaurant job here in town."

"Fair enough." He squared his hat on his head and touched the brim politely. "Good night, Ms. Johnson."

"Under the circumstances, I think you should start calling me Nicki," she said as she saw him to the door. "I prefer it."

"All right. I guess you can call me Jackson."

"If I'm working for you, I think it's more proper that I use your job title or your last name," she replied flatly.

"You called Lou by his first name and he was your boss, too. I hope you don't think working for me is going to demean you… Nicki. I'd never do that."

"Okay…you win. Jackson it is," she said with a smile, wishing her cheeks didn't feel so warm all of a sudden.

Standing at the door and watching him climb into the SUV and drive off, she found herself trying to figure out what he was up to. It was nice of him to offer her a job. However, she wasn't quite ready to view his motivation as totally altruistic.

Still, it didn't matter, did it? She'd be working steadily, and if something else came along, she could move back into town. It wasn't as if she had a lot of furniture to put in storage, or anything else to tie her down. And the fresh air of a ranch environment would be good for the baby.

She rested her hand lightly at her waist and said a silent prayer for her unborn child. She'd already seen a doctor and been told that everything was fine, but that didn't keep her from worrying. Or from remembering what had happened when she'd broken the news to Bobby Lee.

They had been watching an end-of-season football game in her apartment, sharing the sofa that now lay in tatters. Nicki had snuggled up and rested her head on his muscular shoulder. "I have something wonderful to tell you, Bobby Lee."

"Not now, Nicki. The score's tied and they're going into overtime."

Feeling so safe, so filled with joy, she couldn't wait a second longer and blurted, "We're going to have a baby."

The game on TV forgotten, Bobby Lee slowly lifted his booted feet off the coffee table and sat up straighter. He was staring at her as if she had just spoken in a foreign language. His jaw hung slack.

"Isn't that great?" Nicki asked, confused because of his strange expression. "Before we know it, we'll have the big family we talked about."

Instead of smiling and hugging her the way she'd anticipated, however, the tall Texan jumped up and began to yell.

Nicki was flabbergasted. "What's the matter, honey?"

He continued to rant, pace and throw things until his face got so red she wondered if he was going to have a literal fit.

Finally, he returned to lean over her. His volatile mood had caught her by surprise, but that was nothing compared to the intimidating look he flashed her way.

"Thought you'd trap me, huh? Well, you can forget it," he shouted. "I'm too young to settle down."

The feeling of dread that had enveloped Nicki at that time returned in the present. She remembered saying, "But, we love each other. You asked me to marry you."

She shivered, recalling the sarcastic laugh that had

bubbled up from the man she'd expected to spend the rest of her life with.

His sneer had been almost as bad. "Of course I said that, darlin'. It's not my fault you bought the fairy tale, lock, stock and barrel. That's why I like to date older women. They're so desperate they'll believe anything. Besides, how do I even know the kid's mine?"

Silent tears were bathing Nicki's cheeks just as they had when Bobby Lee had revealed his true colors. How could she have been so blind, so naive? Thirty-four wasn't that old, was it? Of course not.

But she had been a terrible fool. She had yearned to believe that someone loved her the way Bobby Lee had sworn he did. That had been her downfall.

Disgusted with herself, she dabbed her cheeks with a tissue. It was a good thing she'd found forgiveness in church and knew that God was merciful because she certainly needed His help starting over.

It did occur to her that perhaps meeting the K-9 cop was a part of the Lord's ultimate plan for her protection. If she hadn't had to nearly get blown up to initiate their encounter, she might have been more likely to assume that divine intervention had been at work.

Thoughtful, Nicki realized she needed to say a prayer of thanks for Jackson's generous job offer. That, she could do. Meaning it from the bottom of her heart was another matter. It wasn't easy to give thanks for a situation that hadn't turned out anywhere near the way she had envisioned.

Her ideas and her prayerful pleas to her heavenly Father had been specific. His answers, however, were far from what she'd expected.

That realization brought a contrite smile. If she truly

trusted God as she'd vowed she did, she would manage to thank Him no matter how things turned out.

Nicki closed her eyes, folded her hands and began, "Father, thank You. I don't understand what's going on but I want to, so please help me. I'm doing the best I can. Honest, I am."

It wasn't a polished prayer like the ones she had heard spoken in church, but it was sincere and straight from her heart.

And, in spite of her misgivings about pretty much everything else these days, she knew God heard her and accepted her just as she was, flaws and all.

That, alone, was enough to bring fresh tears to her eyes and a true spirit of thankfulness to her heart and soul.

Pensive, she walked to the window of the small motel room and looked out, intending to direct her attention heavenward.

The sun had set. Moonlight gave a surreal cast to the dimly lit parking lot, and made the distant hills seem to shimmer—hills she would soon visit when she reported to her new job.

Nicki was actually looking forward to the peacefulness of nights spent on a ranch. There was something special about standing quietly in the twilight and listening to chirps and coos of nocturnal birds and insects. Perhaps there would even be a porch swing where she could sit and let go of her worldly cares more fully.

Lost in thought, she blinked, then tensed. Was that a shadow moving near her parked car? Could someone have followed her? She hadn't thought about hiding her whereabouts by vacating her ruined apartment in secret.

Her only focus had been on salvaging her possessions, and getting another roof over her head.

Nicki held very still and peered into the darkness. The harder she stared, the more the images seemed to flicker and waver.

She switched off the bedside lamp to better hide her presence, then quickly returned to her vantage point. There was nothing out there. No bogeymen, no crooks, no stealthy adversaries of any kind.

"It was my imagination," she insisted, speaking aloud to help reassure herself. "I'm tired and stressed, that's all. There's nobody lurking. I'm perfectly safe."

Nevertheless, she double-checked the lock on her door and threw the dead bolt, as well. If they wanted to get to her, they were going to have to break down the door.

"Which is exactly what the police did when Murke came after me," she murmured, pocketing her cell phone. "And it only took them a few seconds to get in."

She glanced at the bed, then at the closet. If she took the quilted spread off the bed, folded it and used it as a mattress on the floor of the small closet, she'd be fairly comfortable. That way, if anyone snuck in, they wouldn't find her easily. And, as long as she stayed fully dressed, she'd be ready to flee at a moment's notice.

"That idea is so foolish, you should be ashamed," she countered, lecturing herself as if she were two separate people. "Either God is watching over you or He's not. Which is it?"

Heaving a sigh, Nicki whipped the comforter off the king-size bed and started to fold it. Since the Lord had given her a keen mind, she figured He expected her to use it. If nothing bad happened during the night, fine.

If someone did come after her, they might think she'd moved already and leave right away rather than stay to search the room.

As an afterthought, she stuffed two of the three pillows under the blankets on the bed as if she were actually lying there. Yes, it was silly. And, yes, it demonstrated doubt where she should have been showing trust.

But it wasn't all that far-fetched to think that she might not be totally secure, even here. If somebody intended to harm her, she was not going to make it easy for them.

Tucking the pillowcases filled with her clothing under her head and reclining atop the folded quilt, she pulled one edge of it over her like a blanket, then pushed the sliding closet doors closed. Confined to the tiny area she felt much safer, as if she, like her baby, were enclosed in a cozy womb.

Nicki closed her eyes and began to pray as her mind calmed. In the background, normal noises from other motel guests and passing street traffic faded as weariness finally overtook her.

Jackson figured it would be best to speak with his uncle in person before just showing up with Nicki, so he notified his captain of his plans, then headed northeast toward the ranch.

It wasn't a big spread but it was enough to satisfy his urge to be a part of rural Texas culture. He ran about twenty head of Herefords, give or take a few spring calves, and had enough grazing land that he only had to supplement their feed with baled hay during the winter or during an occasional, long, dry spell.

The house was a simple, one-story rock building with a red tile roof and white wood trim. The older barn was painted to match. Neither he nor his uncle saw a need for fancy landscaping, so the lawn area was basically rocks and desert flora with a smattering of wildflowers in the spring. Other than that, the place tended to look deserted unless there were vehicles parked in the yard.

Tonight was no different. There was one lamp burning in the front room. A single bulb on the porch glowed as Jackson pulled around back.

Harold threw open the door and wasted no breath on pleasantries. "What's all this about a homeless woman coming to live with us? I thought you liked our arrangement. No muss, no fuss."

"I know, I know. It was the captain's idea." Jackson held up his hands, palms forward, in a gesture of surrender as he shouldered past his uncle with Titan at his side. "Don't worry…it shouldn't be for long. We need to keep an eye on her and this was the best place to do that."

"Who says?"

"Like I just told you—it was Captain McNeal's idea."

"You went along with it pretty easy. How come?"

Jackson watched Titan head straight for his full food and water bowls. "I can see a need, that's all. Besides, as McNeal reminded me, you hate to cook."

"I'd rather live on peanut butter and stale crackers than let a stranger mess with my grub. What makes you think this woman can do the job?"

"Anybody can cook better than you and I do," Jackson countered. "Didn't the captain tell you? She used to be a short-order cook at the truck stop out on the highway."

"He never said a word about that," Harold replied.

"Just kept goin' on about needin' me to spy on her. What'd she do, anyway?"

"Remember when Rio was dognapped and the captain's father was assaulted, too?"

"Of course. Your team got the guys who kidnapped that Billows kid who witnessed the whole thing, but the police dog is still missing. What's that got to do with this woman we're supposed to watch?"

"We think it's all part of the same overall problem. The rash of murders, the drugs, everything. What we can't figure out is who's killing off all the midlevel criminals in their organization. That's where Nicolette Johnson comes in. Her cousin, Arianna, was part of the gang that's apparently been behind most of the felonies in Sagebrush lately."

"Arianna Munson? Wasn't that case solved?"

"Not entirely. Arianna did kill Andrew Garry, but she also supposedly left behind clues to the crime syndicate's operations. A lot of people, my captain included, think our new cook holds the key to some important code the gang had, whether she realizes it or not."

"What're we supposed to do? Grill her for answers while she grills our dinner?"

Jackson rolled his eyes. "Something like that. Just try to be nice to her, will you? She seems like a pretty decent sort."

"How'd she end up homeless?"

"That was partly my fault. Somebody left a bomb outside her door and I didn't protect her well enough."

The older man eyed the dog licking the last bit of kibble from his bowl. "Titan didn't alert?"

"He did fine. I was too slow. Nicki picked up the explosive device and we just missed getting hurt."

Bushy gray eyebrows arched as Harold began to smile. "So it's *Nicki,* huh? Well, why didn't you say so?"

"Don't look at me like that," Jackson warned. "It's not personal."

"Fine by me. She's probably ugly as a mud fence with stringy hair and missing front teeth. Right?"

He made a face. "Okay, so she's pretty. So what? That doesn't change a thing."

Jackson would have felt a lot more confident that his excuse was credible if Harold had not walked off, chortling to himself, as if somebody had just told a really funny joke.

Truth to tell, Jackson hoped the joke was not going to be on him because thoughts of Nicki were beginning to take up an awful lot of room in his busy mind.

He not only cared about her well-being, he had begun to worry about the health and safety of her unborn child. If that wasn't crazy, he didn't know what was.

SIX

When Nicki awoke the following morning at the motel, she was stiff and sore and sorry she had given in to irrational fear. Nevertheless, she had slept soundly on the floor and was now ready to tackle anything, particularly her new job.

Slowly pushing open the sliding closet door, she got to her feet and stretched. In midyawn, she gazed across the room and gasped. The door she had so carefully locked was standing ajar!

Not only that, sunlight streaming through the doorway revealed that the blankets she had tucked around the bed pillows to replicate her own body had been thrown back, exposing the ruse.

Her wide-eyed stare swept the area in an instant. She was clearly alone, yet her heart continued to pound and her whole body trembled. Her unnamed enemies had been here while she slept. Why they hadn't bothered to check the closet was beyond her. The only reason she could see for her narrow escape was that the Lord must have been watching over her.

Pulling her cell phone out of her jeans pocket as she

rushed to slam and bolt the door, she paged through the stored numbers until she came to Jackson's.

One push of a button and it was ringing on his end. He barely managed to say, "Hello," before she blurted, "They're here. They found me. What should I do?"

"What? Who? Slow down. Where are you?"

"In my motel room. The door was open. They pulled back the blankets. They were in here. They had to be!"

"Are you alone now?"

"I—I think so. I was hiding in the closet and..."

"Okay—I'm on my way. Keep the door locked. I'll call the station for you. Don't come out until they send someone over or I get there."

"I'm really scared," she whispered.

"It'll be all right. Just try to stay calm."

She heard his voice fade for a minute as if he might have tucked his phone under his chin so he could pull on his boots. "Can—can you stay on the phone with me?"

"Yeah." He paused momentarily then shouted, "Harold! Call the station and have them send a unit to the Sagebrush Motel, room 12, code 3. There's been a break-in."

Cupping her phone in both hands, Nicki sank to the edge of the rumpled bed. At that moment, her choices were to sit or fall flat on her face, and she figured she'd be in better shape if she acted quickly.

It was only after she was perched on the mattress and starting to calm down that she realized she might have inadvertently damaged important clues.

She sighed regretfully.

"You still there?" Jackson sounded concerned.

"I'm here. Just disgusted with myself. I made another mistake and sat down on the bed. I'm sorry if it messed up evidence."

"Don't worry. Chances are, whoever was in your room was smart enough to wear gloves," he told her.

Nicki huffed. "Is that supposed to make me feel better? Because if it is, it didn't work."

Jackson had nearly reached the motel when he heard sirens in the background of his telephone connection to Nicki. "Sounds like help is arriving. It sure took them long enough."

"I was about to say the same thing," she replied. "Where are you?"

"Passing the truck stop. I'll be there in a couple more minutes."

"Good. I suppose I'd better go outside and tell your buddies that I'm okay."

"Only when you're positive they're actually coming to the motel. Let them get all the way to your door before you open it."

Although she acknowledged his orders, he was far from positive she was going to obey. There was a streak of stubbornness in that woman that was part bravery, part foolishness. In sticky situations, he was never quite sure which element was going to prevail.

He wheeled into the motel parking lot and slid his gray pickup to a stop behind the black-and-white patrol car. His K-9 unit shared the headquarters building with the regular police, but their system was separate so he wasn't that well acquainted with everyone.

Plus, he hadn't taken the time to change into his uniform. He flashed his badge for identification and nodded a terse greeting as he approached. "Morning. Find anything?"

The taller of the two officers shook his head. "Naw. Just a hysterical female. Probably forgot to latch her door and imagined somebody snuck in."

"You didn't turn up anything suspicious? No pry marks on the door?"

"Nope. Not a scratch."

"Okay. I'll take over," Jackson told them dismissively. "Thanks, fellas."

Nicki was standing outside her room door with her arms folded across her chest when he turned. Her hair was mussed and she looked as if she'd slept in her clothes, but he'd never seen her look lovelier. She was also eyeing him.

"About time. You look a lot more like you belong in Texas when you're wearing jeans and that kind of boots."

"I got ready in a hurry," Jackson said with a welcoming smile. "Apparently, you did, too."

"Actually, I never unpacked. I decided to sleep on the floor in the closet last night and it turned out to be a good thing. Whoever broke in didn't spot me."

He cupped her elbow and led her to his pickup truck, shielding her with his body as if expecting imminent attack. "I want to hear the whole story, from the beginning. What possessed you to move into the closet in the first place?"

"Intuition? An answer to prayer? I don't know. Since I've only been a committed Christian for a month or so, I have no past experiences to judge by. Maybe God put the idea in my head."

"How can you be sure you locked up properly? If you were in a hurry, the door might have popped open by itself. The other cops said there was no sign of forced entry."

Her fists rested on her hips and she stood firm, chin jutting. "You sound like them. I know I locked the door because I'm already paranoid, okay? And I put a couple of pillows into the bed so it would look as if I was still there."

"Well…" Jackson could tell she was getting upset with him but felt it was necessary to be certain something truly had gone wrong.

"Well, unless pillows can kick off their own covers, *somebody* else is responsible," she insisted. "Those blankets were thrown aside just like a person would do if they were trying to uncover a sleeping victim. That could have been me!"

"Okay. I'm convinced." He opened the truck door and pointed. "Get in. I'll go get your clothes, tell the manager to leave the room just as it is and schedule a CSU sweep. They probably won't turn up any clues, but as far as I know, they're not too busy to give it a quick once-over."

"Are we going to your ranch?"

"Yes. Sit tight. I'll be right back."

Although Jackson hated to be even a few steps from her, he had parked where he had full view of her room so he could also continue to observe her from there. The mussed bed was as she had described it. So was the closet. He swept up the pillowcases filled with her clothing, checked to make sure there was no one hiding in the bathroom and locked the outside door.

Hurrying back to Nicki, he pushed the cases across the seat to her and slid behind the wheel. "We'll stop at the office and make sure they understand that your room may be a crime scene, then head for the ranch. That okay with you?"

"I was hoping maybe I could stop and get a few more

things from my apartment. We left in such a hurry yesterday I didn't even think to bring a toothbrush."

"Make a list and I'll pick up anything you need. We're not going back to that apartment. At least not this morning."

He wondered if he'd overdone it with the stern tone, so he chanced a sidelong peek. Instead of the angry glare he had expected, however, Nicki appeared to be stifling a smile. "What's so funny?"

"You are. You don't have to bark at me, you know. I'm a reasonable person. All you have to do is state your case plainly and simply. I'll understand."

"And then you'll do exactly as I say?"

This time she did laugh. "I don't know if I'd go quite *that* far."

"Uh-huh. That's what I figured."

"But I will do my best to use the brains God gave me," Nicki assured him. "In spite of everything that's happened lately, I am learning."

"Have you made up your mind which side you want to be on?" he ventured smoothly, wondering if she'd been frightened enough to want to confess her deepest secrets.

When Nicki glared at him and said, "I have always been one of the good guys, whether you believe me or not, Detective," he was sorry he'd been so blunt.

She seemed innocent enough, at least in his eyes, but that was no guarantee she really was. His opinion had already been skewed, and he was getting more and more convinced that Arianna's dying words might not have referred to Nicki.

But if not her, then whom? And what was the code the woman known as the Serpent had hinted at? Most deathbed confessions were taken as authentic, yet it was always possible that Arianna hadn't known how close she was to taking her final breath, and had been lying in the hopes of diverting suspicion.

Jackson made an effort to concentrate on his driving while his mind spun like a Texas tornado. Everybody, his boss included, thought Nicolette Johnson was guilty. So what was his problem?

He took a deep, settling breath and shook his head in disgust. If he were honest with himself, he'd have to admit that he was starting to really like this woman. Not only was she naturally pretty, she had favorably impressed him with her courage and fortitude, not to mention her intelligence.

Positioning herself in the closet instead of occupying the comfortable bed had been a stroke of genius—one that might not have occurred to him even on his best day. He was, however, far more capable of defending himself from criminal attack than she was.

That was one of his biggest concerns. Although Nicki was admittedly smart and brave, she was still a lone woman against forces of evil that had already committed numerous murders in Sagebrush. Jackson did know one thing. Until they tracked down the person or persons in charge of the criminal syndicate and put an end to their reign, *nobody* would be safe. Least of all Nicolette Johnson and her unborn baby.

Nicki chose to avoid further conversation as they sped out of Sagebrush toward her new job. What was the matter with this man? Why couldn't he take her at her word when she was as much in the dark as the police were? Good old Arianna. Leave it to her to cause trouble, even after she was gone.

A twinge of guilt pricked Nicki's conscience. It had occurred to her to pay her estranged cousin a visit and tell her how wonderful it was to be a Christian, but there hadn't been time. Or had there? She supposed she could have made the time if she'd been convinced it was the right thing to do. Then again, if she had gone to see Arianna recently, there would be an even bigger reason to suspect their complicity.

The landscape changed little as they left the outskirts of Sagebrush. If there was one remarkable thing about south Texas it was its consistency. Trees grew well when clumped near settlements, yet struggled to survive along only seasonally wet streambeds.

Since the spring rains had arrived, there were broad fields of wildflowers, particularly delicate bluebonnets, the state flower. They were not always found in such abundance because everything had to be just right for them to sprout. Happily, this had been a banner year.

Jackson slowed to turn off the highway onto a narrow dirt road. "This is it. Take a good look so you won't miss the driveway when you come and go."

"I'm going to be free to do that?" She was astounded.

"You won't be a prisoner, Nicki. I can't force you to stay at the house all the time. But I do recommend you stick close to my uncle, particularly when I'm gone."

She eyed him suspiciously. "Why? Is he my bodyguard?"

"In a manner of speaking… Harold's a retired former sheriff's deputy. He's usually armed to the teeth."

"What should I expect, a Wild West show?" She gave a nervous laugh. "Am I going to have to wear a sunbonnet, bake biscuits from scratch in a woodstove and draw water from a well?"

"Not hardly."

She could tell from the way Jackson was gripping the truck's steering wheel that he was tense. That sign of emotion took her aback. Here was a guy who faced explosive devices for a living, yet he was nervous about bringing her to his home. What had she gotten herself into? And, come to think of it, how did he expect her to drive away when they'd left her sedan in town at the motel?

"I just had a thought," Nicki said. "How will I get my car?"

"Arnie can tow it again if he has to." Arching a brow, he glanced over at her. "Why? Are you planning a get-away?"

"No. Just trying to get all my ducks in a row. There's a lot to think about. For instance, what about my bed-room suite and the clothes I didn't have time to pack? Or the pots and pans in the kitchen? The fridge came with the apartment, but there was some extra food in there and in the pantry, too."

"The furniture will be stored for you as soon as pos-sible, and I can have the rest of your personal things boxed up. I hadn't thought about disposing of the food, though."

"No problem. I'll phone Pastor Eaton and have him give it to the needy or take it to the teen center for me. That makes more sense than hauling it all out here. Is that okay with you?"

"Sure. That's real neighborly of you."

"You act surprised. I keep telling you I am not a bad person."

"I never said you were," Jackson replied tersely.

"You mean other than being sure I was in cahoots with my cousin and hiding important clues?"

"Yeah. Something like that." He nodded toward a single-story, rock-faced ranch house. "There it is. What do you think?"

The first words that popped into her head remained unspoken. Words like, *plain* and *sad* and *stark.* What she said was, "It has a lot of wonderful potential. I can imagine climbing roses to match the red tile roof twining around the porch posts. And maybe more bluebonnets with marigolds or something else yellow lining the front walk."

"Um… Sure. I guess… Harold and I aren't gardeners, although he did raise some great-tasting tomatoes last year before the weather got too hot."

"Is that him on the porch?" Nicki asked, pressing her fingertips to her mouth to keep from laughing.

Jackson coughed and stared. "Whoa. It's either Harold or Pancho Villa. I'm not sure which."

Nicki lost the battle to remain serious and giggled. The man was wearing an embroidered, black velvet sombrero and vest. A leather bandolero filled with cartridges was draped across his chest, and he was holding a rifle in both hands as if preparing to take part in an old Western movie.

"You did say he had a sense of humor but I was expecting stale jokes, not a vaquero's costume."

"Harold is one of a kind. Come on… I'll introduce you."

The older man made a deep bow and swept his sombrero off his balding head as Jackson led Nicki up the front porch steps.

"Buenos días, señorita," Harold said, propping the rifle against the railing so he could spread his arms wide. "I am pleased to welcome you to our hacienda. As they say, *'Mi casa, su casa.'*"

"Thank you." Nicki offered to shake hands. "It's my pleasure, Mr. Worth."

"Please, call me Whatsit. Or Matchless, if you prefer." He chortled. "Get it? Matchless Worth?"

"Good thing your real name is Harold instead of Les," Nicki quipped.

The older man slapped his leg and began to laugh heartily. "Oh, I like this one, son. She's a corker."

When she looked over and saw Jackson rolling his eyes dramatically, she joined in with a soft laugh of her own. So this was the character she'd been warned about. He had already won her over by going to so much trouble to lighten the mood surrounding her arrival.

"I'll bring Nicki's things," Jackson said to his uncle. "You show her to her room."

"By way of the kitchen," Harold said with a wide grin. "I don't know about you two but I haven't had breakfast yet."

"Let her get settled," Jackson warned. "She's had a rough morning already."

Nicki let the older man take her arm and lead her into the living room, where Titan arose from his bed at one end of the sectional sofa and greeted them like long-lost friends.

They paused long enough to give the big Lab a pat before Harold asked, "What kind of a rough morning?"

"I don't know if I'm supposed to talk about it," Nicki was saying just as Jackson joined them.

"Might as well fill him in," the K-9 detective said.

"Knowing Harold, he's already heard most of it on his scanner."

"A harmless little vice of mine," Harold admitted. "Never could break myself of wanting to know what all was happening around here. Besides, somebody has to keep an eye on that dog and his partner."

"I imagine you worry a lot when they're on duty," Nicki said. The expression on Jackson's face at that moment was so serious, it caused her to frown. Had her innocent comment about worry touched a nerve?

When the time came that she was finally alone with the older man, she was going to ask about Jackson's background. Even if Harold refused to answer, she'd still know more than she did thus far.

Nicki changed the subject. "Tell you what. Why don't I start by looking over the kitchen, and make a shopping list? That way, when Jackson goes to work he can stop at the grocery store in town and pick up what I'll need."

"I wasn't planning on leaving today," he countered.

His uncle laughed. "Don't be silly. Nicki and I will get along just fine. You go on. And take that chow-hound of yours with you before he eats us out of house and home." He turned to Nicki with another wide grin. "The kitchen's through there. I'll go fetch you a pencil and paper."

"I think I've been accepted," she said with relief.

Jackson nodded. "Yeah. Looks like it." He was scowling and making no effort to hide his unpleasant attitude.

"I thought you wanted me here. Why are you acting as if you don't?" she asked.

"Forget it. It's not important."

If Jackson had been the only one involved, she might

have pressed him for an explanation then and there. Since he was not, she figured she could take her time. Harold was no fool, in spite of his joking demeanor, but he could probably be counted on to talk too much if she simply asked the right questions.

One thing she wanted to know was if the police truly suspected her. Another good question would be, what was bugging Jackson? If he didn't want her to stay at the ranch, she certainly was not going to force him to employ her. She'd had to endure enough feelings of alienation thanks to Bobby Lee after she'd told him about the baby. Nobody was going to have that power over her again. Nobody was going to get the chance to dump her like yesterday's garbage. If she wasn't wanted here, she would leave.

Where will you go? she asked herself. *Bobby Lee isolated you from all of your friends, and if you simply leave town, the police will think you're even more guilty.*

Unfortunately, Nicki had more questions than answers. One thing she did know, however. She was innocent of everything except being too gullible.

And that had led to a sin that would have lifelong consequences.

SEVEN

"You got her settled?" Slade McNeal asked Jackson when he reported for duty later that morning.

"Yeah. Harold's making her feel right at home." He arched a brow. "What's new around here? Did any more lab results come in?"

Slade shook his head solemnly. "Nothing useful. We already knew that ballistics on the bullet that killed Andrew Garry didn't match the ones they dug out of one of the low-level thugs and his buddy a couple of months ago."

"What about the gun Derek Murke used to shoot Lexi?"

"No match there, either. I wish we could pin the murders on him, but if he did shoot those others, he used different pistols." The captain leaned back in his desk chair and laced his fingers behind his head. "I hope you have better results getting info from that cook."

Jackson huffed. "I'll be thankful to get a word or two in edgewise. Harold is really taking his so-called assignment seriously. He's running around armed to the teeth. I wouldn't be surprised to find out he's wearing an ankle holster, too."

"At least he's had the right training to keep from shooting himself in the foot."

"That is my fondest hope," Jackson said with a wry smile. "If there's nothing special you need from me right now, I thought I'd take Titan out to the training yard and polish his skills a little."

"Fine with me. Lee's out there working Kip."

"Good. Thanks."

Jackson was looking forward to talking with his old friend, Lee Calloway. They'd been buddies for so long it seemed as if they had always known each other. However, now that Lee was spending every spare minute courting the amnesia victim who'd finally been identified as Lucy Cullen, they didn't have many chances to just hang out.

Lifelong commitment was starting to look like an epidemic among his peers. First Austin Black fell for Eva Billows while the K-9 teams were searching for her kidnapped son, Brady. Then Lucy and Lee got together, followed by Valerie Salgado and FBI agent Trevor Lewis. There was so much romance in the air, it was getting annoying, particularly since Jackson had made up his mind long ago, after a series of failed romances, that marriage and a law-enforcement career didn't mix.

He pushed open the rear office door, led Titan through the kennel area and exited onto the lawn of the fenced training yard. He ordered Titan into a holding crate so he could set up a test in the field, then hailed his old friend with a wave as he approached.

Kip, Lee's black-and-white border collie, was lying on the grass in the shade, panting and obviously taking a well-deserved break.

"Hey, Lee. How's it going?"

"This dog's better than ever." The sandy-haired, muscular officer shook Jackson's hand. "He should be, considering all the practice he's had finding cadavers lately. I'm almost afraid to take him for a walk around town these days."

"Yeah, I know what you mean. Every time Titan sits down, my heart starts to pound and I expect an explosion—even when he's not supposed to be working."

"At least we got to the Munson woman before she died."

"A lot of good that did. We still haven't figured out what her last words meant."

"You will. The captain tells me you're working to gain her cousin's trust. I should think Ms. Johnson would be delighted to confide in you after you saved her skin."

"Yeah, well, I hired her to cook at the ranch but so far we haven't had time to talk much."

"It's sure pretty out there this time of year," Lee said with a contented sigh. "Lucy and I really enjoyed our picnic out there a while back." He brightened. "I have a great idea. Why don't you host a barbecue get-together for our team and we can all check out your new cook."

"That might not be a bad idea. I'll see what McNeal says. I know it would do his kid a lot of good to be around our dogs more. Caleb really misses Rio since he was taken."

"Yeah, I know. Having Rio's sire, Chief, around is nice, but it isn't the same. Caleb never bonded with him the way he did with Rio. They were kind of raised together."

"True. You through training Kip or do you want me to hide and play dead?"

"You smell too good to make a practical dummy," Lee quipped, slapping him on the shoulder. "I know you're not wearing aftershave to impress me."

"No. Of course not."

"I thought maybe you were sprucing up to impress your new cook."

"Don't be silly. Just because *you're* in love and acting silly doesn't mean it's catching."

Lee's grin widened and his dark eyes gleamed. "Who said anything about *love,* bro?"

The warmth spreading up Jackson's neck and coloring his face was telling. It was also very embarrassing. His mind might be made up about staying single for the rest of his life but obviously his heart wasn't so sure.

Suddenly, the urge to return to the ranch and check on Nicki in person hit him like a sucker punch. He stood stock-still, absorbing the unsettling thought and trying to make sense of it.

Was he crazy?

Or was the Lord trying to tell him something?

He hadn't been a particularly faithful churchgoer, but his belief system was strong.

It had also occurred to him, more than once, that he might have been pushed into her life in order to help her, to protect her from whatever evil forces were lurking in and around Sagebrush. There were plenty to choose from. He sure wished he could put names and faces to their deeds, and make sure those who were responsible were locked up.

Leaving Lee and Kip and heading back toward the kennels for privacy, Jackson pulled out his cell phone and dialed the ranch. Nicki probably wouldn't pick up the house phone, but Harold was there.

At least he was supposed to be. Nobody answered.

After counting ten rings, Jackson hung up and tried Nicki's cell—with similar negative results. The hairs at the nape of his neck prickled in warning. His intuition had been right—something had gone wrong.

He unfastened the latch on Titan's kennel box door and ran back into the office with the faithful dog at his heels. Passing the day secretary, Lorna Danfield, he shouted, "I'm headed for my ranch. Taking the SUV. Page me if you need me."

The middle-aged, blonde woman merely waved as if it was normal to see someone racing out the door.

Jackson was thankful that nobody had tried to stop or question him because he wouldn't have lingered to talk.

Harold should have answered the house phone even if Nicki chose to ignore her cell, Jackson reasoned. His jaw clenched. If anything bad had happened to either of them, he was never going to forgive himself.

Nicki had shared coffee and toast with Harold while making a list of necessities for the ranch kitchen. "I'm not a fancy chef and don't pretend to be," she told him. "I hope that's going to be okay with you and your nephew."

"Fix lots of meat and potatoes, and you'll get no complaints from us," he said with a smile. "The freezer's full but I never know what to do with anything except put burgers or steak on the barbecue."

"I think I can manage a little variety and still keep my job," Nicki murmured. "Shall we go to the store?"

His bushy gray brows knit and he shook his head. "Best not leave, at least not 'til Jackson gets home, or he'll have a cow."

"All the more livestock for this ranch," she gibed. "Is that where the rest of these cattle came from?"

"Funny." Harold chuckled. "Actually, we bought most of 'em at an auction up in Odessa. The bull's pure-bred Hereford but the cows are crosses. Gives 'em hybrid vigor."

"So I've heard."

"Are you into ranching?"

"No. I used to date a cowboy." Sobering, she folded her arms across her torso.

"I take it he wasn't a keeper. Did he hurt you bad?"

"Bad enough," Nicki admitted. There was a sweetness behind the older man's question, and kindness in his gray eyes. "I may as well tell you since it's going to be obvious soon enough. I'm pregnant."

"I kinda figured it was something like that."

"You did?"

"Yeah. I've never seen my nephew so protective of anything, man nor beast, before. He may not know it but he's got a soft spot for helpless things."

Nicki's jaw dropped. She was about to insist she was far from helpless when she realized he could have meant her unborn child. In that case, there was no reason to take offense. "The baby, you mean?"

"'Course. I've seen him risk his life in weather that would've kept any sensible man inside, just to go lookin' for one lost calf."

"I don't know my Bible very well, but that sounds like something Pastor Eaton preached about recently."

"One lost sheep, you mean? I guess that could represent all of us. You a believer, Nicki?"

"Yes. I hit bottom after Bobby Lee dumped me, and

the only way to go was up. When I turned my life over to Jesus, I thought things would get better, though."

"Maybe they have and you just haven't seen the outcome yet," Harold offered. "Tell you what. Why don't we leave the kitchen chores for now and take a tour of this spread? Jackson and I are pretty proud of the way we've fixed up the place."

"I'd love to see it all." She patted the cell phone in her pocket to reassure herself it was still there before she smiled and said, "Let's go."

The flatbed ranch truck was sitting next to the barn where he'd last seen it. Harold's private mini-pickup sat nearby and Nicki's car was out front by the covered porch, right where the tow truck had dropped it.

When Jackson arrived, he stopped in the portion of the yard farthest from the buildings. Leaving Titan behind for the present, he stepped out and drew his sidearm. He didn't want to call undue attention to himself in case there was trouble. He also didn't intend to get caught unprepared.

His boots crunched lightly on gravel as he crept closer, and peeked in the windows at the north side of the main house. There were no signs of a struggle. There was also no one visible.

Jackson kept his gun pointed to the sky as he proceeded around to the rear. Loose chickens were scratching and pecking the ground. They didn't seem upset, but that didn't mean a whole lot since hens were far from intelligent.

Still, he mused, they might be acting flighty if there was trouble brewing.

Pausing to listen carefully, Jackson thought he heard

voices in the vicinity of the barn. He was certain of it by the time he'd reached the outside of the front sliding door.

That was Nicki. Laughing. And Harold was chuckling along with her.

Furious, Jackson burst in on them.

His uncle's initial reaction was to make a grab for his own sidearm before he realized who had just popped through the door. A moment later, he started to grin. "Whew! You sure know how to make an entrance, son. Put that gun away. We're fine."

Jackson holstered his weapon but not his temper. "Where *were* you?"

"Right here. Just like I promised we'd be. Who put the burr under your saddle?"

Instead of answering, Jackson glared at Nicki. "Where's your cell phone?"

"In my pocket."

"You might try answering it when it rings."

"It didn't. Ring, I mean." She pulled it out and held it in her palm. "I've had it with me the whole time. See?"

He grabbed it, flipped it open and checked. "How long has it been since you charged this thing?"

"I don't know. Is the battery low?"

"*Low* is not the word for it. It's dead."

"Then that's why I didn't answer it," she said nonchalantly. "It never rang."

Jackson felt as if he were a deflating balloon. These two were acting as if he was overreacting while he was barely able to keep from shouting at them for their carelessness.

"No harm done," Harold said brightly. "As you can see, we're just fine."

"Well, I'm not," Jackson countered. "You scared me out of my mind. When neither of you answered your phones, I thought…"

Nicki laid a hand gently on his forearm, her touch warm through his sleeve. "I'm sorry. We both are. But since you're here, would it be possible to make a grocery run?"

"How can you even think about shopping?"

"Somebody had better," she countered. "If you expect me to prepare a week's worth of food without running back and forth to town, I'll need a properly stocked kitchen."

"Fine. Fine," Jackson grumbled. He knew he sounded peeved but that was just too bad. His heart was racing, even now, and perspiration dotted his brow. If he hadn't been so thankful that he could barely think straight, he knew he'd still be shouting.

"Harold and I will take my car, then," Nicki said. "That way I won't be alone coming home with the groceries, and you can go straight back to work. You do need to do that, don't you?"

"Yeah, sure."

What he wanted to do was grab her by the shoulders, stare her down and make her understand how desperately worried he'd been. The possible tragic scenarios that had filled his mind as he'd raced to the ranch had seemed so real, he'd been sure one of them would come true.

Yet there stood Nicki, smiling sweetly, and behaving as if he were the one with the problem.

I am, Jackson realized with a start. Something about this pretty young woman had brought out the gladiator in him…and he didn't know what to do about it. Only one thing was certain at this point. If he didn't keep a lid on his feelings, he was not only going to be less effective at his bomb-detecting job, he was going to lose his objectivity.

Turning away, he gritted his teeth. He had ceased being impartial with regard to Nicolette Johnson the moment he had met her. And things were only getting worse.

"If we swing by my old apartment on the way home, I can run in and get the charger for my phone," she told Harold and Jackson as they loaded sacks of food into the trunk of her old blue sedan.

When neither man commented, she added, "It'll only take me a second."

Jackson frowned. "Tell me where it is and I'll go up and get it."

"Wish I could. I think it's in a kitchen drawer but I'm not positive." She smiled. "Besides, I want to pick up the potted plants outside on the fire escape, too. They'll add some color to your front porch. It certainly needs it."

"You had this in mind all along, didn't you?"

"Actually, no. I thought of it when I saw the geraniums for sale in the store's nursery department. I did intend to ask about the charger, though. You're the one who was complaining that my phone was dead, and since it's different than yours I'll need to have my own charger."

"All right." Muttering under his breath, he slid into the SUV and slammed the door while Harold and Nicki got into the other car.

"Is he usually this grumpy?" she asked as she started the engine and backed out.

"Nope. I don't know what's gotten into him. He's usually pretty mellow, especially since he's been back in the States."

"He told me he and Titan worked together in the military," Nicki said. "I got the idea it was pretty rough on both of them."

"Yeah. It was." Harold heaved a deep sigh. "And there was the other, too."

"Other?"

"Uh-oh. Shouldn't have said that."

"Maybe not. But since you have, you may as well go on with the story. I'll find out eventually, anyway, and it might help me keep from making Jackson any madder."

"That's debatable." He cleared his throat and shook his head. "There was a girl. She'd promised to wait for him, and I guess she sort of did, until she found out he was planning to become a cop when he got out of the service. Then she hit the road and married a banker. Said she wanted a safe, normal life." He snorted wryly. "Whatever that is."

"That's too bad."

"Yes, and no. She wasn't right for him in the first place. Too prissy and self-centered. Worst of all, she didn't like having animals in the house. Not even Titan."

Nicki chuckled. "That bad, huh? Well, Jackson's life certainly hasn't been dull, particularly recently. What do you know about all these killings?"

"Like your cousin's, you mean?"

"My estranged cousin. The newspaper says Arianna's death is tied to at least two or three others, maybe more. The problem is, Jackson thinks I know something secret, and I don't have a clue what he's talking about."

"Then just bide your time," Harold advised. "My

nephew can be stubborn, but he's fair. He'll see the truth eventually."

"I wish I knew what the truth was. It's really hard to stay out of trouble when you have no earthly idea who the bad guys are or what they're after."

"We'll keep you safe," he promised.

Nicki glanced in her mirror and saw the K-9 vehicle following. She believed both men were sincere. She also knew that they were nearly as blind to the dangers as she was.

Someone was lurking out there in the beautiful Texas countryside, ready to jeopardize her happiness, and perhaps end her life the way they had ended others. The person or persons didn't have a face she could identify or a plausible reason why they wanted to harm her. They simply did. And as far as Nicki was concerned, she was as helpless as a newborn kitten—blind and floundering, looking for comfort and security that were being withheld.

At that moment, just as she was telling herself she had never felt more alone or abandoned, she realized she was far from it. There was a fatherly figure seated beside her. A knight in shining armor was driving behind. And a sweet dog that was just about the smartest canine she had ever met was also along for the ride.

That was her personal army. The individuals the Lord must have sent. How could she question their sincerity or their skills when they were undoubtedly the answers to her most fervent prayers?

EIGHT

Jackson saw Nicki pull into the driveway to the apartment building and stop halfway. He parked behind her.

"I'll be right back. Stay," he told Titan.

As expected, the dog lay down on the seat and acted as if he understood. For all Jackson knew, he did. There were times when his furry partner seemed to almost read his mind.

"I wonder what he thinks of my overblown interest in this woman?" Jackson muttered to himself. The unspoken answer brought a smile and a shake of his head. It was a good thing Titan couldn't express his opinion or he'd probably tell his master he was acting like a fool.

"What if they've changed the locks?" Nicki asked, leaving Harold to wait in the car with the groceries, and falling into step beside Jackson.

"Then we'll get the manager to open up for us. I doubt they've done anything yet, though. We made arrangements to pick up your bedroom suite for storage so there has to be access."

"Are the crime scene people finally through?" she asked.

"Yes. The lab was happy with their samples."

"So, what was the bomb made of?"

He arched an eyebrow at her and cocked his head. "Why do you ask?"

"Curiosity. Is it some big secret?"

"We prefer to keep most details of active cases confidential. I will say I was surprised, though. The explosive wasn't very powerful."

Nicki huffed. "Oh? Tell that to my TV. As a matter of fact, tell it to my landlord."

"You don't need to worry about this place anymore," Jackson said as he led the way up the stairs and tried the door, surprised to find it unlocked.

He held out an arm to block her way. "Hold on. Let me check it out first."

"Do we need to get Titan?"

"I doubt it. You don't live here anymore, so there should be no reason for it to be booby-trapped."

"Oh, that's a comforting thought. Thanks for mentioning it. I feel so much better now."

He could tell from her wry tone that she was being facetious, but nevertheless took his time. Finally, convinced that the apartment was safe, he motioned for her to enter.

"Where do you think you left the phone charger?" he asked.

"In a kitchen drawer or cupboard, most likely. I usually plug it in over the counter." Nicki pointed to the remains of the sliding glass door that led to her tiny porch and fire escape. "The geraniums I want are out there. Do you mind getting them for me? I don't want to spend any more time here than I absolutely have to."

"Sure. No problem."

As Jackson picked his way cautiously through the

shattered glass and rubble, his footsteps crunched as if he were walking on gravel. The drape that had once covered the door was frayed and smoke-tinged, and fluttered in the slight breeze.

He pushed the fabric aside and stepped out, shading his eyes against the glare from the setting sun. Below him lay the back fence of the apartment grounds and beyond that the Lost Woods, a largely undeveloped area of Sagebrush with a wild history of its own. Between legends from the past and current crime statistics, plenty had occurred in those woods over the years.

Jackson was bending to pick up the two small flowerpots Nicki wanted when something in the distance caught his eye. He froze, crouching behind the wooden railing, and blinked to see if he was imagining things. He wasn't.

A tall figure, clad in black, was walking slowly along a path. His body moved like that of a male, and he not only wore a hat that shaded his face, it looked as if he might also be wearing a ski mask.

That anomaly was what originally caught Jackson's attention. Unless the guy was up to no good, there would be little reason to hide his features. Besides, although April weather could be nippy once the sun set, this particular day had been balmy.

From inside the apartment, he heard Nicki announce, "Found it!" and then heard her footsteps approaching.

Remaining crouched, Jackson held up his hand, palm out. His "Shush" was little more than a loud hiss.

To his relief, she froze where she stood, and waited. "What is it? What's wrong?"

"Down there," Jackson whispered. "In the woods."

She tiptoed closer and cautiously peeked around the edge of the opening. "What? All I see is a dog."

"A *dog?*" He scrambled to where she was standing and straightened so he'd have the same vantage point. She was right! Not only was the figure working a dog on a long lead, the animal resembled a German shepherd. Could it be Rio?

He flipped open his cell and pushed speed dial for the station rather than use his radio, and take the chance of the transmission being overheard. If that really was Rio, and the man with him was part of the crime syndicate they'd been after, they might have more men as well as sophisticated eavesdropping equipment positioned nearby.

"This is Worth, K-9 unit 463," he said, turning away and cupping his hands around the phone. "I'm at the apartment on Lost Woods Road, second floor rear, where we had the bombing. I can see a masked individual in the woods behind this building and there's a shepherd with him. It might be Rio. I can't be sure from so far away."

Turning, he peered out once again. "Yes, I can still see them. They're moving slowly, headed southeast. Looks like they're alone, but the trees have leafed out so I can only catch a glimpse when they pass through a clearing."

He paused to wait for orders, and his gaze met Nicki's. She was good and scared, yet safe enough as long as she stayed away from the window, and didn't try to follow him if he was sent to apprehend the suspect.

"What are you going to do?" she whispered.

Jackson pressed the phone to his ear and nodded, listening, before he said, "Copy. We'll stand by."

"We?"

It was more a squeak than a word. If the situation hadn't been so serious, Jackson might have laughed. "I meant Harold and I," he explained. "They want me to observe and wait for backup. There's a chance that isn't Rio but in case it is, we want to be able to track him—and the man—to see what they're up to."

"Won't he get away?"

"Not from the dogs on my team," Jackson assured her. "Austin Black's bloodhound, Justice, is one of the best trackers in the state. And with the help of our narcotics and protection dogs, plus Titan, we can cover all the bases. We'll get him... I hope."

"You had me convinced until you added that at the end." Nicki made a face. "I had no idea police work entailed so much waiting."

"It doesn't always." He forced a smile for her benefit. "Patience is a virtue, you know."

"Yeah, well..."

The wry look she was giving him brought sincerity to his grin. "I know. It's one of the hardest things for me, too. I want results ASAP. I suppose most folks do."

"What do we do now?"

"I wait here and watch. You go down and tell Harold what's going on, then stay with him until the patrol units get here."

Jackson could tell she wasn't eager to follow his orders, probably because she didn't want to be alone long enough to return to her car. Unfortunately, the only other option was to keep her with him and if he did that, Harold might panic and cause a ruckus when he saw the black-and-whites arriving.

"If you're too scared, I guess you can wait up here," he finally said.

"I'm not scared. Not one bit. I just don't want to miss any of the excitement." She shivered. "I don't like it up here, though. Too many bad memories."

Jackson assumed she was referring to the bombing, although he supposed it was also possible that she was upset because she had shared that apartment with her no-good ex-boyfriend. The notion of Nicki in another man's embrace tied Jackson's gut in a knot the size of Amarillo.

"Just go, then," he said brusquely, handing her the small potted plants. "I'll hold down the fort. Harold needs to be briefed, and since he hates to carry a cell phone, somebody will have to deliver the message in person. Are you up for it?"

"Sure. I'm good." Clutching the pots, she started for the door, then hesitated. "You're sure it's safe for me to leave?"

"If I didn't think so, I wouldn't send you," he said. "I'm only seconds away on one end of your errand, and Harold is the same on the other end. We're both armed. Believe me, it's not a big risk."

"Okay, okay. You don't have to sound so impatient. I'm going." She juggled her plants to display the small phone charger before shoving it into a pocket. "I got everything I came for."

As soon as Nicki passed from sight, Jackson was sorry he'd sent her down alone. Yes, he believed it was safe. And, yes, he knew he and Harold would be plenty of protection. Yet there remained a niggling sense of worry that he could not shake.

In the woods below, the man and dog were passing

beneath a canopy of trees, and out of his line of sight. If they continued in the direction they'd been headed, it might be several more minutes before he could actually see them again. That was long enough for him to run to the door and watch Nicki make her way downstairs.

Taking one last look at the area he'd been observing so closely, Jackson sprinted across the small living room, hit the hallway at a run and caught a quick glimpse of Nicki's back.

"Make it okay?" he called after her.

She paused and turned to wave at him. "Fine. I can see Harold."

Jackson flushed, embarrassed. Of course she was okay. It was silly to think that anyone would bother her when she was accompanied by two strong men. *Armed* men. His well-marked vehicle was parked right behind her car, and anybody who had been in Sagebrush for very long knew that Harold, being a retired deputy, was prepared for just about anything, too.

Nicki was with his uncle now, Jackson reassured himself, so she was perfectly safe. He knew that with every ounce of his being. Yet his heart was still racing and his breathing more ragged than it should have been.

He quickly returned to his vantage point above the Lost Woods. Vegetation was thick and lush this time of year due to the spring rains. Even later, when the grass dried and most of the wildflowers were gone, the trees would retain their leaves. Texas cottonwoods and other indigenous varieties of foliage were tough. As tough as the folks who had tamed this country a century or more ago.

A woman like Nicki would have fit right in with those brave settlers, Jackson mused. She was resilient.

Courageous. Willing to do whatever she had to in order to survive.

His breath caught. Was she so determined to succeed on her own that she'd withhold evidence of a crime? Many people in her position might. Despite his instincts about her true virtue was it possible that Nicki was playing him for a fool?

In his heart lay a firm *no.* His fertile mind, however, continued to doubt. Soon, everyone should know the truth. The trouble was, he was already so biased in her favor he wondered if he was going to be able to accept anything except complete innocence.

Turning his attention back to the woods, he forced himself to concentrate on the job at hand. Nobody would be safe until they put an end to the current crime wave. It was possible that the key to solving at least some of the puzzles, perhaps all of them, was right now lurking beneath those trees.

"Where are you?" Jackson whispered into the wind. "Where did you go? Come on, come on. Step into another clearing so I can see you again."

What could that man be searching for? he wondered. And if that truly was Rio, why go to the trouble of stealing him when there had to be other elite, multipurpose canines available.

For an instant, it occurred to Jackson that the theft of that particular police dog might have been a direct attack on Captain McNeal. He dismissed the notion of a vendetta as being too far-fetched. There had to be other possibilities.

They had already tied the deaths of some middle-management criminals like Frist, Garry and even Munson to a powerful criminal organization. The conundrum was why someone involved with them felt it was necessary to kill his or her own men—or why Arianna Munson had apparently murdered Andrew Garry, leading to her own death at the hands of FBI agent Trevor Lewis.

"So, Arianna, what did you mean when you tried to warn your cousin with your last breath?"

Jackson suppressed a shudder. Clueless or not, Nicki was still in trouble. Deep trouble. He pictured her standing in a dry desert streambed while a sudden storm dropped tons of rain in the distant mountains, and a wall of water began to rush toward her. That was the kind of desperate situation she was trapped in. And he had no idea how to rescue her before a destructive wave of wickedness swept her away like a flash flood.

Nicki climbed into the car with Harold and locked the doors.

"What's up? You look a fright. Where's Jackson?"

"Upstairs. He spotted somebody in the Lost Woods and called for backup. I'm supposed to tell you to stay here and wait."

She could tell from the way the older man had tensed and begun to fidget that he was not pleased to have to stand by when something exciting was unfolding. Truth to tell, Nicki wanted to go back to be with Jackson, too.

"We could leave Titan to guard the car and go back," she suggested. "Together, I mean."

Harold's bushy eyebrows knit. "You ready for that?"

"Sure. Why not?" The way his eyes swept over her as if making an assessment gave her pause, but she insisted, "I'm not scared. Honest."

"It's not a matter of courage," he explained. "It's a

matter of duty. Jackson and I are committed to taking care of you, and if that means sitting here and twiddling my thumbs while we wait for more backup, then that's what I'll do."

Nicki's decision was made in an instant. Giving in to impulse she jumped out and leaned down to speak through the open door. "Have it your way. I'm going back upstairs, so if you really want to watch me, you'd better get a move on."

Behind her she could hear the older man muttering under his breath. He was coming all right—huffing and puffing and talking to himself with such intensity, she had to smile. Like his nephew, Harold Worth was the kind of man she could count on in any circumstance, no matter what. That was not only comforting, it buoyed her overall spirits a great deal.

When she reached the top of the stairs, she waited for him to catch up before pointing. "It's down there. End of the hall. Jackson is at the back window looking down into the Lost Woods."

"Lead on," Harold said with a scowl.

Nicki gave him a sweet smile. "You wanted to come up here and you know it, you old faker. I just gave you a good reason to do it."

"Never said I didn't." He fell into line next to her, sighing and shaking his head. "What I didn't want to do was expose you to any more possible danger."

"From who?" Nicki asked. "The bad guy is down in the woods. He has no idea we're watching him."

"He may not but that doesn't mean he's alone. If you're going to play detective, you'll need to learn to think outside the box. See threats behind every door. Assume the worst of everybody until you prove otherwise."

"Is that how you see me?" she asked, lowering her voice now that they were approaching the open apartment door. In her heart of hearts, she hoped he was going to reassure her that he knew she was innocent because that would mean that Jackson probably felt the same.

"I think you're a smart woman who's too naive for her own good, among other things. I also think you've got more guts than half the men I know."

"Thanks, I guess."

"You're welcome." He paused and held out his arm to block her path, reminding her of the way Jackson had also behaved. Without looking at her, he said, "Shush. Slowly now," before he eased through the doorway.

Nicki followed. She was glad she was behind Harold when Jackson spun around and glared at them.

"Didn't you tell him to wait?" the K-9 officer demanded.

"She did," Harold answered for her. "I thought three pairs of eyes would be better than one, that's all. Can you still see him?"

"No." Jackson shook his head. "I lost him over that way, about ten o'clock."

Nicki understood he was referring to the position of the numbers on a clock face and peered in that direction. "I don't see a thing except trees."

"Me, either," Harold added. "How long ago did you lose sight of him?"

"Just a couple of minutes."

"There's nothing over that way except forest, is there?" Nicki asked.

"I seem to remember an old chapel and a graveyard,"

Harold said thoughtfully. He looked to his nephew. "Am I right?"

"I think so. Keep looking."

Nicki could tell from Jackson's expression that he was formulating a plan. She stepped aside to give him room to pass as he reentered the apartment and made another call.

"This is Worth, K-9 unit 463 again," he began.

As Nicki listened, he gave the dispatcher the information Harold had provided and suggested a dual approach to the woods.

"That's right. Nobody uses the chapel anymore, but there are still new burials in the cemetery from time to time. I don't have the GPS coordinates. Tell the units to take Lost Woods Road clear to the end, past the park, then make a right on the dirt road and keep going. The old church is sitting in a grove of trees and the graveyard is behind it."

Nicki didn't look away when Jackson's gaze met hers. She knew he was upset with her, yet she also thought she sensed his grudging respect. Although it was beyond her fondest dreams that he might actually want her with him, she chose to believe that he had at least come to terms with having her there, probably because Harold had accompanied her.

That was okay with her. Almost anything was, as long as she was included as if she belonged.

No, she countered. *That wasn't entirely true.* She had standards, principles, a newly enforced sense of right and wrong. From the moment she had truly become a Christian, she had understood that. She had not been a bad person before, she was simply a better one now.

A flash of light in the distant forest jarred her from

her reverie. She shaded her eyes with one hand and tapped Jackson's shoulder with the other, then pointed.

"Look. Over there! I just saw it for a second. It looked like a reflection of something shiny."

"From what? Could you tell?" He bent over her, almost placing his cheek against hers to get the same perspective.

Nicki caught her breath, astounded by how acutely his nearness was affecting her. "I—I think it might have been from a mirror or something. It's really hard to tell with the sun so low. I suppose I could have imagined it."

"Could it have been reflecting from the chrome or windshield of a car?"

"I suppose so." She strained to listen, to hear other sounds, in spite of her pounding pulse. "Do you hear a motor?"

"I'm not sure. Stay here with Harold."

Jackson left her and raced for the door.

Nicki heard his boots thudding down the stairs. She turned to the older man. "Where is he going?"

"Best guess? I'd say he's headed out there to chase whatever you saw," he said with a shrug. "Uh-oh."

"What?"

"Over there, where you thought you saw the flash of light. There's a cloud of dust. See? It looks pinkish in the twilight."

"Yes! The man with the dog is getting away, isn't he?"

Harold huffed and his shoulders sagged. "Sure looks like it to me."

Closing her eyes, Nicki prayed, *Please, please, please, let Jackson be in time,* then added, *and keep him safe.*

She knew, without actually forming the words, that she wanted to say, *Because he is so very special to me.*

Before she had time to take another breath, she realized that, whether she said so out loud or not, the Lord knew exactly what truths were hidden in her heart.

In the space of a mere couple of days, she had formed a ridiculous attachment to the handsome Texas cop.

She might be wiser than before because of what Bobby Lee had done, but apparently her heart hadn't learned a thing.

NINE

Jackson had radioed his position as he drove into the woods on unmarked dirt roads. Chances had been slim from the outset that he'd arrive in time to overtake whoever had been working that German shepherd, but he'd had to try.

By the time his team had gathered at the place where he'd last spotted the shadowy figure, man and canine had disappeared. So had the sun.

"Titan won't be much use to us in this case," McNeal said, muttering unintelligibly and sounding more than disappointed. "Why don't you head back to the apartment and see if Harold has anything to report?"

"Yes, sir."

Returning to his car, Jackson dialed Nicki, wondering if she'd had the foresight to plug in her phone and let the apartment electricity power it. To his astonishment, she had.

"Hello?"

"I don't believe it! You charged your phone."

"Actually… I can't take credit for that. It was your uncle's idea. Where are you?"

"In the Lost Woods, moving west. Searchers are

spreading out from my original sighting, but it looks like the guy got away. I'm going to check out the area where you saw the flash before I come in, just in case."

"Why don't you turn on your red lights? That will help us see you and maybe tell if you're close."

"Will do." He reached down. "There. Can you see that?"

"Yes. It looks as if you're a little west of the place. Harold and I both saw dust rising over there after you left us."

"How much farther is it?"

There was a short pause before she answered, "Harold says maybe half to a quarter of a mile. He thinks it was near that old church he mentioned."

"Okay. I'll relay your information and keep going. The team is using the bloodhound. They won't disturb him while he's tracking, but I can have a look right now."

"I wish I could be there, too. Any chance Harold and I could come? We'd stay out of the way. Honest."

"You two need to go home and put the groceries away," Jackson said, knowing what her reaction would be.

Nevertheless, it made him smile when she said, "Phooey. There's nothing perishable and you know it."

"Well, it was worth a try. Let me talk to my uncle."

In an instant, Harold was clamoring for more information.

"Simmer down," Jackson said calmly. "There's nothing either of you can do here except mess up the few clues we do have."

"Like what?" the older man demanded.

"A few fresh footprints and some tire tracks from my original observation. Not a whole lot, I'm afraid."

"What about the old church?"

"I'm almost there but I'm going to stage and wait—

unless I see somebody. Austin is working Justice. I don't want to get ahead of that team in case they end up coming this way."

"Fine. We'll take the food back to the ranch, pick up the ranch truck and meet you near the abandoned chapel. Should take us about an hour." He exhaled sharply. "That ought to be long enough for the bloodhound to get his sniffing done."

"No! I don't want you to bring that woman into this." Jackson knew there was too much emotion in his tone, but he couldn't help himself.

He heard his uncle chortle. "*Me* bring *her?* It's more like the other way around. I practically had to hog-tie her to keep her up here after you ran off."

In the background, Nicki was loudly insisting otherwise.

"Okay, okay. I'll meet you in the woods in an hour," Jackson said. "You won't have a reliable phone until Nicki's is fully charged, but you can use the two-way radio in the truck. Meet me where the road forks just before you get to the turnoff for the chapel. Understand?"

What Jackson really wanted was a firm commitment from the retired deputy and was satisfied when Harold said, "Agreed. We'll wait for you. Just don't keep us cooling our heels for too long." He paused to chuckle. "I don't know whether I'm ever going to be able to convince our new cook that she belongs back in the kitchen instead of on a stakeout."

The resulting racket in the background, compliments of Nicki, made Jackson smile as he ended the connection. As long as she was with Harold, he wasn't too worried about her. The way he saw it, she'd probably be safer in his uncle's company than she would be at the ranch by herself.

"And, we still need to keep a close eye on her, just like Captain McNeal said," he muttered.

Could Nicki really be withholding evidence? Everything about her pointed to innocence, yet she was clearly a clever, determined person.

She's also a new Christian, he reminded himself. That wasn't proof of her truthfulness by itself, but it did tend to support her claims. The question was twofold; had she reformed enough for it to make a difference, and had she needed to do so in the first place? Yes, she had made a big mistake by getting pregnant, but that didn't make her a bad person any more than any other sin did. It simply made her human, something they all were whether they happened to be believers or not.

Speaking of being human... Jackson mused. Against regulations he was losing his personal battle to keep from caring too much for a suspect, and there didn't seem to be a thing he could do to stop himself.

Nicolette Johnson had gotten under his skin. Big-time.

Nicki grew more and more enthused as she and Harold drove toward the Lost Woods. He had insisted that they grab a quick bite while storing the groceries at the ranch house, and for that she was thankful. Her easily upset stomach seemed much happier when it wasn't empty.

"I have to admit," she began, "I feel a lot better since I ate. I had no idea that would help."

"Always did wonders for my wife," the older man said.

"You had a family?"

"Yes." His smile was wistful. "Still do. My two kids moved to Florida with my ex and her second husband. Now that they're grown they call or email pretty regularly so it's not so bad."

"Is that how you and Jackson got together?"

"Because we were both alone, you mean?" He smiled to soften the question. "Not exactly. I'd been living in Texas for years before he joined up and was sent overseas. When he asked me to look after his ranch for him, it was a perfect arrangement for us both. After he got home, he invited me to stay on. There's no place I'd rather live so I agreed. I love to explore this country."

"Is that how you learned about the abandoned chapel?"

"Matter of fact, it is. I saw a line of cars headed into the Lost Woods one day and decided to see where they were going. Turns out there was a funeral in the old church graveyard. Apparently, some families have large plots and mausoleums there and keep using them."

"Makes sense. My cousin, Arianna, was buried in Dallas because that's where her parents' graves were. My folks' graves are there, too."

"Sorry for your loss. It's hard being the last one left, isn't it?"

Nicki nodded thoughtfully before she replied, "Yes. I was hit with that realization after I heard that Arianna was gone—although I do have a half sister somewhere back East. I know it's silly, but I feel kind of like an orphan."

She didn't flinch when he reached over and patted her hand where it rested on the seat between them. His knuckles were enlarged and his skin calloused, yet his touch was gentle. "You'll never be alone as long as you're a member of God's family. And if you ever want to add an old uncle like me, I'm available for adoption."

"Thanks," Nicki said. "I'll keep that in mind. It's been so long since I felt as if I was part of a real family that I don't know how well I'd fit into one."

"You'll do just fine wherever the Lord sends you," he said with a smile that crinkled the leathery skin at the corners of his brown eyes, and somehow reminded her of Jackson.

That reaction shouldn't surprise me, Nicki reasoned. Pretty much everything, from police work to cowboy boots and Stetsons, reminded her of that man.

Worse, she could hardly wait until they met him at the planned rendezvous. The mere thought of seeing his face, standing near him, watching him smile, made her giddy with joy. It wasn't the same kind of emotional tie she'd thought she'd shared with Bobby Lee. It was more. Much more.

Mutual? Maybe. Maybe not. She and Jackson hardly knew each other, and time would tell. She was already in plenty of trouble without falling for one of the cops who was investigating Arianna's murder.

Nicki crossed her arms and stared through the truck windshield, realizing how foolish she was being to even dream of such a thing. No man was going to want her now. Not when she was carrying someone else's baby. The chances she might have had for a normal life with a loving husband and children had disappeared when Bobby Lee Crawford had tricked her, used her and deserted her. It was over.

Still, it was not her unborn child's fault that she'd made such a terrible mistake. The baby was as innocent of purposeful wrongdoing as she was.

A sidelong peek at the man behind the wheel of the pickup truck showed his concentration focused primarily on the road ahead. However, he also kept glancing in the side mirrors.

Nicki frowned. "What is it? What's wrong?"

"Probably nothing. Sit still. Don't turn around."

She started to do exactly that and had to stop herself. "Why? What do you see?"

"It's possible we've picked up a tail."

"You mean *I* have, don't you?"

Harold's bushy brows arched. "Okay. You have. Now do you see why I insisted you and I stick together no matter what?"

She huffed, "I guess so. I know Jackson wants you to watch me closely because he thinks I'm holding out on him. Hiding evidence. I wish I were. Believe me, if I knew anything that would get all these idiots out of my life and off my trail, I'd be delighted to reveal it."

"You're sure you don't have even a clue? Anything at all? Did your cousin mail you anything or leave any messages? Think."

"No!" she nearly shouted it. "I am exactly what you see, nothing more, nothing less. I'm a short-order cook with no home, a stack of bills that keep piling up and a bun in the oven that turned my life upside down. All I want is some peace and quiet."

After a short pause Harold said, "I believe you. Pull your seat belt tighter and hang on. I'm about to try to ditch this tail."

He made a snap turn south off the highway and onto a bumpy dirt trail. The truck's engine roared and its heavy-duty springs made the tires bounce like overinflated beach balls.

Nicki's right hand grabbed the handhold mounted above the passenger door while her left clamped the edge of the seat.

"You okay?" Harold shouted.

"As good as can be expected. Have we lost him yet?"

"No. He's still back there," Harold yelled. "Grab the radio and warn Jackson."

"What shall I tell him?" She let go of the seat and fisted the mic at the end of a spiral cord.

"That we're being pursued by a black sedan with tinted windows and those new, bright headlights. If this guy is still with us when we get to the meeting place, there won't be any question of mistaken identity."

"Gotcha. What's Jackson's call sign?

"K-9 unit 463. It's his number, four, plus the vehicle ID."

Nicki triggered the radio and broadcast, "K-9 463, this is your ranch truck. We're approaching the planned rendezvous and we have company. Advise."

"How soon?" Jackson replied.

She looked to her companion. "Five to ten," he said.

"Five to ten minutes," she repeated. "The way Harold's driving it may be even sooner."

"Copy. Keep coming. Don't stop where we had planned. I'll be waiting for him."

Nicki lowered the mic. "He said…"

"I heard him. This may get a little dicey. Hang on."

"As if I'm not already," she shouted over the roar of the engine and the squeaking of the truck as it bounced and twisted over the rough roadway.

Her eyes were wide and she was apprehensive, so filled with adrenaline she could hardly breathe, barely think. How did cops do this without making mistakes or overreacting? Most of the police work she had watched so far had been tedious and rather boring. Being involved in a car chase, however, changed everything. Demonstrated the seriousness of their plight.

And, knowing that Jackson was waiting to leap in to assist them made the situation even more nerve-racking.

For Titan's safety, Jackson had moved him to his crate in the rear of the SUV. Its motor was idling smoothly, headlights off, and the windows were rolled down so he could hear approaching vehicles. The ranch truck was a diesel with a distinctive sound. Mixed with that noise was the higher-pitched whine of a second car.

Jackson's fists tightened on the wheel. "Thank you, Lord, that Harold's driving." If Nicki had been behind the wheel, there was no telling how well she'd have followed his instructions. Probably poorly, judging by past performance.

The light gray ranch truck, referred to in casual conversation as a "dually," had dual sets of rear wheels on each side of the bed and wider fenders to facilitate pulling a stock trailer. Therefore, the truck took up most of the width of the dirt road as it passed, assuring that whoever was following wouldn't be able to easily pass to cut it off.

Jackson was parked where thick brambles hid his patrol car. He let Harold and Nicki fly past his location, then gunned the engine and pulled across the road to block the other vehicle.

A black, compact automobile showed up mere seconds later, its headlights temporarily blinding.

Jackson braced for impact.

The other driver hit the brakes, sending that car into

a skid that almost failed to end in time to avoid a collision. Then, all was quiet.

Jackson jumped out, gun drawn, faced the car over the hood of his SUV and shouted, "Police! Hands where I can see 'em. Now."

At first there was no other movement. Then, the car started to back up rapidly. Jackson would have loved to play Wild West show cowboy and shoot out the tires, but unfortunately it was against department policy to use excessive force unless a criminal threatened bodily harm. If the car had kept coming at him he wouldn't have hesitated to fire.

He thought he heard the diesel sound of the ranch truck in the background. It wasn't fading away as he'd hoped. Apparently, Harold's tail wasn't the only one moving in reverse.

Jackson grabbed his radio to alert other units to the problem, then straightened and waited for Harold and Nicki. They arrived so quickly he was positive they hadn't traveled far after passing him.

He holstered his gun and greeted them. "You could have kept going."

"And miss all this," his uncle said with a grin as he stepped down. "I haven't enjoyed myself so much for ages. Did you get a license number?"

"No, it was too dark. But I did radio a description. Units on the highway may still apprehend them." He looked past Harold and saw Nicki getting out of the truck so he called, "You okay?"

"Fine." To Jackson's astonishment she seemed almost as unruffled about participating in the car chase as Harold did and there was an unnatural brightness to her eyes. That was probably not a good sign. Not good at all.

"Okay. Get back in the truck and let's keep going. I told the others we'd check the graveyard. Austin's bloodhound was hot on a trail that led the other way so that's the direction everybody else headed."

"Okay," Harold said with a smile. "Nice drivin', son."

"You're not so bad yourself, old man." Jackson clapped him on the back. "I see you didn't forget the lessons you learned in the police academy."

"There's nothing like a good dose of adrenaline to bring it all back. You want Nicki to ride shotgun with you the rest of the way?"

"Why?" The self-satisfied gleam in Harold's eyes had caught Jackson off guard, but he quickly figured things out and ended the older man's matchmaking efforts. "You two have apparently been doing just fine. Since your tail is long gone and the excitement is over, I see no reason to change the seating arrangements."

"Have it your way." Harold shrugged thin shoulders beneath his Western shirt. "Probably better that way. She didn't seem to mind getting thrown all over the cab of the truck before, so a little more bouncing around probably won't hurt her."

Jackson was not amused. "That's not funny."

"Want to reconsider then?"

"You guys might want to ask my opinion," Nicki interjected. "I do like sitting up high in that truck, but I'd rather have Titan for company." She looked over at Harold and managed a smile. "No offense."

"None taken." He was peering into the rear seat of the patrol car. "I don't see him."

"He's in his crate," Jackson explained. "I suppose I could let him out—as long as you two promise to behave. No more reckless car chases?"

She spread her hands wide, palms up. "Hey, it wasn't our fault."

"Sometimes I wonder…about both of you," Jackson drawled. "Okay. I'll get Titan and put him up front with us. Then let's get this show on the road. I still want to check the old cemetery. You two can come along so I can keep an eye on you."

"It's not too dark?" Nicki asked.

"That's what flashlights are for." He was leading his bomb-sniffing partner around the SUV as he answered. The dog suddenly balked. Stopped. Jackson knew better than to overlook his canine partner's instincts. "What is it, boy? What's wrong?"

The ebony-coated dog was standing motionless, staring into the forest. Jackson tried to follow the same line of sight with no luck.

"What does he see?" Nicki asked.

"More likely he smells or senses something," Jackson said. "Go ahead and get in the car."

"But…"

"I said—" He was about to reinforce his order when the sharp crack of a shot echoed off the surrounding hills. He didn't have to see the precise point of impact to assume it had hit somewhere close by.

"Get down!" he shouted.

Nicki had been holding the side door open for Titan. She dove inside at the same time the dog did, and they ended up sharing a seat.

Slamming the door and throwing himself behind the wheel, Jackson saw Harold doing the same in the truck. They were at a terrible disadvantage since they didn't know where their enemies were or how many they were facing. The only sensible course of action was to flee.

The dually threw up a rooster tail of dust and gravel.

Jackson whipped in behind it. There was a good chance he'd get a pitted windshield out of following this close, but at the moment he could envision a lot worse consequences as a result of dropping back.

"Hang on!" he yelled at Nicki, taking a quick glance in the mirror to check on her.

Her blue eyes were wide, her cheeks flushed, and she was gripping Titan so fiercely, he wondered why the dog was not trying to wiggle loose.

"Another hundred yards or so and we'll be in the clear," he promised.

"Who's shooting? Are they aiming at us?"

"I don't know, and I don't intend to hang around to find out."

The target probably was Nicki, he concluded, although there were unfortunately plenty of folks who didn't care for cops, either. It was remotely possible they had inadvertently encroached on a moonshine still or a drug operation that was hidden in the forest. It was also possible that the pursuers in the black car had doubled back.

Either way, Jackson was thankful that whoever was shooting had such lousy aim.

"Did we lose them?" Nicki called from the backseat.

Jackson was about to tell her he thought so when a rifle shot clapped. The bullet whined. Zinged.

Both rear side windows of the racing SUV exploded, raining down in tiny bits the same way the glass door at Nicki's apartment had as a result of the explosion.

She shrieked, long and loud.

For an instant, he feared the bullet might have found her, too, and his heart almost pounded out of his chest.

"Nicki!"

TEN

Hugging Titan and huddled with him on the backseat, Nicki wasn't sure what had just happened. She knew there had been a shot. And the SUV had been hit. Beyond that, she was clueless.

The first thing she did was take stock of herself. Nothing hurt, nor was she bleeding, so that was good. Titan seemed okay, too, and was trying to lick her face.

That left Jackson. He was still driving through the woods like a madman but that didn't mean he was unscathed. "Are you hit?" she yelled.

"No. You?"

"We're fine. How about Harold?"

"Still going ninety," Jackson shouted. "Stay down, just in case."

Did he think she was nuts? He must, if he felt the necessity to tell her to duck in the middle of an ambush!

Dropping to the floor on her knees, she pulled the quaking dog closer and held him tightly. *Poor guy.* This terrified reaction must be due to his PTSD. Considering how scared she was right now when she'd had no prior experience being shot at, the poor Lab must be frightened nearly out of his mind.

"Titan is shaking really bad," Nicki called from her position on the floor. "What should I do?"

"Just stay down with him. We're almost there."

"Then what?"

She was positive she heard Jackson make a derisive sound before he answered, "We take cover."

That made sense. At least in theory, she reasoned. Since there was supposed to be a chapel at the cemetery, they might find shelter there. As far as she was concerned, particularly lately, church was the perfect sanctuary.

No place is a good place to die, she countered silently. She knew she'd go to heaven eventually. She simply wasn't ready to depart anytime soon. A new life lay ahead of her and her unborn child. She was not about to give it up without a fight.

Jackson had forgotten there were aboveground burial crypts on the cemetery grounds, as well as the tiny rural chapel. The sun had set behind the tree-topped ridge to the west, giving the horizon an ethereal glow. If it hadn't been for the dust the ranch truck had kicked up, he might have missed locating Harold parking his truck behind a mausoleum.

The small building's stone sides were covered with dead vines, and its once pristine walls had turned a dingy white. There was a carved name over the door, presumably that of one of the main families present at the founding of Sagebrush. All Jackson could read in passing was a capital *A* at the beginning of the inscription.

He chose to pass the place where his uncle had stopped, and park behind the chapel while he radioed his position to the station.

"Out. Both of you," he ordered when he was done talking to dispatch. "Keep Titan on the leash and hunker down between this car and the building. That'll give you better shelter."

"Where will you be?" Nicki asked.

He was amazed at the calm strength of her words, the way she seemed able to adjust to any circumstance and roll with the punches, so to speak.

"As soon as I'm sure we're safe, I'm going to go get Harold and we'll check the area. I'd wait for more backup, but it's going to be pitch-dark soon. If we don't find tire tracks or footprints right away, we may as well give it up for the night."

Although it had occurred to him that their choice to drive all the way onto the grounds might have obliterated any latent clues, he still intended to have a look around.

"At least the dark will help us hide from whoever was shooting," Nicki said quietly.

"It will also help them hide from us," he countered. His gun was drawn, every muscle in his body taut as he paused beside her and scanned the otherwise peaceful grounds. "Are you sure you're okay?"

He heard her sigh before she said, "Sure. I have Titan, and he has me. What more could we want?"

"He's not a protection or attack dog," Jackson warned, "so don't expect him to defend you."

"That's okay. I'll defend him if I need to."

"With what? Are you armed?"

"Of course not. I just meant..." She paused and sighed again. "I don't know what I meant."

"Do you know how to handle a gun?"

"Not unless it's the kind that squirts water."

He almost laughed. "Okay. Tell you what. If you want

to learn, I'll give you shooting lessons while you're out at the ranch. With real bullets."

"I could never purposely hurt anyone."

"I wouldn't expect you to go hunting down the bad guys, Nicki. I just want you to be able to defend yourself, and know how to react properly if you find yourself in danger."

"Well, in that case, I'm willing." She was stroking Titan's head and scratching behind his ears as she spoke.

"Good for you." Jackson started to straighten and move away. "Now stay here." A small smile resulted when he realized how he could ensure her compliance. "I'm counting on you to take good care of Titan. Understand?"

A nod was all the answer he got. It was enough. Nicki was the kind of person who took every job seriously. She would look after the dog, and by doing so would also be safeguarding herself.

He eased out from behind the parked SUV, his pistol in one hand, flashlight in the other. He'd have to circle the chapel in order to signal Harold. That wouldn't be difficult.

The hardest part of all this was forcing himself to leave Nicki. If he followed his true instincts he'd turn back, put his arms around her…and stay that way forever.

That wasn't smart. Nor was it likely. But it sure sounded like a good idea.

Listening intently, Nicki heard Jackson's footfalls even after he was no longer in sight. He'd circled the building slowly, then started to jog.

She also heard Harold's call to him and his reply. If they felt it was safe to shout at each other, there was likely no further danger. Nevertheless, she chose to obey orders and stay put with Titan.

As time passed, the black Lab calmed considerably, although he continued to pant as if he'd just run a marathon. No wonder, considering how scared he'd been.

Truth to tell, the dog wasn't the only one fatigued after their ordeal. Starting to yawn, she eased down beside him and propped her elbows on her bent knees.

"Well, old boy, what would you like to do now? Huh? How about a game of tic-tac-toe? Oh, you don't play? Too bad. I'm very good at it."

The silliness of the one-sided conversation relaxed her. She slid her fingertips through the dog's short, silky hair and wiggled them all the way down his spine, bringing a happy wag of his tail. "You like that, huh? Good."

Time seemed to drag by. The dim glow of the sun beyond the horizon disappeared completely. Nicki was beginning to get concerned. She shivered. How long should it take to canvas a small cemetery like this? Why weren't Jackson and Harold back by now? Could something have happened to them?

Straining to listen, she heard nothing but the onset of nighttime insect chirps and the calls of a few nocturnal birds. No human spoke. No footsteps echoed through the otherwise silent forest surrounding them. No motors purred or raced, not even in the distance.

Loudest of all was the thrumming of her pulse in her ears, and the rapid breathing of the dog lying beside her.

Suddenly, Titan held very still, closed his mouth and stopped panting.

Nicki tensed with him. She leaned closer, trying to see what he was seeing.

It was impossible. The woods were too dark, too

filled with unidentifiable shapes barely defined by the waning moon.

Wind pushed at supple tree branches, making their shadows dance among the headstones and claw at the aboveground crypts like ferocious beasts with long, grasping talons.

She chanced a soft, "Jackson? Harold?"

No one answered.

Her imagination began to create a vivid and terrifying scenario—one in which she was left all alone in the cemetery and villains of every order were closing in on her. On them.

Brushing off the notions as she brushed off her jeans, Nicki stood. The leash was fisted in one hand, the dog obediently poised at her side.

Now what? She had vowed to wait for Jackson's return, yet an awful lot of time had passed—enough to bring the full force of night and cause her to squint, straining to see more clearly. Surely, he hadn't meant for her to stay put this long. Besides, if his dog was concerned, she should also be.

Still standing outside, she eased open the side doors of the patrol vehicle, looking for some sort of weapon, preferably a simple one. There was nothing except a shotgun, and she wasn't going to take the chance of mishandling it.

The storage area behind the backseat, however, provided an L-shaped jack handle. It wasn't too heavy to carry, yet it would certainly be better than being empty-handed.

It was then that she fully realized she intended to go looking for the missing men. Yes, she had promised to take care of the dog but since he was the one who seemed concerned, it made perfect sense to move.

Titan would lead her.

She would protect him.

The plan wasn't foolproof, it was simply the best choice under these circumstances. At least that was what she kept telling herself.

"Come on, Titan." Nicki took a step forward and he kept pace. "That's right, boy. Let's go see what's been bothering you."

To her astonishment, the black Lab seemed to understand—because he not only started off in a straight line, he began to move faster and faster.

Still clutching the metal jack handle, Nicki had to jog to keep up. The leash was shorter than ones she'd seen before, giving her less leeway to maneuver among the headstones and around trees and bushes.

She'd tripped several times before she gave a hard tug on the line and said, "Easy, boy. Slow down."

Titan turned his brown eyes up at her as if he knew what she wanted. His anxiety, however, was still barely contained.

Nicki gave him some slack. That was a mistake.

The dog lunged forward.

She felt the webbing of the short leash slipping through her fingers. It burned as it chafed her skin.

Titan was loose! Running away.

"No!" Nicki shouted, stunned that the usually tractable animal had suddenly bolted. "Titan!"

Glimpses of his orange reflective collar were visible for a few seconds, but the rest of him blended into the darkness far too well.

Nicki set off in pursuit. If he changed direction, she'd

never find him. All she could hope was that his beeline toward his unidentified goal would continue.

She heard his bark fading in the distance as he ran. "Titan!"

Where was Jackson? Where was Harold? *Dear God, help me,* her heart cried out.

Something caught here eye. Was that the dog's reflective collar again? *Praise the Lord. It was.*

Hurrying ahead, she kept her eyes on the place where she'd last seen the bright orange plastic, and threaded a path between upright headstones, showing respect by trying to avoid stepping on the ones that lay flat to the ground.

Rounding a crypt, she stumbled. Felt herself falling.

Self-preservation insisted that she drop her makeshift weapon and use both hands to break her fall.

She landed in the loose dirt on all fours. Something large and hard was pressing against her chest, and the fall had knocked the breath from her lungs. All she could imagine was that she had tripped over the trunk of a fallen tree.

Blinking, she pushed away. Levered herself higher. Saw Titan's nose and wide, pink tongue mere inches from her face.

Nicki's relief at having caught up to the naughty dog was short-lived. There was enough pale light from the moon to show her more than she wanted to see.

The tree trunk had facial features! Wispy blond hair. Sunken eyes. Lips that were little more than a gash across the ashen face.

Nicki gasped.

Screamed.

Threw herself backward and gawked in disbelief for a heartbeat, then screamed again. And again.

There, beside her on the ground, lying as still as death, as cold as ice, was a body.

The dog had led her to a dead man.

Jackson was back at his police vehicle, arguing with Harold about where to start searching for Nicki and Titan, when a high-pitched screech split the darkness. "That's her. It has to be. Stay here by the radio."

He drew his gun and started toward the sound at a run, using his flashlight to choose a safe path. If it hadn't been for a multicar accident on the main highway, they would have had plenty of backup by now. Unfortunately, a hunch about trouble in an old cemetery wasn't enough to warrant a full-blown response when there were specific needs that must take precedence. Jackson knew that was department policy, but he didn't have to like it.

"Nicki! Where are you?" he shouted.

"Over here."

He swung the light beam. Nicki was crouched near the ground with the dog standing over her. All the usable air left Jackson's lungs. He was about to shout for Harold when she waved and clambered to her feet.

He slowed only slightly. Holding his pistol pointed at the sky, he clicked off the flashlight and spread his arms as she ran into his embrace. At this moment, he didn't care what protocols they might be violating. He wanted her as close to him as she apparently wanted to be.

"What happened?" His voice was raw with emotion. "Why didn't you stay put?"

"Titan… Titan wanted to come over here. I guess he sensed something was wrong."

"And you listened to a dog instead of me?" In spite of chastising her, he held tight with his free arm.

"I was afraid for you," she said. Her cheek was against his chest and he could feel her trembling. "I didn't know where you had gone…and I thought maybe Titan was trying to tell me you needed help." She took a shuddering breath. "I'm sorry."

Closing his eyes, Jackson sent up a silent prayer of thanks and just held her. She had gone against his orders for his sake. How could he fault her for caring? He probably would have taken a cue from the dog, too, given similar circumstances.

"Just tell me you're not hurt," he said tenderly.

"I'm not hurt." Nicki leaned away slightly and inclined her head toward the place where she'd fallen. "But the guy over there's not doing so well."

Jackson turned and used his flashlight to illuminate what he first thought would be a grisly scene.

Instead, he saw the body of a young man, probably a teenager, in quiet repose. The boy's clothes were starting to deteriorate—particularly at the cuffs and collar—and his shoes were coming apart, but his body was otherwise pristine.

Playing the beam over the emotionless face, Jackson noted unusual puckering and sallow skin tones.

"This isn't a new murder," he announced, holstering his sidearm. "He looks embalmed."

"That explains the open grave."

"Where?"

She pointed. "Over there. I almost fell into it."

Before he could change his mind, he placed a conciliatory kiss on the top of her head, then took her hand.

"Your new friend isn't going anywhere. Come on. We'll go back to the car and call this in."

"What do you think is going on?"

"I don't have a clue," Jackson admitted ruefully. "If I was going to rob a grave, I sure wouldn't choose a recent one—I'd go for one of the crypts where the rich folks are interred."

"Who was this man?"

"I'm not positive. I don't want to go any closer and disturb evidence." He felt Nicki's grip tighten, and she lagged back so he paused to ask, "What's the matter?"

"My handprints will be in the dirt next to him. When I fell I landed right…" She shuddered and swallowed hard. "It was awful."

"I'll run you by the emergency room on our way back to the ranch, so you can get checked out if you want. I hope you don't believe those old wives' tales about expectant mothers getting scared and hurting their babies."

"Of course not."

"Then don't worry, okay? I'll explain everything to the crime scene techs when I talk to them."

"I'm getting pretty tired of being their guinea pig." She sighed. "I know I'm innocent and just wish they'd believe me."

He wished he could ease her mind. He really did. The trouble was, as far as the police were concerned, Nicolette Johnson was in this mess all the way up to her pretty neck.

It was a lot like being stuck in quicksand. The more she struggled and protested, the deeper she ended up sinking. And he was right there with her.

ELEVEN

"His name was Daniel Jones," Slade McNeal told the assembled officers when they'd had a chance to examine the scene at the cemetery. "I went to his funeral about five years ago."

Jackson had his arm around Nicki's shoulders, much to her relief, and gave her a squeeze of support before asking, "How did he die?"

She could tell that the captain was strongly affected but didn't fully understand why, until he explained further.

"Daniel was resisting arrest for dealing drugs. One minute I had the drop on the kid, trying to reason with him, and the next, he was waving a gun at me. I put one bullet into his thigh to stop him. A sniper finished him off before I even had a chance to cuff him."

"I remember reading about that case," Nicki said softly. She looked up at Jackson. "It must have happened while you were overseas. The newspapers had a field day with the story. They kept insisting it was police brutality and that the victim was just a poor, defenseless kid." She shivered, seeing the similarities to her own life when she added, "His mother was raising him by herself."

"That's right," Slade said. "And it gets worse. Daniel's mom, Sierra, was Detective Melody Zachary's sister. Sierra killed herself when she got the news her son had died." He raked his fingers through his short hair. "All in all, it was a horrible mess."

"The same Melody who's the director of the Sagebrush Youth Center?" Nicki asked. "I didn't know that about her. It makes sense, though. I suppose she feels she's helping other kids, like her nephew, to stay clean."

"Yeah." The captain turned and addressed Jackson. "Since your patrol unit is damaged, use your ranch truck to take everybody home. We can handle this. I'll come out to your spread tomorrow to question everyone again."

Slade's frown deepened. "I'll have a few more questions for you, too, Worth. You know the drill. Please refrain from discussing this evening's events with each other or with any outside parties."

"Yes, sir."

Nicki waited until Jackson had walked her back to his truck before she asked, "Are you under suspicion, too?"

"It's just procedure."

"He looked awfully serious," she remarked.

"That's understandable, considering his prior encounters with the Jones kid. Until tonight, I had no idea the captain was so deeply involved." He paused and glanced back to where floodlights illuminated the crime scene. "I wonder..."

"What?"

"Nothing. We're not supposed to discuss this case, remember?"

She glanced up at him. "Were you planning to talk about what happened tonight?"

"No." Jackson was slowly, thoughtfully, shaking his head. "I was just wondering how a teenager with no money ended up in that section of the cemetery."

"What do you mean? What's so special about it?"

"It's probably nothing. I'll tell you later, after I've had a chance to check a few details."

Harold overheard their conversation. "Tell her what?"

"The choice of grave sites puzzles me, that's all," Jackson said.

"You mean why is a poor kid buried in the Frears section? That's easy. Lots of folks who can't afford their own place end up in there. I imagine, because Captain McNeal and Dante Frears are old friends and former military buddies, there was an arrangement made.

"I was already retired when the Jones shooting took place, but I heard plenty of gossip about it. McNeal was really torn up after it happened. He blamed himself."

"Why? He didn't shoot to kill."

"No, he didn't." Harold was shaking his head. "Just the same, there was some rumor after your captain's wife, Angie, was killed, that maybe somebody was aiming to get back at Slade for the Jones boy's death and blew up Mrs. McNeal by mistake. I guess nobody ever proved a connection."

"Where was Daniel when he was shot?" Jackson asked.

"Come to think of it, right here in these woods. If I was superstitious, I might wonder if there was a jinx on this place."

Nicki didn't believe in such things, but that didn't keep the suggestion of lingering evil from giving her the willies. There was something awfully creepy about running around in the forest after dark, even if she didn't count tripping over an embalmed corpse.

The mere memory of that encounter made her flesh crawl. She had touched him, actually touched him. And although she knew that the young man's soul was long gone from that empty shell, she was nevertheless repulsed.

I should pray for him, Nicki told herself before wondering what good that would do. It was the living, the struggling, the ones still breathing, who needed to be held up in prayer—like the youth center lady named Melody, and Captain McNeal, who kept beating himself up for failing to save a teen who was headed down the wrong path.

And I'll pray for Jackson, she added, feeling her cheeks warm suddenly as she climbed into the truck and scooted to the center to make room for the two men on either side of her, while Titan rode on the narrow seat behind them. She had a good idea what to ask God on the K-9 officer's behalf, and she was going to add him to her prayer list. After all, everybody could use divine help from time to time.

"Like tonight, when whoever was shooting at us missed," she muttered to herself. In the midst of the turmoil, she had failed to give thanks for their survival. Now she made up for that oversight.

They could have all died. It was that simple.

Jackson had assumed his new employee would take a day or two off to acclimate herself, particularly after the harrowing cemetery incident. He was wrong. He awoke to the smell of fresh-brewed coffee and the aroma of sizzling bacon. If Nicki's cooking tasted half as good as it smelled, he was going to be sure to thank Slade for pushing him to hire her.

Harold was already in the sunny kitchen when Jackson entered with Titan at his heels. "Boy, that smells good."

"I wasn't sure what you preferred so I fixed a couple of different things," Nicki said. "How do you want your eggs?"

"Over hard. Are those waffles?"

Her grin was broad, her eyes sparkling. "Yes. The waffle iron in the cupboard looked so new, I wasn't sure if you'd ever used it."

"I don't know that we have," Jackson admitted as he helped himself to a mug of steaming coffee. "Harold and I never fuss. Anybody can fry an egg. The fancy stuff we get when we eat in town."

"Well, I'm taking orders for supper," Nicki said. "There's plenty of meat to choose from in the freezer. What sounds good?"

"Surprise us. We'll love it."

Titan plopped down at Nicki's feet and looked up at her as if she were the most wonderful person he'd ever met.

She laughed. "I think your dog likes me."

"No offense, but he loves anybody who fries bacon. You can give him a little taste if you want, just keep it small. He's on a strictly managed diet."

"Yeah, me, too," Harold chimed in, presenting his empty plate. "And I'm the one who's in charge. Two eggs over easy, all the bacon you can spare and a waffle, please."

"Coming right up." She turned back to the stove. "So, what are we doing today?"

Jackson and Harold both said, *"We?"* as if they had rehearsed speaking in unison.

"Maybe I should rephrase that." Nicki was chuckling quietly. "What am I supposed to do while you two go about your business today? I don't suppose you intend to take me back into town, considering what happened the last couple of times I went."

"Not if I can help it," Jackson replied. He sobered and waited until she was looking directly at him before he continued. "I can't order you to stay here. You're not under house arrest or anything. But if you're smart—and I know you are—you'll lay low for a while. Whoever sent you that bomb and made those other threats could easily have been the same ones who shot at us out by the cemetery."

"Really? I thought that was probably because they didn't want us to discover they'd dug up a body." She gave the frying pan a flip and the eggs landed upside down, perfectly centered.

"I don't think so," Jackson said. He accepted the filled plate she passed him. "Thanks."

Nicki wasn't satisfied. "Then what's going on?"

"Know what *I* think?" Harold piped up. "I think it's all cut from the same cloth, so to speak. The killings, the drugs, the bomb, everything."

"Okay," Jackson said as he started to eat. "How?"

"If I knew that, I'd go to work as a police consultant and make a pile of money," the older man said. "I can't put my finger on the reason, but I keep thinking that the crime syndicate has to be at the bottom of everything."

"That doesn't explain why anybody would dig up Daniel Jones's body. He died five years ago and the rash of killings didn't start until recently." Jackson hesitated. "You know, technically, we're not supposed to discuss the Jones case."

"Horse feathers. If we can't separate one from the other, tough. Maybe the connection is the narcotics."

Thoughtful, Nicki leaned back against the kitchen counter and took a sip of coffee. "Suppose Harold is right. Is there a link between those old drug busts and the people you suspect may be responsible for the latest crimes? I mean, why would a successful syndicate all of a sudden start killing it's own people? That's crazy."

"A power struggle, maybe," Jackson ventured. "I don't know. Nobody does."

"What about my cousin, Arianna? What exactly is she supposed to have done?"

Her question made him raise an eyebrow. "For starters, she not only killed Garry, the Realtor, she was involved in the drug business up to her eyeballs. You must have realized she didn't make all her money running that little restaurant."

"How would I know *that?*"

Nicki's defensiveness was predictable. Nevertheless, he pressed on. "Because you'd known her all your life? In order to live such a lavish lifestyle, she had to have had another source of income."

"I never thought about it," Nicki admitted. "I tried to have as little to do with my cousin as possible. She was—she was…"

"Go on."

Nicki shook her head and averted her gaze. "No. I'm not going to say it. It's bad enough that I'm thinking such awful things about her when she's not here to defend herself. Even when we were kids, Arianna had a mean streak. She was always looking for ways to get me to take the blame for something bad that she'd done."

"Is that what you think she was doing when she mentioned a secret code?"

"If she hadn't added *cousin,* I might have my doubts, but since she did, yes, I do think she was trying to get me into trouble. It wouldn't be the first time."

"Fair enough."

"If it was *really* fair, everybody would believe me when I say I have no idea what she meant about a code or danger."

"The danger part seems to be taking care of itself," Jackson said wryly. "First Murke breaks into your apartment, next somebody sends you a bomb, then we get shot at in the woods. Seems pretty consistent."

"Just what I wanted to hear." Nicki pulled a face. "Not only are there murderous thugs after me, they're reliable, too. How special."

Jackson had to laugh. He finished his meal, wiped his mouth with a paper napkin and carried his plate to the sink.

"I'll do the cleanup," Nicki insisted.

"Sorry. Force of habit. The dishwasher works fine so you shouldn't have too much work to do. After that, the morning is all yours." He turned to her. "Harold will show you which horses are safe to ride and where we keep the tack. Just don't go too far from the house unless one of us is with you."

"Horses won't be a problem," Nicki said, blushing.

"I never learned to ride in the first place, and I don't think it's smart to try to learn now."

"After the baby comes, then," he said, noting that her cheeks flamed and she'd stopped looking at him.

"If I'm still here." Her voice wavered.

In passing, Jackson paused long enough to lightly pat her shoulder. He knew better than to offer a hug the way he had after her fright in the cemetery, but he desperately wanted her to know he accepted her, just as she was.

Subconsciously, he had already determined her innocence—although he wasn't free to say so. In a way, that made the situation worse. Not only was Nicki Johnson clueless about how he felt, she didn't deserve to be under siege. And that was precisely what was going on. Nicki was standing firm against unseen forces bent on harming her, and there was nothing anybody could do to stop the onslaught, except find the culprits and send them to jail.

It was Jackson's fondest hope that he would be instrumental in doing just that.

A sense of melancholy kept nibbling away at Nicki's bright morning mood. She usually greeted each new day with enthusiasm and, standing in the lovely, modern kitchen, cooking for two appreciative men, had only added to her joy. Until Jackson had brought up Arianna, that is.

She followed the K-9 officer out onto the porch and watered her potted geraniums while she watched him briefly exercise Titan before going back inside. The big, black Lab was so full of life, so happy with the slightest praise, Nicki actually envied him.

She could just imagine the look on Jackson's face if she ever admitted she was jealous of the affection he gave his dog! Yet, she was. It was a family thing, a belonging thing. Harold and Jackson and Titan were a tight-knit unit. They cared about each other and it showed. A lot.

Which pointed out the fact that she remained an outsider. She felt like a child looking in the window of a candy store and yearning to taste the sweetness borne of fitting in.

Nicki sighed. She had given her life to Christ and knew He accepted her. So did Pastor Eaton, and probably most of his congregation. Yet, Nicki continued to feel as if she were standing separate. There was a big difference between being a part of a large, impersonal group as opposed to being welcomed by a few individuals who knew your deepest secrets and loved you, anyway.

Perhaps that was what Arianna had been searching for, too, when she'd gotten involved with such bloodthirsty criminals.

Pensive, Nicki leaned against one of the carved porch posts. Titan had been busy sniffing a small patch of scraggly lawn while Harold tended to chores in the barn. Jackson was back inside, dressing for work.

The dog unexpectedly galloped onto the porch and nudged her hand with his nose.

"Yes, I do need a buddy," she crooned, wiggling her fingers behind his ears. "You know that, don't you?"

Instead of continuing to pant and wag his tail, Titan shied away.

"What is it, boy? What's the matter?"

Nicki took a step toward him. He took two steps back. "Titan? It's me. We're friends. Don't you remember?"

The dog cringed, put his tail between his legs and left the porch.

Nicki followed, concerned. "Titan?"

He crept farther away from her, slinking as if he were trying to make himself invisible.

She stopped on the lawn. Watched. Waited to see what he'd do next.

To her horror, the dog approached the ranch truck, the same vehicle they had all ridden in the night before, and plopped into a sitting position next to one set of rear, dual wheels.

His ears were pinned back, his body was trembling.

There was no doubt in Nicki's mind. Titan had just found another bomb!

TWELVE

Jackson was buckling on the belt that held his holster when he heard Nicki start to shriek. She sounded more frantic and panicky this morning than she had when she'd fallen over the disinterred corpse the night before.

He hit the living room at a run and straight-armed the screen door, taking in the entire scene in a flash.

Nicki was bent over, tugging on Titan's collar to force him to go with her. The dog was balking. All four paws slid along the ground, leaving ruts in the gravel.

"What are you doing? Let him go!" Jackson shouted at her.

When she lifted her gaze to his, he saw sheer terror. Her blue eyes were wide, her lips parted, her skin pale.

She made several failed attempts to speak before she finally managed to say, *"Bomb!"*

"Where?"

"Truck."

"How do you know?" By this time, Jackson had reached her side. He snapped a leash on the dog's collar and took command. With one arm around Nicki and the other controlling Titan, he hurried them away.

Harold met them at the door to the barn. "What's all

the yelling out here? You two are scarin' the chickens right off their nests."

"Nicki says Titan alerted," Jackson explained as he passed both his charges to the older man. "You stay put with them. I'll call Boomer and get the bomb squad out here to check the truck."

"If that's where the explosive is supposed to be, I reckon I'll back up a tad more," Harold said, slipping an arm around Nicki's shoulders. "Come on. We'll go into the barn."

She hesitated, twisting away. "No. I want to stay right here."

"Then think of me and the dog," Harold reasoned. "We need to take cover, just in case."

"But… Jackson."

"He knows what he's doing. He's a pro, remember?"

Listening to their conversation as he walked away, Jackson wondered if his uncle was giving him too much credit. He was certainly encountering a lot of glitches, lately. Of course it would help if he knew who his adversaries were. Since the perps had no real names, other than those who were deceased, it was difficult to know what kinds of precautions to take.

Danger had obviously followed Nicki to the ranch, he realized with dismay. Slade had probably figured as much when he'd suggested hiring her in the first place. So, what now?

Jackson kept his distance from the suspected explosives as he reported the situation to dispatch by phone. One important question was whether the bomb was rigged to go off when he started to drive, or triggered remotely to better choose its victims. Either was possible.

Whichever it turned out to be, he knew he wasn't

going anywhere this morning, and maybe not later, either. As long as a serious threat existed, he was going to have to safeguard Nicki. That was all there was to it. When she had accepted the job at the ranch, she had become his responsibility.

Jackson huffed and shook his head. "Who am I kidding? I've been watching out for her, thinking about her, from the first moment we met."

Which was not that long ago, he reminded himself. So, what in the world was going on? Why did it seem as if they had known each other for ages? And why was there such a strong bond forming? Yes, she needed help from someone. But why him? Why now? And why was he getting the idea that divine guidance was influencing him? It had been a long time since he'd felt that kind of unquestionable connection to his faith, to his Lord.

Perhaps this was God's way of helping him transition back into the life he had once enjoyed. He had left the military of his own free will, yet he knew in his heart that Titan wasn't the only one who suffered from disturbing combat memories. The difference between him and the traumatized dog was that he had been able to mask his occasional uneasiness while Titan couldn't.

There were many former soldiers coping with far worse emotional scars, Jackson knew. Men and women who might never feel safe again, no matter where they were or what they were doing. He was thankful that his psyche was still fairly intact, but he also feared that if he failed here, if he failed to safeguard Nicolette Johnson, he might never get over it.

"That's not the real problem," he muttered, pacing the yard and keeping an eye on the truck from a distance. "It's not all about me. It's about her. And that baby."

The basic truth of those affirmations hit him squarely in the gut. The woman was practically a stranger, and her child wasn't his. Yet, he already sensed an emotional attachment. To them both.

He glanced toward the barn. Harold must have closed the bay doors just in case something went wrong. That made sense. However, it also meant that Jackson could no longer personally watch Nicki.

One quick scan of the truck and the otherwise empty yard was all it took him to make up his mind. Boomer and the ATF bomb squad might not arrive for hours, depending on how far they had to travel, and what other cases they might currently be working.

So, in the meantime, he was going to stay close to Nicki. He had to. It was more than a job, now. It was a sacred duty.

Wheeling, he headed for the barn.

Nicki was about to sneeze when the squeak of the door and Jackson's sudden appearance startled it out of her. "Whoa! You scared me."

"Sorry. I wanted you to know that the bomb squad has been notified. Are you okay?"

She had pressed her index finger across her upper lip directly under her nose. "Allergies, I guess. Must be the hay. Do we have to stay out here?"

"I suppose not." He looked to Titan. "I'll take the dog and do a sweep of the yard and house, then we'll talk about relocating."

"Check the house first, will you?" she asked with a forced smile. "I have kitchen chores to finish."

"I hardly think that's important right now."

"Maybe not to you. But I'd feel a lot better if I had something to do besides sit in a barn and sniffle." She could tell from his expression that he was still on high alert so she added, "I can't hide all the time. I won't. Besides, I trust you."

"You should trust the dog more," Jackson said flatly.

Nicki saw a chance to lighten his mood. "I was talking to the dog," she quipped. "But you're helpful, too. He'd have trouble dialing 911 with those big paws."

To her relief, the K-9 officer smiled. It was lopsided and wry but it was a smile, nonetheless. "Has anybody ever told you that you have a strange sense of humor?"

"Often." She chuckled softly. "Since you can't go to work this morning, what's plan B?"

"We wait."

"That's what I was afraid you were going to say." She sighed.

"Patience is a virtue."

Nicki sniffled again. "Yeah, well, it's not one of mine." She gestured toward the half-open door. "Please? Check for me? I want to go back to the house."

"What's the hurry?" Jackson was scowling and staring at her as if trying to read her mind.

"Nothing nefarious, if that's what you're getting at," she insisted. "I feel more at home in a kitchen, that's all. I don't like all this open space."

Harold piped up. "She's scared of chickens, too."

"What?"

It was Nicki's turn to frown. "They startled me, that's all. How was I to know they roosted all over the barn and were so territorial?"

"You have a lot more serious things to worry about

than them," Jackson said soberly. "All right. Nobody can get in or out of here without us seeing them now that it's daylight. If Titan doesn't find anything else wrong, we'll all go back to the house. Harold and I can take turns standing guard from there."

His no-nonsense approach made Nicki shiver. She wrapped her arms around herself and nodded agreement. This mess was all her fault. It had to be, even though she had no idea what was going on. The earlier attacks had been directed at her and these later ones probably were, too, although she didn't know why anybody would put a bomb in the ranch truck when they could just as easily have targeted her personal car.

To eliminate my guardian, she realized with chagrin. Getting rid of Jackson would leave her with one less person to champion her cause, and protect her from whoever they sent next. Murke had been the first, the phone threats and flower bomb had been second. And, chances were, the shot fired at the police car had been the third—not to mention any other times when she might have escaped without even knowing she was under attack, such as from the shadow behind the truck stop that had scared her silly.

And then there was this morning. The threats weren't going to stop. Not even out here where she'd thought she'd be safe.

Tears briefly clouded her vision before she blinked them away, and lifted her chin to affirm resolve. They were not going to beat her. Not now. Not ever. She wasn't alone anymore. God was looking after her. After all, He had sent Jackson, Harold and Titan. What more could she ask? What more could she possibly need?

Jackson was leading his dog out the barn door when she called after him. "One more thing."

He turned. "What?"

"My lessons. Remember? You said you'd teach me to shoot." She let her smile spread as encouragement. "I think it's high time I learned how to protect *myself.*"

Behind her, she heard the older man groan. "She'll shoot herself in the leg."

"I will not," Nicki insisted. "Well, how about it? Can we start before the bomb guys get here?"

"If that's what you want," Jackson said in parting.

Nicki whirled to face Harold. "What makes you think I'll be careless? I won't, you know."

"That's what all novices say until they actually hold a firearm in their hands and have to watch every movement, every second. It's not like taking piano lessons or learning to ride a bike. You can never let down your guard. Never."

"Good," she said, meaning it fully. "Because if I aim at anything, I intend to be able to hit it."

"Even a person?"

She rested a hand at her waist, palm open, to unconsciously cradle her unborn child. "If they threatened my family, I think I could act to protect them," she said. "It has to be better to be able to defend yourself than to have to wait for help to arrive that may come too late." Pausing, she glanced at the door. "Like the bomb squad."

"Gotta agree with you there," Harold said. "Just don't get careless. That's all I ask."

Sober and thoughtful, Nicki agreed. "I won't. If I could have chosen my relatives instead of getting stuck with a criminal cousin, I wouldn't have to learn to shoot in the first place."

"That is where it all leads back to, isn't it?" the older man asked.

"Yes." Nicki had run out of arguments, good or bad. "It has to be because of Arianna. And whatever that code was that she mentioned before she died, I sure wish I could turn it over to the police and simplify my life."

Shivering, she added, "Before more people die for nothing."

Jackson took his time inspecting the ranch house and grounds. It was amazing that Titan had alerted to the tampering with the truck in the first place. Normally, working dogs knew when they were on or off duty, and behaved like the family pet when they weren't wearing their official K-9 gear. Titan's consisted of a Kevlar vest as well as a harness and leash, although if he'd stuck his big, wet nose into a bomb and it had exploded, the vest wouldn't have saved his life. Nothing would.

Finishing with the house and its environs, Jackson praised his canine partner and returned with him to the barn.

He almost burst into laughter when he saw what Harold and Nicki were doing. The older man had grabbed a hen by its spindly legs to hold it still and Nicki was tentatively touching its black-and-white, mottled feathers. The hen wasn't acting particularly happy about being held, but at least she wasn't trying to peck anybody. Yet. One look at Titan approaching sent her into a frenzy of beating wings and loud squawking.

Nicki jumped back. "Whoa. I guess she thinks the dog is a predator."

"Something like that." Jackson couldn't help grinning. "Suppose you two quit playing with that chicken and come back to the house with me? I can give Nicki a crash course in gun safety while we wait for the bomb squad."

"And I can start fixing lunch after that," she replied, eyeing the still-ruffled feathers of the hen she'd been touching. "I'm glad we're not having fried chicken. I don't think my new friend would like that."

"I'd never tell," Jackson assured her. He stood at the doorway, rechecked the empty yard, then drew his gun and motioned for his charges to proceed. "Go ahead. I'll cover you."

Nicki made a face. "I'm starting to feel like one of those mechanical rabbits in a shooting gallery. Run this way and duck, run back that way and duck, then turn around and do it all over again."

"This, too, shall pass," Harold said, cupping her elbow while his nephew and Titan stood guard.

"I have to confess, I haven't been a Christian long enough to know a lot of verses, but that sounds biblical."

"I have my spiritual moments," Harold confided. "Do you go to church regularly?"

"Yes. But under the circumstances, I don't think it would be fair to endanger anyone there by sticking to my normal schedule, do you?"

"Don't worry," Jackson said over his shoulder as she passed behind him. "We'll get this problem of yours solved, and you can start living a normal life again. I promise."

"When?"

"I don't know."

He gritted his teeth, wishing he could give her a more

definitive answer. There was none. Nobody knew how long it would be before whoever was targeting Nicki got tired of the so-called game and quit—or unearthed the information she was supposed to be hiding, and no longer needed to harass her for it.

There had to be something they were not seeing—some clue or hint they had missed. Because if there wasn't, there was no way he could ever hope to guarantee her future safety—not to mention that of her unborn child.

Watching Harold shepherd her through the kitchen door, Jackson felt his gut clench. When all this was over, when he was finally able to think straight, he was going to ask Nicolette Johnson for a real date. And then maybe, just maybe, they'd be able to get to know each other on a personal level without having to deal with outside forces repeatedly trying to harm them.

Or worse.

The way Jackson assessed their present situation, there was no way to tell how much of his sense of commitment was due to his job, and how much might be above and beyond the call of duty. He suspected that he was falling for this victim in spite of his training to the contrary—or his determination to keep their relationship strictly professional.

It wasn't rational.

It wasn't right.

It was simply true.

THIRTEEN

Nicki ended up fixing lunch for nine people besides herself. The ATF crew had arrived to disarm the bomb, and local police were there to secure the area as well as take statements from the three of them.

Listening to conversations in the background as she cooked and served burgers, home fries and sweet tea, she learned quite a bit. First, her cousin had definitely been part of a complicated cabal that was still operating in and around Sagebrush.

Why so many lower-level crooks had been marked for death was an unanswered question, although in Arianna's case, she had died while resisting arrest and trying to kill Valerie Salgado. Apparently her cousin believed the female officer had spotted her leaving the scene of a previous murder—although she actually hadn't.

One homicide after another seemed to be occurring, and they all led back to...to *what?* Nicki wondered. How far back did the influence go? And how in the world was Jackson or anybody on the force going to untangle the repeatedly lethal web of deception?

She was about to ask about the body they'd found

in the cemetery when Jackson's boss, Slade McNeal, broached the subject for her.

"I may ask the new medical examiner to review the original Daniel Jones autopsy report, just in case, but I don't anticipate a problem."

Jackson nodded, and wiped his mouth with a paper napkin before asking, "What can he expect to find? I understood that case was pretty cut-and-dried."

"It was," Slade replied. "Still is. We just want to be sure nothing was done to the body after it was disinterred."

"Do you think there might have been tampering?"

The whole conversation was giving Nicki the willies, and she stifled a shiver. At least she thought she had. When her gaze met Jackson's, she realized that he had been watching her and knew she was distressed.

She managed a forced smile for his benefit. "Go on. I'm interested, actually. I'd never seen a corpse before. It was a shock to fall over him but surprising how well he was preserved for having died so long ago. You said it's been five years, right?"

"Give or take," Slade answered. "I still remember the Jones case as if it happened yesterday. One moment I'm about to read the kid his rights, the next thing I know he's lying dead at my feet from a sniper's bullet." His voice dropped until it was little more than a mumble. "Losing the mother so soon after that was the worst part."

Nicki knew it wasn't her place to contradict a professional, yet her heart ached for the captain. "The papers said that woman—Sierra Jones?—took her own life. It's not your fault. There's no way anybody could have predicted she'd react that way."

"We should have made sure someone stayed with her. I can see that now." A shadow crossed Slade's face. "Back then, we weren't careful enough with survivors. Not the way we are these days."

He was alluding to her situation, Nicki concluded. Was that why everyone seemed so solicitous? Why she'd been offered this job in the first place? That notion did not sit well with her.

Then again, she reasoned, she had desperately needed both a new job and a place to stay. How could she fault the result without questioning God's wisdom in taking care of her needs?

Speaking of which, Jackson had gone over firearms safety with her, and had promised they would do some target shooting as soon as the furor at the ranch died down. Nicki could hardly wait. She wasn't the blood-thirsty type. Not at all. But she was now vulnerable in ways she had never before considered. Learning to protect herself and her unborn child made perfect sense. Whether she could bring herself to shoot another human being, however, was a total unknown.

Picturing herself as the underdog, she recalled the Bible story about a shepherd boy, David, slaying the Philistine giant with a slingshot and a rock. She was certainly up against that kind of uneven contest. Given the greater weaponry available these days, she was glad she'd have more than a pebble in a sling with which to defend herself.

Could she? Would she? Nicki wasn't sure.

One thing was clear, however. As long as she was prepared for self-defense, she'd have a fighting chance. Jackson and his uncle could not be expected to shadow her every move 24/7. She wouldn't want them to even try. There was no telling how long she would remain in danger. What if it was years?

That disturbing thought led her to make a new mental connection. Eyes wide, breathing growing shallow, she nervously scanned the men and women seated around the dining room table.

As if a signal had been given, conversation ceased and everyone stared back at her.

Jackson got to his feet, went quickly to her side and took her hand. "What is it, Nicki? Are you sick?"

"No. No, I… I was just listening to you all talking about murders and I had the strangest notion."

"Well, let's hear it. We haven't exactly been at the top of our game lately. Maybe your viewpoint will help."

"It's about the body. Is there a chance Daniel Jones's murder was the first?"

Jackson scowled. "What do you mean, the first?"

"First of the bunch of killings you're trying to solve right now."

"What makes you say that? Years have passed between that incident and these latest murders."

"I don't know. Maybe it's silly. It just seemed to me that there was no reason to bother digging up his grave unless there was a connection to all the weird stuff that's been going on in Sagebrush." She shrugged. "Never mind. It's a crazy idea."

"Not necessarily. There were drugs involved in all the cases, one way or another. But if the Jones kid was part of the crime syndicate, why send a sniper to kill him?"

"Because the captain was about to arrest him? Like you said, he was young. Foolish. And undoubtedly more likely to cave under police interrogation. Suppose he was shot to silence him?"

"Suppose they *all* were?" Captain McNeal added. "That code the Munson woman mentioned could still be the key. If somebody thought each of them had it and was refusing to play along, that person could have eliminated the others in the process of his or her search."

"Oh, that makes me feel *much* better," Nicki retorted, the color draining from her face. "What if none of the victims knew any more about a so-called secret code than I do? Where does that leave *me?*"

"Up the creek without a paddle," Harold offered. "Don't worry. We'll look after you."

Nicki knew her voice was rising but she couldn't help it. "Who's going to look after *you,* then? It wasn't my car they stuck that new bomb under."

One of the younger ATF officers jumped into the conversation. "I wouldn't worry too much about that, ma'am. This device was designed to send a message without loss of life, just like the one from your apartment. If the guy who made it had wanted to kill anybody, he would have used a lot more explosive force."

"What do you mean?" Nicki asked.

"The truck bomb wasn't meant to cause a fatality. If it had gone off, all it would have done was damage the steering and probably cause a minor wreck. If they want to be serious, they'll set up a device like the one that almost killed that Sagebrush cop a few years back."

Nicki could tell from the way Jackson tensed beside her that the young ATF officer had erred. He apparently wasn't familiar enough with the town to realize what he'd done, but the suddenly charged atmosphere in the room was so disconcerting he looked around in bewilderment.

Jackson spoke up. "The case you're referring to involved our captain's wife."

Red-faced, the crew-cut rookie muttered to himself for a moment before looking at Slade and offering an apology. "Hey, man, I'm sorry. I didn't mean to sound harsh or dredge up…" Running out of words, he gritted his teeth.

McNeal sighed before saying, "It's all right," although Nicki could see that he had to fight to continue to appear unaffected. They all did. The story of the captain's wife's death was a local legend. No one had ever been charged with her murder and, according to newspaper reports, the police had no leads.

Tugging on Jackson's sleeve, Nicki urged him to accompany her back to the kitchen.

He was scowling as he complied. "What is it?"

"I had another idea," she said slowly, purposefully. "Everybody knows McNeal shot the Jones kid, right?"

"Yes, but we also know that wasn't the bullet that killed him."

"Right. According to the official record, it wasn't. But suppose whoever set the bomb in the McNeal car didn't believe it? Suppose they were after your captain and got his wife by accident just like Harold suggested?"

Jackson slowly shook his head. "I can't see how. It's my understanding that they checked all those possibilities. If the bombing had been related to the Jones boy's death, I'm sure they'd have found the connection."

"I wonder… Picture what it must have been like. The whole department is torn up because tragedy has struck one of their own. The captain is already in bad shape over rumors that he purposely killed a teenager, and then later his own wife gets murdered. How clear is anyone's thinking going to be under those circumstances?"

"You may have a point," Jackson conceded. "I'll have a look at the old case files ASAP." His gaze drifted over her shoulder and zeroed in on a plate of cookies. "In the meantime, how about serving dessert so I can invite our guests to pack up their gear and leave? It's high time you got some target practice."

Nicki nodded as she picked up the plate and started for the dining room. "Okay. Bring the fullest coffeepot, if you don't mind, and let's get this show on the road."

It occurred to her that she should be the one doing all the serving, yet she and Jackson already seemed so in tune that she hadn't hesitated to ask for his assistance.

Not only was that odd in this instance, it was something she didn't recall ever doing before. Nicki's core values required her to serve others, not be served by them. She was capable. Practiced. Self-reliant to a fault. She didn't need to be coddled or waited on like some frail female who was unable to stand on her own two feet.

Except that's turning out to be exactly who I am, she countered, disgusted with herself for admitting weakness.

Unreasonable self-reliance had been the trait that had kept her from becoming a true Christian for years, and it had almost stopped her this time, too. Being at the end of her rope with Bobby Lee and the baby was the only reason she had seen the light, so to speak.

Astonished, she faltered. Her hands began trembling

so badly she nearly dropped the platter of cookies before she managed to place it on the table and retreat.

When Jackson followed her out onto the porch, clearly concerned, she averted her gaze rather than allow him to see how unsettled she was feeling.

He came closer, and lightly touched her arm. "What is it. What's wrong?"

Nicki shook her head, still trying to find the words to explain her epiphany to herself, let alone express it so that someone else could understand.

She leaned into him and felt his arm slip around her shoulders, pulling her closer, supporting her physically and emotionally. "It's about my life," she whispered. "I just realized that the things I did that I thought were so wrong were the very things God used to draw me to Him. It wasn't just about salvation and forgiveness, it was about providing a second chance. If I'd been able to see the future, I imagine I'd have tried to fix everything, and might have missed ever becoming a believer." She leaned her head back to look up at him. "Does that make any sense at all?"

"If it does to you, that's good enough for me," he said softly. "I gave up trying to second-guess God years ago when I saw my buddies die in combat while I escaped. I don't think it's wise to try to overthink divine guidance. It'll make your head spin. Just relax and accept it."

Nicki slipped her arms around Jackson's waist and laid her cheek on his chest, listening to his heart hammering in cadence with her own. A few weeks ago, she would never have dreamed she'd be standing on the porch of a rambling ranch house in the arms of its owner, let alone embracing him this way. Yet there was a rightness about it. A sense that what they were doing was not only appropriate, it was mutually necessary.

The words, *thank you, Jesus,* echoed through her mind, her heart, and she repeated them purposefully. She finally saw that she didn't have to understand exactly what was going on before she gave thanks for it. Nor was she through being deeply grateful for her new friends and new job.

In spite of everything that kept happening to her and around her, she was determined to look on the bright side. That vow made her start to smile. If she could manage to see blessings in the act of tripping over a corpse in a dark, deserted cemetery, keep her head when they were being chased and shot at—her grin widened—and be brave enough to actually touch the feathers of a live chicken, there wasn't anything that could keep her from finding hidden blessings in everything, every day.

Like right now, Nicki told herself, knowing she should step away from her protector, yet reluctant to do so.

Then she heard the approaching clomp of cowboy boots and felt Jackson tense. He thrust her away and held her at arm's length. "You okay now?"

Nicki blinked to try to clear her vision, and managed to mutter, "Uh-huh," although she wasn't too sure.

"Good." He turned to Harold, literally passed her off to the older man, and went to rejoin the officers left in the dining room.

The retired deputy didn't say a word. He didn't have to. Nicki could see empathy in his expression and sense that he was on her side. The trouble was, she didn't know which side she wanted to be on. Did she wish

Jackson was interested in her as a person? Was that what his tenderness had meant? Or should she try to keep her distance for everyone's sake because he was merely doing his job?

Believing she was masking her melancholy, she forced a smile.

"He means well," the older man said. "Give him time."

"I don't know what you're talking about," Nicki insisted.

He rolled his eyes and waggled his bushy gray brows. "Oh, brother. Now I've got two of you playing games."

Nicki knew exactly what he meant. She was also determined to keep from admitting it. "There are no games going on, Mr. Worth. All I want to do is stay alive long enough for the police to catch whoever is after me."

And what about future happiness? she asked herself. At present, the concept of falling for the handsome cowboy cop was the most attractive option she could think of. It was also one of the most foolish. Despite the risks, she knew that her heart was teetering on the brink. It didn't matter whether or not Jackson shared those tender sentiments. One false move, one unguarded moment, and she was going to be hopelessly, helplessly, in love with him.

As soon as Jackson had made his escape from the porch, from Nicki, he felt more in control. The regular police officers in his dining room were getting to their feet and preparing to leave. He almost hated to see them go because that would mean it would be even harder to keep his distance from his lovely new cook.

Not that he actually wanted to. Truth to tell, he wished he was still standing on the porch, just the two of them, sharing a mutual embrace. His problem was a conviction that neither of them was behaving appropriately. He certainly wasn't.

Besides, I'm never getting married, he insisted to himself. That thought came to rest as a knot in his gut. *Married?* He hardly knew the Johnson woman. What business did he have thinking such personal thoughts about her?

Perhaps because she was a family in the making, Jackson reasoned. She was tough and resilient and more than capable of taking care of herself, yet she was also vulnerable in ways that would soon be evident as the baby grew. How was she going to make ends meet when she had another mouth to feed, let alone work while the newborn was tiny?

He supposed she could stay on at the ranch indefinitely. That would probably be best for her. The question was, since he was already struggling to keep his distance, how was he going to cope with having her underfoot all the time?

The captain was speaking, drawing Jackson back from his reveries. "I want you to stick close to home for the time being," Slade said. "If we have any more bomb calls, I'll dispatch you. Otherwise, your assignment is witness protection."

"Yes, sir." He cleared his throat as he shook his boss's hand. "One thing more."

Pausing, the captain waited.

"It's something Nicki said. Remember when she asked if there was any chance that the Jones killing and disinterment might be connected to the current crime wave in Sagebrush? Could she be onto something?"

"That's pretty far-fetched." Slade shrugged as if dismissing the notion out of hand.

"I wasn't here back then. Mind if I look into it?"

"Not really, as long as you do your job and don't let it distract you. Start by talking to one of our cold case detectives, Melody Zachary. That might save you some time."

"I know her from around the coffee machine, mostly," Jackson said, thoughtful. "Shoulder-length dark hair, kinda quiet?"

"That's her. We've talked about her background before. When she's not at the station, you'll find her at the center for at-risk teens where she's the director."

Still uneasy, Jackson glanced in the direction of the back porch where he'd left his uncle and Nicki. "It's an at-risk cook I'm most concerned about."

"Have you had any luck gaining her confidence so she'll open up to you about her cousin?"

"I don't think she's holding anything back, Captain. I really don't. Nicolette Johnson is no fool. If she thought she could end this threat by simply confessing, she would. In a heartbeat. I think she's as clueless as the rest of us."

"That's unfortunate." McNeal squared his hat on his head and huffed. "Because if you're right and I'm wrong, that young woman is in for a rough ride."

"Clearly, whoever is causing all the trouble doesn't want to kill her. If they did, they'd have used C-4 or something equally as deadly in their bombs."

"Maybe so. Until they're certain she really isn't hiding the supposed code. Once that happens, if it does, she'll be in even worse danger, and you know it."

McNeal started down the front porch steps, then paused to look over his shoulder. "If I were you, instead of expending so much effort comforting her, I'd let her get good and scared. Maybe that's what it'll take to make her talk."

Watching the other officers climb into their various vehicles and pull away, Jackson couldn't get McNeal's advice out of his mind. *Let* her be scared? That notion galled him. Nicki had already been through hell, thanks to whoever was targeting her. There was no way he was going to stand back and allow anyone to get closer to harming her.

What had already taken place, in spite of his best efforts, was plenty bad enough.

FOURTEEN

To say that Nicki loved her job at the ranch would have been an understatement. Not only did she get to plan meals on her own, whatever she prepared was received with eagerness and gratitude.

She was beginning to settle into the daily routine, and had decorated her private quarters as best she could with a few things salvaged from her ruined apartment. Anything that wasn't either washable or hard-surfaced had had to be thrown away due to the permeating smoke odors. Unhappily, that included the old Bible she'd borrowed from Pastor Eaton. When Jackson had realized how upset that loss had made her, he had provided a brand-new, leather-covered edition.

Now the Bible rested on her nightstand beside an old photo of her parents, ready for her evening devotions. She hadn't known what to call the habit of daily Scripture reading until Harold had mentioned doing the same. One other thing he'd told her was that Jackson, although he called himself a Christian, had apparently given up regular Bible study after returning to civilian life.

Titan had begun following her in and out of the

kitchen, much to her delight and her boss's chagrin. The dog came for tidbits and stayed for TLC, both of which she dispensed gladly.

The big black dog's limpid brown eyes, gazing up at her as if he had never seen anyone he adored more, warmed Nicki to the core every time they met. His master's eyes would have done the same, she was certain, if Jackson had not been avoiding her so much.

Oh, he showed up for meals, all right. But he didn't linger in her presence unless they had specific plans, such as more target practice. Her aim was getting good. Too good. Jackson had remarked on it the last time they'd plinked at tin cans out behind the barn.

"Looks like I can't teach you much more," he'd said. "You're a natural. As long as you remember the safety rules, you'll do fine."

"I wish I had a sidearm to carry in a holster the way you and Harold do."

"That's all we'd need. Arm the cook, and we'd never be able to tell you we didn't like your recipes."

"Very funny. I told you, I don't think I could hurt another human being."

"Then forget about carrying," he had snapped back. "Never draw or point a loaded gun unless you're prepared to use it."

"That sounds so callous."

"No more so than standing there like some sacrificial victim and letting the bad guys finish you off."

"Good point," Nicki remembered saying. Now that she was proficient at shooting, however, she knew she'd feel a lot safer armed. After all, the ranch was far from any neighbors, and there had been times when both Harold and Jackson had been busy with chores and she'd been on her own.

Soon, however, the whole house and yard would be filled with members of the law-enforcement community. She had been making preparations for an outdoor barbecue get-together for two days. Brightly colored paper tablecloths with matching, disposable plates and cups covered long tables, beach umbrellas provided extra shade, and Harold already had a whole pig slow roasting in a pit in the side yard.

The main group of guests would be the K-9 unit and their dogs, something Nicki was certainly looking forward to. She had met a few of the others during the crime responses involving herself, but it would be good to see and meet each dog. She especially wanted to give the injured dog, Lexi, a big hug for acting so heroically during the hostage crisis.

Only a couple of weeks had passed since that awful man had broken into her apartment, shot Lexi and pulled her into this mess. Sometimes, it seemed as if that confrontation had happened years ago. Other times it felt immediate. So did losing Arianna.

There were instances when Nicki still felt guilt for having ignored her kin for so long. And then she'd remember that all her current troubles led back to the cousin who had marked her as a target. Whether the act had been malicious or not, the fact remained that she was still walking around with a virtual bull's-eye on her back.

Sighing, Nicki stirred the bowl of frosting she was preparing for one of the special cakes she'd baked. Jackson had suggested she make more than one kind of dessert, and frosting the white layer cake was the last uncompleted task.

A shout from the rear of the house distracted her. She set aside the bowl and whisk and hurried to the back door. Harold was cradling two watermelons that had to weigh twenty pounds each, and Jackson toted plastic bags of crushed ice.

"I've got the door," Nicki said. "Put the extra ice in the big freezer 'til I see what I'll need. The melons can go on the counter or in the sink. Just be careful they don't roll off."

The "Yes, ma'am" she got from Jackson sounded rather cynical. Well, too bad. If he wanted a nice party, he'd have to learn to follow her orders.

Cowboy boots clomping on the bare floor as he walked, Jackson strode through the main part of the kitchen, and into the pantry where the chest freezer sat.

Harold gingerly placed the melons in the divided sink basins and stood back, breathing hard. "Whew. One more and I'll have 'em all."

As Nicki turned to watch him go, she noticed a flash of movement off to one side. She frowned. Had something just ducked under the kitchen table?

It never occurred to her to be scared. No one had bothered her on the ranch for weeks, and she was certainly not expecting trouble.

She bent. Lifted the edge of the tablecloth. Gasped. Then she screamed, "No!" at the top of her lungs.

The hair on the back of Jackson's neck stood on end. *Nicki!* He whirled and raced back toward her, drawing his gun as he ran.

There she stood in the middle of the kitchen with

her hands clamped over her mouth, her eyes wide and glistening.

"What is it? What's wrong?" he shouted.

She merely pointed at the floor.

He didn't see anything out of the ordinary until he leaned down and peered under the table. Then, he wasn't sure whether to bellow in anger or laugh. Apparently, Titan had gotten tired of waiting for his usual treats and had helped himself. To a whole cake.

Jackson holstered his pistol and turned on Nicki. "You didn't have to scare ten years off my life, woman."

She smiled ruefully. "Oh, my. I am sorry. I just…"

"You've spoiled that dog," Jackson insisted. "It's no wonder he's getting out of hand. I'll have to practically retrain him if I expect him to turn down treats from strangers the way he's supposed to."

"I'm no stranger. Besides, I didn't give him the cake. He stole it."

"Well, the good news is it's not chocolate so it won't be toxic to his system."

"Wonderful." She glanced at the clock over the stove. "I don't have time to bake another one."

"You should have thought of that before you made a house pet out of my working dog. I don't know who I'm madder at, you or him."

Nicki picked up the bowl of now unneeded frosting and gave it a stir. "Bummer. This is starting to stiffen. Without a cake to put it on, I might as well throw it away."

Jackson's hands were fisted on his hips as he glared down at her. "Serves you right for encouraging Titan's bad behavior."

"Oh, yeah?"

"Yeah." Scowling, Jackson stood his ground while she slowly approached, the bowl cradled against her ribs on one side, the whisk in the other hand. There was a look in her eyes that he couldn't exactly read, but he was pretty sure he didn't like it.

"You need to lighten up, mister," Nicki drawled.

"What are you talking about?"

"Your lousy temper. You used to be such a nice guy. At least I thought so before I got to know you better."

"Maybe the problem is that I got to know *you*," he countered. Having her underfoot for the past few weeks had played havoc with his emotions, and he was nearly at the end of his rope. Pretending that he wasn't attracted to this appealing, delightful woman was the hardest thing he'd tried to do for a long, long time. Maybe his Herculean efforts had made him a little touchy, but that couldn't be helped. After all, this was his life she had waltzed into and turned upside down.

The blue of her eyes seemed to deepen. He was so focused on trying to read her expression, he failed to see what else she was doing.

She raised the hand that had been holding the whisk, opened her fist in front of his face and plopped a glob of frosting right on the end of his nose.

Jackson was flabbergasted. How dare she! Who did she think she was? This was his house. She was his guest. No mature adult should even consider doing such an immature thing, let alone expect another person to tolerate it.

As he saw things he had two choices: let her get away with the act or retaliate. The smirk on her face made his decision a whole lot easier.

He grabbed for the bowl. Almost dropped it. Reached inside and filled his hand.

Nicki screeched and whirled to flee.

Jackson let fly.

The sticky, gooey missile caught her in the back of the head.

She skidded into the wall and left a sugary hand-print while changing direction. Coming at him low she clamped a hand on the edge of the bowl and began to wrestle for it.

Jackson whirled like a quarterback carrying a football and held on tight.

Her hand snaked around him, through the space between his side and elbow, and she managed to get more ammunition.

He shouted, "Let go!"

Nicki refused.

The floor was already slippery from their antics and getting worse.

From behind them came a booming, "Hey!" that brought them both to a halt.

Harold was standing in the doorway displaying a grin that threatened to split his face from ear to ear.

Jackson was thoroughly embarrassed, but his adversary seemed delighted with the entire fiasco.

"She started it," he grumbled, before realizing that making an excuse merely contributed to the childishness of the situation.

"If you two are through roughhousing, I suggest you clean up this mess—and yourselves. Our guests will be here in an hour or so."

When Jackson looked at Nicki, he saw that her cheeks were rosy and eyes were still sparkling. In a way, he was glad they had fooled around like silly kids because doing so seemed to have relaxed them both. It had certainly helped him. He had been so keyed up lately, it was a wonder he hadn't bitten her head off instead of accepting her overture of playfulness. She was going to be a good mother. A fun parent who knew how to enjoy herself as well as manage her life sensibly when she needed to.

He was going to miss those things about her when she left, Jackson realized, sobering.

"I'll take care of what's left of the cake and wash the dog," he said flatly. "You go get the frosting out of your hair and change. Harold can mop the floor. He used to do that before you came."

Looking sheepish and still flushed, Nicki grinned at the older man. "Okay, but I'll owe you one."

"You sure will, Ms. Nicki," he quipped back. "And when it comes time to repay me, remember how much I love homemade cherry pie."

"Good thing this wasn't cherry, then!" Nicki giggled. Passing Harold, she cupped a hand around her mouth and spoke in a stage whisper. "I did start it, you know. And I'd do it again. In a heartbeat."

Jackson shook his head and managed to control his own chuckling until she was out of the room. Then he looked at his uncle, blushed and laughed heartily while dragging the cake-sated Labrador retriever out the back door.

Nicki only owned one summer dress, so her choice of what to wear to the party was made for her. A frilly apron tied high over the waist of the full, flower-patterned skirt masked the tiny baby bump. She felt wonderful. Everyone was so sweet to her. And the dogs were magnificent.

All of them were on leashes except Titan, who meandered from one canine visitor to the next, politely touching noses, sniffing and being sniffed, as if personally welcoming them to his home.

The bloodhound, Justice, lay at Austin Black's feet, yawned and looked as if he could barely keep his eyes open. Austin had invited his fiancée, Eva Billows, and her son, Brady, who was currently using the big dog's side as a handy pillow.

In sharp contrast, the little black-and-white border collie, Kip, stayed alert and never missed a thing. It shocked Nicki to be told that Lee Calloway used the sweet-faced dog to locate dead bodies. Lee's petite, blonde companion, Lucy Cullen, didn't seem to mind their gruesome background a bit. As a matter of fact, she had hardly left her husband-to-be's side the whole time they'd been there. Given the trauma of Lucy's amnesia, back when everybody had mistakenly thought her name was Heidi, Nicki supposed it was natural for her to cling to the man she'd fallen in love with during that ordeal.

Then there was Valerie Salgado's Rottweiler, Lexi. Nicki was doubly glad to see for herself that that dog was recovering after being shot in the hind leg, even though she did still limp.

Nicki paused while refilling glasses of iced tea to pet Lexi's broad, black head and speak with the female officer. "I'm so thankful she pulled through," Nicki told Valerie. "When she went down, I was worried the bullet had killed her."

"You and me both. She still has a lot of physical

therapy to go through, but she's coming along," Valerie said with a smile. "How are you feeling, by the way?"

Nicki tenderly laid a hand on her slightly thick waist. "I'm good. Barely any morning sickness." She didn't have to force a smile when she glanced over at Jackson. "I can't believe I ended up with a job like this. Not after all that happened. It's ideal, particularly now. I just hope I can stay awhile."

"Why wouldn't you?" Valerie gestured at her nearly empty paper plate. "This meal is delicious. I can't see anybody in his right mind letting you go."

"I don't know. Sometimes my boss acts as if he doesn't like having me around."

"Or he likes it *too* much. Jackson is a hard guy to get close to. He never has been overly chummy."

Nicki arched a brow. "Really?"

"Yes. As a matter of fact, this is the first time he's invited the whole unit out to his ranch, and I'm really sorry my fiancé, Trevor, couldn't make it, and now that I can see the other kids, I wish I'd brought my niece, Bethany." Her eyes grew misty. "I can't believe how instant motherhood has changed my life."

Touched by the officer's candor, Nicki smiled. "I guess I have a lot of that kind of thing to look forward to. It's not as if I wanted to get pregnant. Not before marriage."

"I know." Valerie laid a hand of comfort on Nicki's arm. "I didn't plan on raising my niece, either, but since that's the way the Lord led me, I can't argue."

"I hope I'm a good mother," Nicki said, sobering.

"You will be. Trust me. It starts to feel natural pretty quickly." Valerie smiled at her. "And if you need any advice about parenting—" she giggled "—ask somebody else."

Nicki rolled her eyes and laughed. "Thanks a bunch. I'll remember that."

Looking around at the other guests she remarked, "Everybody seems to be having a good time. I'm glad."

"Me, too. Lee's been here before because he and Jackson are old friends. And maybe Captain McNeal and a few others have in the course of duty, but we haven't shared social engagements much. I sort of got the idea that Jackson preferred it that way."

"He can be kind of standoffish. Harold says it's because of his time in the service. Titan, too. That kind of thing changes people."

"Hey, daily life here in the States can do that, too," the reddish-haired officer quipped.

"That's certainly true."

As Nicki continued to circulate and top off iced tea glasses, she paused to ruffle the pendulous ears of narcotics detection beagle, Sherlock. He was the smallest of the canines in the Sagebrush unit, and was partnered with Detective Parker Adams. Apparently, that little beagle could smell dope no matter how well it was packaged or hidden.

And then there was Slade McNeal and his five-year-old son, Caleb. The boy seemed unduly shy, but Nicki had been told that a lot of his timidity was due to the loss of his canine buddy, his father's multipurpose, elite German shepherd, Rio. The poor little boy had been mourning since that dog was stolen right out of the McNeal yard.

Nicki could understand feeling so alone and bereft. She had spent many of her teen years experiencing the same thing. That was one reason why she went out of her way to crouch down and speak to the child.

"I have some cookies in the kitchen if you don't like cake," she offered quietly. "I already gave some to Brady Billows over there. See? Maybe you two would like to play later?"

Caleb shook his light brown curls, wrapped his thin arms around his bent knees and averted his gaze.

"Okay." Nicki tried to keep her voice friendly and open as she straightened. The child was clearly traumatized, and needed to be left alone unless he made an overture himself. That condition was certainly understandable. Not only was he motherless, according to Harold, he had formed a strong attachment to Rio, so strong that the loss of that dog had proved a serious setback to his mental state.

And now the sky was starting to look like rain. Gazing upward, Nicki was struck by how much the gray clouds mirrored the child's somber mood. Even she, who had been upbeat and joyful throughout the afternoon and evening, was beginning to be subdued by the overcast sky.

As if providing affirmation that the party would soon have to end, rumbles of distant thunder began.

Jackson joined Nicki. "We can move the tables and chairs into the barn if it starts to rain," he said.

"Unless everybody decides to head home." She'd been watching the others and noted that the animals seemed to be getting a little restless. "We've had dessert, and they ate up almost everything else I fixed."

"With pleasure, I might add. You outdid yourself, Ms. Johnson."

"I'm glad it all came together so well. Especially

after…" Although she was smiling, Nicki also felt her cheeks warming. "I really am sorry about that silly episode in the kitchen. I never should have put frosting on your nose. I don't know what came over me."

"You were keyed up and worried about a lot of things at once, that's all. The frosting fight helped you relax."

"Then you're not holding a grudge?"

The sly smile that lifted the corners of Jackson's mouth told her a lot more than his words. The look he bestowed on her when he drawled, "Well…" was comical, and totally predictable.

If there had not been a sudden crack of lightning and immediate boom of thunder, she might have laughed aloud.

Instead, Nicki and everyone who was gathered in the yard instinctively ducked and headed for cover.

"Looks like the party's over," Harold shouted as he grabbed armloads of picnic supplies and raced toward the kitchen. "Let's get this stuff inside."

Other guests helped clear the tables, then thanked their hosts, bid them a quick goodbye and ran for their various vehicles. Little Caleb and Captain McNeal were the last to go. Nicki made sure the child had his own plastic baggie of homemade cookies to take along.

The letdown after such a busy day was evident in Harold. Nicki felt it, too. Pregnancy wasn't such a bad thing, if you didn't count being scared and elated at the same time, but it had brought unwelcome changes in her stamina. Thankfully, the K-9 unit had eaten well so there wasn't much to store as leftovers.

As soon as she had refrigerated the perishables, she went outside to unwind and watch the developing storm. Under the cover of the front porch, she could sit and relax in safety while nature put on a light show that rivaled Fourth of July fireworks.

Raindrops as big as golf balls spattered into the dry yard and beat a staccato rhythm against the roof. Stiff breezes carried the odor of fresh rain, of wet grass, and washed the south Texas dust away in rivulets like cleansing tears.

Leaning back and giving the padded glider a push with her feet, she closed her eyes and thought of all the times when she'd dreamed of just such an ideal place— somewhere secure where there were people who cared about her, a solid roof over her head and abundant food in the pantry.

A deep breath ended in a sigh. "Don't get too comfortable," she whispered to herself. "This place may feel like a real home but it isn't yours. Remember that."

Subdued, she knew that her time here was fleeting. She also knew how much she dreaded the idea of leaving. Maybe someday, after the baby came and her life got back on track, she'd meet somebody who would share her dreams and accept her for who and what she was, sins and all. It was a far-fetched notion, yes, but it helped her cope…anything but let herself foolishly picture Jackson as a permanent part of her future.

Another clap of thunder startled her into opening her eyes. The flashes were coming closer together now, illuminating the early darkness like a strobe globe hanging from the rafters at a high school prom.

Gray shadows in the distance were distorted by sheets of rain. Tree limbs danced in the increasing wind. Leaves were dislodged before their time and tumbled across the yard.

A door banged.

Nicki startled at the noise, and whirled to see who had joined her. There was nobody there. Not even Titan.

"I must have left the screen unlatched," she mused, turning back to watch the storm.

A gust of wind whipped her hair into her eyes. She raked it back with her hands and stood, deciding it was high time to go inside.

That was when she saw it. Or him. The dark form was no more than a shifting shadow, a morphing shape that might have been a man, or might just as easily been a figment of her imagination.

The harder she peered at it, the less distinct it seemed.

Well, real or not, Nicki was not about to make herself a target.

She turned on her heel.

Ran for the door.

Jerked it open and crashed into Jackson.

She wasn't going to stand there exposed and let someone shoot at her. At both of them.

Before he could say more than, "Whoa," she'd given him a hard push and shoved him back inside.

He may have put out his arms to grab her or simply to steady himself. Nicki didn't care. She slipped her arms around his waist and held tight, unwilling to let go.

"What happened out there?" he asked, sounding nearly as breathless as she felt.

"I—I thought I saw somebody."

When he started to disentangle himself from her embrace she stopped him. "Don't go. Please?"

She felt the change in his posture as he once again pulled her closer and began to gently stroke her back.

His assurance of "You're safe. I've got you" was so dear, so poignant it brought tears to her eyes.

FIFTEEN

A search of the yard the following day had been fruitless, just as Jackson had known it would be. He wanted to believe Nicki had spotted a real prowler, but in view of the storm and the particularly strenuous days she'd spent preparing for his party, he was more inclined to think she'd been imagining things.

That, or the shadow of doubt cast over her was making her so paranoid that she thought she saw a nemesis where there was none.

Yet somehow that theory didn't sit right with him.

During the barbecue, Jackson had heard various members of the K-9 unit asking Nicki leading questions, yet as far as he knew, she had fielded all their queries with ease. At this point, he would just about stake his reputation as a cop that she was innocent.

"Which is what I may have to do," he muttered to himself. It helped to know that Harold believed Nicki's denials of guilt, too. As a matter of fact, the older man was adamant about her innocence.

"What do you have to do?" Harold asked, joining him.

"Just talking to myself," Jackson replied. He scanned the sodden, muddy yard. "Where's Nicki?"

"Inside tidying up. She's not like me. Once I've filled my belly, the last thing I want to do is fuss in the kitchen."

"I've noticed."

"Well, you take after me."

"Never said I didn't." He started for the barn. "C'mon. Let's go where we can talk privately."

"About the girl?"

"Woman," Jackson corrected. "I don't think they like to be called girls anymore."

"Used to." Harold pulled a face. "I miss the good old days when even your granny answered to a polite, *miss*."

"If I remember correctly, Granny could also shoot the eye out of a wild turkey at fifty paces. I'd have called her anything she wanted."

"You've made your point. How is Nicki doing with her shooting lessons? I don't care if she can't hit the broad side of this barn with a scatter gun. Can she be trusted to remember the safety rules?"

"She's fine." Jackson smiled with satisfaction. "Actually, she's a natural marksman."

"I'd still feel better if she wasn't packing. The last thing we need is for her to get scared like she did during that storm and shoot one of our cows."

"She won't. I've shown her where we keep a couple of loaded guns, just in case, but she won't be strapping any on. With the two of us around, she won't need to have a pistol close at hand."

"Which reminds me," Harold began, "I was just coming out to tell you. Your captain called. He wants you at the station for a briefing this afternoon."

"Did he say what about?"

"Nope. And I knew better than to ask."

"Smart man," Jackson said.

"Well, that makes one of us, anyway."

He scowled and studied his uncle's expression. "What's that supposed to mean?"

"Oh, nothing much. I was just thinkin' about how well you and Miss Nicki have been getting along lately. I don't believe I've seen you act playful like that in years. It was a sight for sore eyes."

"What was I supposed to do? She smeared frosting on my face."

"And you could have just wiped it off and walked away mad," Harold argued. "But you didn't. You fought back like a kid would have. I haven't laughed that hard in a long time. Neither have you."

Jackson couldn't help smiling at the memory. "It was fun. Embarrassing when you showed up, but fun just the same. What do you suppose got into her?"

"If she was eight or nine years old, I'd say she had a crush on you. Might anyway. You could do worse."

"Do worse for what? I made up my mind a long time ago that no cop should ever get married. You, of all people, should agree with that."

"Why? Because my wife found somebody else while I was out saving the world? Not all women are that selfish."

"The ones I've met are. Remember!"

"Then look at the matches some of your buddies have made recently. Austin and Eva. Lee and Lucy. Even Valerie Salgado and that FBI guy of hers, Trevor…?"

"Lewis. Trevor Lewis. But that doesn't mean I'm in the market for a wife."

"Or for a family? Is that what's holding you back?"

"No…of course not. I know Nicki's baby can't help

who his father was." He lowered his voice for fear his words might carry enough to reach the kitchen. "His name is Bobby Lee Crawford. I tracked him down. I know where he went after he dumped her and split. I'm just not sure I should tell Nicki, in case…"

"In case she's not over him? I know what you mean but don't you think she deserves the right to choose?"

"I suppose so. I just…"

Harold was grinning widely. "You just don't want her to leave. Admit it. You're falling for her."

"Between you and me, probably." Jackson gritted his teeth and shook his head. "But as far as Nicki is concerned, I'm her boss and temporary bodyguard. Period. Understand?"

"Yeah." The older man shrugged. "I get it. While she's in danger, we'll keep her safe, and when the air clears and she's proven innocent, you can step up and start courting her proper."

"Maybe. Maybe not. Right now, my captain isn't convinced she can be trusted, and if I show any bias, he might remove me from the case. I can't let that happen. *We* can't let that happen."

"For once we agree a hundred percent." He pointed toward the house. "Better go return McNeal's call and see when he wants you there. I'll look after Nicki while you're gone."

Jackson knew his uncle was perfectly capable. After all, the man had been a trained deputy, a seasoned veteran of the force. There should have been no reason to be hesitant to leave Nicki behind…yet he was.

That had to be because he had let himself get too personally involved, Jackson reasoned, chagrined to admit it. Still, as long as Nicki remained in the dark about his feelings, she'd be safe enough. And soon, when they apprehended the masterminds behind the drug gang war and the rash of related killings, he'd be free to share his thoughts about their possible future. He had made up his mind long ago that even if she spurned him as a potential suitor, he was going to make a home for her and her baby.

He still felt that way. Nicki would be exonerated and then he would invite her to stay on at the ranch.

Will I tell her more? he wondered. *Will I tell her I love her?*

The crystallizing of that thought brought him up short. He *did* love her. In spite of his many vows to the contrary, in spite of his superior's opinion of her guilt, he had fallen hopelessly in love with Nicolette Johnson. She had shown him a future filled with hope. Just being around her had banished the shadows of his painful past.

Setting his jaw, he hurried through the kitchen without greeting her. He couldn't. Not now. Not when he was still coming to terms with his emotion.

If he looked in her eyes, he knew she might be perceptive enough to glimpse his true feelings.

And if she looked back at him with the affection he'd been denying for so long, he knew he'd be lost.

In his imagination, he was already embracing her, kissing her, telling her how much he cared. To do so for real, before he was free to share everything, would be a terrible mistake. For both of them.

Nicki's day seemed to drag on forever, particularly after Jackson left for the station. She knew he'd been called in, and while she certainly didn't resent his sense of duty to Sagebrush, she felt unusually lonesome whenever he was away from home.

Even Titan's pleasant companionship wasn't enough to soothe her, although she was thankful the big dog's presence hadn't been needed in town this time.

Harold had done his best to entertain her, too. After lunch, he'd even invited her outside to show her how to care for the horses.

"I really don't want to learn to ride," she argued, trailing behind him while Titan followed her.

"Won't hurt you to at least brush down one of the mares. They're real gentle."

"And big," Nicki said in awe as they drew closer to a corral next to the barn. "Really big. I had no idea."

"A Texas gal and you haven't been around horses?" Harold teased. "What's this world coming to?"

"I grew up in town," she replied. "If I couldn't get around by walking, I rode a bike."

He clipped a lead rope to the halter of a round-bellied chestnut mare and led her out the gate before tying her to a stanchion. "How old were you when you lost your folks?"

"In my teens. Mom went first. That's when I started to hang around with my cousin, Arianna, more." Nicki made a face. "Until I saw her for what she really was."

"Is that when you became a cook?"

"Sort of. I cooked for my father for a while, then went to work doing kitchen prep until a grill job opened up at the truck stop. That's how I found out I was good at short-order work. It wasn't a bad job."

"You're too talented for drudgery like that," Harold said. He handed her a brush, slipped his hand into the strap on a similar tool and demonstrated stroking the mare's coat as he continued. "You should have gone to culinary school to become a real chef."

"Special schooling costs money. I was too busy trying to make ends meet and keep my head above water, so to speak, to even think of getting more education. I learned by doing." She smiled as the brush glided over the horse's smooth hide and the animal's skin twitched beneath her soft touch.

"And then what happened?" he asked.

"I got stupid." Nicki paused the brush and made brief eye contact with the older man before looking away. "It's embarrassing to even talk about, but I suppose you may as well hear it from me instead of through the grapevine. I thought I was in love. I thought Bobby Lee wanted to marry me. I fell for his line that we should move in together and pool our resources so we could save up for a wedding." She huffed. "I'm no kid… I should have known better." She took note of Titan, lying in the shade nearby and panting. "If I'd been smart, I'd have gotten a dog instead."

Harold nodded sagely. Nicki noted that he appeared to be concentrating hard on grooming the mare instead of looking at her, and that helped her continue her story without too much awkwardness.

"Bobby Lee played me like a cheap fiddle. I made the mistake of trusting him and look what it got me."

"Seems to me things are starting to improve," Harold remarked. "At least you have a better job and folks who'll look out for you."

"Until the murderer is caught or whoever has been after me gives up," Nicki countered.

"I take it you still have no idea what your late cousin meant when she mentioned you?"

"Nope. Not even an inkling." She glanced over the mare's withers to see if she could tell whether or not he still doubted her honesty. The kindness and sympathy in his expression was very comforting. "You believe me."

"I do. And for what it's worth, so does my nephew."

"Really? I'd wondered about that, particularly after all those other cops kept questioning me at the barbecue."

"They were just doing their jobs. I could tell they liked you, too."

"It did seem that way, didn't it?" Nicki smiled. "I wish it was as easy to tell about people as it is to tell that Titan likes me."

Hearing his name, the black Lab thumped his tail against the hard-packed ground next to the barn.

Harold chuckled. "Hey, feed me as many treats as you sneak out to him, and I'd follow you anywhere, too."

"You noticed?"

"It's hard to miss. That dog looks up to you as if you were his idol. Come to think of it, you probably are."

"The feeling is mutual. All the K-9 unit dogs are amazing." She sobered. "I sure hope they find Rio soon. I could tell how much that little McNeal boy missed him. The only times he left his father's side at the barbecue was to snuggle with one of the other dogs."

"Yeah. It's been rough for that kid. First he loses his mother and then the dog he counts on for protection and affection gets snatched."

Nicki's hand rested at her waist, fingers splayed over the baby growing within her. "It's going to be hard to raise my child alone, but I can do it. I know I can. Lots of people do fine as single parents."

"Who're you trying to convince? Me, or yourself?"

"Maybe both. I've tried to look ahead, to plan the rest of my life sensibly and sanely. It's hard. I can't tell what to do or think when I know someone is out to get me." She blinked away unshed tears. "What am I going to do, Harold?"

"Pray a lot. Trust the Lord and the folks He's put in your path to help you out. Take one day at a time. That's my motto."

"Mind if I borrow it?" Nicki asked through a forced smile.

"Not at all. Glad to share." He straightened. "I think we've curried her enough. Stay right there while I go get a hoof pick. I'll be right back."

"Is that anything like a toothpick?" she teased.

The sound of the older man's warm laughter was muted as he entered the barn once again.

More relaxed now that she'd become acquainted with the mare, Nicki slipped her fingers through the strands of long mane and wiggled them. The horse turned her head and sniffed, then blew against Nicki's closest arm, tickling her.

She returned the featherlight touch. A few long hairs, like a dog's whiskers, stuck out stiffly, but the rest of the animal's nose was as soft as velvet and warm beneath her hand.

"Okay," she said quietly, "you're not so big and bad after all. But you're sure chubby. What do they feed you, anyway, girl?"

Running her palm gently over the horse's side she felt a bump, then movement. *Of course.* They had something in common. The mare was in foal.

Soon she would be out of shape, too, Nicki mused. That was a given. And even if Jackson had admired her in the past, as she suspected, he was sure to think she looked funny as her pregnancy progressed.

Nicki sighed. Well, that couldn't be helped. It was what it was. She was what she was. God had forgiven her and had used her mistakes to help her heal. For that she was thankful, no matter what.

Perhaps, if things settled down soon, she'd be able to find another position and leave the ranch before Jackson started thinking she was unattractive.

And then what? she asked herself. What difference did it make if he didn't like her looks? They had no chance for future happiness when she would be the mother of another man's illegitimate offspring. If she herself could not fully come to terms with that situation, how could she expect anyone else to?

A shiver shot up her spine. Was she going to be able to love her baby the way she should? Would she be a good mother? A loving parent? Fair to the innocent little one who had not asked to be born, particularly if it happened to be a boy who reminded her of Bobby Lee.

That, and only that, had to be her prayer. Not for herself, but for her baby.

And she must stop pining for Jackson, too, she reminded herself. It was fine to look up to the man, to rely on him—and his uncle—for safety and shelter. However, it was not reasonable to think they might someday become a couple. Her traitorous hormones were leading her astray, that was all.

She had read that that kind of thing might happen, that she could be fooled into believing almost anything when her body was so out of balance.

The mare lifted its head and stomped one of its hooves, jarring Nicki out of her contemplation.

Titan jumped up, too. His hackles rose. A low growl rumbled from deep in his chest.

Both horse and dog were staring at the house, but Nicki didn't hear or see anything out of the ordinary.

She tensed, wondering if she should run into the barn to fetch Harold. To her relief, she saw him coming toward her.

"Titan just alerted," she said, ruing the fact she sounded breathless. "So did the horse, I think."

"What did they do?"

She pointed. "They both started looking that way."

"Did you hear a car drive up? Anything?"

"No."

Titan had moved to heel on her left and was standing as if he were posing for his portrait at a dog show.

Harold drew his sidearm. "You stay here. I'll go investigate."

"Oh, no, you don't. If you're going, I'm going."

"That's unacceptable."

"So is letting you go off and leave me."

"Titan will protect you."

Nicki chuckled nervously. "If I was a bomb I might buy that. I happen to know he's not trained in protection like some of the other dogs in Jackson's unit."

"No, but his basic instinct is working just fine. Look at him," the older man said, taking a step forward.

Nicki stifled a gasp. Someone or something was coming around the corner of the ranch house! A man. A rather portly man.

Her eyes widened as she assessed the scene. Whoever their visitor was, he was dressed in an expensive, three-piece gray suit with Western tailoring. His highly polished boots had already picked up a coating of Texas mud thanks to the recent storm. In one hand he held a businessman's felt Stetson and in the other a crumpled handkerchief. Considering his pristine attire, and the way he was mopping his damp brow and patting the sparse hair stuck to his forehead, he looked far from intimidating.

Smiling, the man raised a hand and waved the hanky before continuing to blot his pudgy face. "Afternoon, folks. My car broke down a ways back, and I need to use a phone to call a tow truck. Can y'all help me with that?"

Harold holstered his weapon and returned the man's grin. "Sure thing. You from around here?"

"Close enough. I'm glad I found somebody home. I was afraid I was going to have to hike on down the road."

"You don't have a cell phone?" Harold asked, closing the distance between himself and the stranger.

"Battery's dead," the man replied. "Guess I forgot to charge it."

"Well, don't worry. You can call from the house. Follow me."

"Thanks. I could use a drink of water, too, please. I'm real parched."

Nicki saw both men disappear into the kitchen. Although Titan seemed to still be upset, the mare had settled down.

Bending slightly, Nicki laid her palm on the dog's broad head and ruffled his ears with her fingers. "It's okay, boy. Just a passing motorist. Nothing to worry about."

The dog remained stiff in spite of pausing to lick her hand. She stood with him and waited for Harold to return. What was the delay? How long did it take to make one phone call?

Finally out of patience, she called, "Hey, Harold, where are you?"

There was no response. Nothing. Not even a wave from the open kitchen window where the men should be getting drinks from the refrigerator, although she did hear the house phone ringing.

Nicki was torn. If she stayed out there with Titan, she'd be safe for a while. But then what? What if Harold needed her? Or what if the businessman had fainted. He'd looked pretty pale and weary when he'd arrived, so that was a possibility.

With Titan at her side, she started for the back door. Climbed the stairs. Opened the screen. And stepped into the kitchen.

Harold was there, all right.

So was the man in the gray suit.

And he was holding a gun.

SIXTEEN

Jackson let the ranch landline ring ten times, then hung up and redialed just in case he'd made a mistake. This time, he let it go until the answering machine triggered.

Frustrated, he punched more keys on his phone and brought up the personal cell his uncle rarely bothered to carry. That call went to voice mail.

Across the desk, Captain McNeal frowned. "Something wrong, Worth?"

"I sure hope not. Nobody at the ranch is answering." Jackson made a wry face. "This isn't the first time this has happened. Between Harold and Nicki you'd think one of them would have the sense to keep a working cell close by."

"I'd expect Harold to since he knows there could be trouble. Not so sure about the girl. She seemed pretty cool and collected during the barbecue, though. Nobody got a thing out of her except polite conversation."

"That's because she has nothing to hide," Jackson countered. "I overheard enough to know you'd asked everybody to quiz her. Now are you satisfied?"

"Getting that way," Slade replied. "Still, there may be some clue she doesn't realize she's withholding. Maybe the Munson woman mentioned it casually, and whatever she said didn't register with Nicki at the time."

"It would help if we had a better idea exactly what we're looking for."

Slade scowled. "Yeah. No kidding."

Listening without continuing to make eye contact, Jackson kept trying various phone numbers. The ones connected to his ranch or his uncle had mechanical responses. The one that was Nicki's simply reported that she was unavailable and had not set up a voice mail account.

Jackson gave his superior a serious look. "I need to go home. Now."

"I agree. Tell dispatch where you're headed and keep us posted." He leaned back in his desk chair and laced his fingers behind his head. "I'm sure it's nothing. Too bad we can't teach your dog to use a telephone."

That notion sat heavily in Jackson's gut as he drove out of town. Titan was at home with Nicki and Harold, giving him one more worry rather than a sense of peace. Since Valerie Salgado's dog had been shot and maimed, not to mention prior minor injuries to other dogs in the K-9 unit, like Kip, he'd been more on edge. He and Titan had survived a war zone. It would be ironic if coming home to the States caused worse damage than the PTSD the Lab was already suffering.

Using his thumb on redial he kept calling Harold's cell. Somebody had to hear and answer eventually.

Surely they would.

Unless something terrible had happened.

Nicki's breathing was shallow, her eyes wide. She knew she was gaping at the stranger, but couldn't manage to pretend that seeing the small, silver pistol in his hand didn't bother her.

Harold was backed up against the edge of the kitchen counter, still armed but apparently convinced that drawing his gun would be foolhardy. She agreed. No one could be fast enough to outmaneuver a bullet, particularly one fired from such a short distance.

The interloper barely glanced her way so she remained motionless, waiting, while the phone in her pocket repeatedly played bars from "Yellow Rose."

Growling, Titan stayed with her.

Finally, the armed man said, "Quiet that dog down before I shoot it, and move over closer to the old man where I can keep an eye on you both. Turn off your cell and put it on the counter with his. Do it. Now!"

Making visual contact with Harold, she saw his slight nod, so she grabbed Titan's collar to control him and took a few tentative steps to comply. "What's going on?"

"I'm about to get what I came for," the man announced hoarsely. Nicki could tell he had not been faking the physical strain from leaving his car on the road and hiking to the barn, but she doubted he'd done so because he'd really broken down.

Harold stepped in front of Nicki as soon as she closed the distance between them. "Whatever you want, you can have. Help yourself. Just leave us alone," he said with a firm tone.

"Butt out, old man. My business is with the woman."

"Forget it. She's off-limits."

Nicki saw their adversary's eyes narrow as he took a step forward, so she raised her free hand with the cell phone in it to signify compliance as she laid it aside. If she'd thought she could have grabbed Harold's gun and fired in time she might have tried, but good sense prevailed. Even if she did manage to get off a shot, she knew the other man would fire, too. And if he didn't shoot her, he'd certainly wound or kill poor Harold and maybe Titan, too.

"I don't want anybody to get hurt," Nicki insisted. She left the little phone and edged away from her erstwhile protector. "Please don't shoot. Just let me put the dog outside. Okay?"

"Good idea. Then shut the door. Don't try any tricks and nobody'll get hurt." He stepped to his left and gestured at Harold with the short barrel of his pistol. "You. Sit in that chair over there and put your hands behind your back so she can tie you up."

Although the older man did move, it was with evident reluctance. "What's all this about? Who are you?"

"What do you care?"

"It's right on the tip of my tongue," Nicki mumbled to herself. "German-sounding, I think. Luther?"

As she continued to guess, she was late looking at Harold so she didn't see him rapidly shaking his head until she'd said, "I know…it's Gunther. Gunther Lamont. I've seen you before. In church, I think it was."

Harold's moan signaled her that she'd made a big mistake. Of course she had. She was too honest to consider the fact that identifying the armed businessman would not bode well for her ultimate survival. Then again, they had no guarantee either of them would live through this long afternoon, let alone greet tomorrow.

Gunther sidled up behind Harold and slipped the old man's sidearm free of the holster, then tucked it into his own waistband before telling Nicki, "Take that extension cord over there and tie him up. Do a good job or I'll shoot him to make sure he stays put."

"Okay, okay." Her hands were trembling, her fingers felt stiff and unwieldy, yet she managed to secure Harold well. She might have tried to arrange an easy escape for him if Lamont had not threatened him with bodily harm.

Nicki straightened and backed away as soon as she was done. With Harold out of commission and Titan banished to the yard, her chances of escape were slim to none.

"What do you want from us?"

"Just from you, Nicolette. I'm an old friend of your cousin, Arianna. Or maybe you know her the way I do, as the Serpent."

"You're part of all that? Why? You're an upstanding citizen."

"Was," Lamont said with chagrin. "I didn't start out looking for criminal connections—they just happened in the course of some slightly shady business dealings that didn't turn out as planned."

"Then it's not too late for you," Nicki insisted. "If you didn't mean to break the law, maybe…"

"Oh, I meant to. And I'm not done, either. Once I get the code from you and know where to look, I'll be home free."

"That code again." Disgusted, she raised her hands, palms up, and stared at him, trying to decide if he had the guts to actually shoot anybody. Judging by the way he was perspiring and the way his gun hand shook, it was a toss-up. He might mean to fire or his nerves might make his finger twitch and pull the trigger. The result would be the same.

"Yes, the code. You may as well confess."

"I don't know what you're talking about. I didn't know what was going on when Arianna brought it up, and I don't know now. I swear."

"Don't try to kid me, lady. It's paces from someplace in the Lost Woods, like a treasure map, only verbal. So many steps to the left or right, then another number from there and another after that. Get it?"

"Um, I think so." Her gaze met Harold's for a split second, and she saw understanding dawn. He was shaking his head, trying to talk her out of doing anything without actually issuing the warning in so many words.

Nicki was not about to be deterred. If she kept insisting she didn't know this code everybody was after, this man might be desperate enough to shoot her sooner, rather than later. And Harold, too.

"Let me think," Nicki drawled, pretending to remember. "Arianna and I used to play a game like that when we were kids. It was based on our birth dates and years of birth. I think I actually may have an idea what she was talking about when she mentioned me and a code."

"That's better." Lamont mopped his beady brow again. "Let's go."

"Where?"

"To the Lost Woods, of course. You don't think I'd be dumb enough to take you at your word and just walk away, do you? You're coming with me. If you help me find where the Jones kid hid the stash, I may decide to let you go."

"Jones?" Nicki's voice rose. "I was right? This whole mess started with Daniel Jones?"

The armed man laughed dryly. "That's irrelevant

at this point. He's dead, and the secret could have died with him if not for your dearly departed cousin."

"How would Arianna find out? Did she even know Daniel Jones?"

"That doesn't matter. Nothing does, as long as you lead me to the spot I'm looking for." He gestured with the pistol. "Move."

"What about the dog? He may be upset when you try to take me away." She hardened her voice as best she could. "If you harm Titan I will not help you. Period."

"Fine. Go get him and tie him up with the old man or shut him in a closet. I don't care. Just make it snappy. I haven't got all day."

Nor do I, Nicki realized with alarm. She hadn't come to grips with the full significance of this situation until that very moment. She could die at any time. So could her innocent baby.

She squeezed her eyes shut for a few seconds and prayed harder than ever before. Words failed her. Her heart did the asking. All she wanted was to live and to protect the people she cared about. And Titan.

It wouldn't have seemed like such a difficult prayer if she had not foreseen disaster for everyone, including and especially, Jackson Worth.

Yet he was her only hope. The only one who might discover her plight in time to orchestrate a rescue.

As she led Titan back into the kitchen and used his leash to secure him to a leg of the table, she passed close enough to Harold to catch his eye and whisper, "Chapel."

Would he understand? Would he remember their recent foray into the Lost Woods and the shoot-out next to the old church...and put two and two together?

She yearned to say more, to explain that she intended to lead her captor on a snipe hunt in the vicinity of the graveyard. However, if she tried to say more, Lamont was liable to overhear and shoot poor Harold just to keep him from sending help. No. She'd have to be satisfied with that one word and trust the Lord to supply the rest.

I do trust God, I really do. I'm just so scared right now. And so worried about Jackson. What if he comes after me and is killed? What then? How will I go on without him?

That was the moment Nicki finally admitted how she truly felt, how much she cared, how deeply she'd fallen in love in spite of the determination to remain unaffected.

Hints of those feelings had tickled at the edges of her mind for days, almost since the first time she'd laid eyes on the handsome Texan, but she'd attributed them to extenuating circumstances rather than seeing them for what they were.

And now? Now, she was sure. She loved the K-9 cop and she cared nearly as much about his dog and his uncle, although obviously not in the same ways.

The hard muzzle of the silver pistol against her spine triggered another wordless prayer. Another silent plea for deliverance. For a way out of this.

As her thoughts spun and her stomach churned, Nicki pictured herself emerging triumphant. She had always had a good imagination. This time, she hoped her dreams would become reality because those nearest and dearest to her were counting on her to think her way out of this dilemma.

And fast.

* * *

There was no sign of life when Jackson skidded to a stop between the rear of the house and the barn. Not even Titan greeted him.

He stiffened, drawing his gun and dropping into a crouch. A mare was tied by a halter rope to a metal stanchion next to the nearest corral. Her head was hanging low, but she didn't seem distressed, other than perhaps being a little weary.

Edging closer, Jackson saw brushes and combs near the horse's feet, indicating that someone had been grooming her. So where was everybody now?

Circling the patrol SUV, he slowly approached the kitchen door. It was closed in spite of the warm afternoon. Something was amiss. He could feel it. Sense it. But *what?*

His hand grasped the knob and turned it slowly. The hinges moved an inch and squeaked.

Jackson froze. He could call out now and announce his arrival, or wait to see what lay on the other side of this door. Since no one had answered his telephone calls, he supposed Harold and Nicki could have gone to the grocery store or something innocent like that... but his instincts kept screaming, *Danger!*

Crouching to present a smaller target, Jackson gave the door a push with his fingertips. The noisy hinges wailed.

He heard a low growl.

"Titan? Is that you?"

The big, black dog barreled into him, trailing half of a chewed leash. The response nearly knocked Jackson onto his back pockets.

Looking past his overzealous dog and ordering him

"off," Jackson spotted his uncle. Harold wasn't merely seated in one of the kitchen chairs, he was lashed to it.

With his sidearm at the ready, Jackson crossed to him. "What happened? Is the perp still here?"

Harold shook his head, his eyes unusually misty. "No. He's long gone. He took Nicki."

"What?" Jackson holstered his weapon then severed the cord with quick, strong swipes of a knife blade. "Who grabbed her...and why?"

The older man got stiffly to his feet and spoke while he rubbed his throbbing wrists. "It was some businessman named Gunther Lamont. He took her at gunpoint. There was nothing I could do after he got the drop on me." After describing the gunman down to the littlest detail, Harold began to pace. "I should have known better. He said his car quit out on the road. He looked so friendly, so harmless, I let my guard down and he got the drop on me like I was a green recruit."

"Do you know where he took her?"

"I think so."

Jackson was already on the handheld radio, explaining to dispatch what he'd found and asking for assistance. He said, "Hold on and I'll tell you more," before looking to his uncle again.

"She was talking about a secret code she and Arianna used to play with when they were kids. I don't know if she meant it or if she was making up the story as she went along, but she told me she was going back to the chapel in the Lost Woods. That's all I really know."

"Lost Woods. Cemetery," Jackson shouted into the radio. "Silent approach. Code 3 but no sirens. Got that?"

Dispatch said, "Affirmative. Anything else?"

"Yes. The subject is Gunther Lamont. Heavyset

white male about fifty. Dressed in a Western-tailored gray suit. Armed and dangerous. He has a hostage. Nicolette Johnson. She managed to let Harold know where they were headed but that's all I know for sure."

"Captain McNeal says we'll also send Austin and his bloodhound, just in case you need them for tracking. ETA approximately thirty."

"I can be there in half that time. If I spot them I'll leave my cruiser where the approaching units can see it and proceed on foot."

He ended the conversation before anyone had a chance to order him to wait. He was not waiting for anybody or anything. Not on your life. Or, in this case, on Nicki's life.

"I'm coming with you," Harold yelled as Jackson and Titan raced for the police SUV.

"Follow in the truck," Jackson shouted over his shoulder. "And grab my hunting rifle."

"Gotcha. Be careful, son."

Jackson was beyond heeding any warnings. Nicki had been kidnapped. On his watch—even though he had been called away. This should never have happened. It was his fault as much as Harold's. He should never have left her. Never have gone to town without taking her along.

Titan dived into his crate, and Jackson slammed the door. When so many threats against her had taken the form of bombs, he had never dreamed that a person would show up at the ranch and literally abduct her. Especially not someone as seemingly far removed from crime as Gunther Lamont was. The guy had a financial interest in half the businesses in town, as well as being active in the Chamber of Commerce and several service clubs. A man like that didn't go around kidnapping innocent women. It just didn't happen.

Only it had, hadn't it? Nicki was gone, and Lamont had taken her.

Jackson's hands clamped on the steering wheel, his boot pressing the gas pedal to the floor as he roared away from the ranch.

Was it possible he had misjudged her? Could she have actually known about a secret code all this time and not confided in him? He didn't want to doubt her, didn't want to even think such a thing. Yet, there it was. Harold had heard her mention a code with his own ears.

Okay. One thing at a time, Jackson told himself. First, he would find Nicki and get her away from Lamont. Then he'd ask her why she'd waited so long to open up about her cousin. It was a fair question. And when he looked into her eyes, he'd know if she was being truthful.

Right now, right here, his heart was telling him that Nicki was every bit as law-abiding as he was. Until somebody showed him otherwise, he was going to trust her.

How much?

Jackson gritted his teeth. With his life.

SEVENTEEN

Long shadows made the Lost Woods seem even more frightening than Nicki remembered, and that was saying a lot in view of the fact that the last time she had been there she had fallen over a stiff, icy body and an open grave.

Her kidnapper had strapped her in with her seat belt, then tied her hands by binding her wrists, making it impossible for her to reach the belt release, let alone open the door and throw herself out. Not that she would have. She and her baby had already come through enough trauma to last the entire pregnancy. She wasn't about to endanger her unborn child's life by leaping from a moving vehicle.

Fervent, constant prayer had been her main objective since this ordeal began. When there was nothing she could do for herself, when all avenues of escape had been cut off, she had naturally turned to the Lord.

Somewhere in the Bible it said to "pray without ceasing" and she could certainly see the point in doing so. She knew she didn't have to be on her knees with her hands folded to speak to God. Nor was piousness necessary. She simply let her heart, her mind, call out with abandon to her heavenly Father.

Unshed tears blurred Nicki's vision. When she blinked they slid silently down her cheeks.

The man behind the wheel of the silver Mercedes was so flushed she wondered if he was going to have a heart attack. Would God save her that way? Maybe. There were certainly plenty of examples in the Bible of Him smiting the enemies of his earthly children.

Gunther Lamont glanced over at her. "What are you staring at?"

"Uh…do you feel okay? Your face is really red. I'd hate to be in a wreck if you had a heart attack or something."

His chortle was choked and far from humorous, although Nicki imagined he'd meant to sound amused. "I feel just fine. And I'll feel even better once you show me where to look."

"I suppose you brought a shovel?"

Muttered curses were the reply. "Never mind the details. Once I see what I need, I'll take care of getting the right tools." A sinister grin lifted the corners of his lips, his smile finally reaching his eyes.

Nicki wondered why his mood had lightened. She didn't have to wait long to find out.

"You just told me half of what I need to know," Lamont said. "I'd been wondering if they'd used one of the crypts, especially if they were in a hurry. Now I know the stash is buried. Thanks."

She shook her head slowly. The man was clearly deranged, at the end of his rope. Desperate. Although the reason for such great anxiety on his part remained unknown.

Nicki leaned back against the butter-soft leather of the luxury car's seat and took deep, settling breaths. The only way she was going to get through this was to keep calm and cool, particularly since her captor was so close to losing control of his emotions. The way she saw it, the more frantic he became, the better her chances of escape, no matter how critical her situation was.

Irony touched at the edges of her mind. Here she sat, kidnapped and in danger of being murdered, and she had just pictured herself wearing a long, white robe and standing with Daniel in the lion's den of the Bible.

Was that so strange? Nicki wondered. Perhaps the Lord was giving her that idea so she'd know to stand firm and not be too frightened.

She huffed. Yeah. And maybe her brain was playing tricks on her as a method of survival. It really didn't matter which was true, or if either notion was logical. All she was certain of was that she was in deep, deep trouble.

Given those parameters, right now, right here, she'd even have welcomed help from Bobby Lee.

That notion struck her as so ludicrous she had to smile. A guy like Bobby Lee would take one look at that gun and hit the trail for parts unknown. As a matter of fact, he had, with far less incentive. Good riddance. Any lingering affection she might have felt for her ex had vanished when she'd realized what real love was like.

It was personified in Jackson Worth.

Nicki simply prayed that she would live long enough to tell him.

The dirt road into the Lost Woods was rutted and bumpy. Since the recent rain it was more muddy than powdery, so Jackson didn't have the benefit of seeing dust clouds ahead to tell him if he was on the right track.

He gritted his teeth. He had to be correct. The alternative was to lose Nicki forever…and he was not going to accept that. Not while he still had breath in his body.

"Father, help me. Help us. Show me the way. Please, God. I have to find her."

Would Titan track her? he wondered. It was possible since she and the dog had bonded so well. The big, affectionate Lab had not been trained to find people, but he was enamored with Nicki so maybe he'd follow her scent.

Titan wasn't the only one who loved that woman, Jackson reminded himself, growing more convinced by the mile. They hadn't known each other nearly as long as he had known a few others he had thought about marrying like Nancy or Ann, yet he and Nicki had clicked in ways he had only dreamed of in the past. She was more than special. She was perfect. At least for him.

He slowed the SUV as they approached the cemetery. Having been there so recently, he was aware of where to park so he wouldn't be seen, and it dawned on him that he had actually been prepared for this very moment. His prayers had been answered long before he'd even prayed them!

Encouraged by that conclusion, Jackson killed the engine, climbed out quietly and circled to get his dog. Titan seemed to understand the need for silence because he didn't bark, didn't even whine.

"Good boy," Jackson whispered, signaling him to jump down. "Come on. Let's find Nicki."

Confused at first, the Lab circled at the end of the

long lead and sniffed the dirt. Then he wagged his tail and looked to Jackson.

"I don't know where she is, boy. But we'll find her. I know we will," he said softly.

In the distance a motor revved, then fell silent. *Praise the Lord.* He had stopped his own vehicle just in time to keep from being overheard the same way. Score one for the good guys.

Gathering all but about ten feet of the braided nylon lead, Jackson started down the narrow road toward the chapel and adjoining cemetery. Since there had been so much official traffic through there due to the Jones disinterment investigation, it was impossible to be certain about fresh tire tracks.

Pausing and crouching, Jackson pointed to what he thought might be the ruts left by their quarry.

By his side, Titan put his nose to the ground and snuffled. Then he raised his broad head and sniffed the air.

"Nicki?" Jackson whispered. "Can you find Nicki?"

Whether or not the dog understood was a moot point. As soon as Jackson straightened, Titan took off in the direction they'd been traveling.

A jumble of unspoken prayers and confusing possibilities filled Jackson's mind as he trotted after his canine partner.

We'll be in time, he kept insisting. *We'll save her. We have to.* The alternative was unthinkable.

Dragging Nicki out of the car increased Lamont's labored breathing. She didn't help him by moving easily, hoping that the more he was forced to struggle, the better her chances were of eventually getting away.

"All right. We're here. Now start pacing it off."

"I have to begin in exactly the right place or it won't work," Nicki insisted.

She took in their surroundings, noting that the sun was nearly set. If she could delay long enough for night to fall, the darkness would give her a better chance to escape unscathed.

"Well, hurry it up. We haven't got all night."

Ah, but we do, Nicki thought, continuing to make circuitous advances toward the abandoned chapel as if searching the ground for the ideal spot. *The longer I can stall, the more chance there is that help will arrive.*

Was that a foolish fantasy? She didn't think so. After all, Jackson wasn't planning to stay in town long, and he'd surely be home in time to enjoy one of her special evening meals. Therefore, he should discover Harold soon and learn what was happening from him.

And then he'd come after her, she thought, smiling slightly in spite of her tenuous situation.

Off to one side, Gunther Lamont still had his pistol trained on her. He gestured with it. "Find the right place soon, or I'll kill you, anyway."

Another intonation echoed from the direction of one of the nearby crypts, making Nicki gasp.

It wasn't Jackson, as she had initially hoped. Matter of fact, the voice didn't even sound human as it said, "You're a fool."

Did he mean her? Or was he speaking to her captor? The instant she made eye contact with Gunther Lamont, she knew that answer. The speaker was not only addressing her kidnapper, Lamont was frightened so badly he'd forgotten himself and lowered his weapon.

Should she make a run for it? Was this her chance? Maybe her only chance?

In seconds, Nicki realized that flight would be futile. Not only was there one man coming out of hiding accompanied by a large brown-and-black dog, he was flanked by two dangerous-looking companions in camouflage clothing: one crew-cut and stocky, the other long-haired and wiry, as well as twitchy.

The speaker was slim, taller than the others, and dressed all in black, including a knit ski mask that covered his head and most of his face. The eyes she saw through the two upper holes weren't normal. They were black, too, except they showed little or no white around the pupils.

Meeting that gaze was like staring into two bottomless pits filled with indescribable evil. The man exuded it as if surrounded by a cloud of palpable wickedness that accompanied him as he approached.

Lamont began to stammer. "I've just about got the answer for you, Boss. A few more minutes and we'll know where to dig."

The man in black snorted. "Bah. I don't need her anymore. I've figured it out for myself."

"Are you sure?" Gunther asked.

Nicki heard the fear in his tone, sensed how terrified he was of the man he had referred to as his boss. She stood stock-still, hoping to deflect undue notice, particularly since the "Boss" was so focused on the quaking businessman.

"As sure as I need to be," the masked man said. He raised a dark-colored pistol he'd been casually holding at his side and pointed it at Lamont.

The gray-suited businessman raised his hands in silent plea, then managed, "Please. No. No!"

"I can't abide failure. As my second in command, you should be well aware of that."

"I didn't fail. She was about to…" He never got to finish his explanation.

The automatic barked…and Nicki saw the muzzle flash. Cringing in horror, she crouched down on the ground and saw her former captor crumple as if he were a marionette, and someone had just cut all the strings holding him erect.

There was no other movement in the clearing. No sound beyond the echo of the shot. Birds had stopped singing. Insects no longer chirped.

Nicki dared to peek from behind lowered lashes. The man in black was staring straight at her. All she could see of his mouth was the slash in the knitted fabric but those eyes—those terrifying eyes—pinned her like a butterfly on a scientist's specimen board.

The Boss turned on his heel and started back the way he had come, the dog at his side.

Nicki could hardly breathe, let alone speak. Her feet felt nailed to the ground, her heart was pounding. And she was so scared, she was afraid she might vomit.

Were they going to leave her? Just like that? After everything Gunther Lamont had already put her through? It certainly looked that way.

She straightened slightly, still trembling, yet beginning to fan a tiny spark of hope.

Then she heard the strange voice again—the voice that was so odd it sounded as if it were being electronically altered.

The Boss didn't bother with explanations to his remaining men. He simply tossed a comment over his shoulder as he left.

"The woman. Kill her."

Jackson pulled Titan closer when they heard a shot and took cover behind the trunk of an ancient, gnarled tree. His dog was shaking, as he'd expected. So was he, at least internally. One shot probably meant a hit, whereas a volley of them would indicate that someone was fleeing, and perhaps getting away.

One solitary gunshot was definitely not a good sign. Not good at all.

He waited a few seconds, then cautiously started forward again, heading in the direction of the sound. Whoever had fired had to be in the vicinity of the chapel Nicki had mentioned to Harold.

That might mean she was the victim, he reasoned, immediately abandoning that notion because his heart refused to accept it. Nicki couldn't be gone. She simply couldn't be. Not now. Not when he'd finally realized she was the right woman for him. It wouldn't be fair.

And how fair was it when your buddies died in combat? he asked himself. *Who says any death is fair?* He, of all people, knew that. He'd seen too many friends killed in combat.

Jackson realized his logic was irrefutable, yet he maintained the soul-deep assurance that Nicki had survived. He had taught her to shoot. Maybe she had gotten her hands on the perp's firearm and had used it to defend herself. The idea might be far-fetched, but it was possible. Anything was.

Pushing forward in spite of his underlying fear that he would soon glimpse her lying lifeless on the forest floor, he kept up a constant, unspoken chain of prayer. Words were inadequate in this instance. Hopes and dreams and heartfelt pleas would have to suffice.

A jumble of voices began to drift to him on the evening breeze. *Nicki?* He held his breath and strained to listen.

It *was* her! She was alive. The bullet hadn't ended her life. But then who had been the target? Or had the shot merely been a warning?

Inching closer, Jackson kept Titan on a very short leash.

The dog seemed to sense the need for stealth because he almost tiptoed, placing each paw without making a sound.

Jackson crept closer.

Nicki was talking. "You don't want to do this, guys. I'm pregnant, so you'll be killing an innocent baby, too, if you shoot me."

Jackson nearly shouted out his anguish. Someone was threatening to kill the woman he loved, and he was still too far away to stop it. How much more time did he have? Should he show himself, charge the scene and try to draw their fire, or might his sudden appearance cause the assassin to panic and shoot Nicki, anyway?

On the other hand, if he delayed too long and waited for backup, what would become of her?

Torn between listening to his head or his heart, he started forward cautiously. He knew what a trained officer of the law would do—should do. But if there was one more shot, he was going to make a run for her... whether it cost him his own life or not.

There was simply no other choice.

EIGHTEEN

Nicki felt better about her chances of survival as soon as she saw the expression on one of the thug's faces soften. His long-haired, younger partner still seemed bent on following their boss's orders, but she believed she may have won one of them over. That was a start.

"I know I'm not showing much yet, but I am pregnant," Nicki explained, focusing on the older of the two men. "If you've been following this case, you know that already. I haven't hidden my condition. As a matter of fact, that's why I was fired from my job at the truck stop."

The one who had chosen to lower his gun nodded. "Yeah. We did hear something about that."

"Doesn't matter," the other insisted. "It's us or her. You know that. If we don't finish her off The Boss will do us, instead, and then send somebody else after her."

"Why should he?" Nicki asked, struggling to keep from sounding as desperate as she was. "You heard him yourself. He has no more use for me. Whatever he thought I knew doesn't matter anymore. There's no reason to shoot me. Or my poor little baby."

"She's got a point," the sympathetic man said. "My

sister just had a kid and it sure is cute. Why don't we let her go?" He turned his eyes on Nicki. "You won't remember what we looked like, will you, lady?"

All she could do was shake her head. Clearly, the younger of the two was far from convinced. That gave her no better than a fifty-fifty chance of survival.

He raked his free hand through his long, stringy brown hair and raised the other arm, pointing his pistol directly at her. "No dice. I ain't gonna die for some dumb broad. If you ain't got the guts to do it with me, I'll do it alone."

Nicki's eyes widened. The round, black hole in the end of the gun's barrel looked enormous. Any second now there would be a sharp crack of sound and a bullet would speed toward her.

This was the end. She'd lost.

Closing her eyes, she clasped her hands and dropped to her knees in prayer. If she had to die, she was going to do it while talking to God.

At least nobody could stop her from doing that.

Emerging from cover, Jackson shouted, "Police! Drop the gun."

Instead of complying, the long-haired man whirled and fired. The shot went wild.

Jackson's returning bullet found its mark and the would-be gangster dropped in his tracks. His partner had his hands raised in surrender before the wounded man finished twitching.

"Nicki!" Jackson shouted. "Are you all right?"

She jumped up and ran toward him. He had to raise his sidearm to keep from pointing it at her. Thankfully, the surviving mobster made no effort to escape, although he could have bolted at that particular moment and might have gotten away.

Barreling into Jackson's arms, she staggered him. Her face pressed to his neck. Her arms encircled his waist. Tears flowed freely. "Thank God you found me!"

Jackson would have closed his eyes and kissed her soundly if he hadn't needed to keep some of his attention focused on the surviving criminal. It was over. He'd succeeded.

"On your knees. Hands behind your head. Now!" he ordered his prisoner, watching the stocky man awkwardly comply.

"I wasn't gonna shoot her," he insisted. "Honest, man. Ask her. She'll tell you."

Nicki clung to her rescuer and nodded. "He's telling the truth. He wanted to let me go but the other guy, the one you shot, was going to follow orders."

Briefly assessing the mayhem, Jackson paused. "Orders? Lamont looks dead. Why do as he said now?"

"It wasn't him," Nicki explained. "There was another man. One they called *Boss*. He wore all black, even had a ski mask hiding his face. His eyes were really scary and his voice was creepy, too." She raised her arm and pointed past the chapel. "He went that way."

"When? How long ago?"

"Just a few minutes. I didn't get a good look at the man you spotted in these woods when we were up in my old apartment, but judging by the way this guy was dressed, it could have been the same person."

She glanced past Jackson's shoulder. "Where's Titan?"

"I tied him to a tree back there to keep him out of the line of fire. We'll go get him in a second."

"Then wh-what's moving out there?" she stammered, looking in the direction he'd come from.

"Harold!" Jackson heaved a relieved sigh. "It's about time."

His uncle was panting and gesturing with a hunting rifle. "I figured I was on the right trail when I found the dog. I heard what Nicki just said. Want me to go after this Boss character?"

"No. It's too dangerous," Jackson told him flatly. "We'll wait a few more minutes for backup and then do a proper search with a tracking dog. The guy we're after is probably too crafty to have left a trail this time, either, but he's bound to make a mistake eventually."

Harold turned the rifle on the man with his hands behind his head, and grinned. "Want me to cuff this one for you? I still remember how."

"Sure. I'll keep him covered." Jackson tossed his uncle the handcuffs from his belt, then waited until he was finished securing the criminal before holstering his gun and concentrating on Nicki.

His hands gently cupped her cheeks, his thumbs whisking away the remnants of stray tears. "Tell me you're all right, sweetheart. Please?"

"I'm fine." She leaned against his palm and smiled. "Now that you're here."

Jackson slowly lowered his head and brushed his lips against hers. He hadn't intended to claim a real kiss. Not yet. But the instant he felt her tender, eager response, he changed his mind.

Nicki already had her arms around his waist. Now, she raised on tiptoe, reaching toward the unbridled affection he offered.

He was breathing hard a few moments later when he

pulled back far enough to gaze into her eyes. "Wow. I thought it would be nice to kiss you, but I had no idea it would be *that* nice."

"Mmm." Her eyes were misty and half-closed. "Not bad." She began to grin. "Of course, I only had a second or two to judge by. Maybe we should try it again so we're sure…"

"I was sure about my feelings for you a long time ago," Jackson whispered, drawing her close again. "I didn't think it was possible to fall so hard, so fast, but I did. I love you, Nicki."

Her smile waned and she opened her eyes to look quizzically into his. Jackson had anticipated her reaction, based on prior conversations she'd had with him and Harold, so he sought to ease her mind.

"I love *both* of you," he said. "Enough that I've located the baby's missing father for you. If you want to go back to Bobby Lee, I'll step aside."

Nicki tightened her arms around Jackson and met his gaze with self-assurance and resolve. "You'll go nowhere, mister. Not if I have anything to say about it. It's you I love and unless you think we should make him help support this baby, I never want to hear that man's name again. Okay?"

"Very okay," Jackson said, kissing her again before adding, "Why would we want anybody else to have anything to do with our firstborn?"

Nicki was smiling when she leaned back to catch her breath. "Firstborn? Are you insinuating there will be more?"

"I certainly hope so," he told her. "And kids need a real mommy and daddy. Will you marry me, Nicki?"

"Are you sure? I mean, you aren't asking just because you saved my life again and feel beholden, are you?"

"I think that kind of thing is supposed work the other way around." He chuckled at her befuddled expression, then placed a kiss on her forehead. "Just say yes and stop torturing me, will you?"

"Yes!" she shouted happily. "Yes."

From across the clearing, Harold yelled, "It's about time."

For Nicki, the remainder of that night and the days following became a blur of confusing details and loose ends, although it was good to see that Jackson and the others had truly believed her when she'd told them about making up a fake secret code to stall Gunther until help could arrive. Unfortunately, even knowing all they did about the fallen hierarchy of the crime syndicate, including Lamont, they didn't have nearly enough information.

Important questions remained. Who was this "Boss" that everyone feared and why had he felt the need to steal Captain McNeal's elite police dog, Rio, when there were other dogs that could do virtually the same thing—without causing undue interest from local law enforcement?

The more Nicki struggled to remember minute details of her encounter with the man in the ski mask, the more confused she became. He was fairly tall, particularly compared to the two henchmen he had brought to confront her and Gunther Lamont. And he moved well, as if he had total control of his muscles as well as his emotions.

There was one thing she was certain of. The Boss

was a cold, calculating criminal who had little or no regard for human life. Reliving the way he had executed Lamont for his apparent failure still made her queasy.

She chose a peaceful evening at home to ask Jackson a few questions. They were seated together on the porch, making the glider swing by kicking their feet, when Nicki broached the subject.

"What I still don't understand is why any criminal would go around killing his own people. It's crazy."

Jackson threaded his fingers between hers and lifted her hand to brush a kiss across her knuckles. "Mmm. Vanilla. I love your perfume."

"Stop trying to distract me. I think it's a fair question." She shivered. "For all we know, there may still be murderers after me."

"I doubt it," he told her with resolve. "Now that The Boss, whoever he is, realizes you don't have a clue about whatever it is he's searching for, he'll probably leave you alone. I think the only reason he told those other two to shoot you is because it was expedient at the time, not because he cared one way or another."

"He kills people just for fun?"

"Oh, I imagine he thinks he has good reasons. But that doesn't mean they make sense to the rest of us."

"You're sure my cousin was one of his middle managers?"

"Yes. Arianna was known as *Serpent* and the Realtor she killed, Andrew Garry, was called *Blood*. They were both involved up to their eyebrows."

"Then what about Gunther Lamont? Where does—did—he fit into the picture? He seemed so normal, at first. I'd even seen him in church. What possesses a person like that to risk everything and turn to crime?"

"Probably money, at least to begin with. Then, once somebody is involved the way Lamont was, it becomes a matter of survival."

"And he didn't."

Jackson slipped his arm around her shoulders and pulled her closer as the swing moved back and forth, lulling them and bringing the peace they both craved. "You're okay and that's all that matters. How are you feeling these days?"

"Fat," Nicki said with a giggle, "and the doctor says I'm only four months along by now. If you're going to give this baby your last name, I think we'd better do it soon—before I start to look too funny."

"You'll never look funny to me, sweetheart. Just set it up with Pastor Eaton. If you want a big wedding with all the trimmings you can have that, too."

"All I need is you—and maybe Harold to give me away. And I'd like to contact my half sister, Mae, and make peace with her, too, if we can find her. Is that all right with you?"

"Fine. We can have a reception out here and invite my whole unit the way we did for the barbecue, only this time I'll have the party catered so you don't have to work so hard."

"Not on your life," Nicki insisted. "I'd love to cook for all your friends again."

"Then we'll celebrate our marriage at a restaurant and you can plan a party here for a later date."

"You don't like my cooking?" Nicki knew that suggestion would flummox Jackson. She wasn't disappointed. He began to sputter and try to find the right words to insist he'd meant nothing of the kind.

She laughed gaily, her blue eyes twinkling in the gold from the setting sun. "Gotcha."

He pulled her closer. Tilted her chin up with one finger. Inclined his head for another kiss—one of many.

Nicki closed her eyes and sighed. They had been through the fires of evil together and had realized their mutual love because of enduring those trials.

This had not been a month she'd care to repeat, yet it had brought out the best in them both. More criminals were out of commission and the future was starting to look so bright it was almost blinding.

As her lips joined with Jackson's and she slipped her arms around his neck, she felt an unexpected flutter in her stomach. It wasn't harsh or painful, simply a sense of movement that caught her by surprise.

She looked up at the man she loved with all her heart and smiled from a joy beyond words.

Her child—*their* child—had just made his or her presence felt for the first time.

They were about to share a new life. In more ways than one.

* * * * *

WE HOPE YOU
ENJOYED THIS

LOVE INSPIRED® SUSPENSE BOOK.

Discover more **heart-pounding** romances of **danger** and **faith** from the Love Inspired Suspense series.

Be sure to look for all six Love Inspired Suspense books every month.

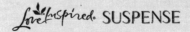

SPECIAL EXCERPT FROM

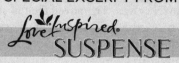

*A serial killer is after a military nurse. She'll fight to
stay one step ahead of him with the help of a heroic
soldier and some brave K-9s.*

Read on for a sneak preview of
Battle Tested *by Laura Scott,*
the next book in the Military K-9 Unit miniseries,
available October 2018 from Love Inspired Suspense.

Two fatal drug overdoses in the past week.

Exhausted from her thirteen-hour shift in the critical
care unit, First Lieutenant Vanessa Gomez made her way
down the hallway of the Canyon Air Force Base hospital,
grappling with the impact of this latest drug-related death.

The corridor lights abruptly went out, enclosing her in
complete darkness. She froze, instinctively searching for
the nearest exit sign, when strong hands roughly grabbed
her from behind, long fingers wrapping themselves around
her throat.

The Red Rose Killer?

It had been months since she'd received the red rose
indicating she was a target of convicted murderer and
prison escapee Boyd Sullivan.

She kicked back at the man's shins, but her soft-soled
nursing shoes didn't do much damage. She used her

elbows, too, but couldn't make enough impact that way, either. The attacker's fingers moved their position around her neck, as if searching for the proper pressure points.

"Why?" she asked.

"Because you're in my way…" the attacker said, his voice low and dripping with malice.

The pressure against her carotid arteries grew, making her dizzy and weak. Black spots dotted her vision.

She was going to die, and there was nothing she could do to stop it.

Her knees sagged, then she heard a man's voice. "Hey, what's going on?"

Her attacker abruptly let go just as the lights came on. She fell to the floor. The sound of pounding footsteps echoed along the corridor.

"Are you okay?" A man wearing battle-ready camo rushed over, then dropped to his knees beside her. A soft, wet, furry nose pushed against her face and a sandpapery tongue licked her cheek.

"Yes," she managed, hoping he didn't notice how badly her hands were shaking.

"Stay, Tango," the stranger ordered. He ran toward the stairwell at the end of the hall, the one that her attacker must have used to escape.

Don't miss
Battle Tested *by Laura Scott,*
available October 2018 wherever
Love Inspired® Suspense books and ebooks are sold.

www.LoveInspired.com

Love Inspired®

Save $1.00

on the purchase of ANY

Love Inspired® book.

Available wherever books are sold, including most bookstores, supermarkets, drugstores and discount stores.

--- ✂ ---

Save $1.00

on the purchase of ANY Love Inspired® book.

Coupon valid until November 30, 2018.
Redeemable at participating retail outlets in the U.S. and Canada only.
Limit one coupon per customer.

52615926

5 65373 00076 2 (8100)0 12382

® and ™ are trademarks owned and used by the trademark owner and/or its licensee.

Looking for inspiration in tales
of hope, faith and heartfelt romance?

Check out **Love Inspired®** and
Love Inspired® Suspense books!

New books available every month!

CONNECT WITH US AT:

Facebook.com/groups/HarlequinConnection

Facebook.com/HarlequinBooks

Twitter.com/HarlequinBooks

Instagram.com/HarlequinBooks

Pinterest.com/HarlequinBooks

ReaderService.com

Love Inspired®

SPECIAL EXCERPT FROM

Love Inspired.

*Though Texan cowboy Toby Christner was raised
Amish, he has no plans to settle down in the new
community along Harmony Creek. But when he meets
Amish nanny Sarah Kuhns, he can't help but wonder
if a Plain life with her is exactly what he needs.*

Read on for a sneak preview of
The Amish Christmas Cowboy *by Jo Ann Brown,
available in October 2018 from Love Inspired!*

Toby was sure something was bothering Sarah.

He thought through their conversation among her
family's Christmas trees. She'd been distressed by how
Summerhays and his wife paid too little attention to their
kinder, but she'd been ready to speak her mind on that
subject.

So what was bothering her?

You.

The voice in his head startled him. He'd heard it
clearly and, for once, it wasn't warning him away from
becoming too close to someone. Instead, it was telling
him the reason why there might be a wall between him
and Sarah.

Maybe it was for the best. Every day he lingered
was another drawing him into the community. Each
moment he spent with Sarah enticed him to look forward

LIEXP0918

to the next time they could be together. In spite of his determination, his life was being linked to hers and her neighbors.

That would change once his coworker's trailer pulled up to take him back to Texas.

Sarah gestured toward the *kinder.* "They're hungry for love."

"You're worried they're going to be hurt when I go back to Texas."

"Ja."

He wanted to ask how she would feel when he left, but he'd hurt his ankle, not his head, so he didn't have an excuse to ask a stupid question.

"The *kinder* will be upset when you go, but won't it be better to give them nice memories of your times together to enjoy when they think about you after you've left?"

Nice memories of times together? Maybe that would be sufficient for the *kinder,* but he doubted it would be enough for him.

Don't miss
The Amish Christmas Cowboy *by Jo Ann Brown,*
available October 2018 wherever
Love Inspired® *books and ebooks are sold.*

www.LoveInspired.com

LIEXP0918